TODD AARON SMITH

BARBOUR
PUBLISHING

For Josie

Visit Higby at
www.higbyonline.com

Edited by Phil A. Smouse

ISBN 1-58660-858-4

Published by Barbour Publishing, Inc., P.O. Box 719, Uhrichsville,
Ohio 44683 www.barbourbooks.com

Member of the
Evangelical Christian
Publishers Association

Printed in China.

5 4 3 2 1

Higby was a happy little monkey.

He loved to swing on his swing. He loved to run and jump and play. He loved to watch the people who came to see him at the zoo.

Everyone seemed to love Higby, too.

One day two boys
stopped to look at
Higby in his cage.
The boys made some
funny monkey noises—
so Higby made some
funny monkey noises, too.

The boys were surprised.
When they began to laugh,
the little monkey hopped
down from his swing and
tumbled over to take a
closer look.

Higby could not believe his eyes!
   One of the boys pulled a shiny red toy from his pocket. The toy moved up and down on a long string that was tied to the boy's finger. *How in the world does he do that?* the little monkey wondered.

Higby watched as
the boy swung the toy
around and around in
an enormous red circle.
What a wonderful toy!
thought Higby.
*I would love to have
a toy like that.*

The boy bent down on one knee. He set the toy on the ground in front of Higby and began to lace up his shoes. "Hurry up!" called his friend as he started to walk away.

The boy tied a quick knot and ran to catch up with his friend.

Higby sighed as he watched the boys disappear around the corner.
Oh, how he wanted to play with that wonderful, amazing,
shiny red. . .

. . .TOY! The boy had run away without his toy!

Higby was very excited. He picked up the shiny red toy. He twirled it and poked it and pulled on the string. The boy made it look so easy—but Higby *could not* get the toy to go.

Suddenly, a hand reached into Higby's cage.

SWOOSH! It swooped down with a flash and a blur and snatched his new toy away.

It was Higby's friend!
The lady who loved him and cared for him and brought his food every day had taken his toy away.

"I'm sorry, Higby, but this is not a toy for a monkey," the zoo worker said.

"We'll put it out here for now. Maybe the person who lost it will come back for it." Higby watched as his friend put the toy on the ledge outside his cage.

Higby looked at the toy. He did not understand. *Why can't I have it?* He sobbed. *What did I do wrong?* The poor little monkey was very sad.

He wanted to play with the toy more than ever before!

Higby reached out of his
cage just as far as he could.
He twisted and he stretched.
But his long monkey fingers
were not long enough. . . .

Then he remembered the little girl.

She had wanted a toy from the zoo gift shop, but her mother said "No." So the girl screamed and cried and pounded her fists— and her mother bought her the toy!

Why didn't I think of that? Higby grinned.

Then he stopped to see if anyone was looking.

He threw back his head and he let out a *SCREAM!* He stomped his big monkey feet and ran around and around in crazy, wild-eyed circles.

But no one had noticed. . .
so he tried even harder!
He bellowed and bawled
and he pounded his fists.
He kicked and he stomped
and he stamped and he tramped.

But no one was paying the least bit of attention.

Higby had thrown a fit, and no one had noticed. He felt foolish and silly, but he still longed for the toy.

Then suddenly, Higby had an idea. . . .

He grabbed his pillow. He flung his arm outside the cage and *FLOOMP!* Higby plopped his pillow down right on top of the toy!

He pulled the pillow toward his cage. The toy dropped right into his hand. His plan had worked. *I got it! I finally got it!* Higby laughed.

Higby put the loop over his long monkey finger.

He opened up his fuzzy hand and the shiny red toy slid down to the floor—*and it came back up!* He did it. It was easy! He was making it go just like the boy had.

Higby was very excited. He swung his arm in wild monkey circles. The toy went around and around and around!

But then something went wrong. The string snapped tight with a *CRACK!* Faster and faster and faster the toy flew as it wrapped itself around Higby's head.

WHACK! The shiny red toy whipped around Higby's ear and smacked him right in the teeth!

Higby's nose hurt. His
teeth hurt. His whole *head*
hurt. Even his eyebrows hurt!
And now, so much worse
than any of those, his heart
was hurting, too.

Higby was so embarrassed. He knew what he did was wrong. He was sorry he had thrown a fit. It didn't do *anyone* any good. Now he was miserable.

Higby found out
the hard way that
he never should
have played with
the shiny red toy.
   The zoo worker
didn't want to ruin
Higby's fun—but she
knew he might get
hurt. Because she
loved Higby so very
much, she wanted
to keep him safe.

Higby tossed the toy back where it belonged.

He thought about God—and he remembered that God doesn't always let us have everything we want.

But now Higby knew that God doesn't want to ruin our fun—He wants to take care of us! God knows what's best, and because He loves us so very much, He wants to keep us safe.

Higby sat down on the edge of his bed. He thanked God for taking good care of him and for loving him so much.

Higby learned that he would not always get what he wanted. Now, though, he knew it's sometimes better if you don't! Higby promised to remember that the next time he wanted something so very much.

THE ELEMENTS OF
FLY FISHING

THE ELEMENTS OF
FLY FISHING

A Comprehensive Guide to the Equipment, Techniques, and Resources of the Sport

Edited by J-stop fitzgerald

Featuring the collection of the
American Museum of Fly Fishing

A Balliett & Fitzgerald Book

Simon & Schuster

To Dad, for introducing me to the sport
and to his Dad for teaching us both

—*f*-stop fitzgerald

SIMON & SCHUSTER
Rockefeller Center
1230 Avenue of the Americas
New York, NY 10020

Designed by Susan Canavan

Manufactured in the United States of America

10 9 8 7 6 5 4 3 2 1

ISBN 0-684-84515-6

Library of Congress Cataloging-in-Publication Data

The elements of fly fishing: a comprehensive guide to the equipment, techniques, and resources of the
    sport / edited by *f*-stop fitzgerald; featuring the collection of the American Museum of Fly Fishing.
        p.   cm
    "A Balliett & Fitzgerald Book."
    Includes bibliographical references (p.   ) and index.
    1. Fly fishing. 2. Fly fishing—Equipment and supplies.
I. fitzgerald, *f*-stop.
SH456.E44 1999
799.1'24—dc21   99-13389
                                                                                   CIP

I came from a race of fishers, trout streams
gurgled about the roots of my family tree.
—John Burroughs, 1884

Every man has a fish in his life that haunts him.
—Negley Farson, 1942

Used trout stream for sale. Must be seen to be appreciated.
—Richard Brautigan, 1967

CONTENTS

INTRODUCTION	F-STOP FITZGERALD	1
HISTORY OF FLY FISHING	PAUL SCHULLERY	5
RODS	RALPH MOON	19
REELS	JASON BORGER	29
LINES, LEADERS, & TIPPETS	DICK TALLEUR	37
KNOTS	GARY SOUCIE	53
FLIES & FLY TYING	JASON BORGER AND JIM ABBS	69
ACCESSORIES	JIM ABBS	85
CASTING	TOM AKSTENS	101
SPECIES	DENNIS BITTON	121
WARMWATER	DENNIS GALYARDT	133
SALTWATER	TOM JINDRA	145
CONSERVATION	PAUL SCHULLERY	159
DESTINATIONS	DENNIS BITTON	173
THE LITERATURE OF FLY FISHING	SANDY RODGERS	201
SHOWS, EVENTS, & SCHOOLS	SANDY RODGERS	209
TERMINOLOGY	SANDY RODGERS	217
PHOTOGRAPHY & ILLUSTRATION CREDITS		226
ACKNOWLEDGMENTS		227
INDEX		228

And if the angler catches fish with difficulty, then there is no man merrier than he is in his spirits.

—Dame Juliana Berners, circa 1450

INTRODUCTION

BY F-STOP FITZGERALD

Welcome to *The Elements of Fly Fishing*. It's not as if there is a dearth of references on this subject; indeed, the many books about the exciting and burgeoning sport of fly fishing stretch across entire sections of bookstores. There are books about how to tie knots and books about fishing for individual species of fish. There are books about tying flies and those about "matching hatches." Many of these books are written by experts in the field, and many are quite good.

What there is a dearth of, however, is a comprehensive book that covers all aspects of fly fishing, from the exotic locations that attract anglers to the fly boxes you'll need to carry in your vest. This is a volume you can turn to when you want to learn—or refresh yourself—about all the elements of fly fishing.

The central concept of this volume is to provide an intelligent introduction to and overview of the many facets of the sport, creating for the reader a foundation upon which to build. Not just the technical features of a somewhat compli-

cated—at least initially so—centuries-old sport, but rather an overview of its many aspects. So while we will take you through the history of fly fishing, we also walk streamside and discuss conservation. And along with our introduction to the many species pursued with a fly—each fly a wonderful creation in and of itself—you will also get a glimpse into the lovely natural surroundings in which you may find yourself while fly fishing.

To me, the appeal of fly fishing lies in this rare combination of a sport steeped in tradition, history, and myth, while at the same time employing the newest technological, space-age gear. Add to that the clever and exciting quarry and the special moments when one finds oneself waist-deep in a roaring stream or watching the sun set on the still of the saltwater flats, and you'll begin to understand the special draws of the sport. These are what have inspired *The Elements of Fly Fishing*.

HOW TO USE THIS BOOK

The Elements of Fly Fishing contains sixteen chapters which cover a broad range of subjects about the sport and can be roughly parceled into four themes: equipment; technique; fishing: yesterday and today; and destinations. The contributors have outlined their respective subjects in a way that is both instructive and fun to read.

EQUIPMENT

Rods. A look at the most fundamental piece of equipment, from its bamboo heyday to the current lightweight, powerful, and responsive graphite incarnation.

Reels. Which reels are most effective in catching which fish.

Lines, Leaders, & Tippets. Learn the difference the weight of these crucial elements makes in everything, from sinking the line properly to propelling the fly forward; and how that affects your presentation to a finicky trout or your approach to the steel-like jaws of the prehistoric tarpon.

Accessories. With so many thick catalogs that specialize in fly-fishing equipment, how do you determine what you really need on the stream? A study of the necessary accessories—and the extraneous ones—from waders to fly boxes.

TECHNIQUE

Casting. A lesson in pictures by an Adirondack guide and master caster.

Shows, Events, and Schools. Where you can go to develop and hone your skills.

Knots. Learning the essential knots with easy step-by-step instructions.

Flies & Fly Tying. Matching the fly to the species' various appetites, and how to tie a few of your own, from nymphs to terrestrials.

FLY FISHING: YESTERDAY AND TODAY

History. How the English developed the sport and what happened when it arrived in America.

Conservation. How catch-and-release makes the crucial difference in maintaining fish species for future anglers.

Terminology. Learning your way around the nomenclature of angling can help you both in your research about the sport and on the stream.

The Literature of Fly Fishing. A carefully selected group of some of the best books on angling.

DESTINATIONS

Saltwater. Fishing for the giants of the ocean in the great wide-open.

Warmwater. Streams, creeks, ponds, and other fishing opportunities in your own backyard.

Destinations. Where to go when you're ready to live it up in exotic places from Iceland to the famous waters of salmon-rich Alaska and from the limestone creeks of Pennsylvania to the flats of the Florida Keys.

OUR CONTRIBUTORS

We have gathered experts in the field who are knowledgeable in the separate facets of the sport and asked them to share their knowledge by focusing on the particulars. We gave the authors some leeway, so at one point you'll be taken on a first-person journey through a casting lesson by Tom Akstens, who demonstrates his unique method of teaching casting in upstate New York, and at another you will explore the favorite knots of Gary Soucie, an author of books about knots and the accessories of the sport. Sandy Rodgers, a journalist and guide in the Florida Keys, takes us to some of her favorite lodges around the world, culls together our glossary of essential terms, and leads the way through the vast literature of fly fishing. Paul Schullery tells us about the historical origins of the sport, drawing on the knowledge that has filled his twenty-five books on the subject. His home in Yellowstone Park is also the perfect platform from which to examine the issues surrounding conservation in fishing today, as well as, quite simply, how to behave on the stream.

And that is just a sampling. Dick Talleur, a knowledgeable enthusiast on lines, leaders, and tippets, tells us how—and why—he bothers to hand-measure his lines before he purchases them. Tom Jindra, the president of the Federation of Fly Fishers, tells us about fishing for some of the giants of the sea. Ralph Moon, a maker of bamboo rods for more than twenty-five years, tells us about the origins of the rod and how the rod has taken a leap into the modern age of graphite. Jim Abbs helps us persevere through the mountain of accessories to find what's really essential. Finally, you will notice many special, entertaining sidebars that bring a rich texture of first-person experiences to our book.

HISTORICAL IMAGERY

The American Museum of Fly Fishing, located in Manchester, Vermont, is a non-profit educational institution dedicated to preserving the rich heritage of fly fishing. It also serves as the repository for and conservator to the world's largest collection of angling-related objects. The archival photography, engravings, and paintings from the museum's collection displayed throughout the pages of this book illustrate the grand history of the sport.

BEGIN YOUR ANGLING JOURNEY

Use this book as a tool when you start discovering (or rediscovering) the many elements of fly fishing. We can lead you to the waters, but you must choose your preferences and learn to study the waters. Look in the banks' shadows, under cover; the fish like it there. Learn how to throw your line so that you can angle the fly—Royal Wulff, grasshopper, or nymph —right above that perfect rock where you saw one jump. Be mindful of your neighbors and respect the stream and surroundings; in turn, it will provide you and your children's children with years of good fishing.

BY PAUL SCHULLERY

I t has been more than two decades since I first fished the Beaverkill—queen of Catskill trout streams—but that early experience with America's hallowed fly-fishing tradition distinctly influenced my view of fly-fishing history.

I was living in Vermont then—having recently arrived from Wyoming—and had traveled down to Roscoe, New York, for a gathering of the Federation of Fly Fishermen. It was early June, time for one of the great eastern mayfly hatches: the Green Drake and its extraordinary spinner, known locally as the Coffin Fly. While Bill, one of my fishing friends, spent the day tying elegant extended-body imitations of the Coffin Fly, I inventoried the obese Humpies, Wulffs, and other heavily dressed, ill-mannered western flies in my own vest. None of them even faintly resembled either Bill's flies or the actual insects I'd seen during a sparse hatch the night before.

That evening, after an early dinner, our party of five adjourned to the river—Cairns Pool, to be exact. We waded toward the rocky far bank, lined up about 30 feet apart, and began casting. I was at the downstream end, feeling a bit overwhelmed by the skills of my companions and considerably awed by the river's history. As I had read so many times, the Beaverkill was the birthplace of American fly fishing. Immortal anglers such as Theodore Gordon, George LaBranche, Edward Hewitt, Lee Wulff, and Ernest Schwiebert had waded and fished those very pools.

But the fish did not materialize for us, so we resorted to the angler's most reliable fallback: pointed remarks about each other's skills. At dusk the first spinner appeared, looking like some bizarre little black and white helicopter humming low over the water. Then, suddenly, the trout— who apparently had been waiting just as impatiently as we had—began to pull the big flies under, and we immediately started casting, persistently if not frantically.

The trout were unimpressed with our efforts. They feasted on the natural insects, shunning even Bill's beautiful flies, which looked so much like the real thing. For a half-hour or so, as the sky became a veritable cloud of fluttering insects, five full-grown, college-educated men were repeatedly humiliated by an unspecified number of small, intellectually challenged animals that didn't even have opposable thumbs. Could it ever have been like that for Theodore Gordon?

Finally, my experience on western rivers asserted itself, and I started thinking—not about the Beaverkill's exalted past, but about what I was actually witnessing there at the moment. The real-life Coffin Flies that were so enticing to the trout were big, long-bodied insects that seemed to lie flat on the water. Something was wrong with the finely constructed, delicate imitations. Did I have any flies that might do justice to the real thing? Rooting around in the grimiest corners of my vest, I found a big, clumsy grasshopper imitation with a crude, meaty yarn body. I tied it on, threw it out there, and immediately experienced the evening's first strike.

The word "Hopper!" quickly echoed down the row of fishermen, as they all dug through their Wheatley fly boxes in search of such a sacrilegious thing. Someone hooked a big one on a Letort Hopper and used up most of the remaining light controlling its wallowing fight. We still didn't catch many, but at least we didn't get skunked.

Over the years, I've come to realize that for all its great traditions and honored experts—for all the generations of brilliant minds trying to figure out how to catch fish—the most wonderful thing about fly fishing may be that most of the time the fish win. Fly-fishing history is a great testament to the discriminating tastes of fish and to the indefatigable commitment of anglers in the face of almost constant failure. If it were otherwise, I am not sure we would have stuck with it as long as we have.

ORIGINS

No one really knows how long people have pursued fly fishing. When discussing the earliest references, fishing historians usually point to a brief account by Aelian, a traveling journalist in Macedonia in about A.D. 200. The ancient angler wrote that because natural insects were too fragile to put on hooks, local fishermen would instead "fasten red wool round a hook and fix on to the wool two feathers which grow under a cock's wattles and which in color are like wax." It is important to note that there is no evidence this Macedonian practice was ever transferred to the European anglers who originated our tradition. Rather, this ancient citation seems to suggest that because fly fishing is such a sensible idea, it didn't have a single point of origin, but sprang up in local variations wherever people were trying to catch fish.

For the last two centuries, it has been commonly (but mistakenly) believed that fly fishing was first formally described in the 1496 British publication *A Treatyse of Fysshynge wyth an Angle*. This early work did provide an excellent introduction to the sport's essentials, including tackle, fly patterns, and even a code of behavior, but it was definitely not

The Egyptians may have been the first to have used a rod to catch fish. This is one of the oldest representations of angling, circa 1400 B. C.

The origins of the fly rod are shrouded in the mists of time, and only by imagination and speculation can we hope to appreciate its early development. Primitive humans presumably learned early that the waters of the earth held a bounteous supply of readily available food.

Undoubtedly, the first attempts to catch fish involved the most rudimentary of methods: hands, spears, fish traps, nets, or poison. Such methods were only moderately effective, dependent as they were upon agility and the proximity of the quarry. In an effort to extend their reach and to improve the catch, early humans discovered that cords with attached hooks of thorn, wood, and, later, bone and rock thrown into the water provided a longer reach.

It was then a short step to the discovery that they could reach even further if the cord was attached to a stick. The distance gained, however, was limited to the length of the stick and the attached cord. Efforts to extend the range led to longer sticks, but there was a practical limit to their length. It will forever remain a mystery where and when some enterprising angler learned that by introducing the element of springiness to the stick, the line itself could be propelled further. But with that single modification, the modern fly rod was born.

—Ralph Moon

the first written reference to fly fishing. References in other languages predated the *Treatyse* by about two hundred years. British writers, who have dominated fly-fishing writing, could be accused of chauvinistically presuming that everything important about the sport originated in Britain, but it is more likely that they simply didn't bother to seek out historical evidence to the contrary—which, to be fair, wasn't all that easy to find.

It was a Canadian medievalist and fly fisher, Richard Hoffman, who did find such evidence, and it has presented us with a whole new picture of early fly fishing. Hoffman's research revealed that even British fly fishing was established long before the *Treatyse* and that indigenous fly-fishing traditions probably existed for centuries in Spain, Switzerland, Austria, and other countries. Use of the *vedercmgel* ("feathered hook") dates from at least the thirteenth century in the literature and unpublished records of German-speaking countries. Hoffman also supervised the publication of *The Tegernsee Fishing Advice*, a manuscript from around 1500 found in a Benedictine Abbey at the foot of the Bavarian Alps. The book reveals some fifty fly patterns in common use five hundred years ago, not only among upperclass anglers but by others as well, including the

*From Izaak Walton's
The Compleat Angler.*

monks at the abbey. Fernando Basurto's *Dialogue between a Hunter and a Fisher*, published in Zaragoza, Spain, in 1539, also cites a mature set of fly-fishing practices different in technique, flies, and equipment from those noted in the British *Treatyse*.

These early publications offer an illuminating window into fly fishing at another time, but it is a fairly narrow and perhaps distorted window. We would have to discover many more such writings to have confidence that we have a realistic view of early fly-fishing practices. Reading the *Treatyse* as a guide to fly fishing in fifteenth century England would be to make the same mistake as reading a single fly-fishing book about the Catskills and assuming it represents how all American anglers prefer to fish, what flies they use, and how they treat one another.

Books published between 1500 and 1800 provide an understanding of what the still-emerging sport

was like in those times. During the 1800s and at the beginning of the Industrial Revolution, massive quantities of periodicals and other publications flooded the sporting world. That written legacy gives an even clearer sense of our past, partially because it helps to illuminate the common threads that run through five centuries of fly-fishing literature. From the time of the *Treatyse*, for example, it is clear that savvy anglers understood that they must imitate the natural foods of fish, who visibly rose for mayflies, stoneflies, and other insects.

Also apparent in the literature is the centuries-old quest for more effective ways to fool fish. When technology or trade brought new possibilities in tackle, anglers were quick to adopt and adapt. These advances included better-forged hooks, silkworm gut to replace horsehair leaders, and the advent of eyed hooks in the mid-1800s. Likewise, more effective flies were created with vast quantities of new fly-tying materials brought to England and the rest of Europe by commerce in the eighteenth and nineteenth centuries. The books also show the expansion of fly-pattern creation. By the time Izaak Walton's *The Compleat Angler* was published in 1653, the original twelve patterns offered by the *Treatyse* 150 years earlier had blossomed into many dozen, differing in style from region to region.

Those anglers were at least as stream-wise as we are today—if not more so, since many of them lived in daily contact with nature and the water. They may have had only a slight grasp of the complexities of ecology and may have lacked the finer elements of modern tackle, but I doubt that those handicaps affected their ability to catch fish. Fly fishing seems always to have had its share of "cool hands," authentic experts who stand out from the mediocre. When I read the better writers from the seventeenth and eighteenth centuries, such as Izaak Walton, Charles Cotton, Thomas Barker (*Barker's Delight*, 1657), Robert Venables (*The Experienced Angler*, 1662), and Richard Bowlker (*The Art of Angling*, 1747), I regret that I will never share a day or two astream with them. It would be worth a lot to watch those early experts in action and then put away a few pints at the local pub while pursuing angling's finer points late into the evening.

THE NEW WORLD

In August of 1766, a young naturalist named Joseph Banks found himself along the Newfoundland tidewater with some time on his hands. He was at the beginning of a world-circling expedition that would launch him on a long and distinguished scientific career (including a term as president of the Royal Society). At that moment, however, the young Banks was focused on the local trout, presumably sea-run brookies, which he found "biting Very well at the artificial Particularly if it has gold about it. . . ." That brief passage, only recently discovered by angling historian David Ledlie, is the first known mention of fly fishing in the New World.

Despite the persistence of a peculiar belief among fishing writers that Americans had no time for outdoor sport until the mid-1800s, most professional historians agree that recreational fishing was quite popular. In the 1600s and 1700s, recreational anglers abounded from Cape Cod's ponds and coastal streams to New Amsterdam's Collect Pond, the Potomac, the Shenandoah, and dozens of other southern streams. It also seems safe to assume that fly fishing was practiced long before Banks made his casts that August day, though evidence is scant. The historical record of fly fishing in late colonial and early post-colonial America tends to be more suggestive than definitive, but by the late 1700s a variety of diaries, letters, and other unpublished sources begin to reveal our fly-fishing ancestors to us. By the 1770s and 1780s, Philadelphia tackle shops advertised a full selection of flies, lures, hooks, rods, and even reels, which were a fairly recent addition to the angler's arsenal.

Anglers fished wherever it was handy, and in the sparsely settled regions there was plenty of great fishing. In the early 1800s, the "salters" of Cape Cod and Long Island and the native brookies of the Cumberland region of Pennsylvania were pursued by avid fly fishers. Anglers traveled the length of Long Island to fish the many ponds and streams that drained into the saltwater. Other early American fly anglers plied their 12- to 15-foot-long fly rods on the gently flowing "limestoners" around Carlisle and Harrisburg, where one hundred and fifty years later Vincent Marinaro, Charles Fox, Ed Koch, and others would develop new American fly-fishing theories. By the time the Civil War erupted, the Catskills and the Adirondacks had become popular fishing destinations, and each region inspired its own unique techniques and fly patterns.

If there is one unifying theme in American fly fishing before the twentieth century, it is a great sense of exploration and discovery. As settlers worked their way west, anglers always seemed to be among the first to arrive, sending back stories of the fishing they found.

It took surprisingly little time for fly fishers to explore most major fisheries in the United States. By the turn of the century, American fly fishing had developed a great variety of local practices, from the Smokies to the Rockies, and from the Florida Keys to the Olympic Peninsula. (For a broader perspective on the variety of fly-fishing destinations, see the Destinations chapter.)

Fly fishing: The inference often hovers like smoke that this might be a secret club, possibly a guy thing. Reality disproves that notion.

E-mail from a noted fly caster prompted my visit to a website named in honor of Dame Juliana Berners. This site (www.1.shore.net/~bjfeibel/juliana.html), and numerous others devoted to women who fly fish, offers advice, news, and scheduled outings. In fact, women fly fishers these days teach casting schools, found corporations that make fly-fishing gifts, and star in fly-fishing videos. Obviously the pastime includes a good number of women, and not merely as participants but as prime movers, yet somehow the perception endures that women are relative newcomers to the sport. This despite the many of us who, paging through old family photo albums, happen upon faded sepia-toned prints of ladies in long skirts casting from grassy banks. While the public may be exposed to the sight of women fly fishing more often nowadays, we've really been involved all along.

Even though simply juggling time enough to indulge in fly fishing's restorative aura seems a tall order, women have produced significant breakthroughs in this elegant sport.

Since we've already mentioned her, let's start with **Dame Juliana**. Her legendary life as nun and noblewoman has generated debate among historians. Whether or not she actually authored *A Treatyse of Fysshynge wyth an Angle* (1496), or merely compiled it from earlier writings, the fact remains that she saw it through to publication. Throughout its five hundred-year history, the essay that basically codified the sport has exerted considerable influence over fly fishing authors and anglers, whether men *or* women.

Sara Jane McBride took her fascination with the life cycles of aquatic insects to fruition by becoming a prize-winning fly tier, and then began publishing an angler's eye view of her observations in distinguished journals as early as 1876.

Fly fishers can thank **Mary Orvis Marbury** for putting together in 1892 the first book that clearly defined American fly patterns and that settled the debate as to what names should be assigned to those flies.

Guiding fly fishers has evolved into a widespread career largely dominated by men, but it was a woman named **Cornelia "Fly Rod" Crosby** who became the first registered guide in Maine. She gained prominence as a sports celebrity in 1895 for her remarkable prowess in shooting and fishing, as well as for her syndicated outdoors column.

Early-twentieth-century trout fishing.

Silver pheasant, jungle cock, and peacock herl feathers contribute to the design of the beautiful Gray Ghost streamer. Tied on the spur of the moment in 1924 by milliner **Carrie Stevens**, who had never tied a fly before, this creation caught not only a huge brook trout, but won second place that year in *Field & Stream*'s competition, and subsequently transformed the way streamer patterns were tied.

During World War II, with so many of the Florida Keys' men occupied with military objectives, sisters **"Bonefish" Bonnie Smith**, **Frankee Albright**, and **Beulah Cass** took over their responsibilities as outstanding fishing guides to the already growing numbers of saltwater fly fishers.

In 1963, **Helen Shaw**'s classic reference book on fly tying, which featured her husband's photographs and her step-by-step instructions, installed itself as the benchmark of clarity for beginning fly tiers.

Also in the 1960s, **Helen Robinson** helped devise the technique still used for teasing the billfish. Contrary to the stereotypical image of the bland librarian, **Kay Brodney**, employed by the Library of Congress, trailblazed through trackless jungles in South America, thus fueling the vogue for adventures among fly fishers.

Joan Wulff, who established a fly casting school with her late husband, Lee Wulff, has made casting her life's work. With 17 national casting titles to her credit, Joan's many years in the sport have made her almost as famous as Dame Juliana.

For generations of women who grew up shrugging into hand-me-down vests and ill-fitting waders, who can now revel in real women's styles, these tokens signal a welcome harvest from our fly fishing legacies. Though five hundred years may be a wink in geologic terms, in fly-fishing years it's a genuine chunk of history; a span of time profoundly affected by reel women.

—Sandy Rodgers

Wagon Wheel Gap, Colorado.

TECHNOLOGY AND COMMUNICATION

With the explosion of popular publications, the Industrial Revolution turned isolated groups of local anglers into a national fraternity, both in England and in America. During the years following the Civil War, American sporting organizations—precursors of today's Theodore Gordon Fly Fishers and Trout Unlimited clubs and chapters—flourished by the hundreds. Anglers found fellowship in these groups as well as a voice in the infant conservation movement that would become so important to the future of their favorite fisheries.

All this social interaction increased the demand for information about fishing and inspired the rise of a whole school of outdoor sports experts. Sporting periodicals and books brought news of the latest thinking and theorizing, and advertised the latest developments in tackle from a growing number of firms specializing in such gear.

Today we take all these rapid advances for granted. We are accustomed to the accelerated rate of new developments in tackle; every year brings new "miracle" rod fibers and fly patterns to our tackle boxes. But during the days of the *Treatyse*, or Basurto, or even Walton, decades passed without widespread advances in tackle, technology, or philosophy—anglers fished precisely the same way at age seventy that they had at age ten. No doubt fishing had its little contentions, as local anglers disagreed over fly patterns or other details; angling has always involved a search for better techniques. But until fairly recently that search was conducted privately, with little interest in—or access to—the findings of fellow anglers.

For most late-nineteenth-century anglers, the dramatic new pace of change was as exciting as it is for today's fly fishers who receive their new Orvis catalogs enthusiastically and consider discussions of new fishing techniques to be among the sport's most engaging pleasures.

Technological changes in fly fishing gear were particularly intense between 1860 and 1900. Although the patrimony of the split-bamboo rod is a matter of debate among tackle collectors, by the mid-1800s people on both sides of the Atlantic were experimenting with ways to make use of bamboo's incredible fiber density and strength. Eventually, anglers developed methods of binding several long, wedge-shaped strips of these fibers together to produce sticks considerably more powerful than rods made of more traditional woods. Between 1860 and 1890—after several centuries of dominance by solid-wood rods of greenheart, lancewood, hickory, and other materials—legions of anglers abruptly switched over to split bamboo (see also the Rods chapter).

At the same time, there were considerable advances in knowledge concerning aquatic food organisms—what fish like to eat. After thousands of years of anglers knowing virtually nothing about the insects that trout eat, scientific and angling writers alike made great progress in identifying specific common insects. Further revolutions took place in fishing hooks and lines. After centuries of woven horsehair lines, refinements led to a variety of vastly simpler lines of braided silk. Previously, anglers had to bind an eyeless hook shank to their line with fine

thread or bind a looped snell to the hook itself to serve as an attachment for the line. In the span of a single decade the metal-eyed hook, popularized first in England by fly-fishing bookmaker Henry Hall, became the standard.

THE DRY FLY

One achievement of the late 1800s—the modern dry fly—is heralded by most fishing historians above advances in entomology, new lines, new rods, and new hooks. The development of the dry fly is also perhaps the most entertaining and instructive saga of competing theories and conflicting personalities in the annals of fly fishing.

Anglers had always worked to keep their flies afloat, particularly because fish feeding on the surface are the most easy to see. A small group of affluent British anglers led by Frederic Halford and George Selwyn Marryat (men with access to the best-managed private waters) raised the floating fly to a high craft. They formalized the casual practice of centuries, deciding on what they thought was the best way to keep the fly afloat and the best way to cast it over trout. Then they applied tight constraints to this process and convinced many anglers that there was only one proper, acceptable form and technique. On the exclusive private waters where the dry-fly men ruled, any other kind of fly fishing was scorned and sometimes outlawed. Fly-fishing snobbery reached a pinnacle at that time, though it has occasionally been equaled since.

The irony was that while Halford and his colleagues made dry-fly technique very systematic, they also created a kind of theoretical dead end in which innovation outside of a narrowly constrained code of technique was regarded as bad form. Of course, it was not long before a champion rose to challenge the stifling restrictions. George Edward Mackenzie Skues, who had learned his fly-fishing theory from Halford's excellent early books (*Floating Flies and How to Dress*

Them, 1886; *Dry-Fly Fishing in Theory and Practice*, reprinted 1990) reacted against the Halfordian code and wrote his own series of books (most notably *Minor Tactics of the Chalk Stream*, 1910, and *The Way of a Trout with a Fly*, 1921). He advocated imitation of the immature stages of aquatic insects, which by definition are found under the surface of the water. This contribution to the sport earned him the title of "the father of nymph fishing" and the eternal enmity of the purists, who eventually hounded him from his favorite stream.

I must resist the decades of debate among various factions in the dry-fly story. There are people who will only fish when there are rising fish in sight and people who will fish under all circumstances. Halford, Skues, and their contemporaries began an intense conversation that continues to this day. Throughout the fly-fishing world, a host of angling entomologists, fly-pattern theorists, and presentation advocates have appeared. As Halford was promoting his dry-fly dogma in England, Theodore Gordon, George LaBranche (*The Dry Fly and Fast Water*, 1914), Louis Rhead (*American Trout Stream Insects*, 1916), Samuel Camp (*Fishing with Floating Flies*, 1913), Emlyn Gill (*Practical Dry-Fly Fishing*, 1912), and many others spent the first few decades of the twentieth century applying competing theories of dry-fly style to American waters.

In their wake, Preston Jennings (*A Book of Trout Flies*, 1935), Art Flick (*Streamside Guide to Naturals and Their Imitations*, 1947), Ernest Schwiebert (*Matching the Hatch*, 1955; *Nymphs*, 1973), Charles Wetzel (*Trout Flies*, 1955), Doug Swisher and Carl Richards (*Selective Trout*, 1971), and many others have brought American angling entomology to a previously unimagined level of intricacy. Today, most major trout streams have at least one book that outlines the important hatches and even maps the most promising pools.

FISHING IN ALL WATERS

When settlers from Europe came to North America, they explored waters that previously had been known only to native anglers. The remarkable diversity of fish species challenged fly fishers to develop new flies and techniques. It was thus in North America that fly fishing also changed from a primarily coldwater sport to one applicable to any water. By the mid-1800s, fly anglers routinely pursued bass, bluegill, and other fish. Even before the Civil War, sportsmen were reporting on successes with a variety of warmwater fish (see also the Warmwater chapter). By the 1800s largemouth and smallmouth bass had inspired countless local fly patterns. At first, most were simply enlarged trout fly patterns in design and shape, but in the early 1800s, a few anglers began experimenting with an amazing assortment of "bugs" made of various woods, hairs, and feathers. These came into commercial prominence in the early 1900s, with several cork-bodied bugs (the Coaxer, the Wilder-Dilg, the Night Bug), and Orley Tuttle's series of deer-hair-bodied Devil Bugs. The bass found an eloquent and persistent champion in Dr. James Henshall, a fisheries professional whose *Book of the Black Bass* (1881) became the bass angler's bible and has been in print almost constantly for more than a century. Bugs, sliders, poppers, and countless other variants appeared—and continue to appear—as warmwater fly fishing became an increasingly popular part of the sport.

By the late 1800s, American fly fishers also were catching a variety of saltwater fish and experimenting with techniques to take the tremendous runs of anadromous fish (those that run up a river) along the Pacific coast. The growth of saltwater fly fishing continued into the twentieth century. The halting experiments in the late 1800s and early 1900s with saltwater fish such as shad, striped bass, bluefish, and a few other relatively small species exploded in the 1950s and 1960s, leading to worldwide searches for the best bonefishing and for other more exotic species. Joe Brooks, Lee Wulff, and a few other anglers conducted occasional experiments with a few species in the Florida Keys in the 1950s, until fly fishers were taking an amazing array of fish routinely. Many skilled anglers, including Stu Apte, Lefty Kreh, and Chico Fernandez, continue to broaden fly fishing in remote destinations around the world. Saltwater fly fishing is, in fact, regarded as an especially fast-growing part of the sport (see also Saltwater chapter).

EVOLUTION OF MODERN FLIES

Saltwater fly fishing also inspired an explosion in fly patterns. In oceans or estuaries, fly anglers may cast any number of singular patterns and imitate a whole community of saltwater species. But perhaps the greatest area of growth in fly patterns is in the imitation of small fish. Streamers, bucktails and their various mutations have multiplied greatly since the days when British and American anglers experimented with just a few patterns in the early and mid-1800s. These innovators proved just how many species could be tricked

Ogden Pleissner, *The Battenkill*, c. 1960.

by fake forage fish patterns. Joseph Bates's encyclopedic *Streamers and Bucktails* (1979) lists hundreds of patterns and variants for flies, opening a larger quarry to fly anglers who might otherwise limit their efforts to fish that only eat small bugs.

Like every other aspect of fly tying, fish imitation has grown from local custom and fauna. Montana anglers wishing to imitate a sculpin may use some local version of the Muddler Minnow with its big deer-hair head, while a saltwater fly fisher may need to imitate a long, snakelike candlefish with a thin, feathery fly several inches in length, or some variation on a "tube fly," made of rubber or plastic rather than fur or feather. This illustrates greatly how "fly" fishing has outgrown its original associations with strictly feather or fur imitations of small aquatic insects.

By the early 1900s, anglers were using "fly" rods to catch almost every kind of fish, from salmon and baby tarpon to bluegill and trout. They were tying "flies" that imitated frogs, minnows, crawdads, grasshoppers, and every other imaginable creature that might interest a fish. As fly fishing evolved, the definition of a "fly" broadened from an imitation of delicate little bugs to a replica of any life form light enough to be conventionally cast with a fly rod. A fly is thus distinguished from a "lure," which may be cast with a bait-casting or spinning rod. The fundamental difference is that in fly casting, it is still the weight of the line that drags the more or less weightless fly along with it. By contrast, in bait-casting and spinning, it is the lure or bait that has the weight, and when it is thrown with the rod, it drags the light line along behind it (see also Casting chapter).

PROGRESS

In 1981, Charles Waterman, one of the best and most entertaining modern fly-fishing writers, wrote *A History of Angling*, in which he pointed out that many of the recent developments in fishing tackle originated through intense competition among professional anglers in bass-fishing tournaments. I compare this situation to the way war makes us better at medicine.

I do not regret for a minute the many advances made in tackle since the 1930s. It is difficult to even describe the extent to which the nylon, fiberglass, graphite, and other truly marvelous synthetic materials have had an impact on fly fishing. If I were to choose only one innovation for daily use, however, it would be the improvements in fly lines. When I was director of the American Museum of Fly Fishing, I peeled enough old gummy silk lines from beautiful antique reels to convince myself that I would have taken up another sport rather than tolerate the nuisance of those lines and the labor-intensive gut leaders that were used before nylon. And my thanks go to the late Myron Gregory, a champion caster who led a relentless campaign in the 1950s to develop a systematic way of designating line weights, which made fly fishing simpler and

more fun (see also Lines, Leaders, & Tippets chapter).

While some fervently believe rods have improved over the ages, I'm not sure there is a great advantage to fiberglass and graphite over the older bamboo and solid wood rods. Although cheap, sturdy fiberglass rods are the reason I could afford fly fishing in the first place, and my very favorite rods are graphite, the new rods have not changed fly fishing all that much for everyday purposes. We still employ the same basic casts; graphite rods just make it a little easier and more efficient. The new materials are lighter and perhaps tougher, so I use them almost exclusively. But sometimes when I get out my bamboo and solid wood rods, I am reminded that fly fishing with organic rods is not that much different—and the rods themselves are a lot prettier (see also Rods chapter).

Yet there are some purposes for which the new tackle is a spectacular improvement. Before nylon, plastic fly lines, and synthetic fly rods, what might be now called extreme fly fishing was very difficult, if not impossible. Steelhead fly fishers who make 120-foot casts hour after hour, big-game fly fishers who want to hook and land a 150-pound tarpon, and anyone who needs to cast a lead-core shooting head any distance at all, can be ecstatically grateful that modern gear makes such enterprises feasible. And anybody who fishes saltwater must be thankful for all the corrosion-resistant alloys that make the experience a lot less exasperating.

St. Albans, Quebec, 1927.

WHO CARES?

For all the noise that many fly fishers make about their sport's splendid history and tradition, few of us know much about it. We love to bow to our past to show that we are part of an honored, ancient pursuit. But many of us don't spend a lot of time learning about it. Today's society—even today's angling society—is very different from the contemplative era of Walton or Gordon. Perhaps we cannot expect more from our hectic, modern world. But fly fishing is like most other complex human activities—it is a product of culture. Like music, art, cooking, or baseball, its depths are enormous. I tell you this not to defend my own enthusiasm for fly fishing's history, lore, and literature, but to encourage you to explore these many facets of the sport for yourself. Just as a symphony is better enjoyed by knowing something about the composer's life and times and the performers' styles and achievements, a river or lake is better enjoyed for knowing its human history, especially the travails and triumphs of the anglers who have been there before you. Then you don't fish just in the present; you fish with everyone else who has fished there, and you learn about life not just as an angler but as a social creature as well.

So, once in a while, look back from where you are fishing now. Read the old books, not just for advice but for their poetry and wisdom. Seek out the old catalogs. Talk to the old-timers. Fish with the old flies. See how it was, and you will enjoy how it is even more.

RODS

BY RALPH MOON

The evolution of fly rods from their primitive beginnings into the modern technological fly rods of today, was never a straight line development, nor was it a rapid development until the past half century. There are only a few references to fishing rods in ancient literature, but those references are a strange mixture of extreme refinement and of crudeness. Some four thousand years ago, Chinese writings and pictures, give us reason to believe that rods of split bamboo, equipped with rudimentary reels and flies made from exotic feathers and bronze hooks had been developed. Further evidence pointing to the technology of split and laminated bamboo construction has been found in references to archery flight arrows made in this manner around 2000 B.C.

In the Western world, we see in some Egyptian hieroglyphics dating from 2000 B.C. illustrations of short, rigid rods with fixed lines. A thousand years later ancient carvings show the Assyrians of Nineveh still using hand lines. Whether the Assyrians were aware of Egyptian fishing rods is unknown, but it is the Egyptians who make the claim of inventing the fishing rod.

Both Plutarch and Shakespeare relate the story of Antony and Cleopatra fishing on the Nile in the first century B.C. It seems that Mark Antony, unwilling to appear less than heroic before Cleopatra, had his military aides swim beneath the barge and attach live fish to his line. Cleopatra soon learned of the ruse and had one of her aides attach a salted fish to Antony's line. Ridiculed by the assembly, Mark Antony attempted to retrieve his dignity by declaring that he had caught the oldest and wisest fish in the Nile. Cleopatra bested him with the riposte that the Egyptians had invented the fishing rod and that it seemed awkward in the hands of the Romans.

There seems to have been little further development in fishing rods, or at least little mention of it, until the beginning of the Middle Ages. The few references that do exist continue to describe the same sort of short rigid rods used in Egypt. In the second century, a Roman naturalist, Aelianus, published a dissertation called the *De Peculari*

This poem, which dates from 1613, describes the method for acquiring an ancient fly rod.

Then goe into some great Arcadian wood,
Where store of ancient Hazels doe abound;
And seeke amongst their springs and tender brood,
Such shutes as are the straightest, long and round:
And of them all (store up what you thinke good)
But fairest choose, the smoothest and most sound;
    So that they doe not two yeares growth exceed,
    In shape and beautie like the Belgicke Reed.

These prune and clense of every leafe and spray,
Yet leave the tender top remaining still:
Then home with thee goe beare them safe away,
But perish not the Rhine and utter Pill;
And on some even boarded floore them lay,

Where they may dry and season at their fill:
    And place upon their crooked parts some waight,
    To presse them downe, and keepe them plaine
                                    and straight.

So shalt thou have alwayes in store the best,
And fittest Rods to serve thy tune awright;
For not the brittle Cane, nor all the rest,
I like so well, though it be long and light,
Since that the Fish are frighted with the least
Aspect of any glittering thing, or white:
    Nor doth it by one halfe so well incline,
    As doth the plyant rod to save the line.

— John Dennys

Quadam Piscato Macedonia and described the Macedonian rods as poles of about 6 feet, with a line of similar length attached.

The first mention of the construction of a fly rod in English literature was made in Dame Juliana Berner's *A Treatyse of Fysshynge wyth an Angle*, first published in 1496, but probably written about 1450. The butt section of Dame Juliana's rod calls for a piece of hazel or willow or aspen a fathom and a half long and as thick as one's arm. The center of this staff is hollowed out with a tapered hole from one end to the other. The middle section of hazel and the tip section of blackthorn, crabtree, medlar or juniper are bound together with cord and fit snugly into the staff. A running device, which she does not describe, is used to pull the concealed section out and in. "And thus," she says, "you will make yourself a rod so secret that you can walk with it and none will know what you are going to do. It will be light and very nimble to fish with at your pleasure." Not only is this the first description of fly

rod building, but it also describes the first telescoping rod.

There is an illustration in the 1496 printed edition that shows an angler using a rod similar to that which Dame Juliana describes. The rod in the illustration is only about 6 feet long, compared with Berner's 18-foot behemoth, but it shows the very rigid butt section with the light and springy mid and tip sections she so eloquently describes. Though this may have been an effective fishing tool, it lacks the grace and elegance of rods of the seventeenth century and later.

It was at that time that rod development began to approach the standards by which modern fly rods are measured. The hallmarks of a good rod are lightness, stiffness, resiliency; the rod is used less as an attachment for the line and more as a tool to manipulate the fly. Fifty years after John Dennys, Charles Cotton in Walton's *The Compleat Angler* told Viator, a character in the book, how to select a rod. "For the length of the rod," he says, "you are always to be governed by the breadth of the river you shall chuse (sic) to angle at; for a trout river one of five or six yards long is commonly enough, and longer, though never so neatly and artificially made, it ought not to be if you intend to fish at ease . . . of these the best I ever saw are made in Yorkshire, which are . . . of several, six, eight, ten or twelve pieces, so neatly pieced, and tied together with fine thread below, and silk above as to make it taper like a switch, and to ply with a true bent to your hand. . . ." Further he says that they are light and even the longest might easily be managed with one hand. Although Cotton's rod remained unusually long, he emphasized that it be light, tapered, and able to bend to the angler's hand.

With some exceptions, very early rods were little more than sticks upon which to attach a line and lure, and it was not until Dame Juliana's description that we begin to see the development of flexibility as a component of rod design. The progression through John Dennys to Charles Cotton is the first indication that the purpose of the rod was to propel the line by means of stiffness and flexibility. From Cotton on, fly rods were made from a wide variety of materials and in almost an infinite number of styles.

MATERIALS

During the early period, woods used for making rods were understandably easily procurable native woods. Oak, ash, cedar, maple, and hickory were the primary materials used for the butt sections, but with the beginning of the British Colonial Empire increasing numbers of rare and exotic woods were imported for making of fishing rods. One of the more popular woods was **greenheart** imported from British Guinea. Greenheart is a fine textured, straight grained and very strong wood which made a heavy slow rod, better suited for fishing still water. Although bamboo became the preferred material in the late nineteenth and early twentieth centuries, there are still anglers who value and continue to use their greenheart rods. Other rare and exotic woods such as ironbark, snakewood, lancewood, degame, paddlewood, purpleheart and pingow also had their brief moments as rod materials.

It was, however, bamboo that emerged as the premier material. In the early 1900s, rodmakers in England began to use cane to form the tips of fly rods. Initially, the slender tip ends of the culms were used as a spliced portion of rod tips. The lack of uniformity of size soon led rodmakers to experiment with splitting the cane into thin strips and laminating them together. The earliest of these tips were generally made with three strips of bamboo with the hard enamel fibers on the inside, and the softer pith on the outside. The sections were rounded and more often than not spliced to sections of lancewood or lemonwood.

The first complete **split-cane bamboo rods** were produced by American rod builders. Samuel Philippe, a famous gunsmith and violinmaker in Pennsylvania is generally given credit for the first six-strip bamboo rod. The methods he used to build his rods have changed little in the last one hundred and fifty years. A whole culm of bamboo is split into strips. After straightening, each strip is cut into a tapering, equilateral triangle shape either with hand planes or more complicated milling and tapering machines. Six such strips, each formed to specifications of less than $\frac{1}{1000}$th of an inch, are then glued

Modern graphite rods are manufactured in a full range of weights to suit any fishing situation from spawning salmon and trophy rainbow trout to Patagonia's high winds and bruising browns.

into a hexagonal rod section. After the sections have been ferruled, the grip, reel seat, and guides are added.

The materials for split-cane bamboo fly rods, like many of the nineteenth-century innovations of fly fishing, came from far away places. The first popular cane rods were made of Calcutta cane, which came from various places in Asia, but was shipped through brokers in Calcutta. During the first decade of this century, another species of bamboo was discovered which had a number of distinct advantages over Calcutta cane. Discovered growing in a small province in China, this superior cane became known as Tonkin Cane. It had a denser and more powerful layer of fibers under its siliceous skin, it grew straighter and longer and more uniformly than Calcutta cane. The denser fiber structure and the straightness not only made it an easier material to work with, but also pro-

duced stronger, straighter, and more attractive fly rods. Almost all quality split-cane bamboo rods are now made with Tonkin cane. The advent of World War II marked the beginning of a decline in the manufacture of bamboo rods. Not only was it virtually impossible to obtain the raw Tonkin cane from China during this period, but most rod manufacturers changed over to the production of goods needed for the war effort. Even existing stocks of Tonkin cane were diverted from bamboo rods to the making of ski poles for the ski-mountaineering troops and other uses. Shortly after the war, in 1950, the U.S. Government placed an embargo on imports from China, and new technologies utilizing man-made fibers such as fiberglass and graphite seemed to sound the death knell for bamboo rods. The Chinese embargo has since been lifted, and although rods made from graphite have now captured the market, there has been a resurgence in the making and use of bamboo fly rods. Tonkin cane rods are now made by craftsmen and small manufacturers all over the world, and many fly fishers have discovered that the vibrancy and delicacy of bamboo fly rods has created a new dimension in fly fishing.

An important intermediate step between handcrafted bamboo rods and hi-tech graphite rods was the introduction of **fiberglass** as a rod material. In the late 1940s, the Shakespeare Company of Kalamazoo, Michigan, manufactured the first fiberglass fly rods. Initially these rods were solid fiberglass, but very soon the Conolan Company of California built the first tubular, or hollow glass, rods. The hollow rods were superior to solid glass in weight and action, and soon thousands were being produced by many different manufacturers. Fiberglass rod manufacturing made fly rods affordable, and soon Shakespeare's white Wonderod took the country by storm; many are still in use today.

The hollow tubular rods are made by cutting sheets of woven fiberglass cloth into a shape that is roughly trapezoidal and wrapping those sheets on a tapered steel shaft called a mandrel. The taper and length of the mandrel correspond to the desired shape of the tip or butt section of the fly rod. The glass-wrapped mandrels are then impregnated with a liquid resin, wrapped with cellophane tape, and heat cured. After it is removed from the oven and cooled the mandrel is extracted, leaving a hollow tubular shaft of fiberglass, which is cleaned, sanded, smoothed and polished. This tube is called a blank, and rod guides and a handle are attached to it. These steps are followed for each section of the rod (usually two, unless it is to be a travel rod of three or more segments).

Fiberglass rods have a slower action than bamboo or graphite, yet some anglers still prefer them. And they do have a number of advantages over bamboo: They are lighter, much less expensive to produce, nearly maintenance free, and immune to the problems of sets and twists, moisture and temperature. But many of the early mass-produced rods had a tendency to oscillate too freely, putting waves in the extended line and reducing distance. They frequently had stiff butt sections and flimsy tips. Although stronger than cane, they were particularly vulnerable to breakage from sharp blows and extreme loads. Many of these problems—and much of the fiberglass rods' bad reputation—came from manufacturers who were more interested in producing a large number of inexpensive rods rather than in ensuring quality and performance. Rod makers such as Vince Cummings and Russ Peake proved that by careful design and modification of tapers, excellent fly rods could be produced from fiberglass.

The limitations of fiberglass were directly responsible for the continuing search for suitable rod-building materials. At the 1973 Federation of Fly Fishers conclave in Sun Valley, Idaho, the Fenwick Rod Company, for many years a leading manufacturer of fishing rods, first introduced the graphite rod. In a very short time these new graphite rods captivated the fishing world—and for good reason. They are lighter than fiberglass; their taper action can be more easily controlled; excessive tip oscillation can be dampened; they are stronger in actual fishing conditions; and they are easier to maintain.

Graphite rods are made in the same way that fiberglass rods are made: A composite material of graphite fibers and resins is cut to a predetermined pattern, rolled on a tapered mandrel, and then baked until cured. The primary difference is in the fiber itself. While glass fibers are relatively bulky, graphite fibers

can be as thin as ³⁄₁₀₀₀th of an inch. More important than the diameters, however, is their inherent resistance to forces applied to them, i.e., their stiffness. This resistance is referred to as the modulus of elasticity, which is simply the ratio of the stiffness of the fiber to its weight expressed in pounds per square inch (psi). Glass fibers generally have a modulus of 6 million to 9 million psi, while graphite fibers may run as high as 70 million psi. A high modulus for the fibers means that a rod may be made lighter, thinner, and stiffer while still offering the necessary elasticity to throw a fly line. There is a trade off between stiffness and brittleness, though, and a too-high modulus results in a fragile rod that can shatter from the mere stresses of casting. Today, most fly anglers use and prefer graphite because of its light weight, fast, powerful action, and affordability.

SELECTING A FLY ROD

One of the most difficult decisions for any fly fisher to make is the selection of a fly rod. The experienced angler will almost invariably select a rod by feel.

Given his own natural rhythms, the choice of length and line weight, and the expected fishing environment, he selects a rod that "feels good." On the other hand, the beginner has no frame of reference as to what feels good, and must depend upon the advice of more knowledgeable anglers. The choice is complicated by the diversity of equipment available.

Fly rods can range in length from "minis" at 4 feet to Goliaths of 12, 15, or even 18 feet. They are made from many different materials. The range of rod actions can encompass a very wide range, from very slow full action rods to quick, tip action rods, parabolic to progressive, dry-fly action or wet fly action. And the range of fishing conditions can defy imagination.

In its simplest terms, a fly rod is a flexible rod that is used to propel the fly line and its attached fly forward. Since the ability to propel the line is related primarily to a combination of the stiffness and the flexibility of the rod, these are the points we need to define, and together they are best known by the term "rod action."

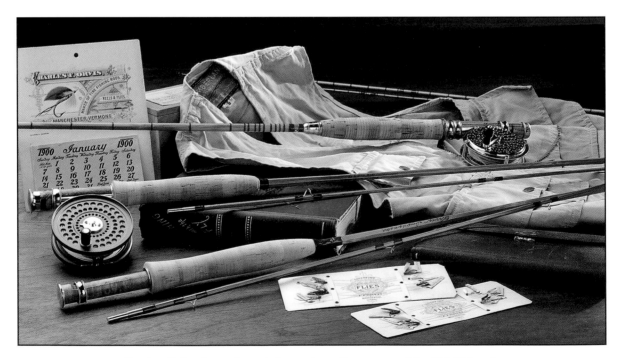

Classic split-bamboo rods made by master craftsmen can sell for $10,000 each.
Their suppleness and delicacy of touch are prized by collectors.

THE PARTS OF A FLY ROD

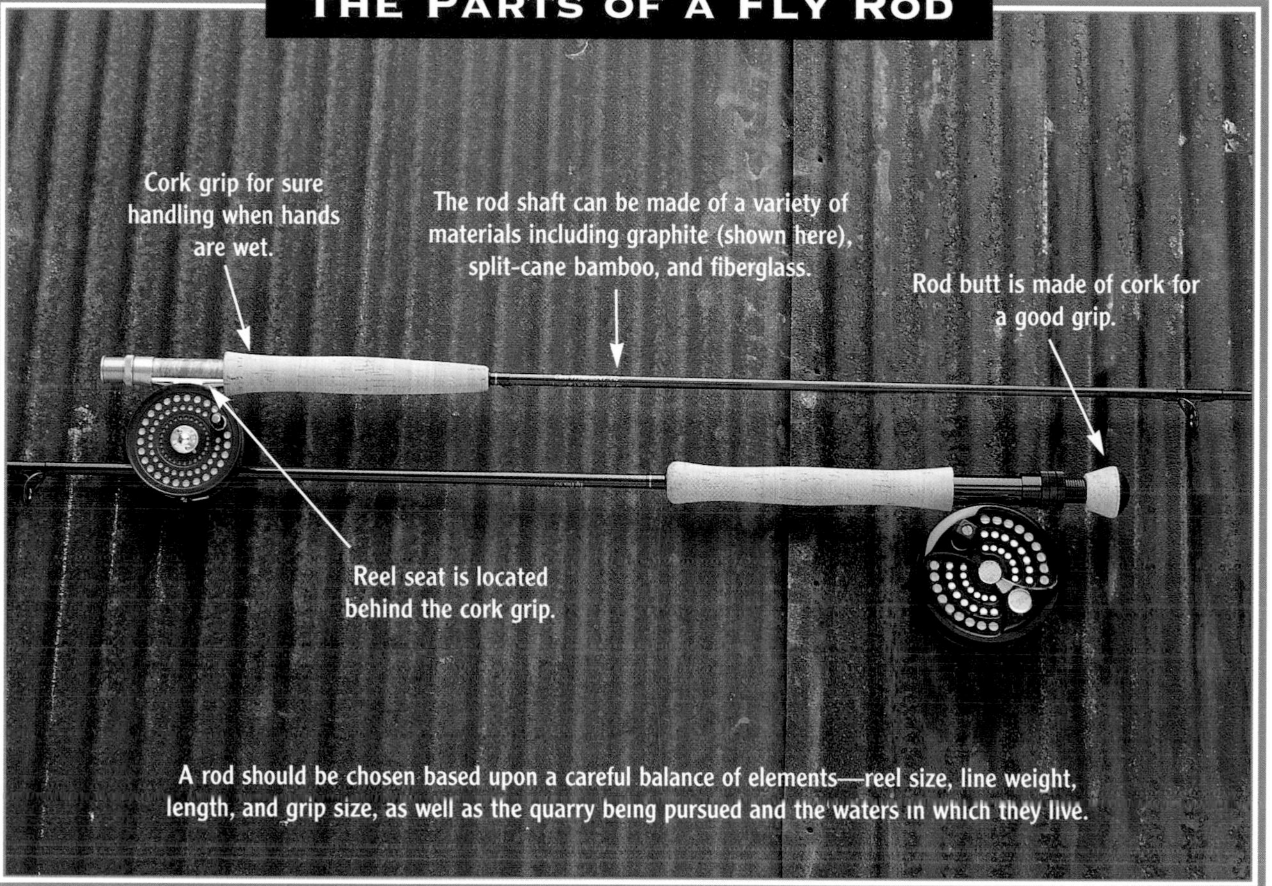

Cork grip for sure handling when hands are wet.

The rod shaft can be made of a variety of materials including graphite (shown here), split-cane bamboo, and fiberglass.

Rod butt is made of cork for a good grip.

Reel seat is located behind the cork grip.

A rod should be chosen based upon a careful balance of elements—reel size, line weight, length, and grip size, as well as the quarry being pursued and the waters in which they live.

ACTION

Most rod makers and casters agree on this fundamental principle to distinguish types of rod action: A **fast-action rod** exhibits the greatest bending at the tip end, generally the upper third of the rod length. A **medium-action rod** bends into the middle third, and the slow-action rod bends down to the handle. There are infinite variations between the stiffest fast-action rods and the most elastic **slow-action rods**.

If you hang around fly anglers for even a short time, you will overhear discussions—even lively debates—about the action of this or that fly rod. Originally, anglers would select the action of the rod based on the kind of flies they wished to use. Fast-action rods are best suited to dry flies as their generally higher line speed enables the angler to dry the

fly in the air. Slow-action rods were better suited for wet flies and for nymphing.

Temperament is another factor that influences the choice of action for a fly rod. Those who have a brisk driving personality generally prefer faster action rods, while those who are slower-paced with a laid-back personality seem to like the medium- and slow-action rods.

Those who fish in salt water, or who often fish heavy flies in windy conditions will find the faster action rods will suit them better, while those who are more at home on small streams under good conditions will appreciate the delicacy of presentation and ease of handling of a slow-action rod.

Finally, since fast-action rods are less critical of timing and more forgiving of casting faults, a beginner might wish to consider using them. The reasoning is that one of the most common mistakes that beginners make is the failure to allow the line to extend fully on both the back cast and the forward cast. A faster action rod under these conditions is somewhat more forgiving.

Regardless of which action is selected, though, it is important that the bend of the rod both statically and in action be smooth. An excessive bend at any location in the rod is a sign of flawed action. A tip that is

These boxes contain antique rod hardware, including guides and ferrules; however, the performance and feel of a fly rod is more than the sum of its parts. A top rod has the individuality and character of a fine musical instrument.

too soft, for example, will oscillate after the cast has stopped and allow waves to develop in the line which limit both distance and accuracy. If the softness occurs in the middle section of the rod, it will recoil in the caster's hand and cause an unpleasant hinge-like effect. A rod too soft in the butt section feels awkward and tip-heavy, and usually lacks power. You don't need a complicated test to find these flaws since they will be obvious when you actually cast the rod.

LENGTH

Fly rods are generally much longer than rods for spin casting or bait casting. A longer rod provides you with the ability to manipulate your line in ways that are not possible with a shorter rod. For example, a longer rod extends your reach and lets you position your fly line on moving water much more efficiently. If you are fishing from a boat, a long rod is valuable because it allows you to keep the line above the water on your back casts. Aside from line control, your fly rod can be viewed as a lever: A longer rod gives you greater mechanical advantage in picking and casting your line. To cast a line of a given weight, a shorter rod requires more work than a longer rod. On the other hand, there is a practical limit on rod length, in terms of both maneuverability and physical weight, since a longer rod weighs more. Like other factors in selecting a fly rod, length may require a compromise. If you are expecting to fish fairly open western waters or lakes, a nine-foot rod is a good choice. If you want to fish smaller waters surrounded by trees and foliage, choose a shorter rod. Short fly rods are, in many cases, more delicate and are fun to use but they do require more skill.

GRIPS

Fly rods come with grips of different shapes and sizes. While their selection is largely a matter of personal preference and feel, you should choose a grip size that matches the size of your hand. All the force of fly casting is transmitted from your arm to the fly rod through your hold on the grip. If the grip is to small or too large, casting will be more tiring than necessary, and if your grip control begins to weaken, your casting will get sloppy. The ideal size differs for every person. Try out several grip shapes and sizes and choose one that gives you the greatest feel of control and strength.

HARDWARE

A well-made professionally finished rod is a work of art. Many fly fishers treasure rods above all other parts of their tackle. Often manufacturers take extra care to make sure that the fly rods they sell are particularly attractive. In addition to the rod blank, a fly rod has hardware to hold the reel: the **reel seat**. Reel seats may be simply no more than two metal bands to hold the reel in place, but more likely they will feature intricately grained, exotic wood fillers with nickle silver fittings that lock in place with screw locks. Then there are line guides that keep the line close to the rod. The guides are attached with fine thread wrappings. This hardware transforms the rod blank into a fishing instrument. The quality of the thread windings and guides, as well as the mechanical smoothness and function of the reel attachment, should be examined. To get some appreciation for this hardware, compare some of the more expensive rods with those in the medium- or low-price range. Nice-looking hardware on a rod is partly cosmetic and partly functional. It won't make you a better caster, but it might make your rod last twenty years instead of fifteen.

PRICE AND OTHER CONSIDERATIONS

Prices of fly rods vary greatly but you usually get what you pay for. A really fine graphite rod will be made from higher modulus fibers with thinner walls and better quality resins, with better attention to design and finish. Cheap rods may contain only a small proportion of graphite fibers and have less attention paid to design and fittings

It is particularly important before selecting a fly rod that the angler consider all of these factors, and explain them to the retailer. An experienced sales person can then make a better recommendation. Before the actual purchase, insist on trying out the rods. Only by casting can you make a good decision. Watch the line on both the backcast and the forward cast; it should extend straight from the rod tip without waves, and should end without recoiling. The line loop should be narrow and well defined. The rod should feel comfortable and present a smooth link between your hand and the line.

There are a few things to beware of. Don't make the mistake that most casters do of seeing how far you can throw the line. Most fishing is under 50 feet from the caster, and within this range is where you should be most comfortable casting. Do not be unduly influenced by someone else casting the rod. Remember that it must feel good to *you*. The fact that another person can cast a tight loop 90 feet does not mean that that rod is good for you.

CARING FOR YOUR FLY ROD

Fly rods are usually not as delicate as most people suppose, but they do require some fundamental maintenance. After use, the rod should be disassembled then wiped off, dried, and replaced in its bag and tube. Graphite rods are very strong but are nevertheless easily broken by scratches, sharp impacts, and excessive straining. Although a light coat of paste wax applied to the rod will help keep it clean and dry, no wax or other additives should be applied to the ferrules. Modern rods have carefully engineered ferrules, and the addition of any material will adversely affect fit and durability. Ferrules should be seated with a slight twisting action without undue force.

The modern fly rod is a technological marvel, and the result of generations of refinements. While none of the separate parts of fly-fishing equipment and technique can stand alone it is safe to say that without the fly rod, there would be little fly fishing done.

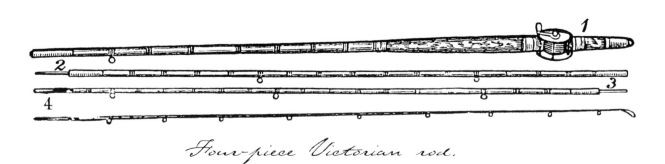

Four-piece Victorian rod.

REELS

BY JASON BORGER

One of fly fishing's great pleasures is the song of the reel as a hooked fish makes a breakaway run—from its frenetic cadence with a bonefish to the syncopated crescendos made by a trout. But fly fishers have not always heard this song; reels were not commonplace on fly rods until the early 1800s. In prior centuries, the fly line was often attached directly to rod tip. Now, however, we are in a "golden age" of fly reels. Advanced machining and aerospace materials have created a striking array of excellent fishing tools. While large companies like Cortland, Orvis, and Scientific Anglers provide good reels for the general marketplace, a boutique market is also in full swing. Manufacturers such as Abel, Ari't Hart, Ballan, Bogdan, Charlton, Governor, Islander, Saracione, and Tibor provide anglers with a variety of elegant and sophisticated possibilities.

Some reels have gone beyond exceptional function to incredible form as well. Computer-controlled machine tools allow shapes to be formed from aluminum, stainless steel, and titanium, with tolerances that previously were impossible. One of Ari't Hart's reels was considered such a design masterpiece that it was exhibited at the Museum of Modern Art in New York.

But whether you prefer extravagant art or pragmatic simplicity, you must know what design features to look for and how to use them.

WHAT A REEL CAN DO

An old fly fishing adage calls a reel "just a place to store line." Don't believe it. A quality reel offers an experienced angler improved control of a fishing situation, and it is an important tool in fighting a fish. The reel allows potentially entangling line to be spooled up, quickly and neatly. When a fish runs, the reel smoothly controls the outgoing line, avoiding the irregular resistances that break tippets and lose fish. In addition, the reel works with the rod to control the pressure on the fish, both when retrieving line and when the fish is running. Depending on tippet strength, species of fish, and where the fish is found, pressure may vary from almost nothing to many pounds.

Of course, there are some fishing circumstances in which the reel is little more than a line holder. An 8-inch brook trout in an 8-foot-wide stream is not going to get very far away very fast. But a 20-inch rainbow trout—or, at the extreme, a bluefin tuna—will quickly obliterate any doubt about the value of a reel. If you have disciplined yourself to fight fish from the reel, you will be better prepared in every situation.

A BASIC REEL

Reels have two basic components: a frame and a spool. The **frame** attaches the reel to the rod via the reel foot and supports the drag system, a friction-producing mechanism that increases tension on outgoing line as a fish pulls it off. The frame also includes a shaft (or similar structure) onto which the spool is mounted, which serves as the reel's axis of rotation. The **spool** holds the fly line and the **backing**, the latter being a thin braided line attached between the spool and the line that offers back-up in case a fish pulls off all the fly line. While many reels have other ancillary parts, all are of this same basic construction.

The size of the reel depends on the rated weight of line being used as well as the amount of backing required. A reel designed for a 3-weight line and 30 yards of backing would not have the spool capacity for a 12-weight line. The reel for the 3-weight line also would be fairly small and consistent with the size and weight of a 3-weight rod. Conversely, a reel sized for a 12-weight line and 200 yards of backing would be cumbersome and awkward when paired with a 3-weight rod and line.

Most reels come with replaceable spools so that different types and, to a limited extent, different weights of line can be quickly interchanged as fishing conditions warrant. For example, an angler can carry two spools, with floating line on one spool and sinking line on another.

THE PARTS OF A FLY REEL

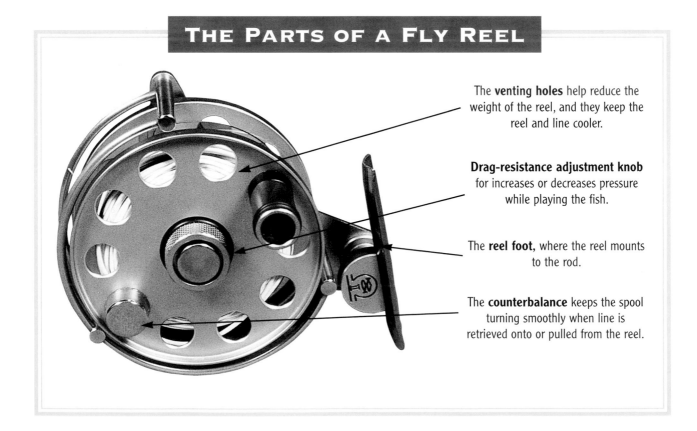

The **venting holes** help reduce the weight of the reel, and they keep the reel and line cooler.

Drag-resistance adjustment knob for increases or decreases pressure while playing the fish.

The **reel foot**, where the reel mounts to the rod.

The **counterbalance** keeps the spool turning smoothly when line is retrieved onto or pulled from the reel.

TYPES OF REELS

Functionally, there are three types of fly reels: single-action, multiplier, and automatic.

SINGLE-ACTION REELS

Single-action reels, which evolved from the Birmingham reels produced in England during the mid-1800s, are the simplest true reels possible: The handle or crank is attached to the spool; one rotation of the handle equals one rotation of the spool (also referred to as "direct drive"). With such simplicity there is little to malfunction, and the reels can be made quite light according to their intended purposes. Single-action reels are used for all forms of fly fishing, from the lightest of trout fishing with 4-foot "toy" rods or salmon fishing with 16-foot, two-handed Spey rods to blue-water billfishing with rods that could double as pool cues.

A subset of single-action reels includes a feature called "anti-reverse." These reels have a clutch mechanism that allows the reel's handle to rotate only when bringing in line. This prevents a rapidly spinning reel handle from banging knuckles or catching on clothing as a fish makes a run. The anti-reverse is primarily used for fast, big fish such as pike, bonefish, and tarpon. The drawbacks of anti-reverse reels include heavier weights and an inability to crank with more pressure than that applied by the drag. Many anglers feel that in certain situations the benefits of anti-reverse reels outweigh their costs; anti-reverse reels have a sizable following.

MULTIPLIER REELS

Multiplier reels, which originated during the Industrial Revolution, are still used today, primarily by Atlantic salmon fly fishers. A multiplier reel uses gear-ratio design; one turn of the handle yields several turns

Single-action reel

Multiplier reel

of the spool. Today's improved construction techniques and high-quality metals have alleviated the mechanical and material failures that caused the multiplier's falling out of popularity in the mid-1800s. But these reels are still relatively heavy and have an internal complexity of intermeshing gears that invites problems, which explains why they are used primarily as specialty tools.

AUTOMATIC FLY REELS

Automatic fly reels retrieve line via an internal spring that is wound up as line is pulled from the reel. A trip-lever on the reel releases the spring, and the fly line is retracted automatically. While automatic reels seem like a great idea, they tend to be excessively heavy, complex, and susceptible to malfunction when sand and other abrasive substances get into them. Moreover, automatic fly reels accommodate a limited range of line sizes and the fly fisher has minimal control over drag settings. Additionally, the tighter the spring gets wound, the harder it becomes to pull line off the reel, and with a tighter spring it is more likely delicate tippets will break. Because automatic reels depend on spring tension to retrieve line, a very big fish may require more cranking power than the spring can provide.

Recently, some of the problems with automatic fly reels have been corrected, and they do have a following in some areas, especially Europe. When using heavier tippets for pan fish, small trout, and the like, automatics are often adequate. However, for most fly-fishing situations, they simply do not offer the desired control. Automatic reels do have one advantage, though:

They accommodate fly fishers who are able to use only one hand.

CONSTRUCTION AND DESIGN

The majority of quality reels are cast or machined—the best tend to be machined—from aluminum or aluminum alloys. Other metals such as brass are used for smaller internal parts. Inexpensive reels may be assembled from plastic or molded graphite, but metals currently provide better fatigue-resistance and durability. Very high-end reels, and those destined for tough use, may be made of more exotic metals, including titanium. Such materials can lend both strength and durability to a reel, as well as serious cachet.

The internal workings of the reel depend on the reel's intended purpose. A reel for trout, bream, and small bass, for instance, may utilize a small-diameter shaft onto which the spool attaches via a spring-actuated quick release. Small fish typically do not generate enough speed to overtax the mechanism, nor do they require a space-age design for drag. That is not to say that such fish do not require a quality reel. Protecting ultra-light tippets is often vital when fishing for trout and other smaller fish, so a well-made, smoothly turning reel can be very important. Besides, a fine piece of equipment is a joy to fish with and, as an investment, it may outlast the angler.

Reel requirements definitely differ for fish like Atlantic salmon and various saltwater species. Certainly, with enough persistence, enormous fish can be landed on simple, trout-style reels. But a reel designed to handle heavy drag pressures and high-speed runs—some fish that live in the open sea may swim over 30 miles per hour—makes the fight much easier to control. For these more demanding tasks, large-diameter shafts with ball or roller bearings, spool locks that rely on screws rather than tiny

springs, and lubricants that are equally at home in automotive engines are de rigueur. Some manufacturers of hard-core equipment also use aerospace adhesives to provide additional bonds to highly stressed parts such as the reel foot.

DRAG SYSTEMS

To offer consistent resistance to a fish pulling out line, most reels have a built-in friction generating mechanism called a drag. In some reels, the drag is not adjustable; it is merely a spring-driven ratchet mechanism to prevent overspooling. Such "pure" designs are still preferred by some anglers, who favor

Above: This reel has a disk drag system, which incorporates a cork pad on one side and a brass plate on the other.

Left: A close-up of the pawl drag system shows the metal band that allows for constant resistance as the line goes out.

tradition as well as simplicity. In reels without adjustable drag systems, the spool's rim is often exposed, allowing anglers to apply resistance directly to the spool with their fingers or hand.

Most fly reels have an adjustable drag. The most common internal reel drag is a **spring-and-pawl**, also called a click drag. One or two pawls, which are typically triangle-shaped pieces of steel, mesh with a gear on the reel spool. The pawls are under pressure

Fly fishers have never enjoyed such a vast selection of reel choices. From anti-reverse to large arbors, it's a buyer's market. With reels manufactured for every type of fly fishing, from small trout streams to marlin on the Gulf Stream, how do you choose?

Do you need a $500.00 anodized wonder reel with a cork disc drag for mountain stream trout? Absolutely not. On the other hand, will a larger version of your stamped, painted trout reel suffice for tarpon? Maybe, for one or two, but it just can't take those terrible stresses day after day. One model can't do it all. Maintenance is a consideration if you plan on using a freshwater reel in the salt. Can it be done? Sure, if you're meticulous in cleaning, but forget once and you'll hear the corrosion build overnight.

Designed to match the size of your fly line and rod, reels should have ample capacity for the amount of backing needed for your quarry. On long-running species, a silky smooth drag is critical. To further complicate matters, many manufacturers offer both direct drive or anti-reverse reels for right- or left-hand operation. As in most things mechanical, simplicity of design often equals longevity. A quality reel is a pleasure to own, will aid you in fighting fish more efficiently, and will ultimately become a family heirloom.

—Bob Rodgers

from a spring, usually either leaf or coil. A knob on the outside of the reel frame allows spring tension to be increased or decreased, thus increasing or decreasing the drag. Many spring-and-pawl reels allow the pawls to be manipulated for right- or left-hand retrieves. Such simple mechanical designs are durable, extremely lightweight, and easy to care for.

Disk drags provide greater stopping power than spring-and-pawl systems, but they weigh more. Nevertheless, a good disk drag is extremely smooth and has very low start-up friction. If a reel has high start-up friction ("stiction") and a fish strikes, the initial resistance may be so great that a light tippet will break before the spool begins to move—and the fish will be lost. Disk drags come in both caliper and compression styles. The caliper design is like the brakes on a car, with pads clamping against a metal disk. The compression design involves the spool, or a spool liner, also contacting a disk. The pads of both styles are made from materials that provide smooth, heat-dissipating friction. The most widely used material is cork composite, but recently carbon fiber has been employed. If you're looking for the big boys of the fly fishing world—salmon, sharks, sailfish, tarpon, etc.—a disk drag is a necessary tool.

The newest type of drag is based on a viscous fluid **turbine**. Basically, a miniature turbine geared to the spool's rotation turns inside a housing filled with a viscous fluid. As the turbine turns faster, the fluid naturally offers more resistance, creating a very smooth drag. Currently, such drags are not user-adjustable, depending instead on the inherent viscosity of the fluid and the blade surfaces of the turbine.

REEL SIZE AND CAPACITY

Other factors in choosing a reel include the reel's weight and the size of the reel's **arbor**—the center of the spool. The smallest arbors allow for maximum line and backing capacity in a given reel diameter, while the largest restrict that capacity greatly.

Large arbors facilitate rapid line retrieval, minimize excessive coiling of the fly line, and, with their longer radius, provide greater (smoother) leverage against the drag's pressure. Large arbors were first popularized in the nineteenth century with the "large barrel" Nottingham reels. However, to match line capacity of a small-arbor reel, a large-arbor spool must be made in a much greater relative diameter. Also, filling a small-arbor spool with backing essentially creates a large-arbor spool of sorts—plus

Ventilation schemes on reels to reduce weight and cool drags often become a reel manufacturer's signature.

it provides some extra insurance in terms of backing on the reel.

Spool width also is a variable. Very wide spools allow for more line capacity, but they do not fill as rapidly as very narrow spools in the same reel diameter. A large-arbor spool with a wide diameter , however, may take up line faster than a small-arbor spool with a narrow diameter, especially during the first few rotations.

Reels come with various ventilation schemes, in the form of holes in the spool and frame designed to reduce weight. Some of these configurations have become signatures for various reel manufacturers.

The weight of a reel is of some importance—remember, you must lift and cast it all day. A reel that is excessively heavy for its purpose is an unnecessary burden and can feel awkward to cast and to handle. But don't feel forced to buy a reel that balances the rod at some certain physical "balance point." While it doesn't hurt to balance your rod and reel, realize that the physical balance point of a rod-and-reel system is dynamic. It changes moment to moment according to several factors, such as the movement of the rod from horizontal to vertical, whether line is being let out or retrieved, how much line is on the reel, and the resistance of the line in the air or on the water.

With respect to reel weight, first consider the best reel you can afford for the job at hand. If the reel

weighs an ounce more or less than your ideal, so be it. If the reel feels intolerably awkward or heavy, look for something else, but do not lose sight of what you need to handle line and land fish.

MAKING YOUR REEL PERFORM

Once you have selected a reel, take some time to become familiar with its drag. To find out how much drag your reel generates, tie the line to a pull-type scale, engage the drag, and see how much pressure is required before the reel turns. Repeat the procedure with different drag settings.

When you set your reel's drag, consider the following general guidelines:

1. Use the lightest drag setting that is applicable to the angling situation.

2. Don't set the drag pressure at greater than half the breaking strength of the tippet.

3. Once you have set the drag for a particular fishing situation, leave it alone. However, this guideline may need to be ignored when dealing with powerful, long-running fish.

Setting drag is a balancing act between overloading (or breaking) the tippet and applying enough resistance to the fish so that eventually it becomes tired enough to be landed. Other factors can complicate the drag-setting process; you may need to use little or no drag to avoid snapping tippets in weeds and extremely deep water.

One of the easiest ways to add drag precisely while fighting a fish is to "palm"—press, pinch, or cup the reel's spool. By palming, you can very quickly and accurately add as much drag as you think your tippet can take, especially if a fish is making a run into fast or very deep water. While exposed rim spools are easier to apply pressure on, you usually can palm enclosed rim spools, if done carefully.

CARING FOR YOUR REEL

Most higher-end modern fly reels are so well made that they will provide you with a lifetime of service with just minor maintenance. The internal parts need

As a designer of fly reels, I am faced with an interesting challenge. I feel a strong urge to honor the long history and traditions of fly fishing, but at the same time the engineer in me demands elegant solutions to the constantly increasing demands placed upon fly reels.

My first fly reel, purchased in 1952 for $3.98, was a Pfleuger stamped reel. It added little to the fly-fishing experience but served me faithfully for 21 years before the brass bushing in the spool finally seized. With no money to purchase a new reel but with a brand new machine shop at my disposal, I decided to create a better reel.

At that point, in 1973, the Hardy Marquis was the standard of the industry, with flat wire springs and click pawls making up the "click regulator" drag system. I polled the experts in the industry at the time—including Lefty Kreh, Russ Peak, and Ned Grey—for their input. Lefty and Ned were both pioneers in saltwater fly fishing and Russ was a custom rod builder with a very traditional frame of mind. I could not have had better input, because the consensus of these revered experts was that the next-generation fly reel should have a very traditional look to it but should also have a smooth, reliable friction drag system with ball bearings between the spool and the spindle.

Soon, my wife, Susie, and I had created our brand new Ross Reel, and we set forth to amaze and delight the industry. (The Ross is different from the Hardy Marquis in that it's not a pawl-and-click reel, but a disk reel.) We then had the privilege of being shown the door of most of the premier fly shops in the West. "A hundred dollars for a fly reel? You must be nuts."

Needless to say, we persevered, and now, twenty-five years later, we are gratified to have contributed an essential reel to the evolution of our beloved sport.

—Ross Hauck

to be well lubricated with an oil or grease intended for such applications. Different reels may benefit from special lubrication on particular internal parts and at specific intervals. For proper lubrication, read your manual or contact the dealer or manufacturer.

While fly reels can take a lot of abuse, one rule must be followed: Never operate a reel after abrasive substances have worked their way inside. Particularly damaging are sand and dirt, which can accelerate wear and damage delicate parts. If you have a spring-and-pawl reel, on-the-water cleaning is easy. Just separate the spool and frame and give them a good shake underwater. If internal parts get dry while you are fishing, a little fly floatant can serve as temporary lubrication.

Disk drags are a bit more complex, but due to internal pressures, disks are not typically as susceptible as spring-and-pawl designs to large particles. A soaked disk, however, can spell reduced performance. If they become dirty, take them apart and wipe them down, replacing grease and oil as necessary. Some reels come with permanently sealed drags, so contamination to that part of the mechanics is of little worry. If fully sealed drags do malfunction, however, you may need to send the reel back to the manufacturer to have it fixed or replaced.

Fishing in saltwater requires special equipment care. Supposedly indestructible reels can lock up solid from salt corrosion. Salt should be rinsed off the reel's workings—as well as from the frame and spool—each day. When your fishing trip is over, take the reel apart, clean it thoroughly in fresh water, and then completely relube it.

Treated well, a reel can become an old and trusted friend. As tools for serious fly anglers, reels are indispensable; as works of art, they are beautiful. And when they sing their siren song, it may even seem that nothing else in the world matters.

LINES, LEADERS, & TIPPETS

BY DICK TALLEUR

An average fly angler can deliver a weightless feathered hook to a trout 40 feet away in a quiet, dinner-plate-sized riffle, across a rushing stream, and despite a billowing morning breeze. This feat may seem like a miracle to a novice, but a balanced fly line, leader, and tippet allow most fly fishers to do it with ease.

To optimize line and leader construction you must appreciate the basic nature of fly casting, which is completely different from casting spoons, spinners, and weighted baits or lures. The key difference is that it is the **line**, rather than the lure or the bait, that provides the propelling momentum. Because the fly has virtually no weight, the weight of the thrown line must pull the fly along. With proper manipulation, the angler is able to whip the line through the air and place the fly at the desired spot.

A **leader** is a tapered transition between the relatively heavy, thick line and the weightless fly. It is the final link in the connection to the fly and ultimately to the fish. It provides continuity of the power developed during the casting stroke, and camouflages the connection to the line. Leaders are made of monofilament materials designed to be as inconspicuous to the fish as possible. Usually, a length of monofilament—the **tippet**—connects the end of the leader to the fly.

For fly rods, lines, leaders, and flies to work as a single unit, they must be in balance. To cast bigger flies, you need heavier lines and leaders; to cast those heavier lines, you need stiffer and stronger rods. Once you understand how different kinds of fly lines are constructed and how they vary, you can consider leaders and tippets of different designs and materials.

FLY LINES

Essentially, a fly line consists of a layer of plastic, usually vinyl, extruded over a core of another material. Modern lines are tapered—larger in diameter at some points along the line and smaller at others—which makes casting much easier and more effective. While it is still possible to buy cheap, untapered (or level) fly lines, tapered ones are generally much preferred.

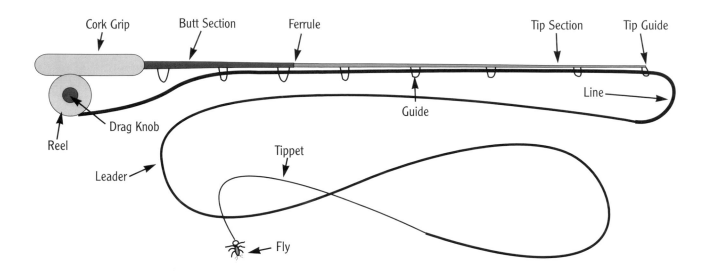

The basic components of the fly casting system from rod and reel to line, leader, tippet, and fly.

Before extruded plastic technology was developed, fly lines had been made of braided silk. The best ones, such as the King Eider, came from England and were very pricey. In order to get them to float, they required constant care and frequent dressing, which means drying the line and applying a floatant after each use. Owning a King Eider was like having a new baby in the house. But in the early 1950s, Leon Martuch patented floating fly lines, which incorporated tiny bubbles in the vinyl coating to make the specific density of the line less than that of water—a key property of all naturally floating materials. Martuch and his son formed a company called Scientific Anglers, which produced not only floating lines (Air Cel) but ones that were designed to sink as well (Wet Cel). For a long time, other companies in the fly line business used the Scientific Angler technology; eventually 3M bought the company.

The earliest system for rating fly lines was by diameter, so that a line could be matched to a rod. Lighter lines had letter designations that were further along in the alphabet: For example, an E line was thinner and lighter than a C line. Lines with a thicker diameter center and tapered on both ends carried such designations as HDH.

By the time I started fly fishing in 1955, several other production methods had joined the Martuch process, and the alphabet system for rating lines was becoming worse than useless because it resulted in very inaccurate and misleading ratings. Plastic line weights varied considerably, even at the same diameter, depending upon how they were produced; none were the same as silk lines. After a period of chaos, a rating system based on line weight was developed and is still in use today. Under the new system the first 30 feet of the fly line is weighed and a numeric rating is assigned. Heavier lines are given higher numbers. Standard ratings specified by the American Fly Tackle Manufacturer's Association (AFTMA) are shown in Table 1. While not shown in this table, lines greater than 12-weight are also available. AFTMA specifies adding fifty grains to the previous weight. Thus, a 12-weight would be in the range of 380 grains, and the 13-weight would be in the neighborhood of 430 grains.

With this line-rating system, holding to specifications is very important—because if people buy a line that is significantly heavier or lighter, it will cast very poorly with the rod with which it has been mismatched. The tolerances of lighter and heavier lines are included because absolute uniformity of weight specifications is not feasible, and subsequently these guidelines will provide a little bit of leeway. Unfortunately, specifications aren't always matched in production from company to company. While quality control is quite good today, some out-of-tolerance lines do escape into the world, i.e., some lines are thicker and heavier than they would be if they were uniformly standardized. This results in imprecise matching of line to rod, and casting is impeded to whatever degree the line is out of specification. So if you have a problem casting a certain line—especially with a rod that you have used successfully with other lines of the same weight and design—the line may be suspect.

SYMBOLS FOR FLY-LINE DESIGNATIONS

Abbreviations are used to indicate fly-line tapers and types. The common ones include DT: double taper (tapered to a small diameter at both ends); WF: weight forward (greater weight in the first 20 to 40 feet); F: floating; F/S: sinking tip (floating body/sinking tip); S: sinking; I: intermediate (sinking); and ST: shooting taper.

These symbols are combined with line weight to give a letter-number system for marking fly lines. DT5F means double-taper 5-weight floating line, and WF7S means weight-forward 7-weight sinking line. This system is used today, but there are so many tapers and sink rates available that additional descriptive information often is required.

TAPER TALK

The many specialized designs we have today evolved from two basic line tapers or shapes: double taper and weight-forward taper. The **double taper (DT)** starts at a certain diameter, is increased to a greater diameter in a section called the belly or body of the line, maintains that diameter for some length, and then is reduced in diameter to the same size as the other end. It doesn't cast as far as the nonsymmetrical tapers, but it forms a lovely, graceful loop in the air, has a uniform feel throughout the casting stroke, and is great for fishing unweighted flies, as it responds very well

to mending techniques (sometimes defined as "throwing" the belly of the line upstream; see the Casting chapter). The overall length for typical double taper lines is 85 to 90 feet, varying with specialized designs. As a bonus, you get two lines for the price of one, since DT lines can be reversed when one end becomes worn. (With the price of fly lines today, that is a significant benefit.)

Upon close examination, you may find that some so-called double-taper lines are not perfectly symmetrical; variations in the properties of materials (especially density) can change the taper somewhat. For example, coatings on fly lines vary considerably. Some contain many more bubbles than others (causing them to float more), and some have harder surfaces for longer wear and better shooting (ability to reach a farther distance). This makes a difference in how these lines cast, which explains variations in the taper.

TABLE 1: LINE WEIGHTS

Weight Rating	Weight, Grains	Tolerance
1	60	54–66
2	80	74–86
3	100	94–106
4	120	114–126
5	140	134–146
6	160	152–168
7	185	177–193
8	210	202–218
9	240	230–250
10	280	270–290
11	330	318–342
12	380	368–392

The **weight-forward (WF)** taper line is just what the name implies: there is more weight at the business end. The standard length is 30 yards, or 105 feet. It starts with a certain diameter, ramps up to its maximum-diameter belly, maintains that belly for a certain length, then tapers down to a relatively thin running line. In a WF line, the tip is sometimes a little heavier than the tip of a double-taper line. The weight-forward taper line was developed for distance casting, the idea being to utilize the belly of the line more effectively.

When the weight is moved forward on the line, the aerodynamics of the cast changes. Compared to the DT line weight, forward lines have a relatively short belly, enabling the caster to aerialize more of the line weight when false casting (the act of casting the line backward and forward in the air, preparatory to delivering it to the water, much like a baseball pitcher's windup). With proper execution, "aerializing" the line weight will optimize the rod's power and enable a fisher to shoot a line considerable lengths.

While any weight-forward line can be used for short distances, there are now more specialized WF tapers for close-in casting. These line tapers are designed expressly for smaller streams, such as Western spring creeks and British chalk streams, where the angler makes a lot of short casts. Here, a taper that puts weight beyond the rod tip while working with a short length of line in the air is ideal. A longer tip and short front taper on these special-ized WF lines enable a more delicate delivery, which is crucial on small, quiet waters.

On American spring creeks and limestome streams, it is seldom necessary to cast a large fly, so these lines with longer tips serve well. On British chalk streams, some very good-sized mayflies are encountered. When it is necessary to cast a larger, more air-resistant fly, adaptations of the leader are usually sufficient to compensate for the lighter, longer tip. The "spring creek taper" is especially good for beginning fly casters; the weight out front loads the rod without a lot of line in the air, making it easier to cast.

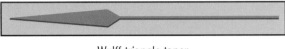

Wulff triangle taper.

One of the more interesting tapers of the modern era of fly lines is the **Wulff triangle taper (TT)**. Lee Wulff designed this taper simply by copying the front taper of the top-quality silk lines he used in his early days as a fly fisher. The typical trout TT lines have 40 feet of continuous front taper, then drop off immediately to thin running line. TT lines are very

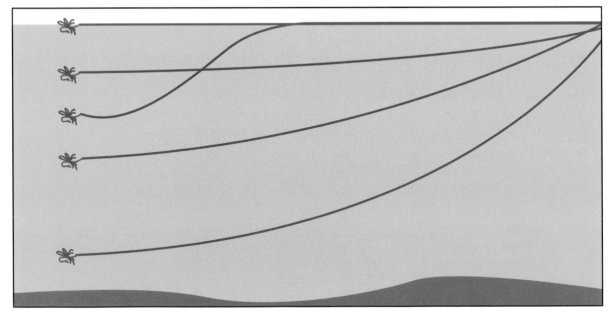

Different fly lines (from top to bottom): floating line, floating line with sinking tip, intermediate line, sinking line, and fast-sinking line.

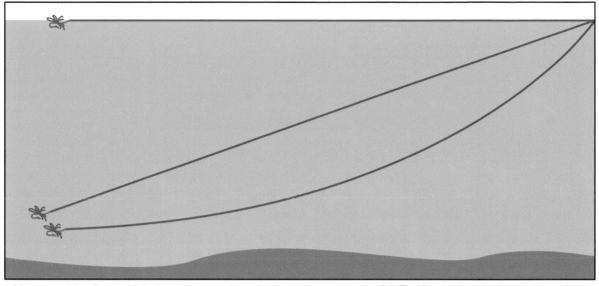

Lines can either float or sink, depending on where the fly can best attract the fish. The floating line (top) sits on top of the of the water. The two types of sinking line, uniform sink line (middle) and regular sink line (bottom), go below the surface.

good for a variety of fishing conditions. The lighter ones make great spring creek lines, as they enable a delicate presentation; they roll cast beautifully. And since their inception, heavier triangle-taper lines with slightly shorter tapers have been developed for saltwater use. These lines are truly designed by fly fishers for fly fishers.

SINKING FLY LINES

Sinking lines are those that are designed to sink at different rates of speed, thus attracting fish that hang out in various depths. **Sinking fly lines** are designated with an "**S**." Over the years, the evolution has been away from full-length sinking lines in favor of **floating lines with sinking tips**, which vary in length, designated "**F/S**." The sinking tips vary in length from as little as 5 feet to almost 30 feet.

Cortland Line Company describes sinking lines by sink rate—or the speed at which they sink. These sinking types are categorized in Roman numerals. A Type I line sinks at 1 inch per second, while a Type II sinks at 2 inches per second, and so on, up to a Type VI line, which sinks at 6 inches per second.

Sinking-tip lines offer some important advantages from a fishing standpoint since they allow the line to reach fish in deeper waters, but they are not a lot of fun to cast. Because these lines are partially submerged, they do not pick up cleanly off the water, which means a certain amount of handwork is involved in preparing for the next cast. Lines with higher sink rates also pose casting problems because they have poor aerodynamics and do not form nice loops, however, the ability to place the fly at optimal fishing depths are well worth the effort.

Slow-sinking lines have a tendency not to penetrate the surface of the water and start sinking immediately, because they are not much heavier than water and may not penetrate the surface tension of the water. A needle floating in a cup of water involves the same principle. A line that resists penetrating the surface can be roughed up a little with some fine sandpaper. These lines sink better as they roughen with age.

One of the more annoying problems with sinking lines is "sag." The belly, being heavier, sinks faster than the tip—it sags. This sag in turn makes it difficult to detect strikes. Some line manufacturers now offer uniform sink tips that effectively counteract sag by varying the grain distribution, so that the thinner part of the line sinks at the same speed as the thicker part.

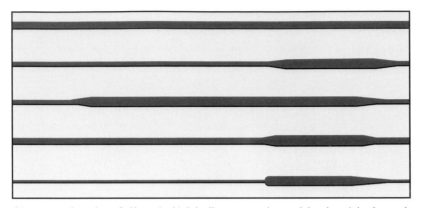

Line tapers from butt (left) to tip (right): (from top to bottom) level, weight-forward taper, double taper, bass taper, and shooting-head taper. Bass and shooting-head lines have a more extreme design, with the heavy part of the line toward the front of the line for casting large, air resistant, or heavy flies.

The selection of a sinking line depends to a great extent on how you plan to use it. Sinking lines are very effective for slow-water fishing, in lakes, ponds, and meandering sections of rivers. In such conditions, the angler has more power to decide how the line will travel, whereas faster streams will inflict a number of other frustrations on an angler, such as dragging the line below rocks, and the like. Indeed, in faster currents, the success of a sinking line depends on the angling technique being employed. I do not like them for drifting nymphs in a natural fashion, especially if the stream bottom is exceptionally rocky or uneven, because they have a tendency to get caught up on things. In such conditions, try a floating line so that the only things that sink are the fly and leader. This enables the angler to use the floating line as a strike indicator. For working a streamer or Woolly Bugger with a shorter leader and quicker retrieve, though, the right kind of sink tip is an asset.

There are also high-density lines that sink like wire. They cast like wire, too, but that comes with the territory. Their effectiveness for certain types of fishing offsets their negative casting characteristics, so they have become very popular. These lines were pioneered by Jim Teeny a number of years ago, but today all of the major line companies offer such fast-sinking products.

SPECIALIZED LINE DESIGNS

Innovation in fly-line design and manufacture has accelerated considerably during the past fifteen to twenty years. In the mid-1980s, a British company introduced a line called Airflo to try to solve the problem of stretchiness in conventional fly lines. This elasticity, not considered a big deal in trout fishing, was a major headache in fly fishing for large saltwater game fish. Because the conventional fly lines were too elastic, it was very difficult to get good hook penetration in the tough mouths of such fish as tarpon and permit.

The original Airflo line had a core made of Kevlar, a high-tech material used in spacecraft nosecones and bulletproof jackets. It is incredibly strong and has virtually no stretch. In theory it was the optimal solution, but in reality it did not work very well. The Kevlar-core lines cast poorly, mainly because they could not be stretched straight like conventional lines—they quickly resembled a Slinky, winding up in frustrating coils that interfered with casting as well as fishing performance.

Now Airflo has a series of High Sense Clear Glass Saltwater Cold Water Fast Intermediate lines (note, this is one type of line that just has a very long name). The lines are built around a virtually nonstretch monofilament core that aids strike detection and helps set the hook. The coating is a polymer that approaches the clearness of glass, greatly reducing the visibility of the line in the water. The head or front taper is 36 to 40 feet in length, depending on line weight, and features a 1.5-inch-per-second sink rate. The coldwater type retains its flexibility in northern conditions, which makes it ideal for striped bass fishing. This line is making rapid headway in the saltwater market.

Meanwhile, Jim Vincent began a company called

Rio to develop advanced fly lines and leaders. His two-handed lines, the Wind Cutter and the Accelerator, are ideally suited to the much faster graphite spey rods of today, and they have virtually revolutionized two-handed casting. There are also Wind Cutter lines for single-handed rods in both floating and sinking models. The VersaTip line, which evolved from the Windcutter, features an interchangeable tip system, which makes it possible to go astream with one line and a selection of tips with different sink rates, and cope with a wide variety of conditions. This is accomplished by the incorporation of a nonhinging spliced-loop system that does not interfere with casting efficiency. Nonhinging means that the action of the line is the same as if there were no loop at all; a spliced-loop is a knotless loop that has been built in by the manufacturer. They are offered in floating and intermediate-sink densities.

For a bold perspective on all this, examine a modern fly line catalog that contains a lot of detail about line designs and tapers. The graphic representations of the tapers and shapings are very explicit, enabling the angler to visualize the designs quite well. The degree of specialization is remarkable. There are lines designed not only for various conditions and types of fly fishing but for individual species of fish—tarpon lines, bonefish lines, striped bass lines, billfish lines, and so forth. There is even a pike line. They all have unique tapers and casting characteristics, even though in some cases the differences are minimal, leading one to wonder about the practicality of all that variation. Do you suppose that a bonefish cruising along in a tidal flat would refuse to take a fly simply because the angler wasn't using a bona fide bonefish line? Would an Atlantic salmon turn up its kype at a fly presented with a pike line? When the fish evolve to that level, I think we are all in big trouble.

LEADERS

The function of the leader is threefold: It transmits the energy of the cast from the fly line to the fly; it serves as camouflage; and it connects to the fly—and ultimately, to the fish. That's a lot to ask of a piece of monofilament. Consider the extremes of fly fishing today, the difference between delicately casting a #26 fly on a spring creek and the labor of working a heavy streamer on a big river or driving a tarpon popper into high wind. Obviously, there is an enormous variety in leader design.

Leaders have gone through even greater development than lines over the past thirty years, thanks to better materials, better manufacturing technology, and improved leader designs. When I first began fly fishing in the mid-1950s, the factory-tapered extruded leaders available in the stores left a lot to be desired. So I began making leaders several years before I started tying flies. I still make most of my own leaders, but more as a matter of choice than necessity, since there are plenty of excellent extruded leaders available today, for every conceivable type of fishing.

The casting characteristics of a leader are of primary importance, because if the angler cannot make a good presentation, camouflage will not help much and hookups will be infrequent. So the first consideration in choosing a leader is how it will cast with a particular rod, line, and type of fly.

The key word in the selection of a leader is "interaction." The line drives the leader from one end, and the fly influences it from the other. The leader allows the energy of the fly line's momentum to be

Modern plastic lines do not require the constant pampering of the old silks. However, a modicum of care is necessary, especially with dry fly lines. Here are the more important steps to getting maximum life and performance from your fly lines:

1. Keep them clean. There are several good products available for cleaning lines. Cortland puts out a little felt pad treated with a cleaning agent that I particularly like. Do not use harsh detergents or petroleum-based solvents, as they will damage the finish of the line. Warm water and mild hand soap works very well.

2. Avoid exposing the lines to high heat. We kill our lines by leaving them in the trunks of cars parked in hot sun, or even worse, by laying them on the rear deck, where they are directly exposed to the sun. We would all be well advised to keep a small cooler in the car, just for the purpose of keeping lines—and camera film—cool.

3. When a line will be out of use for an extended period of time, such as over the off season, take it off the reel and store it on some sort of large spool in loose coils.

4. Be careful what you use to get lines to shoot or float better. I have heard of people applying car polishes, in order to slick up a line for distance casting. I do not know for sure, but I suspect that this might not be good for the health of the line.

5. It is a good idea to straighten a line now and then by pulling it out of the reel and stretching it. This must be done gently, and with discretion. Too much stretching can cause cracks in the finish.

6. Be sure that your reel has adequate capacity. Do not try to force the last few yards of a line onto the reel by jamming it against the spool or frame. Fly lines do not fare well in battles with metal.

—Dick Talleur

---

transmitted to the fly, and the weight and air resistance of the fly determines what kind of connection is necessary. For these reasons, optimizing the leader's performance requires understanding what is happening at both of these ends. As we know, the released power of the rod on the forward cast propels the line in a tight loop. As the line straightens and comes to a stop, this momentum is transferred to the leader. As the loop continues to unfurl—if all has gone well—the fly is delivered on target.

There are various philosophies of leader design. The prominent philosophy is that the butt section of the leader needs to be of such a diameter and texture that a smooth transfer of power takes place from the line to that leader. If the butt section is too limp, power is diminished, perhaps to the point where the leader fails to straighten and the leader, tippet, and fly fall onto the water in a pile. Too stiff a butt section means the line does not bend properly, with poor loop formation, which can also compromise the efficiency of the cast. In general, however, an overly-stiff leader is not as much of a problem as an overly limp one.

Another concept is that the butt should form as tight a loop as possible for effective casting. This is the idea behind the so-called braided-butt leader, where the butt is made of softer, braided material rather than solid monofilament material. Another argument in favor of the braided-butt leader is that it is always straight, which is beneficial. But these leaders have several drawbacks: They do not cast well in the wind, and, because they are quite visible, a long tippet of plain monofilament is required for camouflage. Orvis, perhaps the leading proponent of the braided-butt design, incorporates a loop for adding the tippet to the end of the leader. These leaders have improved in recent years, but I find them to be less efficient in casting than regular monofilament leaders and thus a bit limited from a functional standpoint.

Generally, today's extruded leaders are tapered in a manner similar to the front end of a fly line. The butt portion is considerably longer than the taper nearest the fly, to maximize the transfer of energy. After the butt section, these leaders quickly taper to a tippet of some particular diameter and length. The more sophisticated extruded leaders may vary the stiffness, beginning with a stiffer butt and ending with a limp tippet. For typical fishing situations, this is generally accepted as the best compromise.

SPECIAL SYMBOLS FOR LEADER AND TIPPET DIAMETERS

On a typical package of leader or tippet material, you are apt to see three criteria listed: pounds test, diameter expressed as something-

TABLE 2: RECOMMENDED TIPPET DIAMETER TO FLY SIZE	
Tippet Diameter	Fly Size (in thousandths of an inch)
7X–8X	24 and smaller
6X	18–22
5X	14–16
4X	12–14
3X	10–12
2X	8–10
1X	Big, heavy stuff

X, and diameter expressed in thousandths of an inch. The latter is the most useful. There is a direct translation from thousandths of an inch to the "X" system, as shown in Table 2. There is some 8X around these days, but I have not found it necessary to go down that narrow, even with the tiniest of flies. With today's technology, it may be practical, but I cannot personally attest to that.

READY-MADE LEADERS

Packaged leaders come in a variety of lengths and weights. There is a lot of relevant information on the packages, along

It's possible that this nice-sized brown trout is descended from stock that have lived in the same waters since the Pleistocene.

with the usual promotional rhetoric. In addition to the obvious (length, butt diameter, and tippet diameter), specifications as to stiffness and limpness, recommended line weight, and recommended fly size are often included.

General-purpose leaders for average trout fishing come in lengths of 6, 7½, 9, and 12 feet. A typical 9-foot leader tapered to 3X might have a butt diameter of .023 inches. The tippet would be .008 inches, the specification for 3X. That does not, or at least *should* not, vary. Yet there is sometimes considerable variance in butt diameter for given line weights of leaders from various manufacturers. This is not necessarily all bad; it simply means that the different stiffnesses of materials chosen by the manufacturers require different diameters to produce a similar relativity to the specified line. If a desired stiffness can be obtained with a smaller butt diameter, that should improve aerodynamics because of less air resistance. It also reduces the bulk of the knot that connects the leader to the line. However, that statement should not be considered the last word on butt diameter; there are too many subtleties and variations.

Innovation is as rampant in leaders as it is in lines. A good example of this is an extruded leader produced by the Maxima company, which has long been noted for its monofilament. They start with a butt section of the traditional dark Maxima Chameleon and blend it into a tippet of their newer Ultragreen material.

Specialization is also a very big factor in a modern leader. You can find leaders for the same specialized extremes as you do lines: everything from spring creek trout to tarpon and billfish. Obviously, the fish couldn't care less. This information is for our edification. Personally, I am glad to accept such descriptions, provided there is a rationale to go along with them. For example, I would want to know what characteristics make a leader a bonefish leader, a steelhead leader, and so forth.

And there are valid distinctions. For instance, consider this quote from the package of a Rio Steelhead and Atlantic salmon leader: "Designed with a thick, long butt section that facilitates the transfer of energy from larger fly lines to heavy or wind-resistant flies." That tells me something. Some special features are more obvious. For example, the Climax series, which is offered by Cortland, includes a barracuda/shark leader that has a 15-inch wire tippet. Enough said.

There are also leaders that accommodate various fishing techniques. Some are designed to sink and have sink rates just like some lines. Airflo's Polyleader comes in densities from floating to extra-super-fast sink. They have extruded a tapered coating over a level monofilament core, to which may be added a supplemental tippet. This brings up some interesting possibilities. I have long believed that the ultimate dry fly leader would have about a 2-foot tippet that rode below the surface, to eliminate that highly visible impression in the surface film that is present with all floating tippets, regardless of diameter. Maybe someday I can figure out how to put this together, using one of the Airflo leaders as a starting point.

Obviously, the longer and lighter a leader, the harder it is to cast effectively. What are the limits of a leader? That depends on a number of factors: the skill of the caster, the design of the leader, the size and air resistance of the fly, the capabilities of the rod, the weight of the line, and, of course, the conditions astream. If the wind is blowing a gale, no one is going to be able to work with an overly long leader; but then you will not have to, because the wind roughs up the surface of the water and helps camouflage the presentation. Wind can be hateful, but it can also be helpful.

Umpqua offers a series of spring-creek leaders designed for delicate presentation of smaller flies. Dave Whitlock designed the tapers; he has done a great deal of spring-creek fly fishing in his life, and he knows what works. A typical leader is 13 feet long, has a butt diameter of .019 inches, and tapers to a 7X tippet. If you want to go longer, you can buy one with a heavier tippet and add some lighter material.

It must be recognized that leaders of this sort are tough to straighten in the air, even in favorable conditions. There is no benefit to using an overly long leader if you cannot cast it properly and deliver the fly effectively. In other words, the average angler is better served by using a 12-foot leader that can be handled with proficiency than a 16-footer that piles up in the air and does not deliver the fly on target.

There are highly specialized leaders available for the large-game fly fisher and seeker of recognition in the record books. You can buy leaders with shock tippets in various weights that are connected to monofilament of a specific pound test, which enables a fish to be submitted for record consideration by the International Game Fish Association (IGFA). This requires that the leader be sent to the IGFA for analysis, since records are kept according to the pound test of the tippet with which the fish was landed. These are called tippet class records. There is a small cult of fly fishers that continually strives to catch larger and larger fish on lighter and lighter leaders. The practice encourages playing fish to a level of exhaustion beyond which they will not likely regain strength and survive.

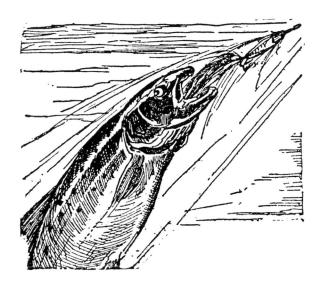

TIPPETS

As flies are changed, or if a strong fish breaks off, your leader-tippet will be shortened. The common practice is to add sections of tippet in an attempt to maintain your original setup. Alternatively, if you change to a smaller or larger fly, modifications in tippet length or diameter on the water offer versatility. For example, you can buy a 7½ foot leader tapered to 3X and use it for fishing a fairly large fly, then tie on a couple of feet of 5X and fish with greater refinement. In fact, you will find that rebuilding leaders astream is an ongoing activity. For this reason, you will want to learn the few simple knots that facilitate this, such as the needle knot or the surgeon's knot (see comments below on hand-tied leaders).

As mentioned previously, the size and air resistance of the fly has a direct bearing on the performance of the leader. Of particular importance is the diameter and length of the tippet. Again, there is a limit here to what is possible. It is very difficult for even the expert caster to deliver a large, bushy dry fly with a long leader and a very fine tippet. I believe in matching the diameter of the tippet to the size and type of fly being used. Apparently, the leader manufacturers agree, since several of them include such information on their packages. In general, if you have a small fly, a light tippet is best, and so on. Guidelines are provided in Table 3.

Table 3: 6–7 Weight Long Leader to Tippet Length		
Long leader, 6–7 Wt.	**Length**	**Diameter**
Section 1 (butt)	42 inches	.020
Section 2	36 inches	.017
Section 3	24 inches	.014
Section 4	18 inches	.012
Section 5	12 inches	.010

Here, attach the appropriate tippet, or if more length and/or a lighter tippet is desired, add another section .008 in diameter and 9 inches in length.

Do not be enslaved by this chart; these are simply general rules. The type of fly, the conditions, and your casting techniques allow for variations. For example, a very air-resistant fly such as a Variant (a bushy fly with extra-large hackle) might require a heavier tippet, whereas a sparsely dressed parachute might allow a lighter one. But remember: The tippet has to do more than just deliver the fly; it has to enable you to set the hook and land the fish. Do not try to get away with a finer tippet than you actually need.

Building Your Own Leaders

As noted earlier, there are some very good extruded leaders on the market today. At the same time, a wide selection of excellent monofilament enables you to make your own leaders. Hand-tied leaders are constructed of multiple sections of monofilament, starting with a fairly large-diameter monofilament connected to the fly line—the butt section—and segments of successively smaller diameters of monofilament down to the fly, creating a stepwise taper.

Hand-tied leaders, whether store-bought or homemade, have one thing in common—they are knotted. (I do not know of anyone who has the equipment in his basement or garage to make an extruded leader.) There are a few situations in which smooth leaders with no knots have an advantage, most frequently when fishing in water that has high algae or vegetation content. The extremely popular Bighorn loca-

tion is a good example. I have fished the Horn and a few other streams that often suffer from a bloom of some kind. After spending most of my time trying to pick globs of green slime off of the knots in my leader, I learned to take a few extruded ones along, just for those situations. Aside from that problem, I like fishing with leaders I have built myself. I can construct them in such a manner that they will cast better than whatever I might buy, and I can fine-tune them to the flies and tackle I'm using at a particular time. I have a formula for making a wind-casting leader that helps ease that obstacle as well. And frankly, I can reduce costs significantly; leader materials do not cost all that much, and knots cost only the small amount of time required to tie them.

Years ago, an old-time Catskill fly fisher, after listening to my long lament about the shortcomings of leaders, laid a real gem on me. "Look," he said, "all you have to do to make a leader that will cast well is to start off thick, end up thin, don't drop more than two or three thousandths per section, and make each piece a little shorter that the one before." Add to that basic proposition a little fine tuning, and you can join the legion of leader mavens.

For general trout fishing, I make my leaders out of a somewhat less flexible or harder monofilament (as it is called). My material of preference is Maxima, although there are some other good ones, such as Mason's. I like Maxima because it can be straightened easily, has good knotting characteristics, and is of such texture as to cast well. However, I usually use something else for my tippets, except when fishing large and/or heavy flies.

Maxima now comes in two shades or colors: the original purplish brown and a misty green, which is a bit softer. I switch at the most critical point, the tippet. The main reason I don't use Maxima for the tippet is that it does not seem of true diameter, especially in lighter weights. This has been true for as long as I have been using the stuff. It has improved somewhat, but I still find significant variations from what is specified on the spool. Thus, when I shop for Maxima, I take my micrometer to the shop, measure the diameter of the material and re-mark the spools. The folks over at the fly shop laugh when they see me coming, but my meticulous measuring pays off. It is a good idea to check any leader material for accuracy of diameter.

Diameter of material is critical in leader-making, though perhaps not quite to the extent that is sometimes stated. In the butt portion and midsection of a leader, you can be a little off on the diameter and still come out with a leader that works fine. The closer you get to the business end, the closer the tolerances become, especially in regard to the tippet.

To connect leaders to the fly line, I like either a needle knot or a nail knot. With small-diameter lines and also with sinking lines, needle knots are difficult to make, so I resort to nail knots. My butt sections are essentially permanent connections to the fly line. Other sections of the leader have to be rebuilt as the leader is used, especially in the forward portion. If you like loop-to-loop connections, you can make a perfection loop in the end of the butt section, which facilitates ease and flexibility in changing leaders. As an option, you can attach a very short piece of heavy monofilament to the line, make a loop, and thus have a completely modular system. My personal preference is to leave the butt section intact as part of my homemade leader.

I use one of two knots for connecting sections of monofilament in leader construction. When working with larger diameters (.010 inches and heavier), I use a common blood knot. When joining smaller diameters, a double or triple surgeon's knot does the job, because it is stronger that the blood knot and thus more practical in critical areas. The double is also known simply as the surgeon's knot. It is also easier and quicker to tie than the blood knot, and has the added benefit of being more stable when con-

Today's angler has a handful of tools to make the job of tying knots possible even in the sternest weather.

necting dissimilar types of monofilament. A double surgeon's knot consists of two overhand knots; a triple surgeon's knot consists of three.

I like to combine my Maxima leaders with a tippet made with one of the newer high-tech monofilaments such as Dai Riki, Climax, Orvis, Rio, or Umpqua for a tippet, thereby gaining the advantage of their greater strength-to-diameter ratio. For a typical leader-to-tippet connection such as .008 to .006, I use a double surgeon's knot. For connecting very fine–diameter stuff, or if I am in a desperate hurry and want to jump more than two thousandths, I add one more turn, and the double surgeon's knot becomes a triple.

TABLE 4: 6–7 WEIGHT SHORT LEADER TO TIPPET LENGTH		
Short leader, 6-7 Wt.	Length	Diameter
Section 1 (butt)	30 inches	.020
Section 2	20 inches	.017
Section 3	14 inches	.014
Section 4	12 inches	.012
Section 5	10 inches	.010

Here, attach the appropriate tippet, or if more length and/or a lighter tippet is desired, add another section, .008 in diameter and 7 or 8 inches in length.

The old rule about connecting monofilament sections and tapering in steps from the line toward the fly was intended to reduce in size no more than two thousandths. With Maxima and other modern materials, it is acceptable to drop three or even four thousandths, in larger diameters. This is helpful in simplifying leader construction and minimizing the number of knotted sections.

In the relationship between the line and the butt section of the leader there is some concern for diameter, but flexibility is also a consideration. I like my lines and butt sections to form an essentially continuous curve when flexed. A sharp bend at the point of line-to-leader connection indicates a difference in stiffness. With similar stiffness for the end of the fly line and butt section of the leader, the power generated in casting will be carried forward into the leader effectively, which enables the delivery of the fly. I do not find it beneficial to use the heaviest butt section I can tie to a given line. This only complicates development of the proper taper, because more step-downs are required. Table 4 shows a butt section for typical line weights (using Maxima and similar materials).

These line-leader diameter rules can be varied a little to achieve certain specific objectives. For example, to make a leader that will effectively deliver a hair bug with my 7-weight outfit, I will start with .021, and drop down from there. For very delicate work with my Scott 8-foot-8 2-weight, on which I prefer a Wulff Triangle 2/3 line, I use a .016 butt.

It's important to understand that dry flies cast differently than wet flies and nymphs, and that the larger and less aerodynamic the dry fly, the more difficult it is to get the leader to lay out effectively. Presentation and the ability to control one's casts and deliveries are the most important ingredients in successful fly fishing. I am more concerned about the ability of the leader to propel the fly and deliver it effectively than about having a slightly smaller-diameter tippet and thus a less visible presentation to the fish on the water's surface. For example, I will fish a big 14 Variant on a 2X or 3X tippet. Sure, a 5X could work if the wind wasn't too bad, but there's no meaningful advantage—plus it invites casting troubles, such as twisting of tippets, poor layout, and reduced accuracy.

On the other hand, I will go as long and light as I have to when the going is tough. If I'm casting upstream over rising trout on a quiet pool with a very small fly, I don't hesitate to use 12, 14, or even 16 feet of leader, tapered to 6X or 7X. This is a problem in significant wind, but if it is windy, the surface of the water will be disturbed, and I can use a shorter leader that casts more efficiently (see Table 5).

When using flies that have any significant amount of weight, all bets are off. Here, the concern is mainly with getting the fly delivered, and much less with delicacy or camouflage. The heavier the fly, the more the deviation from true fly-casting dynamics. Once you're fishing a very heavy fly, you'd better watch out that you don't get bonked in the head. When I fish heavier flies, I use a shorter leader and a heavier tippet. When circumstances allow, I use Maxima as tippet material, as it works better than the more elastic types for larger and heavier flies.

TABLE 5: 4–5 WEIGHT WIND LEADER TO TIPPET LENGTH

Wind leader, 4-5 Wt.	Length	Diameter
Section 1	24 inches	.017 or .018
Section 2	36 inches	.020
Section 3	6 or 7 inches	.017
Section 4	6 or 7 inches	.014
Section 5	6 or 7 inches	.012 or .011

A couple of basic leader formulas are shown in the tables. For long leaders, attach the appropriate tippet (with a reduction no greater than three thousandths), or if more length and/or a lighter tippet is desired, add another section, say .008 in diameter and 9 inches in length. With short leaders, attach the appropriate tippet, or if more length and/or a lighter tippet is desired, add another section, .008 in diameter and 7 or 8 inches in length.

For leaders for lighter systems, simply reduce the diameter of the butt section in accordance with earlier specifications and taper the leader in linear fashion. With very light outfits, you can drop two thousandths per step instead of three if you do not want to end up too fine. I sometimes resort to a special-purpose leader when I have to cast into strong winds. It is weird, but it is really quite helpful when conditions are extreme. Here's a typical formula:

If you are using a tippet that is within .003 of the last section of the leader, use a surgeon's knot. If the disparity exceeds that, attach the tippet with an Albright knot or by simply nail-knotting it to the last section of the leader. I recommend a droplet of ZapAGap on this connection (a great superglue that is perfect for wet conditions).

I have experimented with a relatively new fluorocarbon leader material that virtually disappears underwater—trying it out on some very picky fish—and the difference between it and regular monofilament is significant. But this fluorocarbon monofilament is still undergoing development. It does not have the strength-to-diameter ratio of regular monofilaments, and its knotting characteristics are not quite as stable. For this reason, some producers have been mixing it with other materials. This makes it more user friendly but, of course, detracts from the camouflage effect. It is my understanding that Mirage, an Orvis product, is 100 percent pure fluorocarbon—in other words, it's a very pure product that fish can't see. I have not had any serious problems with knots or inappropriate breaking with it. I use one or two tippet sizes heavier than I would with regular mono, because the unique properties of the material enable me to do so. At the moment, however, it is a bit expensive.

LEADER CARE AND LONGEVITY

Maxima is an inert material, and the knots tend to be very stable and dependable for a long while. With the more stretchy stuff, knots tend to loosen over time. Always re-tie these knots after your outfit sits for several hours or overnight. Also refresh fine tippets often: This will be difficult when fish are rising in front of you, but learning to tie good knots quickly will minimize your frustration and lost opportunities.

Heavy-diameter mono will last indefinitely. I have Maxima that I am still using in leader construction that is probably ten years old. However, finer-diameter mono, especially tippet material, should be replaced yearly, since it can lose as much as 25 percent of its strength in that time period. Even the relatively heavy stuff I use for salmon tippets gets replaced every year. I am still in my Captain Ahab mode, searching for that 40-pounder in Russia, and I do not want twenty cents' worth of leader material to rob me of my trophy photograph.

KNOTS

BY GARY SOUCIE

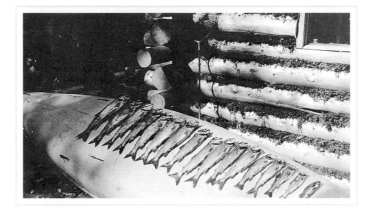

If you want to catch fish, you've got to use good knots. Yet if you ask fly-fishing "experts" which are the best knots, you'll get dozens of different recommendations along with copious and often confusing advice.

Every fly angler seems to have a different opinion about which is the best knot—for every conceivable purpose. By best, anglers usually mean the strongest and most secure knot for the purpose, and that ought to be an objective, directly measurable property. Various fishing books and magazines publish knot-strength charts, but those charts don't always agree. Expert A's strongest knot may often fail under much less pressure than it should when Expert B uses it. Perhaps the difference is that Expert A ties that particular knot better than Expert B, or ties it in a leader material that is better suited to the knot. There are many variables that can confound the situation.

But one simple, real-life principle holds true no matter what the "experts" say: The best knot is one you can tie quickly and well with pounding heart, pumping adrenal glands, and cold-numbed fingers in poor light, high wind, and rocking boat. For most of us, that eliminates a few of the experts' 100-percent favorites. Take the Bimini twist, for example, probably the strongest, most secure knot ever tested, and a perpetual experts' choice. There's just one problem: I can tie a pretty good one in the comfort of my living room, but when I'm out on the water—in the wind or perhaps in a pitching boat—a good Bimini twist is often too tough to tie properly. I usually resort instead to a surgeon's knot, a Spider hitch, or some other 85- to 90-percent knot that I know I can tie correctly and well in real-world fishing conditions.

And there is another consideration as well: A knot must be suited to the specific purpose at hand. Unless you are fishing in saltwater with heavy tackle for big game fish, you probably would never need to tie a Bimini twist. Some knots serve a single purpose, such as attaching a fly to the end of a tippet. Others can be modified to handle a lot of situations. But none can be used for every purpose, so you will need to learn more than one knot.

A conventional fly-fishing rig has five important connections: Dacron backing to the fly reel, fly line to the Dacron backing, leader to the fly line, leader to the tippet, and tippet to the fly. Several specialized knots are used to make most of these connections. Try them all at home if you like, but choose just one in each category for your own fishing—the one that is easiest for you to tie.

THE BASICS

No matter which knot you are tying, the following rules apply:

Choose a knot that is appropriate to the fly-fishing task you have in mind. To make this easy, the knots listed in this chapter are ordered according to their fly-fishing purposes.

Form the knot correctly. Besides learning the basic geometry of the knot, it is critical to make the necessary number of wraps or turns as you hold on to or pull on the appropriate parts of the knot.

Draw up—tighten—the knot properly. First, lubricate the untightened knot with water or saliva. Then, as you hold on to and pull on the correct parts, tighten it with one steady, continuous pull. If you draw knots up dry, or with unsteady jerks, they will deform as they tighten, which means they won't seat properly, and they will fail under pressure.

Clip the leftover ends of the knot close to the knot, but not too short. If you leave the ends too long, they will pick up gunk and weeds and foul up the leader. If you clip them too close, they may slip out under pressure. In fly-fishing knots, ⅛ inch is about the right length for the leftover ends. (Knots that should be clipped longer or shorter are specified in the tying instructions.)

Test the knot before fishing with it, then check it periodically while you are fishing. To test a finished knot, pull hard on it to make sure it does not come apart in your hands. If there is any slippage in the knot, cut it off and tie it again. While fishing, take a look at your knots from time to time, particularly after every fish or savage strike and after freeing a snagged fly. If a knot looks at all suspicious, snip it off and retie it.

TERMINOLOGY

It's not necessary to overindulge in the arcane nautical terms that refer to knots and knot tying, but there are a few words that may be useful. Most knots are formed by making "wraps," or "turns," with one part of the knot around another part. Adept knot-tiers may speed up the process by turning them into "twists," but in the beginning it's better to stick to wrapping turns. Some refer to them as "coils" in the tightened knot, but it is not an important semantic difference. However complicated a knot looks, it has just two basic parts. The "standing part" is the long part of the line or leader. The "tag end" is the part that usually gets clipped away when you are done. Knots used to join sections of leader, or to join the line to either leader or backing, have two tag ends and two standing parts, one for each piece of material. Sometimes, the overlapping strands of material in such knots are treated during the tying as if they are one tag end or one standing part.

THE OVERHAND KNOT

The first knot you must learn to tie is the overhand knot. By itself, the overhand is the worst true knot there is. It is the knot that bad casters like me get in their leaders because they cannot avoid those unwanted, spontaneous overhand knots in their line. We excuse ourselves by calling them wind

Overhand knot

knots, blaming Mother Nature for our own failings. Depending on the chemistry and inherent knot strength of the material in which it is tied, the overhand knot will break at 50 to 70 percent of the unknotted material's breaking point. Why, then, learn to tie it? Because it is used during the formation of many of the knots that follow.

TERMINAL KNOTS

Of all the knots you need to know, the terminal knot may be the most important, because you will use it

IMPROVED CLINCH KNOT

Step 1. Insert 6 to 8 inches of tippet through the eye of the fly. Do not skimp.

Step 2. Hold the fly in one hand and, with your other hand, wrap the tag end of the tippet around the standing part five or six times. Use the tips of the fly-holding hand's thumb and forefinger to hold open a small loop immediately in front of the eye.

Step 3. Bring the tag end of the leader through the loop in front of the fly's eye.

Step 4. Now, pass the tag end through the large loop just formed above the wraps in the previous step.

Step 5. Lubricate the wraps, and then tighten the knot by pulling steadily on the standing part of the tippet while holding the fly firmly. Don't pull on or even hold the tag end of the tippet; this is crucial to the security of the knot. If you must, use a tiny bit of fingertip pressure to keep it from sliding back out of the loop. If the knot looks good, without any loose or unseated wraps, and it does not slip or come apart when tested, clip the tag end fairly close—within ⅛ inch.

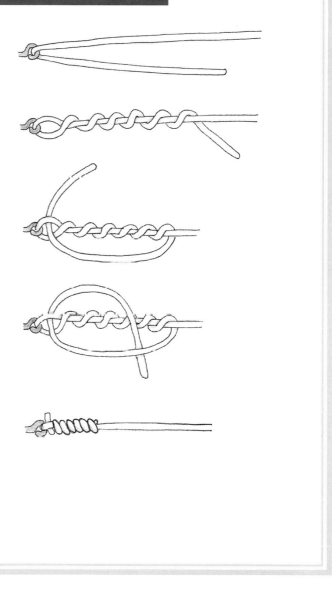

many times a day to tie flies onto your tippets, the weakest link in your tackle. This knot will be exposed to sharp teeth, abrasion on rocks and sand, the constant shock loads of back-and-forth casting, and the other hard knocks of fly fishing. A good terminal knot must be dependable and should hold at least 90 percent of the tippet material's strength.

Old-timers, traditionalists, and tweedies-come-lately like to use the Turle knot or one of its variants. Forget it. Major Turle invented that knot to minimize the weaknesses and shortcomings of silkworm gut, the tippet material of choice back before nylon was invented. It is practically useless in modern monofilaments, cofilaments, and other extruded materials.

IMPROVED CLINCH KNOT

The hands-down favorite terminal knot of fly fishers and most other anglers is the improved clinch knot. It is quick and easy to tie, and if it is tied and tightened properly, it is also very dependable.

Two-Circle Clinch Knot

The improved clinch, tied and tightened properly, is a good, dependable knot, but if you run the tippet twice through the eye before forming the knot, it becomes a two-circle clinch knot—and it is even better. The publicity brigades at Berkley & Company have succeeded in virtually changing the name of the two-circle clinch knot to the "Trilene" knot, after their brand of filament, even though the knot remains virtually the same. Orvis, Ande, Rapala, and a few others have also come up with brand-name knots, but none has enjoyed Berkley's success in getting people to use their knot and their trade name.

Uni-Knot

I use the Uni-Knot or Duncan loop in place of the improved clinch knot because it is more versatile—I do not have to remember a lot of dissimilar knots for the rest of my rig. The knot was invented when Vic Dunaway, longtime editor of *Florida Sportsman*

UNI-KNOT

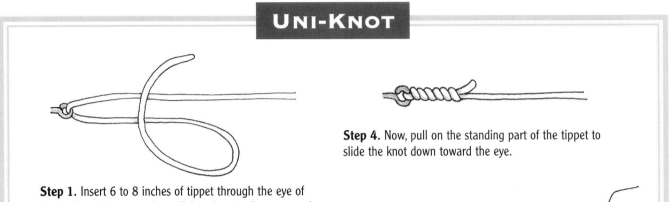

Step 1. Insert 6 to 8 inches of tippet through the eye of the fly. Bend the tag end parallel to the standing part and form a Uni-Knot circle about 1½ inches in diameter, with the tag end pointing up toward the rod and reel, away from the fly.

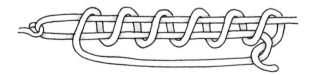

Step 2. Pass the tag end of the tippet through the circle and around both standing parts five or six times, moving up the tippet, away from the fly. Do not let those wraps cross each other as you are taking them.

Step 3. Lubricate the knot and pull firmly on the tag end to snug the wraps down on the tippet. Do not tighten the knot all the way.

Step 4. Now, pull on the standing part of the tippet to slide the knot down toward the eye.

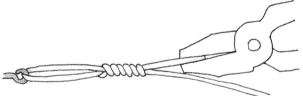

Step 4a. If you want to make a loop, use the thumb and forefinger of the other hand to hold the knot where you want it. Tighten all the way by pulling on the tag with pliers or hemostat (forceps).

Step 4b. If you want to tighten the knot against the eye, keep pulling on the standing part until it is seated against the eye. Now, tighten it all the way by pulling hard on the tag end. Pull on the standing part again, to be sure there is no slippage. Trim the tag end.

Sunrise fishing in the Florida Keys: Whether fising for bonefish, reds, snook, permit, or tarpon, your knots had better be good!

Anglers making the move to saltwater species will have to learn a new knot system for their leaders. It is no myth that saltwater fish are faster and stronger than their freshwater cousins and will test to the limits every piece of your tackle, particularly the knots forming your leader. In most cases, knots used in freshwater will be inappropriate. In the salt, anything less than 100 percent will fail.

Just the construction of a typical tarpon leader will test your knowledge of saltwater leader connections. Starting at the fly line, the butt section of the leader is usually connected to the fly line with a Nail Knot. At the end of the butt section is a double surgeon's loop knot. Looped into that is another double surgeon's loop knot, tied in a doubled section of class tippet formed by a Bimini Twist. At the other end of the class section, another loop is formed by another Bimini Twist. This doubled section of line is tied to the bite leader, or shock tippet, with an Albright or a Huffnagle knot. The fly is attached to the shock tippet with either a Snell or a Homer Rhode loop knot. This one leader requires seven perfectly formed knots to retain 100 percent of the breaking capacity of the line.

Among other must-learn knots for successful saltwater anglers are the Uni-Loop Knot, used to achieve a headfirst dive with the flies cast at permit and bonefish, and a Haywire Twist, used in single strand wire bite tippets for sharks and barracuda.

The old adage states that most fish are caught the night before, meaning preparation is essential to success. Knots should be formed properly and pulled down tightly. If a knot is going to break, you want it to break in your hands, not on a fish.

—Bob Rodgers

magazine, figured out how to turn fisherman Norm Duncan's marvelous little loop, the Duncan loop, into an even more marvelous knot system, the Uni-Knot. It takes more time to tie than a clinch knot, but I can usually tie a Uni-Knot better under real-life fishing conditions.

When both are tied well, the Uni-Knot seldom tests quite as strong at the two-circle improved clinch. But it has an advantage that has won me over. It can be cinched down on itself rather than on the wire of the hook eye. The small loop thus formed gives the fly a bit of extra action, sometimes a desirable trait when fishing wet flies, nymphs, streamers, or other submerged patterns.

You may read or hear that the loop of the Uni-Knot will close down against the eye of the hook under the strain of a fighting fish (true), and that you can pull on the short tag end of the knot to reopen the loop after you have released your fish (false). Because of the fineness and delicacy of tippet material, trying to reopen that loop is a lost cause that usually results in breaking the tippet. If

you want to fish your fly on a loop, snip it off and retie after each fish.

If you don't like all that snipping and retying, tie an overhand knot in your tippet, about 5 inches from the end. Now, when you tie the Uni-Knot, it will slide down only until it runs into that stopper knot, keeping the loop permanently open. Unfortunately, that overhand stopper knot is not as strong as the Uni-Knot itself, and becomes the weak link in your rig. Unless you are fishing strong, heavy tippets, it's best to learn a loop knot that is stronger than the overhand stopper.

NON-SLIP LOOP KNOT

The non-slip loop knot is something like a clinch knot that incorporates an overhand knot. It is used when you need a loop knot that will stay open under the pressure of a fish's weight. It is also stronger than the Uni-Knot.

HOMER RHODE LOOP

Modern saltwater anglers do use the Homer Rhode

NON-SLIP LOOP KNOT

Step 1. Make a loose overhand knot in the tippet about 8 to 10 inches above the tag end. (As you become proficient, you can form the overhand knot a bit closer to the tag end.) Now, pass the tag end through the fly's eye and back up through the overhand knot, so that it enters the knot on the same side of the loop that it originally exited. If you pass the end through the other side of the loop, the knot will not hold securely.

Step 2. Above the overhand knot, wrap the tag end around the standing part seven times. If you are fishing a heavy tippet, take fewer wraps: five turns in 2X (.013-inch diameter) tippets, four wraps in .014 to .025 tippets, three turns in shock tippets testing 50 to 60 pounds, and just two turns in really heavy shock tippets.

loop knot, which is similar to the non-slip loop knot, but only to tie their flies to heavy shock tippets. Even weakened by those overhand knots, a heavy shock tippet is still plenty strong enough.

TIPPET-TO-LEADER KNOTS

Every time you remove (or lose) a fly and tie on another, you shorten your tippet by a few inches. You will seldom want to fish with a tippet that is shorter than, say, 20 inches, so you will be attaching tippets to leaders fairly frequently. If you wish, you can use the same knot you use to build tapered leaders (discussed in the next section). If you do, you will shorten the last tapered section of leader each time you replace tippets, eventually requiring you to replace that tapered section.

LOOP-TO-LOOP CONNECTIONS

Because of the problem of shortening tippets, I prefer to use loop-to-loop connections between my tippets and leaders. They are fast and easy, and save on

lengthening or rebuilding leaders. The actual loop-to-loop connection is known to sailors and other rope riggers as the girth, or reef, hitch. Do it wrong and you have a lark's head, or cow hitch. (Both are sometimes also called ring hitches.)

SURGEON'S LOOP

Before you can make a loop-to-loop connection, you must first tie end loops in the bottom of the leader and the top of the tippet. This is the one knot you cannot make in the Uni-Knot system. Because I go for speed, simplicity, and ease of tying, I use the surgeon's loop. This is nothing but a double overhand knot formed in both strands of the doubled-back leader or tippet.

PERFECTION LOOP

Neat freaks prefer to use the Perfection loop. While it looks better than the surgeon's loop and holds almost as much of the leader's inherent strength, it is not as easy to tie. The first few times I tried tying the Perfection loop—admittedly, while watching a foot-

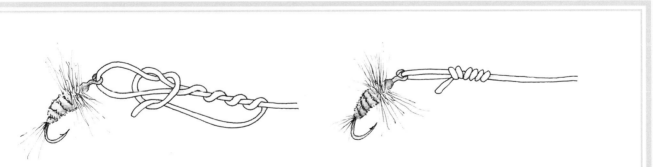

Step 3. Pass the tag end back down through the loop of the loose overhand knot, again making certain that it reenters the knot's loop on the same side that it exited in Step 1.

Step 4. Lubricate the knot and tighten it the same way you tighten the Uni-Knot, in two stages. First, pull on the tag end to seat the wraps snugly against the standing part. Now, hold the standing part of the tippet in one hand and the fly in the other and pull slowly apart with both hands to finish tightening the knot. Clip the tag end.

SURGEON'S LOOP

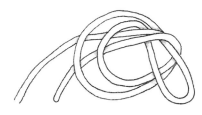

Step 1. Double the tag end of the leader back against the standing part, forming a loop that's a bit longer than the loop you need.

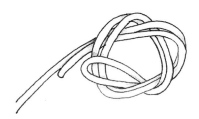

Step 2. Make a simple overhand knot in the doubled line.

Step 3. Now, bring the looped end back through the overhand knot a second time.

Step 4. After lubricating the knot, tighten by pulling on the loop with one hand and on both the standing part and the tag end with the other. The only potentially tricky part of tying this knot is keeping the tag end of wispy tippet material from sliding through your fingers as you tighten the knot. Clip the tag end.

ball game on television—it failed. Discouraged, I decided to stick with the surgeon's loop. Yet those who use the Perfection loop say it is a snap to tie. They are probably right, but it does take practice.

LEADER-BUILDING KNOTS

If you don't want to bother with building your own leaders—you can buy them ready-made from a fly shop—you may be tempted to skip this section. Don't. From time to time, you will have to repair a broken leader or lengthen your leader on one end or the other to compensate for high winds, weighted or wind-resistant flies, or other conditions that wreak havoc on your casting. And if you want to learn the subtle nuances and fine points of adapting tackle to conditions, you will eventually become a builder of leaders. Either way, as repairman or builder, you need to know a knot that

The well-stocked fly fisher should carry several knot-tying tools on the water.

Step 1. Form a small circle in the tippet or leader material, about 6 inches from the tag end. Be sure you form the loop by placing the tag end behind the standing part where they cross. Hold this juncture between tips of thumb and forefinger, with the circle facing upward. With each successive step, you will have to shift your fingertips to re-pinch the new as well as the old parts of the forming knot.

Step 2. Take the tag end over your thumb and back down behind the standing part, forming a second loop in front of the first.

Step 3. Slip the tag end between the two loops, re-pinching everything between your fingertips, leaving the tag end pointing straight up.

Step 4. Reach from behind the first loop and pull the second loop through the first loop.

Step 5. Continue pulling the second loop with one hand while you hold on to the standing part of the tippet or leader. To get it really tight, it is probably best to pull on the loop by inserting some round, smooth object (a pliers handle or the closed jaws of a hemostat) through the loop. Clip the tag end close to the knot once it is firmly tightened.

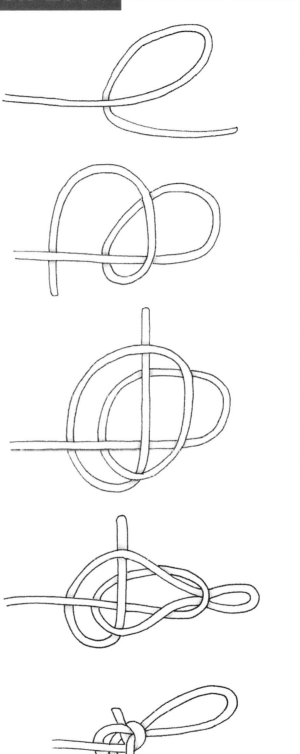

Step 1. Overlap the tag ends of the two pieces of material by 8 to 12 inches. Be sure the tag ends are pointing in opposite directions.

Step 2. Pinching one tag end against the standing part of the other material in one hand, use the other to form an overhand knot in the doubled strands.

Step 3. Pass the other tag end and standing part through the loop a second time, in essence repeating Step 2, forming the surgeon's knot.

Step 4. Firmly grasp tag end A and standing part B in one hand and tag end B and standing part A in the other. Lubricate the knot and tighten it by pulling firmly and steadily on all four parts at once. Test the knot by pulling on each individual strand while holding the other three in the other hand. Clip the two tag ends very closely—about 1/16 inch.

can be used to join two sections of leader material. You have three choices: the surgeon's knot, the blood (or barrel) knot, and the back-to-back Uni-Knot.

SURGEON'S KNOT

The easiest way to connect two pieces of leader material is the surgeon's knot, which is simply a double-overhand knot formed of both overlapping strands of leader material.

BLOOD OR BARREL KNOT

Though not as strong as the surgeon's knot and much more difficult to tie, the blood knot (also called the barrel knot) is favored by many anglers. It is more streamlined than the surgeon's knot, and its tag ends are in the center of the knot. For those reasons, it is less apt to jam against a rod guide when stringing up. And if you tie the blood knot with one extra-long tag end, it makes a right-angle dropper strand to which

Step 1. Overlap the two pieces of leader material so they cross, each tag end extending about 6 to 8 inches.

Step 2. In one hand, pinch together the two pieces of material at the X where they cross. Use the other hand to wrap one tag end (the one aimed away from the fingers that are pinching the X) around the other standing part five to seven times, working up the standing part away from the crossing. Pass the tag end into the gap on the other side of the X and pinch it in place.

Step 3. Now do the same thing with the other tag end, wrapping it in the opposite direction the same number of times around the opposite standing part. Pass the tag end through the small loop formed where the X had been, but be sure to pass it through the loop in the opposite direction from the first tag end. In other words, if the first tag end sticks up, push the second tag end down through that loop.

Step 4. Hold the tag ends together between your fingertips while you lubricate the knot. Holding on to a standing part in each hand, draw the knot up tight by pulling your hands apart. (To keep the tag ends from slipping back out of the loop, I hold them in my teeth as I tighten.) Clip the tag ends very close—within 1/16 inch.

you can attach a second fly. (You can tie the surgeon's knot with a long dropper strand, but it stands off from the leader at an angle and is more apt to let the fly foul the leader.)

The key to properly tying a blood knot—besides keeping it from falling apart while you are forming it—is to pull it up with one smooth, steady, fast draw on both standing parts. Don't jerk it, but definitely pull it faster than you pull most knots. The finished knot will be neat, slim and evenly balanced, with the tag ends sticking perpendicularly out from the middle.

BACK-TO-BACK UNI-KNOT

I generally use the Uni-Knot to connect leader sections. It is less bulky than the surgeon's knot but less streamlined than the blood knot, because the Uni's tag ends are at the exposed ends of the knot. In terms

BACK-TO-BACK KNOT

Step 1. Overlap the two tag ends by a good 6 inches or more and tie back-to-back Uni-Knots in the two overlapping strands, about four or five turns with each tag end through its respective Uni-Knot circle. Snug down each Uni-Knot in turn.

Step 2. Wet both snugged-down Uni-Knots, and pull on the standing parts to slide them together. Trim the tag ends fairly close, but not as close as in the blood knot.

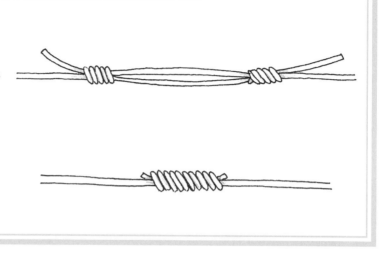

of strength and tying ease, it is also about midway between the other two.

CONNECTING LEADERS TO LINES

The connection between the leader and the fly line must be strong and streamlined and must permit the energy of the cast to be transferred smoothly all the way down to the fly.

BECKET BEND

The first time I went salmon fishing, I was amazed when my Scottish ghillie tied a surgeon's loop in the butt end of the leader and an overhand knot in the end of my fly line, then used a simple sheet, or Becket, bend to join them. (Some old knot books call this use of the sheet bend a jam hitch.) Surely, I thought, the to-and-fro stresses of casting would let that simple connection slip. But it did not, not even during three days of constant casting with a 15-foot, two-handed Spey rod. Unfortunately, I was not able to test the sheet bend's security under the strain of a leaping, head-shaking, upstream-and-down struggle with a big Thurso River salmon. Like many others, I went fishless on my first outing for Atlantic salmon.

NEEDLE KNOT

Most fly fishers prefer to join their lines and leaders with a knot that is a bit sturdier-looking (if not actually sturdier) than my impromptu Becket bend. The needle knot is the old-timer's choice and still the strongest and smoothest permanent connection between the leader and fly line. If fly fishers were still using 6-weight and heavier lines, and if fly lines were always built around a hollow braided core, I would strongly urge that you take the time to learn to make a needle knot. But today's popular 3- and 4-weight lines often are built around monofilament or other solid cores, or have fine-diameter hollow cores made of Kevlar or other high-tech materials. It may be easier to pass a camel through a needle's eye than to get a needle up into and out the side of these modern trout lines. If you want to learn to make needle knots, please look elsewhere for tutelage.

NAIL KNOT

The nail knot has unseated the needle knot among the devotees of permanent line-to-leader connections. Because you do not have to pull the leader into and back out of the line, it is a lot easier to tie. You could substitute a Uni-Knot to make this permanent connection, but I doubt you would like the clunky results.

The nail knot is not as streamlined as the needle knot because the leader extends from the side of the fly line rather than its center. Nor is the nail knot as secure. When you tighten a nail knot, you must pull hard enough on the leader to get it to bite down into the plastic coating of the fly line. Pull too hard, and you will bite all the way down to the core, effectively pulling the coating (and the nail knot) away from the line. The trick is to get it tightened just right—not so loosely that it will slip off the line, but not so tight that it will cut the coating away from the sometimes delicate core.

LOOP-TO-LOOP CONNECTIONS

I prefer to use a loop-to-loop connection between leaders and lines, though many knowledgeable fly fishers worry about the "hinging" effect of the loops. Efficient transfer of energy from line to leader to fly requires that the limpness of the material, from line to tippet, increase gradually and smoothly. To test it, hold the fly line in one hand (a few inches from the end) and the butt section of the leader in the other hand (same distance from the end), and form a bend. The perfect solution is a uniform curve in which the line and leader butt bend alike.

The loop-to-loop connection often causes a more abrupt change in curvature, a "hinge." But until someone comes up with a tool for making needle knots, I like the ease and convenience of the loop-to-loop connection.

BRAIDED-LOOP CONNECTOR

There are many options for putting a loop in the end of the fly line, including a variety of stripping, whip-

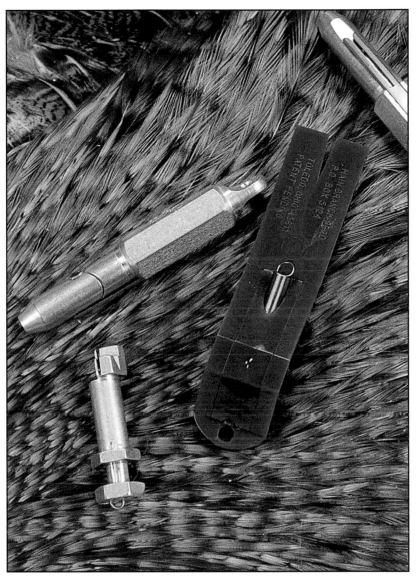

Tools like these three fly threaders, which assist in tying knots, are handy additions to the fly fisher's vest.

ping, and splicing procedures. I prefer the simplicity offered by the braided-loop connectors you can buy in most fly shops. But be warned: The instructions on the package make the process sound effortless; you will have to put more muscle into it than the instructions let on.

CONNECTING FLY LINE TO BACKING

The same knots and connections can be used on the

Step 1. Alongside the end of the fly line, place a finishing nail (pointing down toward the end of the line), a piece of thick wire, a thin metal tube (an inflator needle pointing down the line works well), or a large needle (pointing up the fly line). If you prefer, you can use one of the many nail-knot tools on the market. On the other side of the fly line, place about a foot of the butt end of the leader.

Step 2. Begin wrapping the butt end of the leader around the fly line and nail, holding them all together at the first wrap. Work down toward the end of the line, keeping the wraps parallel and close together, without crossing. Make them snug but not tight. Take at least six or seven wraps, up to as many as ten or twelve.

Step 3. Then work the tag end of the leader butt back up through the wraps by pushing it through the tiny tunnel formed by the gap between the curved sides of the nail and the fly line.

Step 4. Change your grip so that your finger holds all the wraps pinched against the fly line. Pull on the tag end just enough to take up any looseness that has developed in the previous step. Once the wraps are snug but not tight, carefully remove the nail by pulling it up the line.

Step 5. Pulling slowly and steadily on the tag end of the leader but while pinching the wraps in place, tighten the knot against the fly line. Once the wraps are tight, you can release your grip on them.

Step 6. Moisten the knot and then grip the standing part of the leader in one hand and the tag end with pliers in the other. Tighten by steadily drawing the hands apart with equal force. Once the wraps have bitten into, but not through, the fly-line coating, test the knot by pulling on both standing parts, line and leader. Clip the tag end very closely. If you wish, coat the knot with Pliobond or other cement that does not harden when it dries.

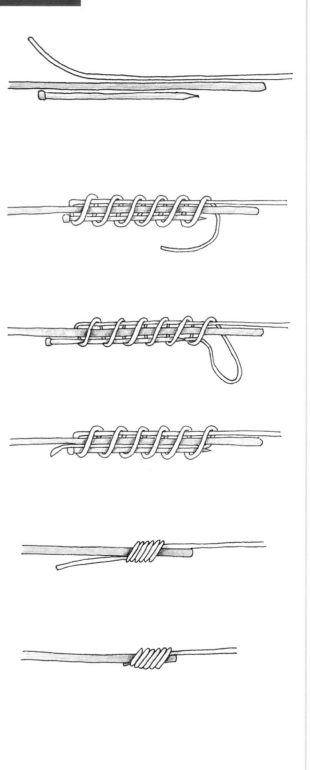

ARBOR KNOT

Step 1. To tie the arbor knot, first tie a simple overhand knot in the tag end of the backing. Now, pass that knotted tag end around the arbor of the reel spool and tie another overhand knot around the standing part, within two to three inches of the knotted tag end.

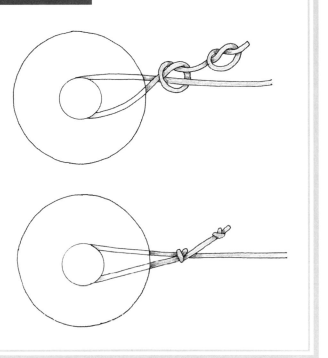

Step 2. Moisten both knots and the line in between. Hold the reel or spool in one hand and pull on the standing part of the backing. The knots will slide together and close up against the arbor. Clip any remaining tag end that is longer than $\frac{1}{8}$ of an inch.

reel end of the line, to connect it to the backing. I use the same braided-loop connectors. If you prefer to use a nail or other knot, remember that streamlined smoothness counts even more on this end of the fly line. If you finally hook into a fish that takes all your line, that line-to-backing connection must fly through all the rod guides without too much rubbing or stubbing. That's why it is imperative to cover that connection with Pliobond or other flexible cement, shaping it with moistened fingers into a streamlined teardrop. Little torpedo-shaped plastic connectors called Leader-Links are used for this purpose. If you can find them in any fly shops, you might want to give them a whirl. My Scottish ghillie used one to connect fly line to backing for salmon fishing.

ARBOR KNOTS

Finally, we get to the knot you will probably tie first, but very seldom—the one that secures the backing to the reel's arbor. I use a Uni-Knot for this purpose, but I tie it with just three wraps around the doubled

standing part of the Uni-Knot circle. The knot does not have to be very strong, just stronger than your tippet. If a hot fish takes all your line and backing, no knot is going to stop it, not even a Bimini twist. As soon as your backing runs out, bang!—there goes the tippet.

Most fly fishers use the aptly named arbor knot. It is strong enough to outlast the tippet and secure enough that it will not work loose and give up the whole fly line and the backing to an unstoppable fish.

FLIES & FLY TYING

by Jason Borger and Jim Abbs

Anglers have always had the same goal: to figure out better ways to catch fish. Two thousand years ago (at least), fly fishers apparently discovered that fishing with artificial flies had several advantages over simply baiting a hook. To begin with, artificial flies are far more durable than natural insects, and a single fly can be used to catch many fish before being lost to a fish or a tree, or simply torn to shreds. Also, many of the organisms that fish—especially trout—feed on are tiny (sometimes just a few millimeters in length); it is essentially impossible to bait a hook with such a small creature. Furthermore, a good fly tier can create a fly that gets a fish to strike because it looks more real than the real thing—to the fish, at least. Or it may look completely unlike anything the fish has ever seen, which may also provoke a strike.

But the creation and design of fishing flies is more than mere sport. Some people view fly tying not as a way to catch fish but as an extension of sculpture, albeit on a rather minuscule level. For those who do fish, however, an enormous sense of

satisfaction comes from catching a fish on a fly you've crafted yourself.

MATCHING THE NATURAL INSECTS

There are two broad categories of flies: matching flies (as they're often called) and attractor flies (sometimes referred to as "searching" flies). The goal of matching flies is to closely resemble (match) the fish's real food organisms so that the fish presumes it is seeing the real thing. Attractor flies, unlike matching flies, do not really attempt to closely mimic a specific food organism. Instead, they are generally representative of life, sometimes employing colorful, even unnaturally hued materials in their construction.

While both a matching and an attractor fly could represent a mayfly adult, for example, the matching fly would be species-specific, down to size and color. The attractor fly, in contrast, would just have an overall look that could be interpreted as a mayfly. When a hatch of a particular mayfly species is ongoing, the matching fly that imitated

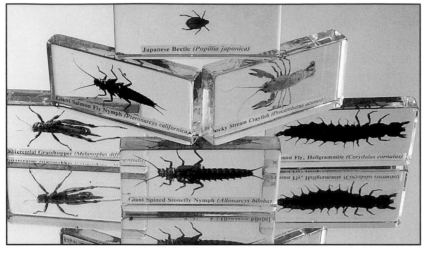

An entymologist's sample display of common aquatic flies.

that particular mayfly species will be the best choice to fish with. At times when there is no hatch activity, the more general attractor fly might be the better choice. It presents the overall impression of life and looks something like a mayfly; a good combination when the fish are just looking for something to eat. Other attractor flies may be far more general, representing only broad categories of food items, or even look very unlike anything a fish sees in its daily routine. Such flies may rely on materials that are eye-catching to the fish (in terms of movement and/or color) for their success.

From an overall materials standpoint, attractor flies and matching flies can use both natural and synthetic materials in their construction, so there is little difference between them in that regard. And as either category of fly may be effective at certain times, they are both used in fly fishing today.

The idea of matching flies has been around at least two millenia, and received distinct recognition in the first known book dealing with fly fishing, A Treatyse of Fysshynge wyth an Angle in 1496. In 1624, a book called El Manuscito de Astorga by Juan de Bergara detailed twenty-four Spanish patterns. The flies of that time had several features that are still used today, including the wound (now also called palmered) "hackles." These hackles were neck or body feathers of various birds wound around the hook shank so that

the hackle fibers stood perpendicular (or at some angle) to the shank. Upright hackles create lifelike impressions on the water, which make floating flies look very real to fish. Hackles also reflect and refract light, making the artificial fly look more alive. De Bergara's descriptions clearly demonstrated the use of multiple hackles to vary stiffness and texture, thereby achieving different degrees of action as well as affecting floatation. This confirms that almost four centuries ago the Spanish were winding hackles similarly to modern fly fishers.

England's Charles Cotton, often called the father of modern fly fishing, came along several decades after the Spanish tiers. He provided the fly fishing and tying sections of Izaak Walton's The Compleat Angler (1676). Cotton preferred many flies that matched natural insects, and he influenced future tiers to look more closely at insect anatomy and behavior.

ATTRACTOR FLIES

The idea of making flies that simply look good to the fish (without the imitation of a specific food organism in mind) has also been around for centuries. One allusion to the attractor philosophy comes slightly after Cotton wrote, when retired English Royal Navy captain Richard Franck described a "dubbing bag" in his Northern Memoirs. The bag was a portable flytying kit, which held "silks of all sorts, threds, thrums, moccadoends, and cruels of all sizes, and a variety of colours; diversified and stained wool, with dogs and bears hair; besides twisted fine threads of gold and silver; with feathers from the capon, partridg, peacock, pheasant, mallard . . . parrot, paraketta, phlimingo [and] mockaw."

Franck's description reflected two different developments. His kit would help him match a particular hatch of insects at a moment's notice. However, the colors of some of the materials were not found in natural food organisms; the exotic plumages were a precursor of things to come in England—the brilliantly ostentatious Atlantic salmon flies. Those flies would become some of the purest attractor flies of all time.

The idea of attractor flies wasn't exclusively the domain of salmon or trout anglers, however. In *Angling in All Its Branches* (1800), author Samuel Taylor wrote about flies for pike: "Another way [to catch pike], is by artificial fly fishing, though many assert that they are not to be taken with a fly at all; I have, however, taken many this way. The fly must be . . . composed of very gaudy materials, such as pheasant's, peacock's, or mallard's feathers. The body must be made rough, full, and round. . . . The whole about the size of a small bird or mammal. In this manner I make this sort of fly, which will often take pike when other baits avail nothing."

Taylor obviously was not attempting to imitate insects or other creatures; rather his pike fly was purely an "attractor" pattern. Had he tied it in subdued hues, perhaps one could argue that he was imitating a wren or another small bird, but his "gaudy materials" served one purpose: getting the fish's attention. The fly appeared to be flashy and hopefully tasty, but beyond that it looked like nothing in the pike's regular diet. The fact that Taylor could catch pike on his psychedelic-style wren when all "other baits avail nothing" confirmed the attractor-pattern philosophy as a sound one.

ATLANTIC SALMON FLIES

In the nineteenth and early twentieth centuries, exotic fly-tying materials flowed into Britain from all over the globe. The feathers of toucans, bowerbirds, quetzals, rails, jungle cock, herons, and bustards were just a few of the multitude of new possibilities.

The "fanciful" school of tying was in full swing at that time, and nowhere was it more apparent than in the attractor-style Atlantic salmon flies. Seemingly every new material that came off the docks from a foreign land was integrated into the dressings. Creatures such as trout and salmon were regarded as "noble" at that time, and therefore one had to use flies that were commensurate with the perceived status of these fish in the animal kingdom.

Hyperspecialization of flies was also a norm, as tiers or "dressers" developed flies to be used on certain rivers or by particular members of the landed aristocracy, after whom they named flies. Of course, these flies usually had little to do with anything a salmon had ever seen or ever would see. And most certainly, such fanciful and artistic dressings are not absolutely neccesary to catch salmon. A common black hackle wrapped around a basic black hook will take Atlantic salmon, but it lacks the verve and cachet of the multichromatic sculptures that were those fancy British attractor flies.

The Atlantic salmon fly's influence on fly tying went beyond materials, firmly cementing fly tying as an art patronized by royalty and politicians. Indeed, the creativity and skill necessary to dress complex Atlantic salmon flies helped to give the sport of fly fishing a separate—and somewhat elevated—identity from other forms of angling. At the same time, those skills were applied to improving the construction of "plain" flies, and all of fly tying became a more artistic effort.

Subimago mayfly

MORE NATURAL THAN THE REAL THING

Four individuals made very special contributions to fly design and function in the nineteenth century, in the midst of Atlantic salmon fly-tying popularity: G. P. R. Pulman, W. C. Stewart, Frederic Halford, and G. E. M. Skues. Pulman was one of the early founders

Classic Atlantic salmon fly designed and tied by Dorothy Douglas.

In North America, arguably the most popular dry fly is the Adams. As a testament to its popularity, a monument was erected in Michigan with the inscription, "Honoring the creation of the Adams fly." Ardent fly fisherman Leonard Hallady created the first Adams dry fly in 1922, near his home on the banks of Mayfield Pond. He named it in honor of his good friend, Judge Charles F. Adams, another enthusiastic angler who loved to fish for brook and brown trout in the nearby Boardman River. The Adams combines brown and grizzly hackle, and many trout anglers claim it to be the best fly ever designed. Some, in fact, declare that if they had to use only one fly for all of their trout fishing, it would be the Adams.

Materials

Hook: Dry fly hook, #10-20

Thread: Gray or black

Wing: Grizzly hackle tips (feathers from a rooster neck)

Tail: Brown and grizzly hackle mixed (moose mane for western waters)

Body: Gray muskrat dubbing fur (underfur)

Hackle: Brown and grizzly hackle mixed (two hackles normally, three for western-style flies)

Tying Steps

1. Tie in brown and grizzly hackle fibers for the tail (six to ten strands), with a length sticking out behind the bend of the hook equivalent to the hook shank length.

2. Twist light to medium muskrat fur ("dubbing") onto waxed tying thread.

3. Wrap dubbed fur-covered thread around hook shank to approximately fifty percent of hook shank length. Taper the body so it is bigger near the hook eye.

4. Select two matched grizzly hackle tips with length appropriate for the hook size you are using (hackle should stand out from the hook by a distance equal to the hook shank length).

5. Lash wings to hook shank and wrap thread around the base of the wings so as to support them in an upright and divided manner.

6. Tie in one grizzly hackle and one brown hackle at the base of the feather (some suggest two brown hackles for western waters) and wind hackle behind and in front of wings. Leave room for the head.

7. Tie off, whip finish (the type of knot used to finish off the head of a fly), and apply head cement.

—Jim Abbs

of the "Impressionistic" school of fly design. Like the Impressionist painters of that era, these fly designers wanted to distill imitations of natural insects to bare essentials, exploring what details must be included and what details could be left out, or expanded upon, in various flies. By doing so, a tier could achieve the impression of life and yet reduce his efforts. And if the designer was really good, the fly could be made to seem more real than the real thing. As Pulman noted earlier, in 1851: "[Natural insects] . . . can be represented without counting the exact number of legs, or microscopically examining the fibers of the wings; on the same principle that, in individual portraiture, what is alone sought to be attained is not minute imitation, but individual character and expression."

Through his impressionistic outlook, Pulman was

also one of the first to look at flies in terms of size, shape, and color, noting that together these features "constitute the character of the insect." Pulman's insights are still significant today.

W. C. Stewart followed the impressionistic precepts of size, shape, and color, but also focused on imitating the behavioral aspects of natural insects. In *The Practical Angler* (1857), he described fishing so-called spiders—wet flies with soft feathers or hackles that moved in the water like the legs of a living arachnid. He particularly suggested casting flies up-current so that the "least motion will agitate and impart a singularly life-like appearance to it." What he did not realize was that he was not imitating spiders at all; rather he was likely imitating the emergent stages of many aquatic insects, including caddies and mayflies. His spiders worked well because they moved well. Building the appearance of movement into the fly through materials selection (and fishing techniques) remains a major element in many modern fly designs.

Frederic Halford revolutionized dry-fly designs and their practical use from the late 1800s through the first decades of the 1900s. His *Modern Development of the Dry Fly* (1887)—brilliantly written and convincing—laid the foundation for modern dry-fly innovation. He even went so far as to print a color system in his book to allow anglers to match insects' natural hues with their fly-tying materials. Most of his design ideas are still used in standard dry-fly patterns. Halford also promoted Stewart's up-current fly delivery as the best way to achieve a natural drift.

G. E. M. Skues added insights into pre-hatch stages of aquatic insects, as well as promoting new materials to achieve the desired impressions. In fact, he suggested to his readers that they wet their materials to be certain that the materials would match the coloration of the subaquatic organism being imitated. His innovations were as brilliant and decisive as Halford's and were based on a thorough, in-depth understanding of the insects he sought to imitate.

AMERICA MAKES ITS MARK

In the first half of this century, fly fishing in the United States was closely linked to the English schools of Halford and Skues. No wonder, then, that the early innovators of fly design in this country based their work so firmly on the efforts of their European counterparts. James Leisenring, Art Flick, Harry Darbee, Edward Dette, and Edward Hewitt made up the "Catskill school" of tying because they lived in that region of New York State and they based their imitations on the food organisms of its waters. They modeled their thinking on what they read in the English literature and their writings also reflected the European thoroughness and focus on innovation of that time. For example, in *Tying and Fishing the Wet Fly* (1941), Leisenring recommended carrying a book of materials to match insect coloration on the water in natural light (*à la* Halford). Hewitt was a brilliant observer of nature, and his imitations accurately reflected the naturals. He even devised a technique to create flat bodies in some of his insect and fly imitations. Normally, when you wrap thread around the hook, it makes the body round. Hewitt's method would become useful if you wanted instead to create a flat-bodied insect, such as a "clinging" mayfly nymph, a nymph whose body is strongly flattened and that clings to varied objects in swift water.

Flick gave up fishing for an entire season and devoted that time simply to collecting and observing the insects of his beloved Catskill waters. Such observational prowess has motivated some modern fly designers to don scuba gear so they can study insects in their natural environments.

Darbee and Dette pushed the craft of Catskill tying to its highest level, seeking the finest materials for their designs (in the manner of Stewart). Harry Dar-

TYING A GOLD-RIBBED HARE'S EAR

While many fly fishers consider fishing with surface flies to be the most fun, about 70 to 90 percent of a trout's food consists of underwater insects. This means that if you want to catch fish, particularly trout, you must use flies that imitate those underwater creatures. In trout streams and many lakes, a nymph is a general name for immature forms of aquatic insects that live beneath the surface. When it comes to nymphs, there is one fly that every trout angler must have. This fly, which appears to have originated in Britain, is called the Gold-Ribbed Hare's Ear. Like many flies, the name of this nymph is based upon the materials used in its construction.

Materials

Hook: Mustad 3906B (slightly longer than a standard hook), #8-16

Thread: Dark brown or black

Tail: Guard hairs from the face or ears of English hare

Body: Guard hair and underfur from face and ears of an English hare

Rib: Gold oval wire or flat gold tinsel

Wing case: Turkey tail feather or goose wing quill, dyed black

Thorax: Longer guard hair, with a little underfur from face and ears of an English hare

Head: Dark brown or black tying thread

Tying Steps

1. Tie in a small bunch (size of pencil lead) of hare face guard hairs at the bend of the hook for the fly's tail. Also, tie in gold oval wire or flat tinsel at the bend of the hook.

2. Apply dubbing wax to the tying thread (much like ski wax), and twist the hare's fur fibers on to the thread to create a strand of fur yarn.

3. Wrap fur yarn strand forward two-thirds of the length of the hook shank toward the eye. Taper from back to front—smaller to larger—to simulate the fly body. Tie off.

4. Wrap gold wire or tinsel forward in an even spiral fashion to create a segmented look for the fly's body.

5. Tie in a section of turkey tail or goose quill at the two-thirds point of hook shank.

6. Using hair longer than that used for the fly body, create another strand of fur yarn, with the same dubbing wax and twisting action.

7. Wrap the fur strand toward the eye of the hook, creating a hump that represents the thorax of the fly. Leave room behind the eye for the fly head.

8. Fold the segment of turkey quill forward over the fur hump, creating a wing case.

9. Whip finish the thread behind the eye to form a head and coat with fly-tying cement.

—Jim Abbs

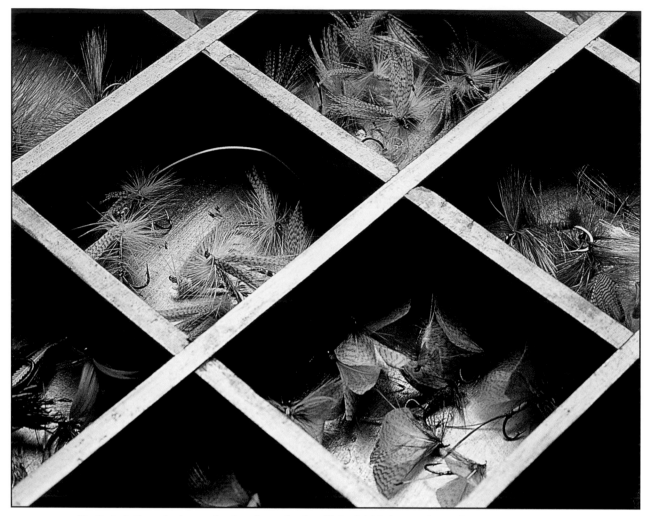

Mayfly imitations: In the words of angler and writer Silvio Calabi, the mayfly is a "graceful, fragile creature, poised and alert—as quintessential an insect as the trout is a fish." The four stages in the mayfly's life are egg, nymph (larva), dun (subimago) and spinner (imago).

bee's work in this area led to the refinement of certain strains of chickens bred to produce hackle especially for fly tiers—the so-called genetic hackle.

In 1951, Jack Atherton released his book *The Fly and the Fish*, in which he put forth eloquent and thoughtful support for impressionistic designing. Atherton compared fly construction to the aims of portraiture (like Pulman), using the works of artists like Renoir and Monet as examples. Furthermore, he was interested not in how the fly looked to humans but rather in the impression it made on fish in the water.

THE MODERN AMERICAN ERA

In 1955, Ernest Schwiebert's seminal work, *Matching the Hatch*, initiated the truly modern era of fly innovation. His vast angling experience, beginning as a child, gave him an insight that changed the way impressionistic fly tying was to be perceived. He collected insects from all around the country and developed an eclectic mix of imitations that swept like a firestorm through American angling. His work launched a cadre of young anglers—including Rene Harrop, Mike Lawson, Doug Swisher, and Carl Richards—whose innovations molded our current way of thinking about fly design and fishing. Among their creations were the "no hackle dun," a mayfly imitation that was more realistic than other mayfly patterns of the time, and "trailing shucks," representations of the partially discarded skins of hatching insects that were enormously important in our understanding of the features that trigger strikes by fish.

Doug Swisher and Carl Richards's book, *Selective Trout* (1971), moved these new ideas of fly designing to the forefront. No longer would anglers be satisfied with Catskill-style patterns when such highly effective flies that elegantly matched size, shape, color, and behavior were within their grasp.

Another angler, Dave Whitlock, was also a pioneer of modern trout-fly design, though he is best known as the modern father of warmwater fly fishing and fly tying.

Following on the heels of those early pioneers of modern impressionistic fly design were John Betts, Gary Borger, Al Caucci, Jack Gartside, Gary LaFontaine, Darrel Martin, and a host of others. With their input, fly innovation has expanded exponentially.

With the surge in modern fly innovation have come materials that are specific to fly tying. No longer do tiers have to go to craft or knitting stores and dig around in the yarn bins. Fly shops and catalogs now carry materials that are either packaged versions of the craft-store stuff or manufactured explicitly for tying flies. This explosion of materials was driven by fly tying, but it is also driving fly tying. Today, fly tying has entered the era of synthetics.

With the proliferation of these materials, tiers are being offered a whole new spectrum of possibilities in color, shape, and design parameters that allow previously unachievable effects to be created easily.

SALTWATER'S NEW DIMENSIONS

In the 1960s and 1970s, while trout insect imitation was exploding, saltwater fly tying was still in its infancy as far as fly innovation was concerned. However, people like Stu Apte, Dan Blanton, Trey Combs,

Bill Cutherwood, Lefty Kreh, Pete Parker, Bob Popovics, and Lou Tabory began to create more realistic and varied designs that brought saltwater tying into a more modern era. Since the 1980s, an intense interest in saltwater fly fishing has spurred the development of many new designs. More importantly, these new tying techniques have influenced all areas of fly fishing. Epoxy and hot-glue are two of the materials that the saltwater world has helped popularize. Such materials are now commonplace in a huge variety of designs, even for trout.

Advances in equipment have brought advances in fly design as well. More refined rods and reels mean that larger, faster, and meaner fish can be pursued with greater ease. At the extreme, flies have grown to be a

The Glass Minnow is a versatile saltwater fly developed by Carl Hanson, who uses them in the turtlegrass flats of Florida. The fly is tied with bucktail and monofilament snelled over foil, with a double wing that's green and brown.

foot or more in length, often with moveable or articulated parts or tube designs. These flies have changed perceptions of what a fly is, and how a fly can be used. The mere sight of a huge size 6/0 offshore streamer—twenty times bigger than most flies—is enough to get even the most jaded fly angler excited and ready to catch whatever could eat it. In essence, saltwater fly tying helped (and still helps) create a new fishing industry.

Joe McCusker, a volunteer at the American Museum of Fly Fishing, shows how today's fly tier uses a palette of traditional and synthetic materials.

Recently, saltwater fly designing has taken even further steps forward, with more emphasis being placed on matching the hatch. George V. Roberts, Jr.'s *A Fly-Fisher's Guide to Saltwater Naturals and Their Imitation* (1994) was the first book to thoroughly examine the relationships between natural food organisms and fly designing as it related to saltwater.

FLIES BY MASTERS OF THE TWENTIETH CENTURY

Today, cutting-edge fly-design ideas are coming from all over the world. One of the newest innovations, which utilizes both natural and artificial materials, comes from France. In an effort to create proper surface impression and body shape, Christian Billard devised a method for creating premade bodies for mayflies, caddis, stoneflies, grasshopper, streamer flies, and others. His Tube Bodiz, as they're called, allow even a novice tier to very quickly and easily create effective and durable impressionistic, efficient designs.

Of course, individual tiers or even schools of tying are not solely responsible for advancing equipment development. The enormous number of flies that are tied commercially each year—millions of dozens—promotes the case of more advanced equipment and, to an extent, materials. For fabricating the more difficult or tediously repetitious fly patterns, high quality, technically advanced fly-tying vices such as rotating head designs have become commonplace. Tools have been refined to meet the demands of hard-core commercial tiers as well as those who simply want the best. Scissors of surgical steel, machined aluminum hair-stackers, and ceramic-lined bobbins all have come about as a result.

THE ELITE FLY DRESSERS AND THEIR CREATIONS

Fly tying is not only about catching fish but also about art. Among the best-known artistic tiers are the dressers of complex and impossibly beautiful Atlantic salmon flies. Although both historic and modern iterations of these flies are still tied for fishing, many of today's best Atlantic salmon fly tiers produce flies primarily for collectors, with examples often fetching hundreds of dollars apiece. These tiers display great levels of skill in manipulating materials; learning from their techniques could help any tier improve the crafting of other, more modern, flies. If you wish to expand your horizons as a fly tier, at least page through Paul Schmookler and Ingrid V. Sils's *Rare and Unusual Fly Tying Materials: A Natural History, Volumes I and II* (1995). The books not only discuss the exotic materials used by salmon fly tiers, but also are full of stunning plates depicting the work of both old and new masters.

Also working toward the outside of the "fishing-only" realm are the realists—tiers who employ materials and methods to make flies that look more like the real thing. While these realistic flies are used for fishing, they are more often collected, since they can be so time-consuming to produce. Through their experimentation, tiers such as D. L. Goddard, Poul Jorgensen, and Jean-Louis Teyssie bring new materials and techniques into the domain of fishing.

On the cutting edge of the cutting edge lie those few fly dressers who are completely redefining the boundaries of materials and method—the super-realistic tiers. Steve Fernandez, Herb Klein, Bob Mead, Paul Schmookler, and Bill Logan are among those who aim for near-perfect reproduction of the natural organism. As practical fishing flies, these creations are of little use; they are often too stiff to move in a lifelike way with water currents and typically too fragile to withstand the rigors of actual fishing. But as microscopic sculpture, they are amazing.

Bill Logan approaches the pinnacle of what can realistically be achieved. His flies are truly photorealistic, so much so that they have even fooled entomologists. Logan uses a combination of underbody sculpting and the microscopically precise application of tying materials. His truly masterful manipulation of thread, wire, feathers, and epoxy is almost beyond belief. It is not unusual for him to spend 150 hours tying a single ¾-inch-long fly.

This seemingly nonfishing-minded work has practical applications, however, since the specialized techniques for creating super-realism can often be integrated into the construction of fishing flies. This allows tiers to achieve new effects and create flies that work better on the water.

Designing and crafting flies for catching fish is as ancient as fly fishing itself. Flies have gone from vague representations of insects to brilliant, gaudy combinations of exotica, to scientifically-based designs, to near-perfect reproductions of the natural

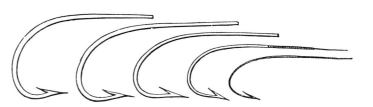

world. And the beauty of the process is that all of those ideas, patterns, principles, and traditions still exist today. Fly tying is truly an art for all time.

FLIES IN GREAT VARIETY

Tying your own flies extends the challenge and thrill of catching fish. When you first catch a fish on a fly you tied yourself, your tying abilities have been confirmed in the only way that counts. If you are inquisitive and persistent, this will happen sooner than you think. And, after you start catching fish on your own flies, buying them will never be the same.

Over the centuries, fly tiers have developed a language of their own to describe the parts of a fly and the materials used to make them. As new flies are developed or old ones are changed, they are given colorful names derived from rivers, famous anglers, or other fanciful namesakes. Many flies are tied with materials and special techniques that have been passed down over decades or even over centuries. When a fly tier refers to a fly pattern, he is referring to those materials and the special tying techniques that have been passed down generation after generation.

DRY FLIES

Some of the best known flies are dry flies, which float on top of the water and are used to entice fish that are feeding on the surface. How many times have you visited a lake or a river and seen circles on the water, especially in the early evening? Very often, those circles are from fish disturbing the surface to eat insects or other food that is on or near the top; dry flies try to imitate that food. Some of the best-known dry flies include the Adams (the most popular dry fly in America), the Royal Coachman, the Hendrickson, the Quill Gordon (developed by a famous New York angler of the 1880s), the Cahill (light and dark), the Rio Grand King, the Green Drake, the Ausable Wulff, the H&L Variant (President Eisenhower's favorite fly), the Royal Wulff, the Elk Hair Caddis (the favorite caddis pattern), and the Trude (from a collaboration between an Idaho rancher and a mayor of Chicago).

STREAMERS

Streamer flies of different colors, shapes, and sizes imitate minnows, salamanders, crayfish, frogs, and even leeches. Some streamers' wings are made of feathers, while others are made of fur or hair. One set of streamers—bucktails—uses tail hairs from a deer. Famous streamers include the Mickey Finn, the

The realistic fly-tying movement, although not necessarily useful on the water, yields some stunning patterns as shown here with the MacEnerny Adult Dobson Fly.

Llama, the Dahlberg Diver (a famous pike and bass fly), the Muddler Minnow (the most popular of all streamers), the Woolly Bugger, the Gray Ghost (developed by a famous woman fly tier), and the Hornberg (named after the game warden who invented it).

NYMPHS

In most lakes and streams, underwater insects and other small life forms are a major source of food for fish. Many of these are immature forms of flying insects (like mayflies or caddisflies) that hatch and live the first part of their lives under water; others never leave the water at all. Most trout streams host tiny freshwater scrimp (called scuds) that are trout favorites. There are thousands of popular nymphs, including the Gold-Ribbed Hare's Ear (with both an English and American version), the Prince Nymph (a California creation), the Red Fox Squirrel Nymph (developed by Dave Whitlock), the Pheasant Tail (developed by English riverkeeper Frank Sawyer), the Zugbug and the Montana Stonefly.

TERRESTRIALS

Terrestrials imitate creatures such as ants, grasshoppers, and crickets, which live on and in the ground but become lunch for fish when they fall into a creek or lake. Well-known terrestrial patterns include the Letort Cricket (from a famous creek in Pennsylvania), Dave's Hopper (from Dave Whitlock), the McMurray Ant, the Black Crowe Beetle, the Inchworm, and the Henry's Fork Hopper (from a famous river in Idaho).

HOOKS FOR FLIES

Flies are tied on many different kinds of hooks. They vary in the shape of the hook bend, how the eye of the hook is constructed, the way the eye is oriented (up or down), whether the bend is straight or offset, and so on. Many of these hook styles are hundreds of years old and were designed for particular kinds of flies. For example, nymph hooks have a longer shank and thicker wire than hooks used for dry flies. For

Tackle salesman's kit, showing sizes and samples of hooks.

streamer flies, the hooks are very long because these flies imitate fish foods with elongated shapes. For very small flies, a turned-up eye creates a larger hooking opening (gap). A final and most important feature of hooks is size. Hooks are sized according to the gap of the hook (the distance between the point and the shank). For fly fishers, there is a tremendous variation in size, depending upon the life form that you are trying to imitate. For very small midges, you are likely to use a fly that is a size 24 (1.5 mm hook gap), while for a bass bug you may choose a size 2 (9 mm hook gap).

A BOUNTY OF MATERIALS

There is simply not enough room in this book to list all the materials used to tie flies. Originally, most flies used natural substances, including feathers, hair, furs, and silk. As noted earlier, with the expansion of the British Empire in the mid-eighteenth century, fly tiers had access to exotic feathers, hairs, and fibers from all over the world. Even today, many of the popular patterns reflect those origins. But most fly tiers and fly anglers are seldom restrained by tradi-

tion. New materials and tying techniques have always been sought. In the last forty years, synthetic materials—primarily from the garment, upholstery, and carpet industries—have replaced some of the natural materials and in many cases have led to the creation of completely new fly patterns. The use of synthetic materials in some instances arose because of the unavailability of the natural feathers and furs from exotic and now endangered species, such as polar bears and certain seals. To illustrate the variety of tying materials, it is only necessary to examine a handful of modern flies.

ROYAL COACHMAN

The Royal Coachman has wings made of white duck feathers, a tail of golden pheasant, a body of peacock herl, legs or hackle of brown rooster neck feathers, and a band around the body of red silk floss.

CATSKILL CURLER

The Catskill Curler, a famous fly pattern from upstate New York, has a tail of wild pig hairs, abdomen and wing case of turkey tail feathers, a front body (tho-

When it comes to an all-around fly, perhaps none is more popular or famous than the Muddler Minnow. This fly commonly is used to resemble a minnow, a grasshopper, a cricket, an emerging green drake, a stonefly, or even a tadpole. The Muddler Minnow is so respected that there are fly shops and even fly fishing clubs named after it. This fly came from Minnesota, but Montana's Dan Bailey popularized it with the addition of marabou (a soft underfeather) that is often used in a yellow or white color.

Materials

Hook: Mustad 9672, #2-10

Thread: Brown or gray

Tail: Dyed red hackle fibers

Body: Flat gold tinsel

Wing: Marabou plume feathers (soft underfeathers from turkey, chicken, or other fowl), squirrel hair, peacock herl

Head: Deer hair, with some of the fibers angling backwards to form a collar

Tying steps

1. Attach thread at the rear of the hook and tie tail on top (seven or eight fibers for a #6 hook). Wind thread about two-thirds of the way back toward the hook eye. The tail should extend beyond the bend of the hook the equivalent of one hook gap.

2. Tie in length of flat gold tinsel. Wrap the tinsel toward the tail in close, even wraps back to the tail, and then wrap it forward over the first layer to the original tie-in point.

3. Tie in a large clump of yellow marabou, one-fifth of the distance back from the eye of the hook. This wing should extend beyond the hook bend. Trim off excess and apply cement to base.

4. Select a right and left section of a mottled turkey wing quill and place their concave sides together. Tie these sections of turkey wing quill directly on top of the squirrel hair underwing. Wind the thread back toward the eye.

5. Tie in four to six strands of peacock herl on top of the marabou.

6. Tie in a small clump of deer body hair (a little bigger than a wood matchstick), with the tips pointed toward the rear of the hook and the cut ends pointed forward. "Spin" the deer hair by bringing the thread around the deer hair and hook shank and pulling it toward you. The deer hair will flare. Add more deer hair on the other side of the hook, and continue with small clumps until the front one-third of the hook shank is covered with flared deer hair.

7. Remove the fly from the tying vise and trim the flared deer hair to form a shape with a rounded top and a flat bottom. Different tiers prefer different shapes.

8. Whip finish and cement head.

—Jim Abbs

Lee Wulff pushed the barriers of the sport. Here, shortly before his death, he experiments with solvents as a means of creating flies without thread.

rax) of tan ostrich herl, legs from the tail of a ring-neck pheasant, and a head of turkey feathers.

GRAY GHOST

The Gray Ghost has a body of orange silk floss wrapped directly on the hook shank, a rib of flat sil-

Streamer flies, like the Gray Ghost (above) are used to seduce fish that are feeding on minnows.

ver tinsel spiral wrapped over the floss, a wing made of golden pheasant crest, a shoulder (immediately behind the head) of silver pheasant, and a cheek (on top and in front of the shoulder) of jungle cock (now endangered but grown domestically).

HOW TO START TYING FLIES

There are several painless ways to learn to tie flies. The most popular is to take a short class at a local fly shop or through a fly-fishing club. They offer the opportunity to ask lots of questions about technique, equipment, and materials. There also are many fly-fishing shows and conclaves held each year, where hundreds of amateur and professional tiers demonstrate their skills. You can also try videos and books, but these are most useful after you have already learned some of the basic skills and techniques firsthand.

FLY-TYING TOOLS

Tools for tying flies are not expensive, and initially you only need a few. As a general rule, avoid fly-tying kits; most of the materials are not useful and the tools are overpriced. Instead, go to a fly-fishing show or join a fly-fishing club for advice on what to buy and where to buy it. You can get started tying flies for less than $100.

Vise. The vise is the most important, and the most expensive, tool required to tie flies. It holds the hook securely as the fly is tied or dressed. There are many different types of vises: C-clamps attach to a table edge, while others sit on top of the table with a pedestal. A pedestal base can be moved anywhere, while a C-clamp is usually less expensive and you can adjust the height.

Scissors. At least one pair of small, sharp scissors with fine, narrow points is important for the detailed work of fly tying. This is not an area in which to cut costs. The blade should be of a high enough quality to hold a good edge with repeated use. You should also make sure the finger holes are large enough that the scissors can be picked up easily.

Bobbin. This fairly inexpensive device is used to hold the fly-tying thread and to maintain correct tension on the thread as the fly is tied. Bobbins for fly tying come with tubes of varying length and diameter.

Hackle pliers. This tool is used to grip feathers (hackles) and hold them securely as they are wrapped around the fly. Feathers are quite slippery and must be kept under tension to be wound on properly.

Bodkin. Basically, this a needle inserted into a handle (about the size of a pencil) used for applying head cement, picking out stray fibers, cleaning the eye of a hook, and so on.

Whip finisher. This tool is used to wrap thread on the fly in a way that not only secures the materials but provides a smooth surface. Used especially for the head of the fly, it generally requires practice to use properly.

Half-hitch tool. This metal shaft with an indentation in one end is used to make a "half-hitch" knot to hold fly materials in place. The tip of a ballpoint pen (without the ink cartridge) can serve the purpose quite well.

The record-breaker,

A monster trout,

"George's dream"

ACCESSORIES

BY JIM ABBS

Fly fishers often look like walking hardware stores, with vest pockets bulging and strange little tools hanging all over the place. Some people might be put off by all that gadgetry, and it's true that all you really need is a rod, reel, some line, and a few flies. But for some kinds of fishing and some settings, you will eventually want more thingamabobs.

Most fly anglers believe that the artifacts of fly fishing—lines, rods, reels, flies, and gadgets—make the sport especially interesting and challenging. Fly fishing is, after all, more strategy and planning than action, more prediction and scheming than athletic skill. In fact, it is rumored that the Boy Scouts' famous motto—"Be Prepared"—was spawned by their founder's fly-fishing experiences. The story may or may not be true, but the message is clear: The ability to anticipate on-the-water eventualities can separate a truly successful fly fisher from a mediocre one.

Likewise, the penalty of being unprepared can be tormenting. Imagine a trip to the waters of your dreams (Montana's Madison, the Catskills' Beaverkill or Hampshire's Test in England) and not being able to keep your fly afloat while 18-inch-plus native trout keep sipping high-floating naturals. Imagine sighting a school of feeding bonefish on a secluded Christmas Island flat and not having the right size of tippet to cast that #2 Clouser Deep Minnow properly. Imagine finding those giant Bighorn rainbow tailing on midge pupa and lacking that 1/300th-ounce microshot necessary to just break the surface tension and suspend a #24 Brassie in the top 4 inches of water.

Preparing to catch a particular species (or even an individual fish) on a specific river is sort of like planning a military engagement with a familiar enemy. The practiced fly angler soon realizes that for each month, each time of day, and each weather pattern, one must consider what insects or aquatic food the fish are likely to prefer. In anticipation of these questions fly fishers load up on flies of different colors, sizes, and shapes. In order to cast small or large weightless or weighted flies, anglers also need the correct rod, line, reel, leader, and tippets, along with twenty-five to

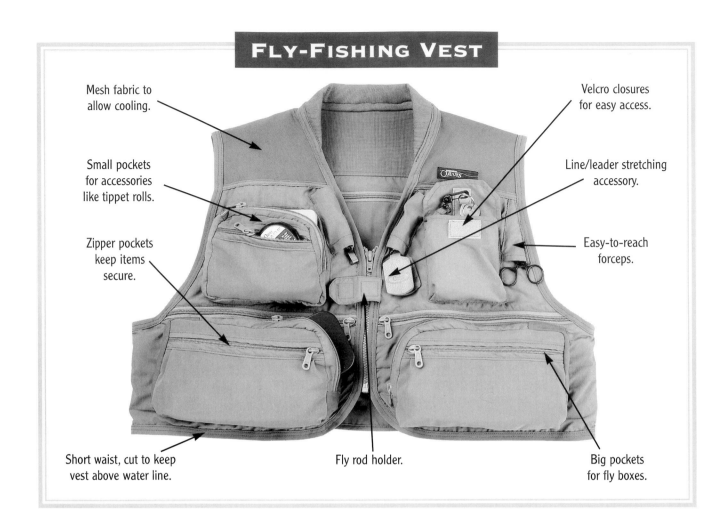

Mesh fabric to allow cooling.

Small pockets for accessories like tippet rolls.

Zipper pockets keep items secure.

Velcro closures for easy access.

Line/leader stretching accessory.

Easy-to-reach forceps.

Short waist, cut to keep vest above water line.

Fly rod holder.

Big pockets for fly boxes.

thirty other related accessories. With the burgeoning popularity of fly fishing in the 1990s has come an explosion of devices, whatchamacallits, and widgets that claim to aid the cause of catching fish. Many inventive anglers devise their own special tools and solutions, finding useful items in sewing baskets, junk drawers, and other ordinary household repositories. Others pore through fly-fishing catalogs and hang around fly-fishing shops to examine and question all that is new.

There is a reason why the challenge of being ready for any eventuality can become nearly an obsession with fly fishers. Most fly anglers carry all of their equipment on their backs, attached to, or in the pockets of a vest. This is necessary for trout anglers because it simply is not possible to wade in the middle of a river and fish properly with a tackle box in one hand. Warmwater anglers on the other hand, often replace a vest with a pocketed float tube (see the Warmwater chapter).

FLY-FISHING VESTS: AN OBSESSION WITH POCKETS

Before legendary fly fisher Lee Wulff invented the modern fly-fishing vest more than fifty years ago, anglers carried flies in their hatbands and other materials in shirt pockets. Back then, it could be argued, fish were more abundant and less inhibited in their willingness to strike a fly, and angling equipment didn't need to be so sophisticated. Today, however, the angler's vest is both a symbol and a storehouse for what a fly fisher needs in the way of proper accessories.

Vests come in just a couple of colors: tan to match the streamside vegetation in the dry West, and forest green to blend with eastern foliage. Inexpensive vests are made of cotton or cotton-synthetic blends, but for warm-weather fishing, a synthetic netting-mesh vest (with mounted pockets) is cooler and lighter. For fly anglers who hike into remote wilderness or high mountain destinations, vest-backpack combinations are available.

Obviously, it is possible for the fully outfitted fly angler to use a different fly vest for each fishing opportunity—one each for eastern and western trout streams, a third for steelhead and salmon, and yet another for winter fly fishing. Fly fishing in warm-water streams and rivers requires yet another set of flies, leaders, and related accessories. It may be convenient to have all those different vests, but it is also practical to use just one vest and simply exchange fly boxes and other equipment. A third solution is to use modular chest packs or fanny packs, which can be configured flexibly by changing one or more elements (each of which has three to five pockets). While there are vests that can be purchased for less than $40, high-end vests and the versatile vest/chest-pack/fanny-pack systems generally cost $100 to $130.

FLIES AND FLY BOXES

Have you ever looked into the tackle box of a well-equipped—and well-heeled—spin angler? There are buzz baits in several dozen sizes and colors, twenty or thirty varieties of plastic worms and other mold-injected critters, floating diving minnows, sinking diving minnows (all in several sizes and colors), and much more. This variety reflects the realization that different times and places require different lures.

The same is true for the fly angler, except that tradition and practicality require that a fly fisher carry flies on his back rather than in a tackle box. Happily, flies by definition are fairly lightweight. Before you fill your vest pockets with boxes of flies, though, you need to figure out how many flies you really need. If you are just starting out, fifteen to twenty-five flies—mixed between some top-water and under-the-water patterns—will suffice for a single species on a particular creek or river. Go to local

fly shops and talk to old-timers to find out which flies you need to get started. But no matter which flies you select, you'll need several duplicates of each, because they do get lost—in trees and hopefully in fish—or otherwise ruined. An old and true axiom suggests that if you are not losing flies, you are not fishing correctly. The ideal trout feeding spot is often right next to a log or under an overhanging branch, ideal spots for flies to get snagged and lost.

A minimum of seven fly boxes are needed to begin the battle with trout: one each for mayflies, caddisflies, stoneflies, terrestrials, streamers, nymphs, and attractors.

Store and organize your flies in small boxes in your vest. The least expensive fly boxes are semitransparent plastic with multiple compartments. Many fly anglers use these, but there is one major shortcoming: If you open a compartmentalized box in a breeze or accidentally tip it, you may lose a lot of flies at once. You could easily dump $30 worth of flies in one momentary mishap. Another problem with compartmentalized boxes is that you have to poke around within small individual compartments to find the exact fly you want. Slightly more expensive boxes have a liner or some material (foam or clips) into which flies can be hooked so they stay put, making them easier to find and to organize by color, size, or other feature.

So how many fly boxes do you need? A good rule is to use as few as you need to keep your flies at your fingertips. Some fly fishers like to have a box for each category of fly, which helps in finding a particular one in the heat of battle (when a hatch is on). If, for example, trout are your quarry, a good starting point is a fly box for each kind of aquatic insect—one each for caddisflies, stoneflies, and mayflies. You also will need a fourth box devoted to terrestrials (land insects such as grasshoppers, ants, beetles, leaf worms, etc.), and yet another box each for streamers and nymphs. A final box might be used for so-called attractor flies, those that don't imitate any particular insect or fish food item but simply seem to attract fish.

That's seven fly boxes to start trout fishing, but more experienced—and specialized—fishers use many more to accommodate different colors and sizes as well different stages of those insects. Caddisflies alone are available in larval (worm), emerger, and adult forms, in sizes from 4 to 15 millimeters, and in at least four or five color combinations. Multiply that by the variety of insects, and you can begin to imagine the storage problem. Some fly fishers have twenty to thirty fly boxes and vary the ones they carry depending on the season and the hatches. If you fish steelhead, salmon, saltwater, or warmwater, you'll need additional fly selections and possibly additional vests.

SINKING THE FLOATER AND FLOATING THE SINKER

Most fish—especially trout—like their food to look and behave properly. When fish are feeding on surface insects or other topside critters, your fly must float like the naturals. Ideally, for a classic dry fly, the

Presentation of flies either on the surface film of the water, within the film, or submerged in the water is critical for success. The sinkers (center) and floatants (bottom) pictured here all aid in getting and keeping your flies where fish are feeding.

feathers (hackle) should indent the surface like insect legs, thus giving your prey the impression of the real thing. If the fish are feeding on or near the bottom, it is critical to get that fly at the same depth as the rest of the fish's food, namely on or near the bottom. When the fish are rising to make dimples on the surface but don't strike your perfect floating imitation, you may find that the successful fly is neither floating or sinking but in the surface layer (film) of the water. By properly selecting your flies or tying them yourself with floating or sinking materials, some of these incompatibilities can be overcome. We generally tie floating flies with lighter hooks and material (synthetic yarn, polypropylene) that does not absorb water. Sinking flies usually have heavier hooks and water-absorbing yarns or fur. Many tiers add lead to these nymphs, streamers, or other sinking patterns.

However, very often the fly materials and design are not sufficient to make your fly behave the way you want. To help keep them on top, for example, it is generally necessary to waterproof dry flies before they are dunked and to dry them off every once in a while to keep them floating properly. In addition, after you catch and fight a fish on your perfect dry fly, the fly will require a radical drying out before it will float properly again. To accomplish the proper floatation, you need (or may want to use) several products. There are a very large number of **fly floatants** on the market, most of which are good to excellent; these are applied to the fly before it is first cast. Most floatants are basically some sort of oil or grease waterproofing mixture. A related item is a special **towel** or **chamois** to dry a fly that has gotten wet. Finally, for the totally slimed-up and soaked fly that has been submerged in the mouth of a fighting fish for five minutes, there are **drying crystals** (in a little shake 'n' bake bottle) and dry-cleaning solution, both of which accomplish miracles in removing moisture and other gunk.

To get your flies to sink, on the other hand, you can use a fly weighted by **lead** wrapped around the body as it is tied. In moving water, subsurface insects that serve as a trout food source often drift with the current, in a natural fashion. By contrast, flies that are overweighted are difficult to cast and generally do not move in a manner similar to a living insect or other water critter. Fish reject food that does not drift properly. Additionally, overweighted flies also hang up on every rock or branch. Underweighted flies, by contrast may not get down to the feeding level, and the

fish simply do not see them. Importantly, the amount of weight necessary to get a proper drift depends on the speed of the current and depth of the water, which varies from river to river and in different parts of the same river. The best solution for getting your flies to sink just the right amount is to add weight as necessary when you are on the water. **Spit shot** is an obvious choice, and this is available in a range of sizes, from very small (microshot) to larger sizes that are also used for spin angling. Unfortunately, concentrated weight on a leader tends to cause tangles and hang-ups. Alternatives include small matchsticks of lead, a lead putty that can be better distributed, or even mud to help your fly sink more naturally. Out of concern for the environment, it is worth noting that there are some weights that are made of nonlead materials and thus are less toxic to migratory birds and other living things.

LITTLE TOOLS THAT SAVE THE DAY

A century-old poem emphasized the need to take care of details, declaring that "for the want of a nail," a

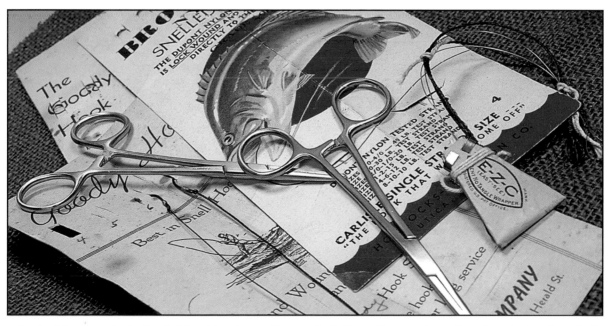

A pair of forceps and a leader stretcher (above), as well as a pair of pliers, a thermometer, and a release tool are important tools for the fly fishermen and can make the difference between a good day on the water and a poor one.

horse, a soldier, a battle, a war, and, in turn, a country were lost. It is often the same with fly fishing.

Early this season, I was nymph fishing for jumbo bluegill on a favorite Wisconsin lake, and as I excitedly removed a fly from a beautiful fish, my $3 **forceps** (also called a **hemostat**) slipped from my hand and sank all the way to the bottom. As it turned out, this little misadventure spoiled a potentially great afternoon. Without the hemostat, I was unable to retrieve flies from those selective 10-inch killers, and very quickly my supply of #14 flashback nymphs was gone. My sad story has several lessons. First, I should have had the hemostat connected to my vest with a retractor (sometimes called a zinger), or at least a length of fly line. Most often you are connecting flies and making adjustments to your gear over water as you wade, and anything that is dropped is lost permanently, unless you want to go for a swim. This problem is made worse by the fact that, while fly anglers are sociable folks, most of us fish by ourselves or at least some distance away from

Feeding and movement of many species is connected to water temperature so a thermometer can prove invaluable.

our companions. If you loose a critical tool, help is not often nearby.

Sometimes the tool you need is peculiar to a certain fly-fishing situation, making a critical difference between a good day and a poor one. I was lucky enough to fish the Bighorn River in the early 1990s, and there was an early- to mid-season period when midge pupa (very little flies, about 4 millimeters long) were deadly when fished just below the surface. This was particularly exciting fishing because those Bighorn trout averaged 16 inches—a 20-incher was not unusual—and the flies were tiny. To set up the rig for these suspended pupa, I needed to crimp a microshot of about .06 inches in diameter on a tippet of about .005 inches, about 4 inches above the fly. Forceps did not work because the teeth were too big for the microshot (sometimes nicking and weakening the tippet), and it was impossible to reliably crimp the shot with my teeth because of its small size. If the shot was not securely attached to the line, it moved down to obstruct the tiny fly or just fell off. For pinching on that microshot, the critical tool (for me) was a pair of little 3-inch pliers with a spring-open jaw and no teeth. I still carry this tool today even though I have not used it in four years.

There are a number of such tools that fly anglers sometimes find useful, including several ingenious devices to tie knots, a small **spring-loaded clip** that holds flies to keep them from blowing away as you tie them on, a small **file** to sharpen hooks, a **small measuring tape** (for bragging rights), and a **thermometer**.

This handy fly retriever unsnags flies from trees, bushes, and anglers' other natural hazards.

Some of the more unusual gadgets carried by fly anglers include a **fish stomach pump** (similar to a basting syringe and used to examine the contents of the fish's stomach to see what it has been feeding on), a miniature **monocular** (for spotting flies and trout at a distance), and a small special-purpose **calculator** that determines the weight of a fish from its length and girth. Of course, there are new and better tools coming along all the time, like a digital micrometer to determine the diameter of a tippet, all-around (but very expensive) fisherman's pliers that not only cuts very heavy and very light monofilament but also can mash split shot and remove hooks as well, and several devices that allow you to remove a fly without even touching the fish.

Do you need all of these things just to go fly fishing? Our grandfathers did not have them, but they also used larger flies to catch fish that were less picky, and had more time to develop the fine skill of tying elaborate knots on a stream in the dark. These old-timers also clipped monofilament tippets by biting them, a practice that horrifies dentists because it damages teeth.

FLY-FISHING SPECTACLES

A top-quality pair of polarized sunglasses is perhaps the most important fly-fishing accessory after rod, reel, and line. This is a fact that I, and no doubt many others, learned the hard way. For me, the lesson came one afternoon on the upper Brule River.

It was the third strike that I had missed. The afternoon light was a mixture of shadows from the overhanging white pines and a low in-your-face sun splashing through the bottom branches. At the very head of the pool where the huge browns were feeding, the light on the water changed. At that critical spot my fly was repeatedly lost between the shadows and the surface glare of the sun on the water. Why didn't I have the right polarized sunglasses in my vest? What I needed was the light-brown tinted pair, perfect for low, late-afternoon light. I had only the darker gray, good for bright noontime fishing but almost worthless late in the day. My only choice was

UV protection is essential, even on overcast days. Here in the Florida Keys, wildlife artist Tim Borski wears sunglasses and a balaclava.

to cast further upstream where the light was better, away from the feeding area, in the hope that a lone fish would oblige. Meanwhile, my fishing partner was landing his fourth fat brown. He had wisely packed the right sunglasses.

To get to this reach of the upper Brule River, we had hiked two tough miles from an old logging road. The late-afternoon caddis hatch was exactly as anticipated, and a #14 emerging sparkle pupa fished in the water's surface film, was the critical fly. Everything was perfect—except that I couldn't see the fish strike my fly.

In my experience, this frustration is an all-too common one. The dominance of the visual sense in fly fishing is both a blessing and a curse, especially on the flats of the Keys. On the plus side, many believe that fly fishing is uniquely exciting because it permits you to visualize the critical, all-important triumph of an actual fish striking your fly. There is almost nothing like the adrenaline rush you get when your eyes confirm that you fooled that cautious wild creature, giving the cue to set the hook properly. On the other hand, when you cannot see well, it all fails.

Sleek, elegantly-designed fly-tying vise that will last forever with minimal care.

In spinner or baitfishing, when a fish strikes, the event is telegraphed via a taut line to the fishing rod; you feel it. The fish is often hooked without much more than a sharp reactive pull at the moment of sudden resistance. By contrast, in fly fishing, the line cannot be tight because fish will reject a fly floating unnaturally on a taut line and so you can usually only detect the strike visually.

Say the fly is 35 feet away, half-submerged in the surface film with maybe ⅛ inch showing above the reflective water surface. Unlike a lure, flies have only a single hook (with very limited self-hooking potential). Flies made of feathers and fur are detected as unnatural almost instantly—within hundredths of milliseconds—based on the fish's acute senses of taste, smell, and oral touch. So if you set the hook too soon, the fly may not be properly in the fish's mouth. Alternatively, if you are but a moment too late, the fish will have already rejected it. The narrow window of opportunity challenges your skill and punishes your failures. Proper sunglasses improve your chances, often critically.

BASIC CONSIDERATIONS

Sunglasses are not an accessory on which to cut costs. Here are a few tips that may help you choose the best pairs for you.

▶Avoid the very inexpensive sunglasses commonly displayed on revolving stands in drug stores, souvenir shops, and even some sporting goods stores; the polarization is often limited and the poor optics cause distortion.

▶Buy polarized lenses; this is the only way to reduce the critical glare and protect your eyes from ultraviolet light.

▶If you wear corrective lenses, consider a pair of prescription sunglasses.

In deciding on sunglasses, the first real choice is the color or tint of the lenses. Two kinds of light, ultraviolet (UV) and infrared (IR), which cannot be detected by the human eye, are present in large quantities in the light spectrum. Both can damage the retina unless you wear proper filtering lenses. For

example, cataracts, which severely limit visual acuity, are due in large part to exposure to ultraviolet B radiation. Secondly, there is a shorter-wave blue light, on which the human eye focuses imperfectly. It causes "blue blur" which in time also can damage the retina and reduce your ability to see details clearly. Haze, fog, rain, and snow intensify the effects of blue light. Proper polarized sunglasses will protect your eyes from UV and IR rays, glare, and blue light.

Polarized sunglasses with different tints filter different wavelengths of light, and darker glasses filter out more light. For many fly anglers, no single pair of sunglasses is optimal for every fishing need.

A very important consideration is a pair of **photochromatic lenses**, which are now available in plastic as well as glass. Basically, these lenses get lighter or darker with variations in external light. In midday, with a bright sun, the lenses are dark, giving you protection. As evening approaches, or in the shade, the lens become lighter. With these sunglasses, you may be able wear the same ones all day. If I had photochromatic lenses on the Brule, I would have been able to see my flies in bright sun or shade.

MAGNIFICATION

If you are over forty (and aren't all great fly fishers?) and fishing especially in low light conditions, threading a .007 inch tippet through the eye of a tiny #20 fly hook can be very difficult. For this reason, sunglasses with additional magnification—in the form of a bifocal magnification in the lower part of the lens—

A handy clip-on magnifier assists anglers trying to tie that #24 midge on a darkening action-filled hatch.

are very popular. Some fly fishers carry a pair of dime-store readers with a magnification of 1.5 to 2.0 diopters in their vests. Other, more expensive, options include flip-up magnifying lenses that attach to your sunglasses (but may also scratch them), stick-on fresnel lens that act like bifocals, or flip-down lenses that attach to the brim of a baseball-style fishing cap. All of these solutions help, but none is perfect. The best solution is a pair of sunglasses that have been fitted for your particular needs (and deficiencies) and produced by an ophthalmic professional.

ARTIFICIAL LIGHT

It was almost 8:00 P.M. by the time we got on the water, and even though it was early June, the sun was very low. We intentionally started late knowing that the best time for big feeding browns on the Tomorrow River was right at dusk, sometime around 9:00 P.M. Within a few minutes we were all into fish, albeit small browns and brook trout. As that first hour passed, the number of rising fish increased, and in the canopy of cedar, the light had faded considerably. The first challenge of the night came as I had to replace a fly bedraggled by one too many fish. For onstream light I use a small lithium-powered flashlight hooked to the front of my vest to project right where I tie on my flies. I turned away from the water, sensitive to the claim that light can put evening trout off their feed. This kind of artificial light is but one of several options for night fly fishers.

Because of the tendency of big brown trout and large-mouth bass trout to feed at night, more and more fly anglers fish after dark. Night fly fishing is also much less crowded and better fits the 8-to-5 workday. Fish you would never see during daylight feed at night. The Pennsylvania state record brown trout—an

11-pounder caught by Joe Humphreys—was a night-caught fish. Some hatches, like the famed Midwestern hexagenia hatch with 2-inch flies, occur almost entirely after dark and attract the biggest fish. While it is outside the scope of this chapter to consider the strangeness of fly fishing in the dark and listening (rather than watching) for a big trout to strike, the need for a special light should be obvious. Several solutions are available to nighttime fly anglers: a **flashlight** with a pocket clip and flexible neck to aim the light on the fly, a **light with a magnifier** that lies flat against your chest until you need it, and a **headlamp** that attaches to a headband like a miner's light. The light need not be designed for fly fishing—any flashlight will do—but you must keep both hands free to tie flies or make other adjustments.

PROTECTION AGAINST THE SUN

One of the byproducts of being an avid fly angler is that bronzed Montana fishing guide look. Unfortunately, it has become painfully—and mortally—clear in the last decade that we need to avoid exposure to direct sunlight. Medical scientists have shown that even the mildest suntan is evidence of damaged skin and could eventually lead to skin cancer. If you burn easily, rarely tan, sometimes freckle, or have a fair complexion with blonde or red hair, you are even more vulnerable to skin cancer. (These problems are made worse at high elevations, where many of the more famous western trout rivers are found.) The hard truth is that no matter what your complexion, suntanned skin is a step closer to developing cancer because the sun's damage is progressive. Every year you increase the chances of joining the estimated seven hundred thousand Americans who develop skin cancer and the seven

Hats shade the face and neck from the sun and keep an angler dry in bad weather.

thousand to ten thousand who die from the disease. Moreover, the incidents of malignant melanoma, the most deadly form of skin cancer, has been steadily rising. These problems are especially acute for the occasional angler, who gets almost no sun most of the year and then is overexposed for a couple of months in early summer. One way to avoid these problems is to make sure your fly-fishing accessories include proper clothing and adequate sunblocking agents.

According to the American Cancer Society, a few simple steps can significantly reduce the risk of developing skin problems. First, use a sunscreen of at least SPF 15 before going out in the sun, and apply it again if you stay out for more than four hours. Keep some in your vest. Second, wear long-sleeved, tightly woven cotton shirts and long pants. Finally, discard that baseball-style hat. It doesn't provide any protection for the sides and back of your neck, nor for your ears or the side of your face. The far better alternative—according to skin cancer researchers at the National Farm Medicine Center—is a **wide-brimmed hat**. Increasingly, fly fishing shops and catalogs are offering better hats. An inexpensive and cool solution (temperature-wise) is a woven-straw hat. While floppy hats and long-sleeved shirts may look a little eccentric, remember that it is better to be an odd fly angler than a sickly or dead fly angler.

MOISTURE AND TEMPERATURE CONTROL

While some anglers prefer to fish when the sun is shining and the sky is blue, there is little question that the feeding habits of many species require braving less friendly elements. In many parts of the country, trout streams are open all year, offering more solitude—and colder weather—in winter than during the popular spring and summer seasons. Steelhead and salmon fishing often take place in

Wading shoes are felt-soled or studded to provide traction on slippery surfaces underwater and along river banks.

inclement or cooler weather. Likewise, warmwater and saltwater fly fishing is not always comfortably warm but sometimes uncomfortably hot.

To make fly fishing possible, or at least tolerable, in inclement weather, several major companies have designed and marketed separate lines of clothing for the angler. **Water-resistant hooded jackets** with big pockets for fly boxes and extra fabric permit the active movements involved in casting. These jackets often come in a shortened style for fairly deep wading without getting the bottom of the jacket wet. Some of this clothing is compressible so it can be rolled up and put in the back of your fly-fishing vest, to be used when the weather changes unexpectedly. Many of these vests, coats, shirts, and pants take advantage of the new breathable materials as well as lightweight fleece for maximum comfort. The serious cold-weather angler can also find **fleece liners for waders**, and **fleece or neoprene fingerless gloves** (some with rollback index fingers or thumbs) for easy line handling and also to keep hands dry and warm.

The hot-weather fly angler faces a different set of problems, and clothing manufacturers have been

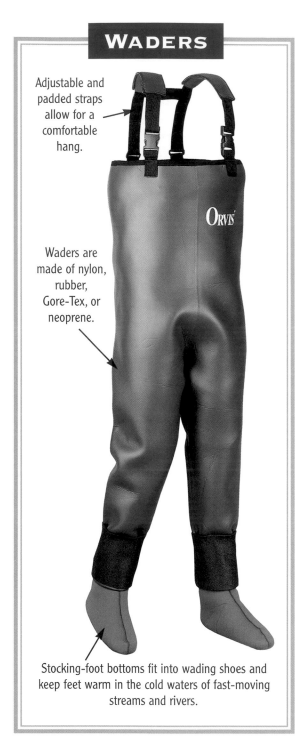

WADERS

Adjustable and padded straps allow for a comfortable hang.

Waders are made of nylon, rubber, Gore-Tex, or neoprene.

ORVIS

Stocking-foot bottoms fit into wading shoes and keep feet warm in the cold waters of fast-moving streams and rivers.

Many shirts have very large vents in the back to allow air movement, and big pockets for fly boxes. Along with shirts and pants to keep you cool, mesh vests provide even the most demanding fly fisher with enough pockets to carry flies and other necessary accessories yet still stay cool.

WADERS AND THEN SOME

Not too many years ago, fly fishers were especially conspicuous in their bulky, ill-fitting chest waders constructed of heavy rubberized canvas. These waders had clumsy boots that made it difficult to walk very far without blisters, significant fatigue, or serious missteps. Rubberized canvas waders also acted as a body sauna, causing as much moisture inside (from perspiration and condensation) as outside. For those who survived, waders were undoubtedly one of the least pleasant aspects of stream or lake fishing. Ten to fifteen years ago, lighter waterproof nylon improved the situation somewhat, but not completely.

All of that has changed. The vast majority of fly fishers now use **stocking-foot waders**, worn inside wading boots that look and fit like hiking shoes. The waders themselves are made of several different materials, from latex rubber to breathable fabrics like Gore-Tex. The oldest of these are latex rubber, and these continue to be used by some very serious trout anglers. All latex rubber waders are inexpensive and if punctured can be patched just like an old car tire inner tube.

A second and more popular alternative material is closed-cell neoprene, the same material that is used for wetsuits. **Neoprene** waders are quite comfortable (once you get them on) and feel like stretchable blue jeans. Neoprene is easy to patch, and if you take a dunk the neoprene keeps you warm. Unfortunately, most neoprene waders have the same sauna problem as the old rubber waders, making for a very wet next-to-skin experience. Nevertheless, for winter fishing, neoprene is a great help. One manufacturer offers a neoprene wader with a fleece lining, which wicks away moisture from perspiration. Obviously, neoprene in the warmer months is too

even more active in providing very lightweight, quick-drying, and breathable clothes for these extremes. Pants come with zippers that allow them to be converted to shorts. Shirts with roll-up sleeve tabs let you expose as much of your arms as you like.

warm, especially if you have to walk any distance to your favorite spot. A final issue with neoprene waders is the fact that they fit like a body stocking and the peculiarities of your shape, including bulges, will be exaggerated.

Finally, there is one last alternative—better and more expensive. The most comfortable waders to date are made of **Gore-Tex** or similar material. Perspiration and condensation from inside these waders pass through to the outside, while outside moisture is kept out. These waders are thus very comfortable in warmer settings and can also be worn in winter with fleece lining.

When selecting waders, make sure they fit comfortably. If they are too small—or tight in the wrong places—you will not be able to move properly. If they are too big, the constant rubbing of surfaces, against both you and one another can be a source of painful chafing as well as premature wear. Also worth mentioning is that ill-fitting waders will make you look rather peculiar.

Wading shoes are worn over stocking-foot waders just like conventional boots. They generally are constructed of synthetic leather and have high tops, like hiking boots. Several kinds of materials are used on the soles to aid surefootedness. Felt soles are preferred for slippery stone and rock bottoms, with studs (carbide or tungsten) embedded in the felt to offer extra traction. Some companies also offer soles designed for sandy surfaces (river bottoms, beaches) with a special cleat that is guaranteed not to fill up. Wading traction can also be improved with stretchy stud-bottomed sandals that slip over wading shoes like overshoes. **Korkers**—full foot-length sandals with aluminum studs for weedy streams or ice—have been around for a long time. If cost is an issue, some anglers

Waders, vests, shorts, and other fishing apparel are made for especially for the female angler in both women's and girls' sizes as worn by angling writer Margot Page and her daughter Brooke in a Vermont river.

wear tennis shoes with stocking foot waders, but these are almost suicidal on slippery rocks.

Some wader accessories are considered essential by most fly fishers. One of these is a **wading belt** (web or neoprene) to keep your waders from filling up with water—and sinking you—if you happen to take a spill. A wading belt might save your life. To keep gravel from abrading stocking foot waders and causing leaks there are also special **wading socks** (neoprene or heavy cloth) with a fold-down top to keep gravel out of your boots.

The proper use of a net can help increase the chances that a large fish will survive after it has been hooked, played, and landed.

If you expect to be fishing trout rivers and streams that require a lot of wading, you also may want to invest in a **wading staff**, which is basically a longish walking cane (45 to 60 inches long). It provides a critical third point of stability when moving over rocky, muddy, or unknown river bottoms, or in fast current. In western rivers, even knee-deep water can be forceful enough to knock you off of your feet, especially if you take a false step. A wading staff can prevent that from happening. The best and most effective staffs are made of hardwood or bamboo. Unfortunately, they are clumsy to carry, and your fly line will forever be wrapping around them. A good alternative is a folding wading staff made of six or eight sections held together with a shock cord. These are carried in a belt holster and with a snap of the wrist the sections are straightened and ready to use.

LANDING THE FISH

When you hook a fish on a fly and work it to the point where it can be landed, you have several choices. Small and large fish create different challenges. If the fish is small (like many trout and bluegill, and most bass), it can be landed by hand. This is preferable to using a landing net because your fly and leader can often get tangled in the net, and the net itself can damage the fish, reducing its sur-

vival potential if you want to release it. For smaller fish that are going to be released, you may want to use a **release tool**. With a release tool—basically a small hook at the end of a 4- to 8-inch handle—you can release the fish without even getting your hands wet. Release tools are available commercially but also can be made from a coat hanger or a piece of wooden dowel and an eyehook.

Larger fish, especially in fast water, often require a **landing net**. Using a net allows you to get the fish in and released more quickly, before it becomes exhausted. Of course, an exhausted fish has a much lower chance of surviving if released. Nicely finished hardwood landing nets are items of beauty in themselves, and many anglers come to treasure them almost as much as they do a split-cane bamboo rod. If you use a landing net, use one with a soft material for the netting. Nets made of nylon are especially damaging to fish. Some of the new landing nets are shallow for easier fish release and have a netting that is slightly elastic so the fish cannot easily flip out.

TRAVELING WITH ALL YOUR STUFF

Now that you have collected a rod, reel (or two, with extra spools), a bunch of fly boxes, a vest full of stuff, waders, boots, hat, socks, and whatever else you just can't live without, you'll soon discover that it is more than a little clumsy to load and unload this bulky and odd-shaped assortment in and out of your vehicle. These complications increase if you want to take a trip by commercial airline. To help fly fishers travel safely and without damage to their equipment, several companies have marketed specially designed fly-fishing luggage. There are padded rod cases for up to six rods (two, three, or four-piece), special padded reel carriers (holding up to six reels), bags for carrying fly-tying gear (including all the thread, feathers, fur, tools, and hooks), a special bag with mesh ventilation for wet wading shoes and waders, and a carry-all bag that holds almost everything but the fly rods. Even for those who do not travel extensively, this luggage is very convenient and practical.

Other items that are especially useful for even short trips include a fabric-covered and padded tube that lets you transport your rod and reel without taking the assembly apart. This allows you to be ready to fish all the more quickly, without any compromise of safety for your most expensive items.

WHAT ELSE COULD I NEED?

Believe it or not, there are yet other items that the fashionable and fully supplied (some say oversupplied) fly fisher might need or just want. To keep up with the latest gadgets and the perennial must-haves, visit your local fly shop or get on the mailing lists of a few fly-fishing catalogs. Another great way to stay on top of all the good stuff is to join a local fly-fishing club, which gives anglers the chance to show off their new accessories and talk about their own homegrown inventions. This kind of sharing has been part of fly fishing for at least one hundred and fifty years.

A final caveat regarding all of these wonderfully clever gadgets: Fly fishing is a commercial endeavor to some, and there are all manner of devices for sale, some of which are not easy to use and basically lack practical value. As proof, there are many gadgets that were all the rage two, three, or four years ago that simply are not around anymore. Buyers beware!

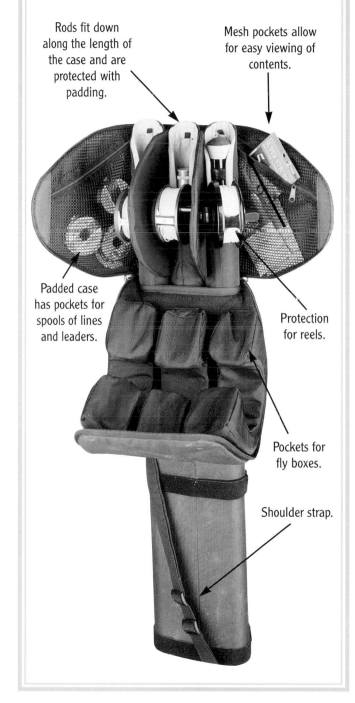

GEAR CASE

A gear case is an essential piece of luggage for the traveling fly fisherman. It has specially-designed compartments for all your fishing gear, including vented pockets for wet shoes and waders.

Rods fit down along the length of the case and are protected with padding.

Mesh pockets allow for easy viewing of contents.

Padded case has pockets for spools of lines and leaders.

Protection for reels.

Pockets for fly boxes.

Shoulder strap.

CASTING

BY TOM AKSTENS

Fly casting has evolved over hundreds of years as a solution to an interesting problem: You're here, the fish is over there, and you want to put a fly that weighs next to nothing in front of its nose. The great casting instructor Joan Salvato Wulff once asked a rhetorical question that sums up the challenge astutely: "How far can you throw a feather?"

Some British anglers on lochs and reservoirs still employ a method called "dapping," an age-old solution to the perplexing challenge of throwing a feather. Using a very long rod and a relatively short line, the angler swings the line into the air, and the fly floats downwind. The obvious limitation to this technique is that the fly can't go any farther than the combined length of the rod and the line—about 25 feet. You'd be dead out of luck with a fish rising 40 feet away. Modern fly casting depends instead on the weight of the line and the capacity of the rod to store energy like a spring and propel a loop of line through the air for considerable distances. The fly merely goes along for the ride.

In the first half of the twentieth century, classic split-cane rods from the shops of Leonard, Edwards, Divine, and Payne evolved in response to the angler's need to present a fly delicately at 30 to 40 feet on the relatively small rivers of the Northeast. The best cane rods of this period were remarkably refined casting tools, especially at short to medium distances. However, since they were (at that time) individually handcrafted, these rods could put quite a dent in a fly fisher's wallet.

In the 1950s, fiberglass rods and plastic-coated fly lines began to take over the marketplace as technology put affordable, functional tackle into the hands of a greater number of anglers. But most of these rods had very slow actions by today's standards. As a result, casting instruction in the 1950s and '60s tended to emphasize the double-haul (see the Hauling and Shooting Line section) and other techniques to develop line speed and attain distance. Longer casts (and big cowboy hats) were the order of the day on large, windy western rivers such as the Madison and the

A PERFECT CAST

Throughout your fishing experience, you will have good casts and bad: some that are better than expected, others that will make you wonder if you'll ever get it right.

And there *will* be casts that are absolutely perfect!

A perfect cast is a thing of beauty. It is like a note of music extended and held. In all other sports the moment of impact separates you from the very thing you are projecting in beautiful flight—but the execution of the perfect cast can be seen and felt, from its inception until the fly touches down on the water.

—Joan Wulff

Yellowstone, which had already been "discovered" by Dan Bailey and other pioneering fly rodders.

The introduction of graphite rods in the 1970s revolutionized casting, a revolution that has accelerated with compound rod tapers and other advances in rod design. Graphite rods have faster actions and store energy much more efficiently than bamboo or fiberglass rods and thus generate higher line speeds. Graphite rods are also remarkably light in the hand. With these modern rods, a caster of average competence can throw 50 feet of line for hours, even in windy conditions—a feat that could have taxed the skills of an expert forty years ago.

The inherent power of graphite liberates the modern caster from the gymnastics that were often needed to get maximum performance from a fiberglass rod. At the same time, a good graphite rod allows for very precise presentations at medium range, although it does have a completely different feel than the classic cane rods that set the standard for accuracy. So, while you should still learn how to put a haul in your cast for a few extra feet to reach a tailing bonefish, graphite lets you concentrate on perfecting your timing and your technique. It is not too much of a stretch to say that in the graphite era

the most important lesson you need to learn is how to let the rod do the work.

LEARNING TO CAST—SOME PRELIMINARIES

In Norman Maclean's renowned novella, *A River Runs Through It*, a minister teaches his sons to cast with this admonition: "Casting is an art performed on a four-count rhythm between ten and two o'clock."

The rhythmic incantation of "ten o'clock and two o'clock" brings many of us back to our own first casting lesson. In my case, the lesson was forty-three years ago, when I was eight years old. My Uncle Julie was my teacher, and even though the lesson took place in a suburban backyard in Massachusetts rather than on a brawling Montana trout river, the mantra was the same: "ten o'clock and two o'clock, ten o'clock and two o'clock."

Today, however, most fly rods are so improved over their bamboo and fiberglass predecessors that the traditional casting arc can be shortened considerably, giving greater control and more line speed. Ten o'clock and one o'clock would be a more appropriate arc for an average beginning caster using a well-designed graphite rod.

As you develop your casting skills, you will find that you will shorten or lengthen your arc depending on circumstances. The clock-face description is simply a convenient way to visualize what the rod is doing in the air. Use it as a learning tool but do not become a slave to it. You do not want to cast like a robot; the goal is to develop a casting stroke that feels natural and comfortable.

It's worth mentioning that my Uncle Julie was a golf pro and therefore had a lot of experience with processes that are designed to store and release mechanical energy. Aside from the fact that they're long and tapered, golf clubs and fly rods have at least one other thing in common: They store energy on the back swing and release it on the forward swing. And, as any golf pro will tell you, "It's all in the backswing."

In order to have a fly rod work efficiently, you

need to load it efficiently from the very beginning of the back cast with a smooth application of power. As a matter of fact, if you load the rod efficiently to begin with, you can pretty much relax and concentrate on letting the rod do what it was designed to do—load and unload, load and unload, load and unload—storing and releasing energy with each back cast and forward cast in the casting sequence.

Remember that there is really no mystery to casting with a fly rod. It does not require any extraordinary physical skills, and the mechanics of casting are quite simple and straightforward. With a solid foundation in the proper technique and basic mechanics of casting, your skills will continue to develop over the years.

Finally, please bear in mind that the instructions in this chapter are for right-handed casting—holding the rod with your right hand and using your left hand to control the loose line.

EQUIPMENT

Before you start casting, take a few minutes to get to know the system you will be using, so that you will understand how it has been designed to store and release energy so efficiently.

You should be practicing with a balanced outfit—your rod, reel and line should be rated for the same weight line (as described in the chapter on lines and leaders). An 8½ or 9-foot rod for 5- or 6-weight line is a good choice. Select a rod made of second- or third-generation graphite; the latest graphite composites are often too stiff for comfortable use. It would be like giving a recreational skier a pair of Alberto Tomba's slalom skis. A stiff rod makes it difficult to feel the rod "load up" with the weight of the line when you are starting out.

Begin by looking down the rod

from the grip to the tip. Now run your finger and thumb over the front 20 feet of fly line and the leader, pulling slowly and feeling the taper of the line and leader. You will notice that the entire system, from the fairly heavy rod grip to the end of the leader, is continuously tapered to allow for a smooth transfer of energy as you cast. It is this taper that allows the rod to release the energy to form a loop with the fly line, and allows the transfer of energy that will straighten out the loop as it travels through the air.

THE GRIP

Most casters use the "handshake" grip to hold a fly rod. To do that, extend your hand as if you were getting ready to seal a deal with a handshake, and set the handle of the rod in your palm. Close your fingers and rest your thumb on top of the handle. The handshake grip feels natural and actually provides a very solid foundation for casting heavier rods (7-weight or higher) and large flies. But it makes it too easy to move your wrist back and forth like a hinge as you cast. Excess motion—such as flexing your wrist or twisting your upper body—should be kept out of the casting process, because it tends to allow energy to be

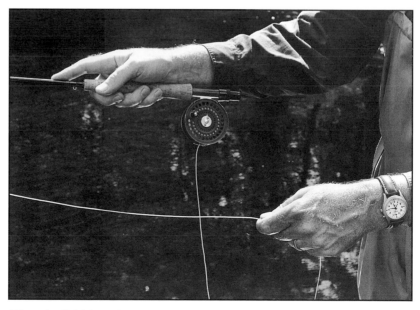

The grip: Hold the rod handle comfortably with your index finger on top, while your left hand controls the line.

The casting plane: Move the rod in a plane about 45 degrees down from overhead to avoid snagging the fly on nearby trees or setting it on the water too soon.

the air, so that you can perfect your timing.

STANCE AND PREPARATION

Next, stand in a relaxed posture, facing the direction in which you want to cast. Your shoulders should be loose and comfortable; your elbows should be by your side. Your weight should be on the balls of your feet, so that you have good balance and can feel the rhythm of the casting motion. Your upper body should be relaxed and still. Above all else, remember that fly casting is a matter of timing, not strength. If you are straining like Schwarzenegger, you're already sunk.

One more detail: Make sure you are wearing glasses or sunglasses. Things can get a bit hairy if a sudden gust of wind brings your line toward you unexpectedly. It is a good idea to have your eyes covered and protected.

It is fine to practice casting on the lawn, but a small pond is even better. Your flyline will come off the water with more resistance than it will off grass, allowing you to load up the system more efficiently. Still, if you're using grass, straighten out about 25 feet of fly line (not counting the leader) in front of you. Point your rod tip at the end of your leader, where your fly would be. There should be no slack anywhere in the system. Eliminating slack and starting with your tip down at water (grass) level will give you the greatest possible mechanical advantage in terms of loading your rod. Hold the loose fly line comfortably with your free hand, slightly above belt level.

THINKING IT THROUGH

Now you are ready to cast, but first visualize the arc that you want your rod tip to make as it travels through the air. Then turn slightly toward your rod

wasted or "spill" out of the system. Your wrist should be relaxed but still and reasonably straight, as it would be if you were driving a nail with a hammer. Do not use your wrist as a hinge.

With this in mind, there's another grip I recommend because it helps keep your wrist still and straight. I learned it from my Uncle Julie, and I still use it—even when I'm casting a 9-weight into a headwind on the Rhode Island coastline. Simply hold the rod handle comfortably with your index finger on top. Then let your fingers wrap round the handle naturally. It's fine to choke up a bit with this grip; if it feels comfortable, the tip of your index finger can even rest on the rod blank itself. Regardless of the grip you use, your hand should hold the rod securely, but it should be relaxed. The rod is your partner—don't try to strangle it.

Now get ready to cast. Double a section of fly line over itself and run it through the guides. Make sure you have a 7½ or 9-foot leader attached to the end of your line, but leave off the fly. In the place of a fly, you might find it helpful to loop a half-inch piece of fluorescent yarn to the end of your tippet—the kind of yarn fly shops sell as "strike indicator" material. This will help you follow the travel of your cast in hand so that you will be able to watch the rod tip form that arc. Remember, you're going to stop your back cast at one o'clock, and you're going to wait at one o'clock until the loop of the flyline has a chance to straighten out behind you, which will load the rod for the forward cast. Then you're going to accelerate the rod forward, stopping at ten o'clock and waiting again for the loop to straighten out in front of you to load the rod for the next back cast. Visualize where ten and one o'clock are. It is probably a more compact arc than you think it is.

It will also help to visualize the plane along which your rod will travel as it makes its arc. For different fishing situations, you may wish to vary the casting plane from vertical to horizontal. Often a casting plane 35 to 45 degrees down from vertical is most comfortable.

THE BASIC CAST

Now begin the pickup for the **back cast**, starting with your rod tip barely touching the water or grass. Without flexing your wrist, smoothly accelerate the rod tip up to one o'clock and stop. Turn a bit sideways so that you can watch the travel of the line in the air as it straightens out behind you. Just as the line begins to straighten out completely, accelerate the rod forward and stop the tip at ten o'clock. Wait until the loop of line has nearly straightened out again and then accelerate the rod back to one o'clock.

Count the rhythm to yourself, exaggerating the wait on both back cast and forward cast: "Ten o'clock annnnnd one o'clock annnnnd ten o'clock annnnnd one o'clock. . . ." If you hear a snap in the air on your back cast, it means that you are "cracking the whip"—not waiting long enough for the line to straighten out behind you. Follow the line in the air visually—and be patient.

Try several false casts, keeping the fly, or yarn, in the air as your rod travels back and forth from ten to one. To end the casting sequence, stop one of your forward casts at ten. Wait at ten until your

Basic Cast Step 1: The resistance of the line coming off the water loads the rod with energy.

Basic Cast Step 2: Stop the back cast at one o'clock and wait for the line to straighten behind you.

Basic Cast Step 3: Stop the forward cast at ten o'clock and wait for the loop to turn over.

Presentation and follow-through: Stop forward cast at ten o'clock, wait for the loop to turn over, and then follow the fly with your rod tip until it touches the water. Don't "throw" the line forward.

loop has straightened in the air, and then allow your rod tip to drift down toward the water, following the fly. Do not try to "throw" the line forward; relax and let the rod do the work.

The tip should come to rest just above the water's surface, ready to begin your next back cast with the maximum mechanical advantage.

Here is a quick review of some essential points for you to be mindful of as you practice.

1. Keep slack out of the system.
2. Begin with your rod tip at water level.
3. Do not use your wrist like a hinge.
4. Stop your rod tip at one o'clock.
5. Wait for the line to straighten out behind you and begin to load the rod before you start your forward cast.

There are two more things to remember as you practice this basic cast. The first is that the best time to apply a bit of power (to load your rod and build up line speed) is at the very beginning of your back cast. Do not try to recover a botched cast by trying to throw or push your line on the forward cast. Many modern graphite rods are designed well enough to let you get away with this, but you will be compromising your technique for the future when you want to cast for

distance. Distance is a function of line speed, and to get line speed you must load your rod efficiently at the start of the back cast. Further, if you try to add power to your forward cast, you are likely to develop a "tailing loop," the most common error of casters. If it seems as if your line is trying to hook itself, you are throwing a tailing loop.

Second, when things go haywire—as they inevitably will at some time or another—stop, relax, and go back to the "thinking it through" stage. Trying to recover a casting sequence that has gotten out of timing and fallen apart will simply cause you endless frustration. It's best to just stop, untangle yourself, lay out a new 25 feet of line, visualize what you're trying to do, and then start over. In fact, I've found that no matter how well the initial casting session is going, many beginning casters "hit the wall" after about twenty minutes. Practice for a half-hour at most, then take a break. You will do much better when you go back to it.

FROM CASTING TO FISHING— THE TRANSITION

An essential point of technique that often seems to be ignored in fly casting instruction is the transition between casting and fishing. Interestingly enough, the transition is something that you do with your hands, as much as with your rod and line.

Let's go back to your practice casting sequence— to the point where you present the fly, stopping your forward cast at ten and then letting your rod tip drift down to the level of the water, following the fly as it falls through the air. At the point where you stop your cast, your rod hand has the index finger on top of the blank and your line hand is comfortably holding the fly line at about belt height. When your tip stops at ten, and as it drifts toward the water, rotate your wrist, turning your rod hand over—towards you—about 40 degrees, controlling the fly line by grasping it between your middle finger and thumb. At the same time, bring the index finger and thumb of your left hand up to meet the thumb and middle finger of your rod hand. Now your hands are in position to strip (pull in) line, which is the basic action of fishing with a fly rod. Your grip should be secure but your hands should be relaxed—not a death grip.

Strip in the line a few times. Keep your rod tip pointed at your fly while you use your line hand to pull 6 inches of line through the middle finger and thumb of your right hand. Now slide your line hand back up to meet your rod hand and strip another 6 inches. When you are actually fishing, you might strip line fast or slow, an inch or a foot at a time, but notice that your line hand is always behind your rod

hand. And notice that your rod tip is always pointed directly at your fly, a few inches off the surface of the water. In this position, you are always ready to begin another efficient back cast or to set the hook on a striking fish.

It is important that you take the time to learn the mechanics of the casting-to-stripping transition correctly. Practice hand turnover and line stripping diligently and you will soon be making the transition unconsciously from casting to fishing. Remember that what you do with your hands at this point will be basically the same, whether you are fishing for 10-inch brook trout in a beaver pond in Michigan's Upper Peninsula or for big "chopper" bluefish in Vineyard Sound.

One thing you will have to contend with when you strip line is the coil of loose line that piles up at

Stripping line: At the end of the cast, your left hand should come up to meet your right. Strip line by moving your left hand toward you. Your left hand should not reach in front of your right while you are stripping line.

your feet or on your lap. In moving water, coils of line have an uncanny ability to tangle around your legs and wading staff; in a boat, they seem to reach out and wrap themselves around oarlocks, cleats, and the neck of the family dog. Keep the runaway spaghetti to a minimum by casting accurately and stripping only as much line as you need. You will also learn to cast out extra line by false casting and letting out a bit of loose line each time the loop begins to straighten out on your forward cast.

THE ROLL CAST

The **roll cast** is one of the most useful skills in fly fishing. It allows you to present a fly even if you are fishing a brushy stream or from the banks of a pond where there is no room for a conventional back cast.

It also forms the foundation for the roll cast pickup, a good way to get your back cast going and load your rod, even when you've developed some slack in your line. The roll cast is best executed in two distinct movements, with a definite pause between them. To learn and practice the roll cast, you should have about 25 feet of line in front of you on the water. I do not recommend trying to learn this cast on your front lawn; the resistance of your line on the surface of the water helps you load the rod properly.

Make sure you have good footing and balance, since your weight will shift if you are roll casting correctly and following through completely.

First, raise your rod tip to the twelve o'clock position. Your rod should move in a smooth, continuous motion. You are not trying to lift the line off the

Roll Cast Step 1: Raise rod to twelve o'clock and pause.

Roll Cast Step 2: Push out and reach with your right hand as your weight shifts forward.

water at this point; the line should just slide along as you raise your tip. Pause at twelve o'clock and count to three to make sure that you don't try to make the roll cast in a continuous motion. The elbow of your casting arm should be bent at a 45-degree angle and your weight should be slightly back on your right foot. Now, forcefully push your right hand out (as if you were trying to push open a very heavy swinging door), and then down, until the forefinger of your casting hand points directly in front of you. As you complete the motion, your weight should shift slightly from your right foot to your left. The line will have lifted off the water and will be "rolling" over itself in front of you. Follow through by extending your casting arm completely in front of you, parallel to the water.

There is no back cast at all in the roll cast. There is not even a little wiggle or "hitch"—even if the trees give you room for one. The rod is loaded by the forward push of your casting hand, which slides the line along the water and lifts it into the air.

THE ROLL CAST PICKUP AND THE LEISENRING LIFT

The same motion used in the roll cast can help you get your casting sequence going when you have developed some slack in your system and cannot start an efficient conventional back cast. This problem occurs most commonly when you're fishing a dry fly upstream in fast current; if your line-stripping technique isn't fast enough to keep up with the drift of the fly, slack can build up in your line. Slack also

Roll Cast Step 3: Push out and reach with your right hand as your weight shifts forward.

Roll Cast Pickup Step 1: Begin roll casting motion.

Roll Cast Pickup Step 2: Start your back cast as the line is straightening out in the air in front of you.

Roll Cast Pickup Step 3: Stop your back cast at one o'clock to load the rod and begin basic casting sequence.

might be a byproduct of an intentional technique such as the S-cast (see below) or the **Leisenring lift**. The Leisenring lift sounds like something out of Wagnerian opera, but it is really quite simple. In fact, you have already done it.

James Leisenring was a Pennsylvania angler who discovered in the 1930s that he could imitate the motion of a nymph swimming toward the surface to emerge simply by raising his rod tip to twelve o'clock in a smooth, continuous motion. Sound familiar? If you tie a nymph on the end of your tippet, let it sink, and then watch the end of your leader as you do the first half of the roll cast, you'll see something very interesting. Notice the little V-shaped wake that appears as your fly comes to the surface? I'll bet the nearest trout noticed it too. In fact, the lift is probably the single most effective technique for fishing a nymph in still water—and it's also deadly in moving water.

But the lift leaves you with lots of slack if you lower your rod tip to water level and try to cast conventionally. You can roll cast your line to solve that problem, but even the best roll cast will not give you the most delicate or accurate presentation of your fly. Another option is to use the roll cast to begin a conventional casting sequence. It sounds difficult, but it's really just a matter of putting together two things you already know. The key, again, is to visualize what you're going to do before you try to do it.

As you follow through to conclude your roll cast, your rod tip will be in front of you, parallel to the water at about nine o'clock. Your line will be rolling over itself in front of you. As the line begins to straighten, pull your rod back to the one o'clock position. Wait for the loop of line to straighten out behind you to load the rod, and then bring your rod tip to ten o'clock to begin the normal casting sequence.

THE STEEPLE CAST

The steeple cast is another way to deal with close quarters where there is not enough room for a back cast. It is a technique worth knowing because you

can generally get a bit more distance and accuracy with a steeple cast than you can with a roll cast.

This cast begins like the basic cast, with your tip at water level. Load your rod as usual, but stop your back cast at about eleven o'clock, with the elbow of your rod arm straight. This will send your back cast almost directly overhead.

Wait until the rod begins to load again, and accelerate forward to ten o'clock and complete your cast as usual. The key to the steeple cast is to build as much line speed as possible on the back cast, because gravity will be working against you as your loop travels directly overhead.

MENDING LINE AND THE REACH CAST

The water in a trout stream moves in complex patterns and at different speeds as it encounters obstructions and flows over variations in the bottom topography. In

Steeple Cast: Stop your back cast at eleven o'clock, with your arm extended. Wait for the rod to load (left). Complete the forward cast with your arm fully extended (below).

Mending Line Step 1: Mend line by drawing a semicircle in the air with your rod tip (top).
Mending Line Step 2: Mend as soon as your fly touches the water (bottom).

fact, one of the keys to reading a stretch of trout water is to understand that fish like to conserve energy by holding a position in slower water, close to a faster current that will carry food in their direction. But a problem arises when you are casting across current that is moving either faster or slower than the current where your fly will land. Your fly may be pulled across the surface of the water by these intervening currents acting on your line, making the fly look unnatural to the trout. There are two basic ways to overcome the drag that will inevitably result as a fast tongue of current grabs the belly of your fly line and sweeps it downstream: mending line and the reach cast.

Mending line has sometimes been described as "throwing" the belly of the line upstream—a motion that would be likely to send any trout within casting distance scooting for cover. As with most situations in fly fishing, a bit of subtlety produces better results. Unless you are fishing a very long line, it is best to mend by simply drawing a 180-degree arc with your rod tip as soon as your tip reaches the surface of the water at the end of your casting stroke—upstream to compensate for fast current; downstream for current that's moving slowly. As you complete the arc, your rod tip comes back to the surface of the water. This allows your fly to drift freely until the fly line, which is now upstream from the fly, catches up. The key is to mend early; if the fly starts to drag even a tiny bit, it's over. Mending line skillfully gives you a lot of control over the movement of your line, leader, and fly in the water. Accomplished Atlantic salmon anglers sometimes "stall" a fly in front of a fish's nose by repeated mending, in order to provoke an angry strike.

The **reach cast** accomplishes the same effect as mending line, but it is even more effective because you compensate for the effect of the current while the line is still in the air. There are two versions of this cast: the reach and the **cross-body reach**. In either case, you should make sure you have solid footing because your follow-through will take you off balance, which can lead to an unwanted soaking in a fast-moving river.

The mechanics of the reach cast are the same as the basic cast, until your rod tip reaches the ten o'clock position on your forward cast and your loop is on its way to the target. Then, rather than drift your tip down toward the water in your usual follow-through, sweep the rod either across your body or away from you at a 45-degree angle. At the conclusion of the cast, your elbow should be straight.

THE S-CAST

Every rule has exceptions—including the rule about

Cross-Body Reach Cast Step 1: As your rod tip reaches ten o'clock, sweep the rod across your body.

Cross-Body Reach Cast Step 2: Follow through with your arm extended.

Cross-Body Reach Cast Step 3: Follow through with your arm extended.

The S-Cast: As your rod tip reaches ten o'clock (above) move the tip briskly from side to side (right).

avoiding slack in your line. There are times when you will purposely want to put slack into the system. One of these is when you are in an awkward wading position and the only way you can reach a rising fish with a dry fly is to float it downstream. Another is when you're confronted with a very complex current flow, and it's just not possible to solve it using a simple mend or a reach cast. In both of these instances, you'll want to introduce enough slack into the line so that the fly will have a chance to float some distance before the line starts to drag it. The best way to put a controlled amount of slack in your line is to use the S-cast.

Begin with the basic cast. As you stop your forward cast at the ten o'clock position and begin to follow the fly down toward the water with your rod tip, give the tip a few brisk sideways movements. Your rod tip should only travel a foot or so from side to side.

By the time your tip reaches the water to

complete your follow-through, your line will have formed a series of S-curves on the water. As your fly drifts naturally in the current, it will straighten out these curves before it starts to drag.

DEALING WITH WIND

There must be an unwritten law somewhere that the wind blows in your face at least 80 percent of the time you're fly fishing—and all the time when there's a rising trout 75 feet away. The wind itself is bad enough, but the means many anglers use to compensate for it actually make matters worse. Lots of casters try to power their fly into the wind, and in the process they rush their back cast and then try to gain line speed on their forward cast. The result is usually a tailing loop, a "wind knot" in the leader, and an inefficient, inaccurate cast.

The most important thing to remember when you are confronted with a headwind is to keep the discipline of your casting stroke. If you need more line speed, apply a short haul at the start of your back cast (discussed later), and try to keep your loop compact. Learning to stop your forward cast a bit early—at about eleven o'clock—will help you propel a compact loop into the wind.

It also helps to remember something that any sailor knows: Wind velocity over water can increase as you get farther above the surface. So keep your forward loop as low as possible when you are casting into a strong headwind. When it's really howling, you'll need to keep your loop as close to the surface of the water as possible. It might help to cast sidearm, or even to get down on one knee. On the other hand, it might be time to head back to the lodge for a nice warm bowl of soup.

Crosswinds can also bedevil the fly caster. It's possible to adjust for moderate crosswinds by aiming a couple of feet to one side or another of your intended target or by lowering the plane of your casting stroke to sidearm. But a gusty crosswind coming at you from your rod side can be downright dangerous; a sudden blast can fling your fly right in your face during your back cast or stick it in the back of

Casting into a headwind: Lower your casting plane toward sidearm. Shorten your casting arc, stopping your forward cast at eleven o'clock.

your ear during your forward cast. I learned that the hard way one stormy afternoon on the East Branch of the Delaware about 25 years ago, when a #16 Blue-Winged Olive lodged in my cheek up to the bend in the hook.

HAULING AND SHOOTING LINE

A well-executed double haul really is a thing of beauty. And in the days of fiberglass rods, it was very often a necessity, since most of those rods had soft actions and did not develop line speed very effectively. **Hauling line**—giving it a quick downward tug with your line hand at just the right moment—

Hauling Line: Add a haul on your back cast by tugging on the line with your left hand (top) as the rod loads up and the line begins to accelerate (bottom).

many competent anglers get the distance they need in 99 percent of their fishing situations simply by maintaining good casting technique and letting the inherent power of the rod take care of the distance. Still, there will be times when you need to add that extra 5 or 10 feet to get your fly to its target. Start by learning the single haul.

As with everything else in fly casting, hauling line is a question of timing and finesse, not strength. Lay out 25 feet of line, as you did to begin practicing the basic cast. Position your line hand about midway between belt level and your rod hand. Begin your back cast with the rod tip at water level. As the rod really starts to load and the line starts to accelerate back, give a tug with your line hand. Then stop your back cast at one o'clock and continue with your casting sequence. You have just added considerable speed to your fly line. You can put a haul in your back cast during a sequence of back and forward casts; just give a tug as you start to pull the rod back from the ten o'clock position.

It will probably take awhile to get a feel for the timing of the **single haul**. The important thing is to remember that the haul is a short tug on the line just as the rod is fully loaded and the line is beginning to accelerate. Bear in mind that you can increase line speed a lot with a tug of only a few inches or so. If you haul more than a foot or so of line, you will probably complicate the mechanics of

will accelerate your line and add distance to your cast. **Shooting line**—allowing the momentum of the cast to carry loose line through the guides—is another way to add distance.

It should be noted that with today's graphite rods,

your cast unnecessarily and add cumbersome slack between your rod hand and your line hand.

The **double haul** simply adds a second haul during the forward cast. It's a useful technique to know, but with today's rods a well-timed haul on the back cast will generate all the line speed you're likely to need. In any case, the easiest way to learn the double haul is to start a casting sequence without hauling at all, and gradually try to add a haul on the forward cast just as the rod is fully loaded and about to drive the loop forward. Once again, like many other sporting activities, good timing is the key to a successful haul.

You can shoot line for extra distance at the end of your basic casting sequence, whether or not you've added a line haul. If you have reasonable line speed, you can shoot a surprising amount of loose line by simply continuing your forward cast to nine o'clock as you straighten and lift the elbow of your rod arm. Stop the rod tip abruptly at nine o'clock and, as you do, allow loose line to shoot through the guides. Don't release the line completely with your line hand; you'll maintain line control much more easily if you let the loose line slide through your fingers and, as it does, bring your line hand up to meet your rod hand in the transition we learned earlier. Even when you shoot line, your hands should be in posi-

Shooting Line Step 1: Straighten and lift the elbow of your right arm as you continue your forward cast to the nine o'clock position.

Shooting Line Step 2: Control the line with your left hand as the excess line shoots through the guides.

Fly fishing is one of those endeavors in life that really is an endless journey. There is always more to learn and more to experience, always a next step. Even experienced anglers find it helpful to get input from expert casters, and there are excellent instructional materials available today as well.

Many instructors, like myself, give individual fly-casting lessons. Nearly all fly-fishing lodges and quality fly shops offer classes, and a number of fly fishing schools offer specialized classes in various aspects of casting.

Fly-casting books and videos have proliferated so much in recent years that looking through the fly-fishing shelf at any large bookstore can be a bewildering experience. Following is a selective list of books and videos from among the many worthwhile titles available. Each of these masters offers their own unique perspective on fly casting—after all, there is no "right" way to roll cast, or "wrong" way to double haul.

Ed Jaworowski's book, *The Cast*, is a comprehensive reference on fly casting, illustrated with hundreds of photographs by Lefty Kreh, who has been a major figure in fly-casting instruction for decades. Lefty is not shy with his opinions, and he can back them up with more than forty years of teaching experience. His books and videos, such as *Lessons with Lefty*, convey his authoritative perspective on the art of casting a fly. Joan Wulff's book, *Flycasting Techniques*, and her videos, *Dynamics of Flycasting* and *Flycasting Accuracy*, would be valuable additions to any fly caster's

bookshelf and video collection. Mel Krieger is a gifted teacher whose books and videos have been favorites with many of my own students; his *Essence of Flycasting* is particularly recommended for its straightforward clarity. Doug Swisher's *Basic Flycasting* takes a fresh look at fly casting mechanics. Swisher has been a respected innovator in fly fishing tactics for more than two decades, and this video adds a new dimension to casting technique.

—Tom Akstens

tion to strip line as your fly touches the water.

Accuracy—and Other Lessons

In trout fishing, accuracy is much more important than distance. Most of the trout you catch will be hooked within 30 feet of where you are standing—and most of them will not have moved more than a foot to take the fly.

The first rule of accuracy in fly casting is to always have a target in mind. Even when there are no rising fish in sight and you are simply casting to cover the water, pick out a visual target (it might

be a seam where two currents meet or the beginning of a bubble line) and try to hit it. It sounds a bit strange, but you should learn to hit your target by casting to a spot about 2 feet in the air above your actual target on the water. This way, your flyline will never land on the water with the kind of noise and commotion that will spook every fish in the river.

If you cast to a target every time you put the fly on the water, your accuracy will take care of itself, but you can easily practice accuracy on your lawn as well. Rig the end of your tippet with a half-inch of fluorescent yarn, put your fishing hat upside-down on the ground about 30 feet away, and try to land the bit of yarn in your hat. As your accuracy improves, extend the range to your target to 40 feet, then to 50.

Other exercises can also help you develop casting proficiency. If you're just starting to get the hang of things, try to keep your yarn "fly" from touching the ground for ten backward and forward false casts. When you have managed that, try twenty, then thirty. This will really help you develop your timing.

Practice casting while you are sitting in a chair, or sitting cross-legged on the ground. This is great training for canoe fishing, and it's a sure cure for the "wiggles"—unnecessary twists and turns of the upper body that plague some beginning casters. Practicing on one knee will prepare you for small-stream fishing, where stealth is often essential.

Of course, the best practice of all is to actually be on the stream. If you get enough opportunities to fish and if you maintain sound fundamentals in your casting technique, the day will arrive when it comes so naturally to you that you won't have to think about it at all.

BY DENNIS BITTON

The fish hit with amazing speed and took off almost instantly toward the far horizon. I was in a panga off the shores of Loreto, Mexico, about two-thirds of the way down the eastern shore of Baja California. The fish was a dolphin, otherwise known as dorado, Spanish for "colorful" or "golden."

This fish certainly was colorful—blue-black on its back and shoulders, brilliant silver on its sides, a spot of yellow on its belly, and iridescent specks all over its body. Its head was bigger than its body, and its body was thin from side to side, yet tall from top to bottom. It looked like a torpedo, complete with big V tail. After several minutes of working the line, the dorado was alongside our boat, flashing like a Las Vegas neon sign, from bright blue-silver to fluorescent blue-green to pure gold.

Many of us rarely take expedition fly-fishing trips like this; in fact, we fish relatively close to home most of the time.

Still, most of us dream about catching a species we've never fished before. As beginners, we probably do best with what is nearby and easy. Bluegill from a pond, small brook trout, rainbow trout, or Rocky Mountain cutthroat provide almost guaranteed success. Farm ponds, lakes, and reservoirs offer big rewards for largemouth bass, sometimes smallmouth bass, bluegill, and crappie.

Rarely does a body of water have just one fish species in it. Multiple species coexist in the same waters, and some actually help each other out. For example, often a species will make a nest, then abandon it, only to have it be taken over by another species looking for shelter. Also, some fish eat the eggs that drift downstream from prespawning females that are moving upstream. You can take numerous species on a fly rod. If you live near saltwater and have some knowledge of which fish are in your area each month, you can quickly work out a fishing schedule by planning to be at a specific spot at a specific time. On vacant months, go for freshwater species.

Some fly fishers leave home to fish in climates completely different from their own. When the snow is deep in the Rockies, anglers often fly

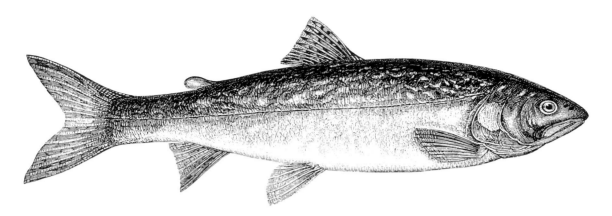

Lake trout, which can weigh 40 pounds or more, inhabit the deep, clear lakes of the northern United States, including the Great Lakes.

south to Mexico or Belize for permit, bonefish, and assorted members of the tuna family. And when the summer sun is baking Texas and Arizona, fly fishers head several states north in pursuit of trout, pike, and largemouth bass, or they go all the way to Alaska or British Columbia for steelhead or Pacific salmon.

Wherever their destination, anglers are challenged by numerous species, all exciting to catch for different reasons. The following is a thumbnail sketch of some of the more popular species of fish.

FRESHWATER SPECIES

There are thirty to forty freshwater fish species that will readily strike artificial fly patterns. **Trout** and **bass**, both freshwater species, are probably the two best-known sportfish for fly fishers.

TROUT

One hundred years ago, most fly-fishing authors lived in East Coast cities and wrote almost exclusively about catching trout (although fly fishers were not located exclusively on the East Coast). Consequently, everybody fished for trout, and local populations of native **brook trout** (*Salvelinus fontinalis*) were almost completely wiped out. By 1900 there were hardly any left. **Brown trout** (*Salmo*

trutta) were shipped in from Europe—as eggs or as fingerlings—to replace dwindling local populations of native brook trout. These European imports proved to be more wary than their predecessors. In the early- to mid-1900s, yet another species was introduced to the streams: **rainbow trout** (*Salmo gairdneri*). This sturdy species took fish hatcheries by surprise, because it could tolerate the hatcheries' conditions much better than any other species of trout. Fish also have a different group mentality in hatchery waters; while rainbow trout work well in a school, brown trout tend to be loners. Also, hatcheries' waters have artificially regulated pH balances and temperatures, which fish respond differently to than they do to their more volatile natural waters. As a result, rainbows are now farmed more than any other fish, and are readily available in a multitude of American waters on both the East and West coasts.

The nice thing about trout is that they are so prevalent. Most fly fishers know where the closest trout waters are. **Cutthroat** (*Salmo clarki*) and **golden trout** (*Salmo aguabonita*) are found mainly in the Rocky Mountains, with the golden usually at much higher elevations than the cutthroat. Brookies are still thinly spread from coast to coast, while brown trout have been in so many waters for so long that people often think they're natives.

When I was a young boy, my great uncle in Mackay, Idaho, told me that the brook trout in the stream flowing through his pasture were "natives, good homegrown locals, worthy of respect." Besides, they were good eating, and since "they didn't have scales," they fried up nicely in bacon grease. A few years later I found out that neither the rainbows or the brookies were native to the area. In fact, there had been no trout species in some of the smaller central Idaho streams for hundreds or even thousands of years. People introduced trout before the turn of the century, but not much before. And technically, brook trout are members of the char family, with skin and no scales. At least my great-uncle got part of it right.

Today most fly anglers in search of trout look for cold water—preferably cooler than 60 degrees Fahrenheit, never warmer than 80, and hopefully not below 30. During the summer, all of the northern states, Alaska, and Canada are good spots for rainbow and brown trout.

Fish in lakes and reservoirs generally are bigger than those in rivers; the smallest trout are in streams that feed rivers. Browns and rainbows grow up to 20 pounds or more in flat water; and any river trout that weighs 5 or 10 pounds is a real prize. Most fly fishers are content with 12-inch trout, regardless of species.

The other really great thing about trout is that they'll eat a very broad variety of flies and insects, for the simple reason that trout are exposed to all kinds of food that gets blown across the water, everything from grasshoppers to dragonflies.

BASS

Largemouth (*Micropterus salmoides*) and **smallmouth bass (*Micropterus dolomieui*)** provide more hours of fishing entertainment than any other species in America. Most of those hours are spent by non-fly-fishing anglers, but many of them now include a "long rod" with their spin or bait casting gear. True to their name, largemouth bass *do* have big mouths, and can be identified by the position of the corner of their mouths, where the lower jaw and upper jaw come together. If that spot ends just in front of the eye, the fish is a smallmouth or "bronzeback." If the mouth/jaw line extends past the eye, it is a largemouth, "bucketmouth," or "hawg." But even without looking at the jaw, you can easily identify a largemouth by its blue back and silver sides, which are distinctly different from the brownish, green, and yellow colors of the smallmouth species.

Big largemouth bass weigh 10 to 12 pounds, with some monsters reaching 20 pounds or more. Big smallmouth weigh a mere 5 pounds, although most fly fishers are happy to land a 3-pounder in a flowing river. Fly fishers seek largemouth mainly in lakes, reservoirs, and ponds, using a boat or some sort of personal floatation device (see the Accessories chapter). Fly patterns depend somewhat on available food sources, but the most popular are the spun-deer-hair poppers, a top-water attractor fly pattern with a huge variation in color, design, and size. Watching a largemouth bust your fly as it comes leaping out of the water is one of the universal images of fly fishing. Smallmouth bass in rivers are pursued much like

"Like an operatic hero, the Pacific salmon dies after mating," observed British biologist J. B. S. Haldane. Salmon are a widely distributed fish. Atlantic salmon run up rivers in the northeastern United States, Iceland, Scandanavia, Scotland, and Russia. Pacific salmon range from California, north to Alaska, and east to Siberia.

trout. A variety of patterns work well, with the same basic divisions as trout fishing: terrestrials, minnow patterns, and sometimes floating or emerging insects (see the Flies & Fly Tying chapter).

SALTWATER GIANTS IN FRESHWATER

SALMON AND STEELHEAD

Salmon and steelhead are anadromous fish who travel from saltwater back to freshwater streams to lay their eggs. While steelheads are technically rainbow trout, they acquire the nickname "steelhead" when they move into salty waters: Their skintone changes to a silvery hue, and because they are in wide-open areas where food is readily available, they fatten up before returning to freshwater for spawning. **Atlantic salmon (*Salmo salar*)** are quite possibly the world's most esteemed fish. For centuries, fly fishers from coastal Europe to Connecticut have sought this fish. Most fly fishers will take Atlantic salmon (on one of the gaudy Atlantic salmon fly patterns) weighing between 10 and 20 pounds. Now and then, record-book fish weighing almost twice that are caught.

These legendary fish live most of their lives in salt-water but return to the streams of their origin to spawn. Adult Atlantic salmon, upon returning from the northern Atlantic Ocean to their ancestral spawning streams, have a blue, green, or black hue to their backs, and their sides are bright silver. Unlike their Pacific counterparts, Atlantic salmon survive the spawning process and return to the sea.

Pacific salmon (*Oncorhynchus* spp) and the family of **steelhead**—a variety of rainbow trout that grows up in saltwater but returns to freshwater to spawn—are creatures of the northwestern United States. They spawn in coastal streams from northern California to the Arctic Circle in Alaska, having spent their growing years in the Pacific. There are six separate species of Pacific salmon: chinook, pink salmon, sockeye, coho, chum salmon, and cherry salmon (which live only in Asia). Unlike Pacific salmon, steelhead survive and return to the ocean after spawning. Both species were once protected from extinction by natural factors such as overproducing eggs, spawning in many streams, and spawning at different times to avoid droughts, floods, ice, fire, and predators. Now some of these species are at risk, but for the moment there are still plenty of fish—and the further north you go the better the situation gets.

Of the subsets of the salmon family, **chinook** (*Onchorhynchus tshawytscha*) are the largest, often reaching up to 50 pounds. Most commonly, they are caught by trolling off a boat in the ocean. Only once did I have a chinook on my hook, albeit very briefly. It was an incredible thrill and felt like hooking into a fast moving submarine. **Coho salmon** (*Oncorhynchus kisutch*) are also exciting fish to catch. They often leap out of the water once they're hooked. They, too, are usually caught by trolling. Water temperature is one of the major factors in drawing these spawners from saltwater to freshwater, so anglers in search of coho carry stream thermome-

ters. Fish who are moving upstream are directed by instinct and scent. They will wait at the mouth of a river for water temperatures to cool down, which is often caused by precipitation. This is why, often, anglers will fish in lousy weather conditions. If fish were to travel in warmer temperatures, they would risk damaging their eggs in potentially exposed reed beds (where they lay their eggs).

Anglers have been nicknaming fish forever, and nicknames get confusing—particularly for subsets of the salmon family. Chinooks are called kings; chums are called dog salmon; cohos are called silvers; pinks are called humpbacked or humpies; and sockeye are called reds.

Salmon and steelhead fishing should not be com-

This small, colorful pollock is released after striking a fly in the rocky waters of Maine.

area more than a century ago. It has two claims to fame: the timing of its freshwater spawning runs and the tastiness of its flesh. Little is known about the shad's life in the sea, but every three to five years, a generation of spawners head for shore. Once at the mouth of a stream, the fish wait for a comfortably cool water temperature and then move upstream. Shad will go into any stream anywhere, so their biological survival is not dependent on a few watersheds. Dedicated fly fishers go after them anytime from December to May, ice or no ice.

The shad (family **Clupeidae**) is not a big fish. A big one weighs 10 to 12 pounds (most fly fishers take them from 2 to 8 pounds). Fly patterns need to be small because the shad has a small mouth. Bright colors seem to work well.

SALTWATER SPECIES

There are at least thirty species of saltwater fish that are eminently catchable with a fly rod. All saltwater fish are predators, living by nature's most basic law: eat or be eaten. For example, the **dorado** of the waters of Baja and the Gulf of Mexico feed on local baitfish, known as sardinata and cabellitos, much smaller than the dorado. The dorado are actually **dolphin** (*Coryphaena hippurus*). Anglers usually pull in dorados that weigh between 5 and 15 pounds. They are well regarded for their beautiful colors, which pulse from excitement during the chase for the fly and when they're caught, as well as for their exotic locale.

The mopst popular fish species in the Bahamas, Florida, and Mexico's Yucatan Peninsula are bonefish, permit, and tarpon. Catching all three in the same day is called a Grand Slam. Praised for their wariness, these three are difficult to catch. Just the right pattern has to be cast to just the right spot to induce a strike.

pared with any other type of fly fishing. The fish can get pretty large (the largest chinook on record, for example, is 126 pounds, though they rarely surpass 60 pounds; the largest steelhead on record is 42 pounds). Each of the many species can be found in a different setting at different times of the year. Terrific places for steelhead and salmon are the feeder streams to the Great Lakes. Brought in decades ago, the fish established themselves in that region and now support a growing number of fly fishers in Minnesota, Wisconsin, Michigan, New York, Indiana, Illinios, and even Ohio.

Because the tradition of chasing salmon is so long in the tooth, fly fishers for steelhead and salmon probably carry more flies than any other anglers. Indeed, the patterns are endless and have evolved over a hundred years. Synthetic materials make new patterns glossier and more tempting than ever.

The effectiveness of steelhead anglers is determined by how many fish per day are raised or hooked, with few actually brought to hand. Good salmon fishing is often quite different. Because they travel upstream in large groups salmon tend to be caught in droves; occasionally, the day's haul is so great that an angler must quit fishing due to sore arms.

SHAD

Like the other fish in this section, the silver-colored **American shad** (*Alosa sapidissima*) is an anadromous fish native to the East Coast of the United States, but it was transplanted to the San Francisco

BONEFISH AND PERMIT

Bonefish (*Albula vulpes*) and permit are saltwater flats feeders who take advantage of high tides to move in over reefs and flats in only 12 to 18 inches of water. There they pick up crustaceans and minnows, though their nervous eyes are always on the watch for bird, human, and ocean predators. Both fish will take fly patterns that imitate small saltwater crabs. Accuracy of casting is critical; good polarized sunglasses help immensely. The challenge is to set the crab pattern down ahead of the moving fish without spooking it. The distance in front of the fish depends, at least in part, on how fast your fly sinks. Once it is close to the bottom, you can twitch the fly a few times to attract your quarry. Often, the fish sees it on its way down and simply rushes forward to suck it in.

A bonefish is sleek and slim, with a pointed head and a definite snout, and the mouth tucked slightly back and under. These are stealthy fish and tough fighters, whose bodies are very round and firm, the sign of a strong fish. Its overall coloration is a brilliant silver, which creates a mirror effect, so anglers look for the fish's shadow instead of the fish itself. Size is not the bonefish's drawing card—most weigh less than 10 pounds—but the challenge of taking a bonefish with a fly makes it arguably one of the most popular saltwater species. It is a challenging fish to catch because it is known for being a finicky eater that makes a fast and long run as soon as it is hooked. In fact, bonefish have been known to wear out reels. Most anglers who have taken bonefish with a fly rod proclaim it to be the ultimate high.

By contrast, **permit** (a family with multiple genera) are shaped like a big silver saucer, and they have a dark-colored back. Their eyes are well forward, and

Little Digger, a recent watercolor by Tim Borski, pictures mudding bonefish on the flats off Isla Morada in the Florida Keys.

Fly-fishing pioneer Lee Wulff is perhaps best known for his statement that "fish are too valuable to only catch once."

Bluefish. This ferocious "wolf of the sea" feeds in deadly packs, often close to the surface, killing more food than it can possible consume.

they have a vertical tilt to their forehead. A permit's long, dark-gray or blue-black dorsal and anal fins sweep back over its entire length, making the species easily identifiable. Once on, permit fight well. A 10-pound permit provides a real battle. Super-sized fish weigh between 20 and 40 pounds.

TARPON

Tarpon (*Megalops atlantica*), found in the waters off Florida, will readily hit large streamer patterns if the fly fisher can get within casting distance. Of course, there is the problem of trying to land one of these bruisers. Tarpon have very large and bony mouths, and their ancient-looking scales are huge. Someday, a fly fisher will catch a 200-pound tarpon, but today's angler should look for fish weighing closer to 100 pounds. In fact, many experienced tarpon fly fishers prefer fishing for 20- to 40-pound juveniles, also known as "baby tarpon."

REDFISH

The **redfish (*Sciaenops ocellata*)**, also known as the red drum, is another popular fly-fishing target along the Gulf of Mexico shoreline and the Florida peninsula. Redfish feed in murky flats, providing opportunities for those fly fishers who aren't going out in

boats but instead casting from the ocean's edge. Redfish feed head-down, tail-up. Fortunately for the fly fisher, the tail has an "eye," a dark, round spot on a silver-bronze background that makes spotting it easier. Redfish have elongated bodies with predominantly square tails. Their snouts are slightly rounded, and their upper jaw protrudes a little beyond the lower one. Their backs and sides are bronze or copper over silver or gray. In Texas, Louisiana, and even in northern Mexico, the popularity of redfish has created entire subcultures based around fishing camps devoted to its pursuit. Fly patterns like the Clouser Minnow work well in the murky waters, but veteran fly fishers say whatever you throw, make sure it has some Flashabou or Crystal Flash (reflective material) on it, preferably in two bright colors.

NORTHERN SALTWATER FISH

Not all great saltwater fish are found in tropical waters. Perhaps the earliest and most legendary saltwater fly fishing was for **striped bass (*Morone saxatilis*)** and **bluefish (*Pomatomus saltatrix*)** on the northeast coast of the United States. These fish, approached by boat or from beaches, have provided great fly fishing for generations. Striped bass are found everywhere from northern New England to the

Atlantic coast of Florida as well as the California Coast. These fish enthusiastically strike flies and range in size up to 30 pounds. Thanks to conservation efforts, striped bass are once again present in generous numbers, providing sport for many fly anglers.

EXOTIC-LOOKING SPECIES

The term "billfish" actually refers to three types of fish: marlin, swordfish, and sailfish. It is not a scientific term, but is commonly used by anglers. Marlin are mammoth fish and often reach upwards of 1,000 pounds. The swordfish is the least often of those caught by fly fishers, but the fight is a challenge that's tough to rival. It's now common practice to lure these giants (up to 1,500 pounds) to the surface using hookless "teaser" baits, bring them near the boat rapidly, and let the fly fisher cast a big saltwater pattern in front of the fish's bill. Fly-fishing challenges do not get bigger than this—and traveling to Costa Rica, Venezuela, or Australia to fish for swordfish is fabulous. Sailfish are also exciting fish and are pretty as well: Long dorsal fins leap out of the water when they're hooked, creating beautiful splashing spectacles. However, in general, sailfish do not grow as large as the marlin and swordfish do.

Sharks are not often thought of as candidates for a fly fisher, but two species in particular provide great sport: the **lemon shark** (*Negaprian revirostris*) and the **blacktip shark** (*Carcharhinus limbatus*). Both feed in saltwater flats and will eagerly take a well-presented fly. Neither species gets very big their first five years—2 to 3 feet would be considered a good size—and both have provided tremendous sport for fly fishers having an otherwise boring day. Despite being sharks, these fish are generally not dangerous to fly fishers wading the flats.

IS THAT ALL THERE IS?

Almost any fish can be caught on a fly rod. Because catching fish with fly-fishing methods is so much fun, many unusual species are now becoming popular. One of strongest fighting fish, found virtually everywhere in the United States, eagerly feeds on insects. That fish, at home in shallow water in many large lakes, is the common **carp** (*Cyprinus carpio*). Before you turn up your nose, consider how much fun it would be to hook a 25-pound fish on your fly rod.

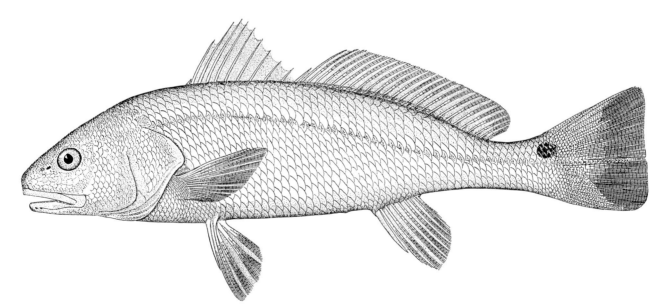

Redfish or red drum. Called "the copper warrior of the tides," this superb game fish is an aggressive feeder and readily takes a fly.

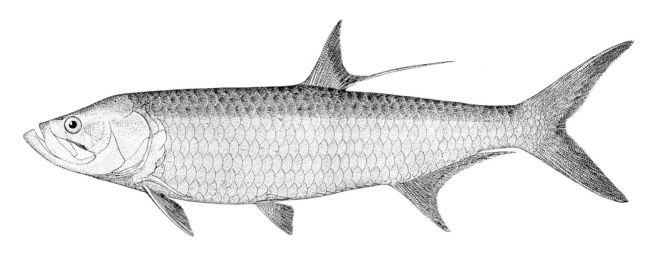

The fearsome tarpon busts rods, rips reel, and stops hearts.

Northern pike (*Esox lucius*) can be found in large lakes in the northern United States and have a reputation for eating just about anything. **Muskie (*Esox masquinongy*)** are found in the Great Lakes and are considerably larger than their cohabitors, the Northern pike. The **black crappie (*Pomoxis nigromaculatus*)**, a member of the sunfish family, tends to be found in quieter waters of the eastern United States and Canada, and is easy to catch since their mouths are so big and they go for just about any lure you can think to use. The **white crappie (*Pomoxis annularis*)**, also a member of the sunfish family, is one of the more popular freshwater panfish; it likes to hang around in rivers and lakes of the eastern United States. **White bass (*Morone chrysops*)**, which actually resemble a bluegill more than a bass, are very easy to catch and are found in streams and rivers. This is a small and abundant species, usually weighing no more than 2 pounds.

Interest in species diversification is powering much of the current growth in fly fishing. Taking innumerable species of saltwater fish on a fly rod has captured the imagination of thousands. But the more traditional warmwater fisherman who fishes for bass, bluegill, crappie, and catfish has also found the concept of matching a fly rod's delicacy or strength to that of the quarry a fabulous challenge.

Any fish species anywhere is a potential challenge for a fly rod. Not all fish can be caught on a fly rod, but the numbers that are moving from the "impossible" list to the "it has been done" list increase every year. Most people fish with a fly rod to have fun. The more species they pursue, the more chances they have to have fun. Thank mother nature for making it so simple.

WARMWATER

BY DENNIS GALYARDT

At the tender age of twelve, I read a book called *America's Favorite Fishing*, by F. Philip Rice. That book changed my way of fishing—and my life—forever. Rice's advice was unambiguous: "If you want to learn to be an expert panfisherman, then you simply must learn to use the fly rod."

I had never seen a fly fisher in eastern Nebraska, but I craved fishing action. It didn't matter what kind. I had heard about coldwater species like trout, salmon, steelhead char, and grayling, but certainly had never caught one. Instead, warmwater species were the kind I found in the sandpits, farm ponds, and small reservoirs that studded the cornfields just outside of my town: bluegill, crappies, bass, and catfish. When I learned that fly fishermen catch the most panfish, I consulted a Herter's catalog and started saving my money. By spring, my brand-new fast-taper, power-butt fiberglass rod, click reel, and level line were ready for baptism.

Trial and error is the best way to describe my fly-fishing development. In my first attempts, I almost hung myself with the fly line. I did catch some fish right away, but I sorely needed assistance. My otherwise helpful father could offer little advice, being a relocated Kansas catfish angler who only rarely sought other species. The library was my only hope. On Saturdays I rode the bus downtown and checked out books on fly fishing. I read, practiced, and experimented for years. My greatest help came from a tattered edition of Ray Bergman's *Just Fishing*, which I bought for a dollar at a used-book sale. I read the old literature and authors like Brooks, Bergman, Knight, Dalrymple, and Lucas. They taught me how to roll cast, tie blood knots, reel with my right hand, and fight fish. I put aside my spinning rods and tied my own flies and bugs.

Finally, after about fifteen years, I considered myself proficient at fly fishing. I even converted my father to the fly rod. Today, after forty years of fly fishing, my enthusiasm, excitement, and love of the sport remains unabated, and it all started with warmwater fly fishing.

If you attend a fly-fishing conclave and talk to

the old-timers, you'll probably hear a lot of stories like mine. Why does poking a fly rod around tiny warmwater ponds, murky lakes, and backwoods streams endear itself to so many? Why are the ranks of warmwater fly fishers increasing at a rate never before seen? To understand these phenomena, you need to understand how American fly fishing developed over the years.

A WORTHY HISTORY

Before colonists arrived in North America, fly fishing had been refined in Europe to a pure form, but almost exclusively for trout, particularly in Great Britain. In America, native brook trout were so abundant that many other species were initially overlooked. But it was not long—around the late 1700s—before fly anglers began also fishing for bass, using flies originally designed for trout. While the written history is meager, bass and other warmwater species became increasingly popular with fly fishers over the

Panfish provide good sport on a fly rod. These frisky fish will take bass bugs, wet flies, dry flies, and streamers.

next sixty years. As different parts of the country were settled, with new challenges and new waters, fly fishing for a variety of nontrout species was encouraged.

If warmwater fly fishing has a patron saint, it is Dr. James Henshall, who promoted bass as a worthy game fish in his classic book, *Book of the Black Bass* (1881). Henshall's ultimate compliment towards bass, "inch for inch and pound for pound the bass is the gamiest fish that swims," spoke true about the fighting spirit of the species. It wasn't until the early 1930s, however, that angler-writers like Ray Bergman, John Alden Knight, and Robert Page Lincoln really started to "sell" warmwater fly fishing. Bamboo fly rods, flies, bugs, lures, and even leaders for bass appeared in the magazines and catalogs. Specialized bass fly tackle companies emerged. Tackle houses like Weber promoted fly fishing for all species. E. H. Peckinpaugh developed and marketed the first bass bugs. Big name outfits like Heddon, South Bend, and Pflueger got into warmwater fly fishing and promoted lures, bugs, flies, rods, and tackle. Fly fishing for bass became so popular that most good bass anglers of the day carried two fishing outfits: a bait casting rig for plugs and a fly rod for bass bugs. When one did not work, the other did.

Warmwater fly fishing flourished through the depression and into the 1940s. All this time, however, bass received most of the recognition. Bluegill, crappies, rock bass, white bass, and pike were seldom mentioned. They were considered "kids' fish" by most advanced fly fishers. The feeling was that you'd only fish for bass if you couldn't fish for trout. Today that attitude has changed—warmwater species have become some of the most popular targets—but warmwater fly fishing almost died during the 1960s. In those years, most anglers found fly fishing too complicated, and stuck to their spin casters. Spin casters ruled the waters, but as the human population grew, the fish population shrank. Pollution made many waters unfishable, and large bag limits decimated the number of fish in others. But fly anglers, who turned to other waters and more conservation-oriented fishing methods, maintained their interest in warmwater species.

KIND TO BEGINNERS

One reason that warmwater fly fishing has seen such continued growth is that it provides an elementary way to get into the sport. By the time I married, in 1971, I could consistently catch panfish and bass on flies at any of the local ponds. My new wife, Amy, had only fished for perch with worms and bobbers. Teaching her to fly fish seemed a natural step; in my mind, I knew the perfect pond, the best season, and the correct tackle.

I chose the third weekend in May and a quiet cove on a local farm pond. All Amy needed was a 7½-foot, 5-weight fiberglass rod and a handful of flies and poppers. Bluegill were spawning. After casting practice on our lawn, we relocated to the pond. While her first casts were rumpled tangles, eventually her flies landed near the shoreline cover and the spawning bluegill obliged. Strikes were missed, line landed with splashes, but still the bluegill assaulted her flies to defend their nests, and she started catching fish. While big bluegill can become very selective later in the season, the average sunny turns into a kamikaze during spawning. With their aggressive abandon and their strong fighting ability, bluegill give a beginner lots of exciting action. Because of this early warmwater experience, my wife Amy has bluegill to thank for getting her excited about fly fishing. If you are a beginner and have not tried bluegill on a fly rod, it is a terrific way to start.

WARMWATER MOBILITY

Another phenomenon has contributed to the popu-larity of warmwater fly fishing: the **belly boat**. In its earliest form, this "personal watercraft" was actually a truck inner tube with a board tied on the bottom for a seat. The angler would put his legs through the tube, sit on the board, and use swim fins to paddle around the local pond or lake. It was cool and comfortable on a hot summer's day, inexpensive, very portable, and deadly for sneaking up on warmwater fish. The whole rig weighed less than 25 pounds and was small enough to fit into the back of a station wagon. The mobility provided by belly boats tremendously increased fly-fishing opportunities for warmwater anglers. And fish did not seem to be frightened by these small craft, so anglers could go into small coves and bays that would not be fishable from a larger boat or from shore.

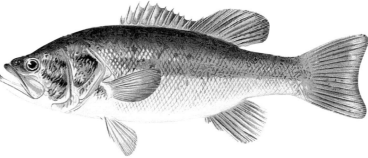

Largemouth bass will eat absolutely anything that swims, crawls, flies, wiggles, or walks.

Since their commercial introduction more than twenty years ago, these small watercraft have become extremely popular, and have undergone many improvements. Today belly boats, or **float tubes** as they are now called, feature a U-shape design for easier entry and exit. They come with a tough nylon covering for the tube (or specially-designed floatation bladders), zippered pockets for flies and other accessories, and sometimes a space for a small cooler.

There are also one-person mini-pontoons, or **kick boats**, in which the angler sits 4 to 10 inches above the water on a seat that straddles two 60- to 75-inch-long pontoons. Kick boats are usually paddled with

A belly boat is used to float out into the middle of a lake on a mid-summer day. This personal watercraft is deadly for sneaking up on warmwater species.

swim fins, but some manufacturers have devised rowing frames.

Even elaborate personal fishing craft seldom weigh more than 50 pounds and can be easily transported in most station wagons or sport utility vehicles. Fishing from a float tube or kick boat gives you a special intimacy with a lake or river, much like wading does for the stream angler. If you want access to waters in which warmwater fish can be caught on a fly rod, a personal watercraft is an essential investment.

CLOSE TO HOME

For the frazzled city dweller, warmwater fly fishing can provide relaxation for an evening or even an hour. Most cities have fishable waters within a thirty-minute drive, if not within the city limits. Those ponds, drainage canals or creeks may not be world-class fisheries, but they often sustain four or five warmwater species. Casting poppers, streamers, microjigs, or wet flies in these waters is simply a wonderful way to decompress. And every once in a while the 7-inch bluegill snapping at your popper turns out to be a 17-inch bass. My shore-bound spinning friends often have been amazed at my evening catches of fifty-plus panfish and bass, as I paddled serenely along on quiet Midwestern summer evenings, watching the sun slowly set—less than fifteen minutes from my suburban home. As Zane Grey said in the 1930s, "Fishing is a state of mind during which you can't have a bad time."

BIG GAME

Not all warmwater fishing is tranquil, however. Some denizens of freshwater lakes are as voracious as any

The voracious strike of a great northern pike will shatter the calmest morning.

saltwater fish. Members of the **pike** clan (*Esox*) are barracuda-like and wonderful fly-rod targets. Not anything like hand-fed, soft-fleshed hatchery pets, these fish are the top carnivores in their home waters and are more than willing to attack any creature that comes their way. They lie in wait for fish, frogs, mice, birds, and one another. Armed with an arsenal of backward-pointing teeth, pickerel, pike, and muskellunge are awesome predators that often push the 4-foot mark. Pike and **muskie** offer the ultimate thrill for the warmwater fly fisher.

Every spring I travel to the north central states for a week of fly-rod float-tubing for pike. If the timing is right and surface temperatures are near 60 degrees, exciting water action is virtually guaranteed. When a member of the pike clan strikes, it aims to kill. The violence of a pike surface attack back in the weeds looks and sounds like a toilet flushing. Often pike leave a clearly visible V-wake as they drive in to slash your fly. Inexperienced anglers sometimes get the jitters and miss the strike by setting the hook too soon. Big poppers, Dahlberg divers, 2/0 deer-hair "rats," and 8-inch slinky streamers trigger the aggression of these bad boys.

Wire shock leaders are imperative to prevent pike bite-offs and can be easily made using Larry Dahlberg's "twist melt" method, whereby nylon-coated wire is heated by a candle flame and twisted around itself to form a loop. The melted plastic coating bonds to itself and even a really huge pike in the weeds cannot undo it.

In their focus on killing the big fly, **northern pike** seem not to be inhibited by the very visible 20-pound test wire. Landing one of these alligator-like fish takes some skill. Carrying a net in a float-tube is a bit awkward, so I land my pike by hand. After fighting it to a standstill, I bring the beast alongside the tube and grip it behind the gills across the back. Because northerns often inhale the fly deeply, an extra-long hemostat is essential to remove a hook from their mouths, which are razor-sharp toothy traps.

FLIES

Flies for bass and panfish have had a colorful history paralleling the evolution of warmwater fly fishing in America. Early enticers were primarily aimed at bass and resembled giant trout patterns. Often tied on #2 through #10 hooks, antique bass flies seldom looked like living organisms and were often wrapped with "double gut snells" to avoid breaking off on the strike of a ferocious bass. In the 1920s, bamboo fly rods became more reasonably priced and enticed many fisherman to try this form of angling. Fishing for bass and other warmwater species was also considered more sportsmanlike than in the previous century, so tackle companies started producing fly-rod lures for bass and panfish. Spinners and tiny plugs—miniature

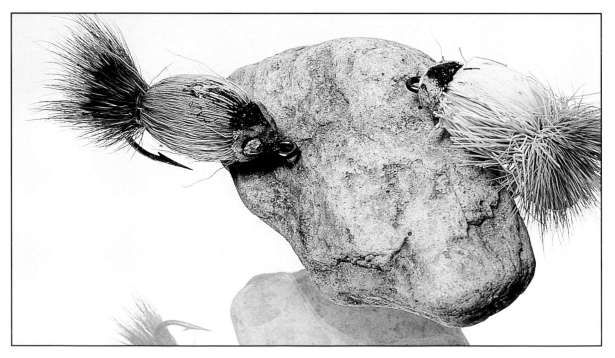

A bass bug imitates the fish's omnivorous diet like these primitive deer-hair mice.

versions of casting baits—as well as bass bugs and streamer flies became the state of the art for taking bass, panfish, and assorted freshwater dwellers. These lures often were heavy and wind-resistant, making them difficult to cast on the bamboo or steel rods of the day. Weight-forward lines, used almost universally by modern bass fly rodders, were uncommon, which made casting even more difficult.

BASS PATTERNS

Because **bass** eat absolutely anything that swims, flies, crawls, wiggles, or walks, bass flies imitate countless aquatic and terrestrial organisms. These include flies that take on the appearance of insects, amphibians, rodents, worms, crustaceans, fish, and even birds. With all of these creatures to mimic, materials and colors incorporated into modern bass flies are as varied as cereal boxes in the grocery aisle.

Currently, many warmwater fly anglers prefer **deer-hair bass bugs**. These intricate creations resemble mice, frogs, dragonflies, and even turtles. Hard-bodied bass bugs with painted cork or balsa wood heads and vivid tail feathers still catch countless fish each season. Underwater creations made of rabbit fur strips, long slinky feathers, or flexible hairs also tempt warmwater fishes into striking.

If you are just starting to fish bass with a fly rod, the array of flies can be bewildering. A simple selection of bass flies will catch largemouth, smallmouth, and Kentucky bass all over their range. As any experienced bass fly fisher knows—and the novice will soon learn—there are at least three styles of bass flies: top-water, floating-diving, and subsurface attractors.

Since fly fishing for bass is most efficient in water no deeper than 6 feet, it is not productive for the beginner to try to probe to greater depths. Therefore, sinking flies, while a very important aspect of the bassman's arsenal, do not have to be elaborate or varied in design. My favorite is a wormlike pattern tied with a rabbit fur body and a 4- to 6-inch strip tail. It is weighted with lead eyes and sinks instantly but slowly. I fish this fly (tied with a weed guard) around vertical structure such as trees, dock pilings, and rock bluffs. Bass often take this writhing imitation as it descends. Watching the line for movement is essential in hooking fish. Dark colors seem to work best under most water conditions, with basic black topping the list. Other underwater patterns that imitate crayfish, leeches, and nymphs are all productive.

One subsurface fly that is commonly overlooked is a microjig that weighs about $\frac{1}{80}$ of an ounce. These little jigs are difficult to find ready-made in catalogs or fly shops but are easy to tie. I often fish these small jigs suspended under a strike indicator or tiny bobber. It is amazing the number, size, and variety of fish that these diminutive lures attract. While almost any color will catch fish, black, brown, chartreuse, and yellow are excellent producers.

At mid-depths, from just under the surface down

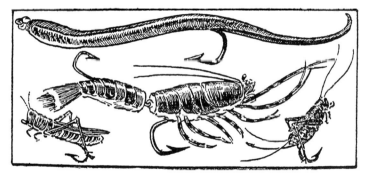

A sampling of flies.

to about 3 feet, floating-diving flies excel. My favorite is a bug designed by Larry Dahlberg in the late 1970s. The Dahlberg Diver has a deer-hair head and trailing feather tails and legs. While this style of bug has been modified over the years, the basic design —a collared head that forces the fly underwater when it is retrieved (hand-over-hand stripping in of line) —has caught more bass for me than anything else I've thrown in the pond. Almost all of my patterns contain dark and light materials for contrast. I often tie this fly with rubber legs and in colors that are more attention-getting than imitative of any food organism. I cast these floating-diving bugs near surface

This deer-hair frog pattern will draw strikes from bass or pike when presented realistically.

or plastic and are painted. Deer hair is sculpted and trimmed to form a body. Bugs are often decorated with bulging eyes, wiggling legs, and floppy tails. When twitched, popped, or simply allowed to remain still on the surface, bass bugs take countless fish every season. Deer-hair mice, frogs, grasshoppers, and dragonflies all catch fish and are wonderful to animate through the water—but many catch as many fishers as fish.

All good bass flies should have some sort of weed or brush guard and come in an assortment of sizes from #8 through #10. Flies must match the weight of the fly line and rod. Lighter-weight lines work best for smaller bugs and flies. A half-dozen flies that sink, swim, and float will suffice at first. But part of the fun of fly fishing is matching fish foods and experimenting with new materials and patterns. You should probably buy a fly box bigger than you think you will need; if you are like most of us, it will soon be full.

cover, allow a moment for the fly to rest, plunk it a time or two, then give the line a long, hard pull. This causes the fly to dive 6 to 18 inches underwater, leaving a long trail of bubbles. Motion like this is irresistible to bass and other gamefish—they seem to line up to attack this "super fly." Other mid-depth flies include unweighted or lightly weighted wooly buggers, muddler minnows, marabou streamers, and sculpin patterns. These flies imitate leeches, salamanders, and baitfish that wind up in the stomachs of big bass.

On the surface, the fly-rodding bass fisher needs but a few good bugs to attract fish that are looking up. There are two basic types of bass bugs, hard-bodied and deer-hair. The hard ones are made of cork, balsa,

PANFISH FLIES

Flies for panfish can be as simple as a wooly bugger or as complicated as a delicate damselfly imitation. But for all-season productivity, the ultimate weapon for just about anything that a fly rodder can catch in warmwater is a $1/80$ of an ounce microjig tied with black rabbit fur, crystal flash, and white rubber legs, fished under a Styrofoam indicator. It is the best thing I've ever used for panfish. Bluegill, smallmouth bass, crappies, largemouth bass, green sunfish, rock bass, channel catfish, yellow perch, white bass, drum, carp, bullheads, and even gar have all fallen for the black microjig. I make them in other colors—chartreuse, white, yellow, and brown—but the black always outfishes the rest.

The tiny strike indicator helps to suspend the $\frac{1}{80}$-ounce jig over weeds, sticks, stumps, and rocks where panfish hide from their nastier neighbors. Many of these, such as the crappie, are not aggressive; a gentle jigging motion under the indicator tempts timid biters. Usually the biggest panfish are the most cautious and move slowly to inhale the tiny fly. If the indicator moves, set the hook with your line hand rather than the rod tip. After the fish is hooked, raise the rod tip to absorb the shock of the first run and to fight the fish. Most panfish give a good account of themselves on the fly rod, and bluegill in particular are great fighters. A 9-inch gill can outfight any other fish its size.

But is this really fly fishing? Tom Nixon, an innovative fly fisher who wrote *Fly Fishing and Fly Tying for Bass and Panfish* (1968), and Jack Ellis, author of *Bassin' With a Fly Rod* (1995), would probably approve. They both advocate unusual fly-rod baits for warmwater species. Their fly patterns, such as the Calcasieu Pig Boat, Sowela, and Grinnel Fly, and even fly-rod spinner baits and plastic worms are unorthodox but productive. Some trout anglers complain that split shot, strike indicators, and sinking lines do not really belong in the fly fisher's tackle bag. But warmwater fly tiers are not traditionalists. We like to go past those limits—and we have a tendency to take ideas from our hardware-slinging brethren, those fisherman who cast spoons, spinners, plugs, and other forms of "hardwood" as opposed to large baitcasting plugs, spoons, and spinners.

Warmwater fishing at its best in the lily-padded St. John's River, Florida.

Peacock bass are a boutique fish pursued by well-heeled anglers in the lakes of Venezuela and now in southern Florida.

EQUIPMENT

While float-tubing my favorite waters, I often carry two fly-rod outfits on board. One is a rig for bass and the other is a lighter setup for the bluegill, crappies, and sunfish that inhabit the same waters.

My bass equipment includes a float-tube, chest-high neoprene waders, a pair of flippers (the longest I can buy), a 9-foot, 8-weight graphite fly rod with a weight-forward floating line to match, and a single-action reel. Leaders are tapered to about 10-pound test. Sometimes in ultraclear water a 9-foot 4X leader is in order, but many bass come from weedy shallows, so my leaders are usually short and strong. My bass fly boxes carry weedless deer-hair bugs, a mouse, a frog, and some hard-head cork or plastic bugs that produce a noisy pop. Also useful is an assortment of subsurface slinky critters made of black or purple fur on hide strips. These bunny leeches should have lead eyes

and weed guards to help them probe the depths. In a flotation vest (required equipment for float-tubers in many states and suggested for all others), I carry extra tippet material, fly floatant, and a hemostat to extract the fly from a deeply hooked fish.

CONSERVATION

Throughout North America, there are literally tens of thousands of small and medium-sized lakes that have the natural habitat to support abundant wild populations of warmwater fish. These lakes—in both rural and urban areas—could offer great fishing for kids, adults, and families, if given a chance. The greatest limitation on top-quality warmwater fishing is overharvest. Just a few proficient anglers can wipe out a quality bass or panfish population in just one season by consistently killing their legal limit. Contrary to the common notion that panfish populations cannot be harmed by over-fishing, studies show that even bluegill suffer from too many twenty-five or fifty-fish bag limits. While not as publicized as trout conservation, conservation and preservation of bass, all panfish, and even "rough fish" is also important.

My own experience has proven to me that warmwater conservation of fish populations can really work. Late one summer, I slipped my float-tube into the water at the far end of a 300-acre lake just twenty minutes from my suburban home. The sun was just beginning to rise. With a surface temperature in the high 80s, I anticipated slow action for this mid-August morning. The lake was clear to a depth of about 18 inches, and water level was near normal. I decided to fish a long, rocky point that practically cut the small reservoir in half. This manmade jetty serves as a crossover point for joggers and bicyclists as they circle the multipurpose recreation site. I eased within 40 feet of the rubble shore that I planned to fish.

A few casts later, a bass, 14 inches, jumped out of the water to pounce on my Dahlberg Diver. Excited, I looked downstream, and spotted my friend, Tip, and was glad to see a fellow fly fisher from the local club. He followed me along the same shoreline, breaking a general rule of "never fish behind another fly fisher." As the morning progressed, the bass kept up their attack, and we caught a number of them, including five between 15 and 19 inches.

That could never have happened two years earlier. When the lake had first opened, within a short drive of half a million people, it was fished constantly. Soon 11-inch bass were the biggest fish. With encouragement from the local fishing clubs, the Fish and Game Commission decided to experiment with size and kill

Yellow-barred perch

limits on several popular species. First, a 15-inch size limit went into effect. Within a season, the average bass size increased to 13 or 14 inches; most bass over that size wound up on stringers. Bluegill size limits were raised to 8 inches, and crappies to 10. Anglers asked for still more restrictions, and an even more protective rule was instituted. All bass less than 21 inches had to be released and the limit was just one bass per day.

When Henshall championed black bass back in the late 1800s, they were considered to be a commoners' fish or even a rough fish. Today bass are considered to be "America's premier gamefish" and our most sought-after species. Fly fishers have come to realize that warmwater gamesters like pike, panfish, smallmouth, and carp deserve their attention, even devotion. Warmwater fly fishing is again attracting thousands of anglers. Like many anglers' great-grandfathers knew almost a century ago, the fish that inhabit the warmwaters from Canada to Mexico provide unending thrills. If the quality of coldwater fisheries deteriorates any further than it already has, warmwater species will certainly become the sport fish of the future.

SALTWATER

BY TOM JINDRA

The target was about 40 yards ahead of us. A nice redfish from what I could see, and I could see a great deal. He was rooting around in mere inches of water, having found a buffet of crabs and other forage on the edge of a shallow weed bed. His dorsal fin was exposed to the air, tapering back to the submerged "wrist" that marks the beginning of the tail. And the tip of his tail fin was also exposed, giving me the benchmark I needed to estimate a fish of 5, maybe 6, pounds. He cruised back and forth, accelerating occasionally to pick up a morsel before it could escape—but he never moved far. He seemed content to stay put as long as the food held out and we did nothing to spook him. So I urged my buddy, Steve Whipple, to bring the boat closer for a clean shot.

A good fish drives everything from your mind. Only moments before, I had been focused on the heat and humidity that are so much a part of summer on the Louisiana coast. I had also been watching the thunderheads building to the west out over the Gulf of Mexico. One of those storm cells, if it crossed our path, would be enough to run us off the water. But for now, the weather could wait. I had a fish in my sights.

Steve leaned into the pushpole, driving the 16-foot boat toward our target, and I stood on the bow with my 7-weight rod. But about 70 feet out, the mudflat rose up and buried the keel. We had reached our limit and could go no further. So I flipped my fly line into the air, sending the small yellow popper on its way. Then I waited to see what might go wrong, knowing that the possibilities were endless. If my fly fell off to the left, it would tangle in the weeds. If it were off to the right, the fish might never see it. It could simply go too far, spooking the redfish by putting the line across its back. Or I could easily step on the line, meaning my cast would not go far enough.

But today everything fell just right, and my 2-inch bug settled silently where I aimed. I dropped my rod tip to the water to avoid any slack in the line and began a gentle chugging retrieve. The redfish answered by turning toward the commotion, slowly at first. Then, closing the gap with a quick burst, he smashed the bug. I struck back when I felt the weight on my line. Then I jabbed again to plant the barbless hook firmly, triggering an explosion of mud and water as the red began his instinctive run for deeper water.

Clearing my excess line from the deck so I could fight the battle from my reel, I held on through the dogged runs so typical of a redfish. Moments later, I removed the hook and gently returned my coppery prize to the marsh, repeating to myself the words of the immortal Lee Wulff: "A good game fish is too valuable to be caught only once."

No one who has ever pursued a redfish on the flats will doubt that this species meets Wulff's standards for a good game fish. The redfish has, in fact, become a favorite target of saltwater fly fishers throughout the southeastern United States. It is a favorite because it offers everything a fly rodder could want: size, numbers, a widespread distribution, and a fondness for shallow water. And shallow water makes this species highly susceptible to sight-casting with flies.

The redfish is only one of the many saltwater fish available to fly rodders. If you filled a room with saltwater enthusiasts just from around the United States, you would be overwhelmed by the host of species they could name: redfish, bonefish, tarpon, striped bass, mackerel, tuna, sharks, and billfish. And that's a very short inventory of prospective targets. We could add bluefish, cobia, flounder, lingcod, salmon, spotted sea trout, and many others without compiling a complete list. Each fish has its own geography and behavior, and each demands a distinct set of angling techniques. In listing saltwater fly-fishing prey, we find ourselves describing a sport so diverse that it hardly seems fair to consider it a single endeavor. It is enough, however, to divide it into three primary forms based on three differing regional traditions: South Florida, the Northeast, and offshore.

We sometimes have a tendency to think that

Guide Seth Taylor fishes for stripers and the occasional bluefish from the cold rocky Maine coast. The population of striped bass in the Atlantic has boomed in recent years after having been on a decline due to overfishing and pollution.

these three forms define the geographic boundaries of saltwater fly fishing; nothing could be further from the truth. Rather, these three schools represent the primary approaches to utilizing fly tackle in an ocean environment, and the resulting techniques have been used effectively throughout the world. The lessons learned on the South Florida flats, for example, have long been proven throughout the Gulf of Mexico, the Caribbean, and in the South Pacific. And techniques that had their origins from New England south to the Chesapeake Bay have for many years found a home on the West Coast and anywhere else that saltwater game fish are found. Meanwhile, offshore fly fishing springs from both the South Florida and Northeastern traditions. Yet offshore fly fishing is distinct because it targets species that were never before thought possible on fly tackle. Regardless of the geography, these special offshore tactics are effective wherever fly casters encounter pelagic species (those who live in the open sea).

THE FLORIDA TRADITION

Those of us who fly fish on the coast tend to think of South Florida as our mecca. We even go so far as to describe it as the birthplace of saltwater fly fishing, but that is not entirely fair. History suggests that the British had taken their flies down to the sea in the early 1800s. Records also demonstrate that fly fishers were exploring the coast from New England to the Chesapeake Bay by the 1830s. The legacy of these early American anglers was a solid corps of fly fishers who were consistently taking stripers and blues in the Northeast by the 1950s and 1960s, while Florida fly casters were still perfecting their techniques on bonefish and tarpon. During those two decades, traditions were also being established on the West Coast, particularly on the Baja California peninsula in Mexico. Yet it was Florida that really latched on to our imagination for one very important reason: It offered an abundance of game fish

that were susceptible to sightcasting in the shallow waters known as flats.

The redfish, or red drum, has proven a boon to the angling communities of the south and Gulf coasts.

The flats are extraordinary. Far from being the barren expanse perceived by some, these shallow edges of the sea are among the most fertile real estate in the world, bringing together a rich blend of land, water, sun, and air—all the basic ingredients for sustaining plants that form the bottom rung of any food chain. Other organisms follow: Small animals such as worms, shellfish, and various baitfish feed off the detritus that falls from the cordgrass, turtle grass, and other vegetation. These smaller creatures in turn provide the forage that attracts and sustains the large predators that anglers pursue.

Not all flats are the same. The most obvious differences lie in the flora and fauna and how this mix of plants and animals changes with latitude and temperature. Few animals from the tropics, for example, are suited to coping with the cold waters of New England, just as creatures from the North Atlantic are poorly adapted to tropical heat. The impact of the tides also changes. As you travel away from the equator, tidal range becomes increasingly dramatic. On a given day in New England, for example, an angler can anticipate the water rising several feet. Meanwhile, his counterpart in the Gulf of Mexico

Guide Bob Rogers lands a redfish in the shallow water of the Florida Keys. These fish are known for their lightning-fast runs and powerful battles in skinny saltwater flats.

may measure the tidal variation in inches. This is an important distinction for the sportsman, for these smaller tides encourage the presence of predators such as bonefish, permit, and redfish—the so-called "tailing" species on which sightcasters rely.

Most fishing relies on detective skills: You assemble the best available information, and then you test for the presence of fish by making a cast. Sightcasting requires these same detective skills, but what makes this sport so exciting is that finding fish is only the beginning. When a target is spotted, the angler becomes a hunter and must stalk the prey. While maneuvering for position, the hunter often experiences a surge of "buck fever." In his 1950 book, *Salt Water Fly Fishing*, Joe Brooks described sighting a tailing bonefish. "You shiver and shake and tingle all over and your mouth goes dry," he wrote. "It is one of the great moments of all fishing experience, and the thrill of seeing his first tailing

fish has turned many an expert into a tyro. It is a thrill that does not diminish with time."

Despite your jitters, you fight for calm because you must still determine the proper approach to your target. If you have found a tailing fish, it may hold its position long enough for you to maneuver into casting range. More often, the target is moving, leaving you to calculate its speed and direction, and your odds of intercepting it. Whatever the situation, you become acutely aware of every sound and motion you might make. Even stepping too hard on the gunwale can trigger the alarm by causing a shock wave as the boat dips in the water. And you are instantly aware of any mistake, because it will cause your prey to scurry off for deeper water.

But if you have successfully maneuvered into position, the game continues and the tension grows. You still have to put the cast in front of your fish, and that means casting with accuracy. You also have to cast quickly. Saltwater gamefish are loathe to wait in any one spot and will routinely change direction or move out of range if you take too long; so you learn to deliver a fly with no more than three backcasts. "Quick and to the point" becomes the mantra of any fly fisher who frequents the flats.

Amid the growing tension, you begin asking yourself whether you have the correct fly. The answer comes soon enough. If your fish flees or ignores the fly, you know you have chosen poorly. Being snubbed is, of course, part of the game. No matter how good you think you may get, the flats will inevitably put you in your place with fussy or flighty fish, or no fish at all. But that makes it so much sweeter when you see the fish accelerate toward your fly, inhale, and begin its initial run.

No species has been more important to this sport than the bonefish. Some would argue that the tarpon is the true sightcasting king, and it would be impossible to overlook this impressive animal. But there are relatively few places outside of the Florida Keys where sight-casters can tackle tarpon on the flats. Bonefish, on the other hand, make sightcasting accessible as well as exciting. While tarpon and other big game fish require boats, bonefish flats are typically shallow enough for wading, though boats are also used. Nor do bonefish require the heavy tackle so necessary for large tarpon. But the greatest factor is that bonefish tactics are not limited to south Florida. The Caribbean is also well known for its bonefish flats, and fly fishers have discovered bonefish throughout Central America and even in the South Pacific.

Bonefish tactics are also effective on other flats species, chief among them the redfish or red drum. With a more northerly range than the bonefish, the red drum has made sight-casting on the flats accessible throughout Florida, in the other Gulf states, and north into the Carolinas. And by the 1980s, fly fishers from cities as widespread as Houston, New Orleans, and Jacksonville demonstrated that you do not have to live in Miami to enjoy a weekend on the flats.

THE NORTHEAST

As the tide swept our 20-foot boat toward the submerged rocks, Captain Mike Hintlian stressed the importance of the first cast. Make it count, he said. The target was a marker that warned boaters to keep a safe distance from the reef. If I missed, I might get a second shot, but a third attempt was unlikely. By then, the current would drag us out of range. Mike wasn't asking me to do anything difficult—the distance was a little long, but it wasn't unreasonable with the 10-weight rod and shooting head I was using. The problem was that I had never fished New

Tailing redfish exhibiting intense feeding activity are a welcome sight to flats anglers.

England before, and I had spent the whole morning fighting butterflies. I tried and tried, and yet I could not shake the image of big stripers and bluefish charging out from under the rocky ledges. Finally I told myself that this was just a routine cast, like those I practice at home.

You can sense a good cast as the rod accelerates and bends overhead, loading the graphite with energy like a tensed spring. Suddenly, your hand stops and the spring straightens, unleashing the power and throwing your line. If you have done it right, that short burst brings the rod to life. If you have done it wrong, the rod is little more than a stick swinging in the air.

In this case, as soon as I released my line toward the rocks, I knew that I was simply swinging a stick, and I watched the cast fall apart far short of its mark. But before I could grumble about the flubbed attempt, Mike was telling me to try again; there was still time. So I stripped in line like a demon, rolled the shooting head back into the air and false cast. And I reminded myself to focus on technique, that it beats muscle every time.

We were drawing away from the reef when I released the second cast with a smooth acceleration and sharp stop. I did not know if I could cover the growing distance; every cast has its limits, even with shooting heads. But this time I felt the life in the rod, and I knew I had hit a good stroke. The running line shot off the deck, and the shooting head straightened on the water. "Close enough," Mike said. "Let it sink."

I wasted no time retrieving when Mike gave me the word. It had seemed like forever, and I was sure the fly I was using, the white deceiver, had settled too deep into some crevice. But it was too late to change that now, so I began a quick, sharp retrieve—one strip, two strips. The third strip stopped with a jolt, and I felt the friction burn as the line cut into my fingers. I thought the fly was snagged in a rock and I would have to break off. Yet this rock was moving away too fast to account for the boat's drift. I had a fish down there, so I jammed the hook home and held on as my "rock" began its first powerful run.

Soon, the rock became a 10-pound bluefish, and as it slipped into Mike's net I marveled at its gunmetal blue back, big shoulders, steely flanks, and forked tail. I also admired, from a safe distance, its impressive dental work, easily capable of taking off a finger. Then Mike eased my fish back into the dark, clear Atlantic waters. There was still plenty of fight left in that bluefish, and I was happy to share it with the next angler who might come along.

When fighting a good bluefish, you have to wonder why this grand sport lost its popularity, but it clearly happened. Perhaps it's because bluefish appear and disappear in random patterns—no one has figured out why bluefish run in such irregular cycles. One year they're abundant, and another year they're rare.

Though bluefish have always been a staple of fly fishers in the Northeast, the historical basis for the

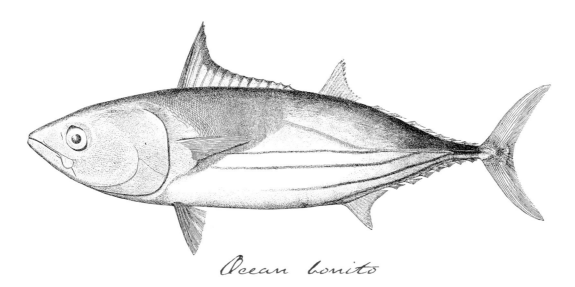

Ocean bonito

Piers and jetties attract feeding seabirds, fish, and fishermen as they do here in Kennebunkport, Maine.

sport is striped bass. Unlike bluefish, striped bass populations are better suited to changing water conditions. Stripers are widely distributed and could show up just about anywhere, whether deep in an estuary or out in heavy surf. This makes them a whole lot easier to get to than bluefish, who prefer much deeper waters in general. Add to that their enthusiasm for eating flies and their jolting strikes, and the striper became a prime target for the fly rod. The weakness was that stripers were a prime target for just about everyone, and for too many years anglers of all persuasions failed to find a bass that was not worth keeping. The result was an inevitable crash. The collapse began in the 1970s; by the 1980s biologists were calling for emergency regulations and an end to unlimited fishing. Given that situation, it is no surprise that fly fishers began looking elsewhere for their sport. The good news is that efforts to rescue

the striper worked, and as word of the recovery spread, fly fishers began returning to the waters of the Northeast coast. Today, the bass are once again a regular part of fishing in the Northeast. Fifteen years ago, I thought they were gone forever. It is good to be proven wrong.

OFFSHORE

To understand the difference between fishing rivers and streams versus fishing offshore, all you have to do is imagine the difference between going camping in the mountains versus going to the beach. For the most part, the fishing techniques are the same. Your concept of clear water becomes a little skewed when you do most of your fishing in the Louisiana marsh. The influence of the Mississippi River makes you think anything short of *café au lait* is crystalline. So I marveled at the clarity as I looked down into the

The swift and powerful false albacore has challenged fly fishers along the Atlantic coast.

waters of Mexico's Sea of Cortez. Five feet, 10 feet, 20 feet—I could only guess the depth of my vision, but I knew I could see far. Far enough that I soon lost interest in the shortage of dissolved solids and began to focus on the dorado schooling below.

Dorado, also known as dolphin but not to be confused with the mammal made famous on "Flipper," seemed to come out of nowhere. The water had been empty when Jesus, our guide, shut down his panga's outboard beside the floating bed of sargassum weed. Jesus was far from discouraged. Reaching into a livewell, he removed three sardines, each perhaps 3 inches long, and tossed them overboard. Disoriented, the baitfish skittered momentarily on the surface. When they gained their bearings, they vanished into the sheltering weeds. Jesus paused, then reached for three more sardines, but the second silvery trio never made it into the weed bed. They had scarcely touched the water when the surface erupted around them; the

dorado had arrived. Swinging my 9-weight rod into action, I lobbed a large white deceiver 30 or 40 feet onto the water and began stripping. But the dorado needed no more time to find the fly than they took to locate the second bunch of sardines; I am not even sure that I had a chance to set the hook. All I know is that my reel was screaming, my fly line had vanished from the spool, and the greyhounding fish had taken who-knows-how-many yards of backing as he headed for the horizon. The only thing I could do was hold on.

Dorado are remarkable fish regardless of your tackle, but they are especially good on the fly. They are agile, they are fast, and a 15-pound fish is nicely matched against a 9-weight rod. More than anything, they are beautiful, with colors that are incomprehensible for anyone who has never seen the live fish.

On the wall of my living room is the mount of a 20-pound dolphin that I caught while trolling from a charter boat in Florida when I was twelve. My mother had visions of fillets when the skipper returned my brothers and me to the dock. But the angst of having such a fish carved up for dinner was more than I could bear, so my dolphin found its way to the taxidermist instead. More than thirty years later, friends who have never seen a dorado remain suspicious of the bright greens, blues, and yellows of my fish. I explain that their skepticism is justified. I doubt any artist will ever capture the dolphin's true brilliance.

TACKLE

With the diversity of species and circumstances, saltwater fly fishing defies any attempt to specify a single rod- and reel-outfit as standard tackle. The demands of anglers looking for 200-pound tarpon or marlin, for example, are far removed from the needs of those hoping to hit a school of spotted sea trout. And a day on the flats is radically different from tackling a New England jetty at night. In short, you need to know the probable conditions as well as the fish you expect to encounter; versatility and flexibility are always assets. But if you are likely to err, do so on the side of being too heavy, even though ultralight is very much in vogue now. Some anglers have the skill to fight large fish with the lightest rods. I have one friend in Louisiana, Captain Danny Ayo, who would use half-weight rods and spiderweb tippets if they were available, and I am confident he would still boat the largest fish quickly. But that level of skill and experience is uncommon, and few of us really know how to push our tackle to its limits without breaking those limits. The result is often a fish that is fought to exhaustion, and there is nothing in our sport more pointless than killing a fish we meant to release.

Saltwater fish will, in fact, fight to the death. For example, I find few species more exciting than a good ladyfish. The strike is electric and the battle a spectacle, because ladyfish will expend everything they've got against the rod. But if you do not play them quickly, they will go belly up the moment you return them to the water, and that is a sad sight.

So where do you start in selecting the correct rod? A good beginning is a local fly shop, a guide, or a friend who is familiar with your waters. You'll soon develop enough experience to use your own judgment.

If I had to pick a single rod for everything other than big game or offshore use, it would be a 9-foot graphite rod for a 9-weight line. A 9-weight rod should handle just about any inshore fish you might encounter, although it is too light for something such as serious striper fishing with big flies in a heavy surf. For that, you want a 10- or even an 11-weight, and I would begin with a 10-weight as my standard rod if I routinely visited waters where 20-pound fish were likely. For serious tarpon fishing and offshore work, a 12-weight is standard equipment, but a 14-weight rod is more appropriate for billfish. Luckily for me, I do not have to limit my gear, and so I routinely carry two rods: one heavy and one light, with a 7-weight as the light. I will include a third if conditions dictate, but carrying three rods is only justified if you are going to cover quite a variety of situations in the course of the day.

If picking the right rod sounds complicated, finding the right line may seem overwhelming. It does

not have to be. Begin with a standard weight-forward line matched to your rod. If you have a 9-weight rod, for example, you want a 9-weight line. Some experts advocate mismatched tackle, such as a 10-weight line on a 9-weight rod, and their reasons are usually sound. You may even adopt their advice as you gain experience. But tackle manufacturers also deserve

A few off-shore fly rodders have been taking sailfish on big streamer flies since the 1950s, but the practice of fly fishing for these acrobatic giants has taken off in recent years.

credit for knowing their products. So before you ignore the factory's recommendation, be sure you understand why.

Your most versatile line will be a floating or perhaps an intermediate line. Again, knowing the local conditions will help you decide. I spend most my time on shallow redfish flats in perhaps a foot of water and have found a floating line works best. For

Bonefishing in the tropics of Mexico, Bermuda, and the Bahamas brings blue sky and bluer waters.

deep flats or the surf, you will probably be better off with the slow-sinking intermediate line. You should also have a fast-sinking line for deep holes and channels. Having a high-density line that really goes down fast is essential if you are going to fish offshore.

Leaders are very much a matter of individual taste, as long as they turn over correctly and the knots do not fail. I have tried just about every leader style possible, and I prefer traditional compound leaders that step down one piece of monofilament at a time, from a heavy butt to a light tippet. I include a shock tippet of wire or heavy mono for some species. The exception to using a tapered leader is with fast-sinking lines, where you can simply loop the tippet directly to the fly line. Just remember that the tippet should always be lighter than the fly line and backing. I recently met a fellow who lost his fly

line to a big dolphin. I asked him the weight of his tippet, and he said 40 pounds. Well most fly lines break at 20 pounds of pressure, and standard backings are rated at 20 to 30 pounds. You can use heavier leaders if you like, but I find replacing a foot or two of mono leader much more economical than losing 30 yards of fly line.

Reels are also a matter of personal taste, and you will have to decide for yourself whether to buy one of the big-ticket models or opt for economy. Either type works so long as you understand the tradeoffs. Any single-action fly reel built with a decent drag and corrosion resistance will handle most saltwater fish, and there is no better proof than the bargain-basement Pflueger Medalist 1498. But no one in his right mind would expect to get as many years from a Medalist as from a Pate, Seamaster, or Abel. So if you want one reel to last a lifetime, spend the big bucks.

ROADSIDE SALTWATER FLY FISHING

Wander along the roads that follow any coastline and you'll see anglers trying their luck from the shore for local saltwater species. Even if you are among the nautically challenged, you can reap the benefits of a successful day on the water.

We have fished without using any flotation devices, often mere steps from our truck, in places as diverse as the Pacific Northwest for salmon, the Gulf Coast of Texas for tarpon, and the Florida Keys for bonefish. Redfish in both the Indian River Lagoon of Florida, and the Laguna Madre of Texas can easily be reached from roadside. In the Northeast, fly fishers enjoy a long season of striper fishing from the shoreline. A recent trip to the Outer Banks of North Carolina for false albacore found us in a boat offshore casting toward scores of wader-clad anglers along the bank, who were casting toward us.

Sometimes it requires a bit of research to uncover prime fishing spots. Once your maps have led you to a likely region, fly shops can often provide more detailed directions and assistance. If finances allow, spending a day with a local guide can keep you from wasting your time in barren water. You'll get help with techniques, tackle, and fly patterns that work best in the area, too. But even if you go it alone, chances are you will discover great fishing just steps from the road, somewhere along the edge of every state that borders the salt.

— Bob Rodgers

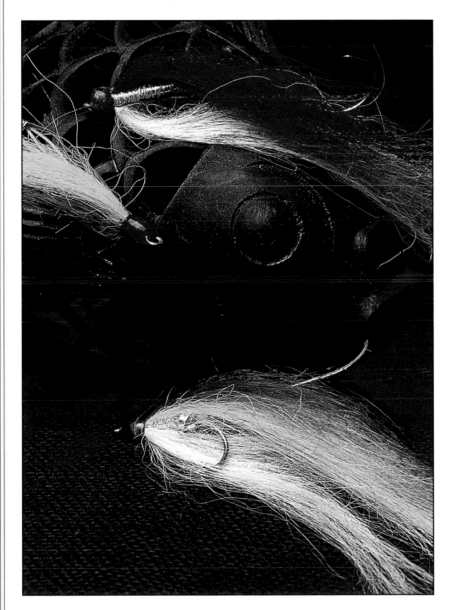

Winston Moore's billfish fly has helped him capture over 138 Pacific sailfish.

If you go cheap, plan to replace it every so often.

But I consider one point non-negotiable: Every saltwater reel should have a big spool, and again, I use the Medalist 1498 as my standard. A big spool is important because it translates into line capacity for handling big fish. Just as important is the fact that big spools retrieve line faster than small spools, which is essential when you're trying to clear excess line from the deck or when a fish runs toward you.

D. L. Goddard's Mylar Needlefish, made of mylar tubing and epoxy, has proven itself to be a killer fly for stripers in the Chesapeake Bay.

FLIES

You can usually start a fight among fly fishers by asking what constitutes a proper fly, and that is especially true among the saltwater crowd. Myself, I tend to fall among the traditionalists who specify that the design should not impart a wobbling or spinning action to the fly. Synthetic materials may be used, but they should be used in the same manner as natural or other traditional materials. On the other side of this friendly debate are those who constantly look for new materials and new ways to use them. Whatever side you're on, it is important to recognize that, though some flies may prove more effective than others, there are no secret weapons. The perfect fly is worthless if you cannot find fish and cannot make a proper presentation.

If I were asked to choose one fly for all my saltwater fishing, I would quickly ask to expand my choice to three. One would be a Clouser minnow, in chartreuse and about 2 inches long. That choice of color and size reflects my penchant for redfish, but you can easily vary these elements to suit your own needs. This bucktail is weighted with an inverted hook, so it dives nicely and is perfect for bouncing along the flats to imitate a shrimp or crab. Or you can pick up the pace to simulate a fleeing bait fish.

In short, the Clouser can mimic just about any forage anywhere.

Lefty's Deceiver is another of the all-time greats. This streamer is a universal baitfish imitation and is especially effective when tied about 3 inches long in white with a blue or black back.

No saltwater fly box would be complete if it did not include popping bugs. I prefer very clean and simple ties, unlike the traditional bass bug with its heavy hackle and rubber legs. The heavy dressing is simply unnecessary. All those accessories also increase wind resistance, which only complicates casting. Not everyone shares my fascination with poppers, nor are they always the best flies to use. But when they are hitting, it is hard to imagine anything more exciting than a good gamefish crashing to the surface to get his prey.

Are these the only saltwater flies you will ever need? Certainly not. There are many more flies from which you can choose. But a box filled with a good variety of Clousers, deceivers, and poppers is remarkably versatile no matter what gamefish you pursue.

You should note that I have not mentioned fly "patterns." The reason is that saltwater has few true fly patterns like those found on the trout stream. The word "pattern" suggests that the tier is following a specific recipe, with little or no variation from one tier to the next. A light Cahill dry fly, for example, is pretty much the same fly throughout the country. The situation is similar with an Adams or elk-wing caddis. That is almost never the case with the so-called saltwater "patterns." Instead, saltwater flies are better described as styles, with tiers introducing their own improvements or embellishments. It is a very free-spirited approach.

Whatever flies you choose, you should bend down the barbs on all your hooks. Barbless hooks are easily removed when you release a fish, and a quick release is an important factor in ensuring a fish's survival.

For those who are not concerned about the fish, there is another very good reason for using barbless hooks: They are also easier to remove from yourself. Some very good casters have hit me, and I have even hit myself. It is bound to happen when fly casting in a small boat or in windy conditions, and the hook always hurts going in. But it hurts a lot less coming out if the barb has been removed, and pulling out a barbless hook is much easier than making a run to the nearest hospital.

CONSERVATION

One of the beauties of fly fishing on the coast is the realization that the sea is so vast. It is possible to travel for hundreds of miles without encountering another person. But that vastness has also been the undoing of many of our saltwater fisheries, because it encourages us to think of the sea as an unlimited resource.

The sad truth is that the limits are real; it is just that we sometimes fail to recognize them. Most of the time, we pin the blame on commercial interests—and they certainly have been guilty of behaving badly often enough—but they are not alone in their guilt. So-called sportsmen have also done their share of the damage. When redfish stocks in the Gulf of Mexico were collapsing in the 1980s, the National Marine Fisheries Service revealed that commercial and recreational fishermen were harvesting more than 90 percent of the fish from inshore waters, and had been doing so for several years.

Yet overfishing is only one part of the problem. We must also contend with pollution, and with developers who would turn our coasts into one long string of condominium complexes and shopping malls. These problems do not lend themselves to easy solutions. Every summer, for example, a vast algae bloom develops in the Gulf of Mexico, depleting the water of oxygen and causing a dead zone covering thousands of square miles. The bloom is caused by nutrients carried by the Mississippi River from places as far away as Montana and Pennsylvania. Part of the problem is agricultural runoff rich with fertilizer; part of it comes from people fertilizing their lawns. And how are we ever going to convince some fellow in Montana that the Gulf is dying in part because he wants his yard to look healthy?

The good news is that solutions are possible, and the solutions begin with individuals. The coasts need people who vote their convictions. The coasts also needs people who recognize that we do not have to turn every last barrier island into a condo city or fill in every last salt marsh to make room for more shopping malls. Sometimes, the coasts need people who simply pick up after themselves rather than leaving their trash to be washed away with the tide. There is no such thing as an unlimited resource; we have disproved the premise too many times. But the sea can last for an eternity if we work for it.

CONSERVATION

BY PAUL SCHULLERY

Fly fishers are true conservationists; they have to be. The sport requires careful and constant attention to aquatic ecosystems. If something goes wrong—if, say, pollution kills off a species of delicate insects that local trout depend upon for food—a fly fisher can't help but notice. When the environment is contaminated, the angling is damaged along with it.

There are many other reasons why fly fishing is conservation-oriented. Rather than impose his will on his surroundings, a fly fisher succeeds by blending in, by imitating nature. To do so requires empathy and the imagination to see oneself as a brown trout or a salmon, qualities that naturally instill a sense of stewardship. Consequently, fly fishers have very often distinguished themselves, not only on behalf of better fishing but also to the benefit of entire natural systems. If you are just starting to fly fish, this is the group you are joining, and conservation will—by definition—become very important to you. We need your help.

In the late 1800s, when the conservation movement first emerged, most anglers' primary goal was to ensure abundant fish, even if that meant building big hatcheries and growing the fish domestically. But many sports enthusiasts eventually realized it was not possible to "conserve" just one species. They discovered that to protect their favorite quarry, they had to protect whole ecosystems. Taking care of deer habitat and grouse cover, for example, benefitted wetlands, while keeping a trout stream free-flowing and clean meant a greater abundance of species on the ground and in the air.

By the early years of the twentieth century, President Theodore Roosevelt's very visible conservation efforts broadened public support for conservation to include not just sports enthusiasts but bird-watchers, garden clubs, foresters, and a growing number of people who simply considered themselves nature lovers. Some were completely opposed to hunting and fishing, for moral reasons or because they wanted to appreciate natural places without violent intrusions. (A great irony—and tragedy—of the modern conservation movement is that environmentalists with different interests often have become as antagonistic toward one another as they are toward the real enemies of the natural beauty which they want to protect.)

Fly fishers occupy a very unusual niche in this conservationist-environmentalist spectrum. We practice one of the oldest blood sports, but unlike most other anglers and all hunters, we are able to do so without killing. Fly fishers use old tools, but in new ways. And our attitudes are changing along with our definition of what constitutes good sport. One very important example from today's conservation debate relating to trout fishing illustrates those changes and the complexities of the issue.

WILD TROUT, NATIVE TROUT

Fly fishers in the United States have gone from the "good old days" when streams were teeming with native fish, through a time of great overexploitation at the turn of the century, to the modern era of efforts to restore long-ruined fisheries. The first response to dwindling populations of native fish one hundred years ago was for hatcheries to regularly dump fish into streams and lakes. People became accustomed to catching these farm-grown fish. In fact, many people were quite satisfied with the situation, if for no other reason than that hatcheries can provide far more fish to catch during a season than can a wild trout stream. Hatchery fish are still popular in many parts of the country and probably always will be.

Today, though, most fly fishers put a far higher premium than did their grandfathers on catching wild trout that have

lived for generations in the same stream. Because they're not raised in pools or fed on commercial pellets, these fish provide better sport and have far higher aesthetic values to most fly fishers than do fish recently planted from a hatchery truck. To catch a wild trout, many feel, is to experience a more direct contact with nature in its uncultivated form.

Preference for wild trout usually comes with a growing appreciation of wild habitats, because in order to fish well, fly fishers must attune themselves to a stream's ecology. I learned to fish in Yellowstone Park, where no fish had been stocked for decades, and each fish represented many generations of breeding, growing, and adapting to those waters. When I moved to other parts of the country, I had a twinge of disappointment in catching fish that had been in the stream only a few days and were obviously maladapted. In most cases, very few hatchery fish survive their first winter in the wild. They are either harvested or die because they cannot adapt to the unpredictability of natural conditions.

In the last decade, there has been yet another redefinition of wild trout fishing. While it is contentious and controversial, it is also very important. A growing number of anglers want not just wild trout, but wild trout that are also native, meaning a species that has always lived in that water, not one introduced into those waters to live wild. The ancestors of brown trout in most eastern American streams may have been there for more than a hundred years, for example, but they evolved over

Brook trout

millennia in Europe or Great Britain. By contrast, ancestors of brook trout in some eastern American streams—or rainbow trout in some Western streams—evolved in that very water over thousands of years. The form and function of these native fish was created by the mountains and waters around them. To some, this issue seems frivolous, and the distinction subtle, but it has become important to a growing portion of the angling public.

The issue of native and wild fish causes practical conflict when anglers disagree over how a given stream should be managed. Should we remove non-native fish and restore the native species in order to re-create a stream's original state? Many anglers, to give a common example, oppose the idea of replacing established trophy brown trout introduced to the stream at some point with much smaller native fish, whether brook, rainbow, or other species. This controversy is often fervent, and it shows no signs of being resolved any time soon.

While anglers debate the issue, restoration of native species is becoming a greater priority not just to wildlife managers but to the general public as well. Conservationists who traditionally have focused on mammals and birds have shifted more of their attention to fish because of the increased understanding of the importance of wetlands, adding to the nonfishing public's interest in restoring native species. To a nonfisherman who cares about preserving intact ecosystems, it is obvious that native fish are more desirable, if for no other reason than their unfortunate rarity.

ALL FISH, ALL WATERS

The conservation issues surrounding trout apply as well to every species of fish. As trout hatcheries were flourishing, anglers and fishery agencies also worked to "improve" countless other warmwater fisheries. Many native fish (walleye, northern pike, largemouth and smallmouth bass) and some non-native ones (most notoriously carp) were moved from native ranges into faraway lakes and streams to create better fishing. As with the decline of trout and salmon from 1870 to 1920, warmwater fisheries were destroyed through pollution, overharvest, and even commercial fishing in many larger waters. Conservation of these fish requires the same basic steps as conservation of trout: protection of habitat, control of harvest, and general respect for the aquatic ecosystems of which they are a part.

Saltwater species present more difficult problems. Oceans are the ultimate depositories of all the pollution we dump into streams and rivers across the continent. Commercial demands for the ocean's fish are far more intense than for freshwater fish, and modern, high-tech industrial fishing is devastatingly effective. Good management policy is hampered by incredibly complex international maritime laws and treaties. Many ocean species follow extended and often poorly understood migrations, moving to different habitats that cross legal jurisdictions. These obstacles, which sometimes seem insurmountable, underscore the immediate importance of trying to protect saltwater species.

Still, there are significant angler-conservationist success stories. Fly fishers enjoy excellent fishing for a variety of Alaska salmon because of a carefully regulated harvest that allows everyone a share. We also now celebrate the recovery of the striped bass along the Atlantic Coast. Likewise, due to intensive pressure by anglers, limits on commercial inshore netting on the Gulf Coast have already yielded improvements in fishing for redfish, sea trout and

With fly fishing placing much of its emphasis on style rather than efficiency and on the experience rather than the reward, the sport has understandably been the leader in the practice of "catch-and-release." This small but rapidly growing movement has followers all over the world, mostly as a result of the missionary work done by American fly fishers. There are times, however, when some of us get so carried away with our slogans and enthusiasm that we forget our own fishing beginnings and refuse to consider other points of view.

Some time ago I was brought back to earth by an incident in one of my fishing schools. I usually show a movie called *The Way of a Trout*, which concludes with a strong plea for catch-and-release fishing. Right after the final dramatic scene, which ends with the release of a large rainbow trout, an eleven-year-old boy impulsively jumped up and said, "I wouldn't a let that fish go!" As he sat down, a little embarrassed, he explained, "I wouldn't a let that fish go. I've never caught a fish that big." In the awkward silence that followed, I realized that most of the people in that room—and, for that matter, the vast majority of all anglers—wouldn't have let that fish go, either. I don't remember exactly what I said to that class and to that young man, but I do remember feeling awfully inadequate.

The apparent contradiction of catching and then uncatching a fish is not only difficult to understand, but also offers an argument in favor of keeping fish. A famous naturalist recently suggested that sport fishing is a perversion in itself, and that the only reasonable justification for fishing is to acquire food. After all, some would say that humans by our very nature are hunting animals who survive by killing and eating lesser animals, and in a way those innate acts are genuine and honest. But to make a sport—a kind of game—out of that experience, and possibly to traumatize a wild animal for sheer pleasure, may well be a diversion that lessens a person's dignity.

For most civilized humans, killing and eating the catch is probably the closest thing to the basic hunting experience; the kill is the logical conclusion of the hunt, and no one should ever be made to feel ashamed or guilty about wanting to consummate a fishing experience by keeping the catch. However, there are also valid arguments to be made in favor of catch-and-release fishing.

First, it is indisputable that many heavily fished waters have benefited tremendously from catch-and-release fishing. Where there are simply too many people and too few fish, regulations requiring the release of fish improve the situation dramatically.

An additional philosophical consideration may in time be even more important to the sport and to the fisher. On occassion people strive to be something more than just brute animals. *Noble* is perhaps a good word to describe a concept that permits us to satisfy our innate need to hunt and then to return our prize to the wild. Maybe it is simply some modification of our instincts that will permit us to survive on this crowded planet.

Finally, most of us make this decision emotionally. It was not too many years ago that I kept everything I was able to catch. I started to release fish because of regulations in some of the waters I frequented, and because of pressure from my friends and the fishing community. It was uncomfortable at first, and I found myself resenting the whole catch-and-release program. Then a funny thing happened that I can't really explain: I began to enjoy releasing fish. And now when I feel a fish move through my hands and see him swim away, it makes me feel good. It makes me feel very good.

—Mel Krieger

Some anglers question placing hatchery fish in wild waters, but many species have benefited from federal and state hatchery programs.

other species. These are bright spots in the conservation story, but we have a long way to go.

CATCH AND RELEASE

One hundred and fifty years ago, on several eastern trout waters, a few forward-looking anglers were already concerned about depletion of fish. Hatcheries were one attempt at a solution. But even then, a few anglers had other ideas. They knew, as we do today, that a small fish put back would grow into a big fish. They also seemed to understand that fish do not swallow flies as deeply as bait, and thus have a better chance of survival if released.

In 1840, a writer in *Spirit of the Times*, an early sporting periodical, complained that the trout harvest from Long Island ponds was too indiscriminate: "We wish it were possible to put a stop to pond fishing on the Island until May-day, by which time the trout would be active, rosy, and in good condition for the table, and then allow them to be taken with the fly only."

Why did this writer want to have only fly fishing in his favorite ponds? Was it because he knew that fly-caught fish were easier to release alive than were bait caught fish? Or was he merely reflecting a local distinction by which snobbery also came into play? (People of higher social status were more likely to fish with flies, a "gentleman's" sport.) He may have been a conservationist or just a snob—or more likely a little of both.

Whatever the case, because fly fishing allowed for the successful release and survival of undersized fish, some fisheries had set up fly-fishing-only rules by the turn of the century. In 1904, the New York Adirondack League Club—which controled many private lakes, ponds and streams—instituted fly-fishing-only regulations on the South Branch of the Moose River. Over the next few years, the club applied this same regulation to some of its lakes as well.

Instituting fly-fishing-only regulations was easy on private waters, but on public waters anglers using other types of equipment viewed such exclusive restrictions as undemocratic. Moreover, by 1900 many public waters were heavily stocked, and the public was already conditioned to regard hatchery fish as acceptable, even preferable. As long as there were plenty of fish to take home, not many anglers cared where the fish came from.

But in the 1930s and 1940s, the concept of fishing for fun rather than for food began to take hold. This idea grew from the leadership of fisheries biologist Albert Hazzard and his colleagues, and was popularized by the strong advocacy of thoughtful anglers such as Lee Wulff, John Alden Knight, and Ed Zern. Fly fishing's advantage as a way to catch fish without killing them was further recognized. So, as political circumstances allowed, a few public waters also became fly-fishing-only. In 1941, for example, a con-

certed effort by a group of Washington fly fishermen led to a fly-fishing-only regulation for steelhead on the Stilliguamish River. Almost ten years later, the Firehole River in Yellowstone National Park was made fly-fishing-only.

In the 1960s and 1970s, with rising national environmental awareness, no-kill regulations spread to many other streams, such as the Beaverkill in New

York and the Yellowstone in Yellowstone Park. Eventually, even commercialized fishing tournaments on many bass waters and saltwater fisheries adopted catch-and-release rules. Today many U.S. streams, rivers, and lakes apply regulations aimed at sustaining a robust fish population. Fly fishers played an important role in that change.

But experience with regulations has provided more data about how fish are affected by various kinds of tackle. This new information challenges the old attitude that fly fishing is the only conservation-minded way to fish. Fly fishers have been almost smug in the assumption that their catch was easily released—and would probably live. And dozens of scientific studies proved beyond any doubt that bait tastes and feels so good (and natural) to the fish that they swallow it deeply, and removing the hook often kills the fish. At least half of all bait-caught fish, especially trout, die.

But the good news for fish—if not for fly fishers—is that those same scientific studies proved that fish caught on spinners and lures survive just as well as those caught on flies. If you fish with a lure or spinner that has only one hook or one group of hooks—like the treble hook on a Mepps Spinner or Daredevil—you will on the average kill no more fish during release than will a fly fisher. Lures that are more harmful to fish are those with several hooks, such as a Rappala—a plug with multiple treble hooks. These multihook lures tend to harm the fish during the fight, because if the fish is caught by one hook, it will often be gouged on the sides, gills or eyes by the other hooks.

These studies thus indicate that fly-fishing-only waters can no longer be justified biologically as a means to maintain fish populations. No-bait and no-kill regulations are equally effective. For this reason, many waters are labeled no-kill, which means that only catch-and-release fishing is allowed. The method is left up to the angler, as long as it does not involve bait. Another reason that fly-fishing-only waters are uncommon is that fishery management agencies cannot afford to be too exclusive. Fishing license fees pay the bills, and the public has been quick to resent any regulation that smacks of elitism by restricting what kinds of anglers are allowed.

Some states still maintain some fly-fishing-only waters, arguing that fly fishing is a distinct enough fishing method to require some waters where it can be practiced without conflict. These fly-fishing-only waters usually are places where longstanding tradition and local preference already make fly fishing the method of choice.

BARBLESS HOOKS

A second issue that fly fishers may need to reconsider is the use of barbless hooks. For years, most fly fishing writers advocated these as a way to reduce mortal injury to the fish. It is true that a barbed hook is not critical to good fishing; as long as you keep a reasonably tight line, the fish will not get free. There also is no question that releasing a fish caught on a barbless hook is much less hassle; often it is not even necessary to touch the fish. All you have to do, once the fish is close enough to reach, is run your hand lightly down the leader, grasp the hook shank, and turn it right out of the fish's mouth. (If you tie your own flies, you can buy barbless hooks, but I usually use a small pliers to flatten the barb back against the shank of the hook.)

While releasing a fish from a barbless fly is easier, several independent studies have shown that barbless hooks do not differ from barbed hooks when it comes to fish survival. Averaged over a very large number of fish hooked and released, there is no statistical difference in the number of fish that will die if you used barbed rather than barbless hooks. Many fly fishers object to these conclusions in light of their personal experiences, which indicate that barbless hooks are better. But scientists cannot rely upon the small picture, i.e., personal experience, when the mortality rate among huge numbers of caught-and-released fish consistently proves otherwise.

Douglas Adams, *Salmon Fishing: A Likely Pool,* c. 1890

Despite these studies, however, I still recommend barbless hooks, if only because they save a lot of time and hassle. My flies snag less on weeds, trees, and clothing—and I do not believe they cause me to lose fish in the process. Most importantly, if there is another fish rising, I want to get that first fish released quickly and get my fly back in the water.

ARE WE GOOD ENOUGH?

We fly fishers have long considered ourselves distanced from other blood sports because we do not have to kill our quarry. Many of us release practically every fish we catch. However, not everyone believes fly fishers are great conservationists. Today the movement to protect wildlife is very broad-based in our society, with a growing number of people who don't approve of killing wild animals for sport or even for food.

In the minds of these people—and to the astonishment of many fly fishers—releasing fish makes us even worse than the traditional sportsmen who kill and eat wild creatures. To many animal rights activists, whose legions are growing astonishingly quickly while anglers' are not, catch-and-release fishing is morally worse than catch-and-kill. They insist that while we cause pain and suffering, we do not saying, "If there is a moral compromise involved in my fishing, it is one I consider worth the price I pay in exchange for the enrichment and joy the sport brings me." But it is something all of us would do well to give a little thought to.

PRACTICAL CONSERVATION STEPS FOR FLY FISHERS

So what can a lone fly angler do to protect and conserve fisheries?

GET INVOLVED

First, join other fly fishers—and other anglers—to preserve the ecosystems upon which aquatic life depend. Most of us can support excellent conservation efforts underway on our favorite waters by sending money or by participating in stream cleanup projects. Local Theodore Gordon Fly Fishers and Trout Unlimited clubs work on stream restoration, attend local hearings, and serve as watchdogs on rivers, lakes, and streams that need attention. They sponsor clinics that teach children and adults to fish, and they educate the public as well as fellow anglers.

Fishing technique and etiquette are passed down through the generations from parents and grandparents to their children and grandchildren. Fortunately fly fishing demands more concentration and coordination than power.

even have the justification of sustenance. In their eyes, we torture fish for fun. We hook them, we watch them exhibit terror at the end of our line, and then we let them go so that they can be put through the same outrage again.

Most anglers have considered these ideas and have come to some personal decision based upon their individual ethics to justify how they interact with wild creatures, especially fish. It may be as simple as

But the larger conservation and environmental organizations make a big difference for anglers, too, simply because they care about the same things: protecting wild habitats. Look around your region, ask questions, and find out who is doing work that suits your interests. The National Wildlife Federation, the Audubon Society, and many other groups are important partners in fisheries conservation because they focus on protecting whole ecosystems. The Nature Conservancy acquires and protects key lands and has literally saved whole trout streams for

MAKE A CATCH-AND-RELEASE TOOL

Several commercially produced catch-and-release gadgets allow the safe return of fish, often while the fish is still under water and often without even touching it. But you don't have to buy one of these tools to be a conscientious fly fisher; you can make your own from a 3-inch-long wooden dowel and a coat hanger or cup hook. Just follow the simple instructions below to make a small catch-and-release tool for trout and small bass. For use on boats and with larger fish, you may want to lengthen the handle and increase the diameter of the wooden dowel.

1. Drill a $7/16$-inch-diameter hole two inches deep into one end of the dowel.

2. Cut and straighten a 4-inch piece of the coat hanger.

3. Cover 2 inches of the wire with epoxy glue and insert it into the hole in the dowel.

4. Bend the other end of the wire into a hook shape. You can also use a cup hook or an open-eyed screw hook in place of the coat-hanger wire.

To release a fish, hold the leader in your left hand to keep pressure off of the hook. With the release tool in your right hand, hook the leader and slide the tool toward the fish. With the hook of the release tool in the fish's mouth, raise your right hand. This movement inverts the fish hook, and the weight of even a small fish will usually disengage it. If that does not happen, position the tool over the fish hook and flip it out. For best results with this tool and technique, use barbless hooks. Practice makes perfect!

—Jim Abbs

Catch and release: A small brown trout is released to live—and fight—another day.

Salmon hatcheries have played a large role in bringing dwindling stocks back to watersheds where they had been overfished or adversely affected by development.

public use and enjoyment. The Orvis Company is one of several major fly fishing outfitters that have taken a leadership role in raising and donating hundreds of thousands of dollars to help protect the environment and save important fisheries.

EDUCATE YOURSELF

A serious part of being effective in fisheries conservation is being well informed. Conservation activists, who participate in discussion, debate, litigation, and lobbying, and who follow the media closely, advise that you cannot know too much. It is not enough just to care and to be convinced you are on the right side. You also must know what you are talking about. People who threaten healthy fisheries are going to provide as much scientific and economic evidence as they can to defend their actions, and many of these people are very thoughtful and persuasive. Countering their efforts requires an educated and well-funded stance.

There are a host of threats to healthy fisheries. Acid deposition, the result of national and even international industrial practices, has killed many eastern trout waters. Logging, grazing, and building practices have devastated aquatic ecosystems, especially in the West, on both public and private lands. Overfishing has brought many marine species to the brink of extinction—the price paid for all those wonderful fish dinners served in restaurants. Problems on this scale may best be addressed by large conservation groups acting together.

ACT LOCALLY

Problems that affect you most directly often are on your favorite waters. If you live in the East or Midwest, for example, one of your neighbors could be a farmer who drives his tractor across your stream and lets his cows water in it. To effect a change, you may have to find out if there are any laws against such behavior and, if not, whether such a law may be enacted. But before you take any action, try a friendly conversation with the farmer, or perhaps suggest that your local fishing group could build a fence to help keep the cows out of the water. Do not start with the assumption that you have to go to court, even though you must be prepared for that possibility. Always start by being civil. Local work often succeeds best when it is neighborly rather than arrogant or confrontational.

WHAT YOU CAN DO TODAY

Let's say you belong to the right organizations, keep up on the issues, and act locally. What can you do as an angler out there on the water, every day, to help?

LET THEM LIVE

Despite the complications, practice catch-and-release. You do not have to make a religion of it. If you like to eat fish, keep a few on occasion. But be moderate. By letting most of the fish go, you will be doing the single most important, immediate, thing to ensure tomorrow's fishing.

STEP LIGHTLY

While it may seem insignificant, make sure that you personally do not harm any stream or lake, even in a very small way. If each of us took special care to have minimal impact on waters by not polluting or littering, by respecting lake or stream banks it would make a big total difference.

FIGHT EXOTIC INVASIONS

We all need to consider the impact of exotic organisms—not just fish, but all kinds of life forms, plant and animal— that find their way into new waters. Dr. Michael Soule, the father of the new scientific discipline of conservation biology, points out that aquatic ecosystems are

especially vulnerable to exotic species because they are so thoroughly interconnected. He also regards invasion of exotics as the single greatest threat to remaining wild ecosystems—even more perilous than destruction of habitat by humans.

Anglers share a lot of the blame for this problem. There are still anglers who think it is perfectly reasonable to take some species of fish from some water whose ecology they don't understand, carry it across many miles of land, and put it in some other water they don't understand. This Johnny Appleseed mentality has cost untold millions of taxpayer dollars to

White River National Fish Hatchery in Vermont is home to a mature Atlantic salmon development program, from egg fertilization to fingerlings to parr and mature silver-sides.

restore waters as exotic fish have wiped out local fisheries. In each case, and in each region, the situation differs, but the principle is the same.

Protecting against exotic invasions is a worldwide challenge. As mentioned earlier, there are limited waters in the U.S. with purely native fauna and flora and no exotics. In my part of the West, there are only a very few, isolated high-country lakes and headwater streams unaffected by exotic species. While that may sound discouraging, it highlights the need to be careful. Such risks are everywhere and involve all kinds of plants and animals.

In major trout rivers of the West, we now have a very serious example of damage by an exotic organism, whirling disease. Whirling disease, transmitted by a transplanted European fish parasite, can damage a river's rainbow trout population very significantly. It is transmitted in mud or silt. To reduce the transmission of whirling disease, remove all mud from your car, your boat, your boat trailer, and your fishing tackle, so

no little organisms can be transported to the next place you fish. Drain and dry your boat, your cooler, and even your waders. Do not carry fish to another water, alive or dead. And finally, do not accidentally bring any aquatic plants with you (on your motor, on your anchor, on your waders) when you leave the stream. If everyone is informed and acts accordingly, it will make a difference.

FISHING ETIQUETTE

Fishing manners are important to conservation because we are trying to find civil ways to share the things we love in a world with an increasing population. If we want to maintain fly fishing in its traditional form, we need to convince people that we are caring, trustworthy souls who are good to have around.

Longtime fly fishing outfitter Bud Lilly has pointed out that the recent upsurge in the popularity of fly fishing has brought to the sport many peo-

Arguably fly fishing's greatest quarry, the tarpon has been known to melt reels and break rods and men.

ple with no previous outdoor experience. They know how to behave perfectly at a dinner party, but they have not been taught any fishing manners.

I cannot tell you how to behave on every lake or stream. It is more complicated than choosing the right fork, because it depends upon local tradition. On one stream, it may be acceptable for anglers to crowd in shoulder-to-shoulder, while on another stream that behavior will get you in a fight. On one lake, all boats may crowd together over the best spot, while on another there is some unwritten rule about spreading out. In some streams everyone wades, while in other waters everyone tries to fish from the bank and not disturb the water. Because of these variations, you must first determine what the local etiquette requires, and then obey it.

There are some general guidelines, however:
▶Never cast to fish where someone else is fishing to unless you have permission.
▶Stay well back from the bank as you walk along a stream or lake, especially if you see an angler casting to fish. It is very easy to spook fish that another angler just spent half an hour stalking.
▶If you are going to pass behind another fisher and you are not sure he has seen you, let him know so he does not hit you with a back cast, and then remember that experience when you're fishing and someone walks behind *you*.
▶Be pleasant, but if a friendly greeting to another angler is not returned, do not force it; some people are social by nature, and others prefer to fish alone.
▶Be helpful. If you can spare a fly that has been successful that day, you will probably make another angler's day too—but don't push it. If there is any doubt at all of how you should behave, ask.
▶As Izaak Walton said, study to be quiet.

An increasingly important aspect of fly fishing etiquette has to do with access to private water. In the U.S., this has become an issue of growing concern, even a crisis. Many landowners simply do not

Marquetry fishing scene.

want the nuisance of allowing access because they have had bad experiences with other anglers who have littered, left gates open, and otherwise abused the landowner's generosity. Try to follow these simple rules:
▶Always ask permission, and always accept rejection courteously.
▶Never offer to bring the landowner some fish, as if that were a reward for his hospitality.
▶Clean up other people's messes if it seems reasonable to do so.
▶Go out of your way to make the landowner's experience with anglers a very good one.
▶Remember that a landowner who respects fly anglers is more likely to view these private waters as important. A great deal of premier fly fishing water is bordered by private land, and thus landowner conservation is critical.

DESTINATIONS

BY DENNIS BITTON

Most fly fishers begin fishing close to home. But the first time you travel to a distant place to fly fish, you'll be absolutely filled with high hopes of beautiful waters and great fishing. When you return home, you'll have spectacular memories, not just of the big fish you caught, but of mountains, lakes, trees, saltwater flats, big rivers, small creeks, sunsets, first light, mist, and late-night meals. And the more places you visit, the more abundant those memories will be.

There are more extraordinary fly-fishing destinations than most people could visit in a lifetime. So how do you choose where to go?

Most fly fishers are species-motivated. They want to catch a new species, and they will go where they have to go for good odds of hooking up. Some look for trout all over the world. Others do the same with marlin, tuna, or Atlantic salmon.

Then there are the destination addicts, fly fishers who find a magnificent spot and just can't stay away from it. I daydream about the confluence of the Ventuari River and the Orinoco River in southern Venezuela. I have been there twice, and I will go again the very next chance I get.

No matter what place you choose as your vacation spot, you will have a chance to experience local culture (and cuisine), observe new plants and geological formations, and see native animals and aquatic life in a way other travelers seldom do. Fly-fishing destinations are often wilder than normal tourist spots and offer adventures that simply don't exist on the beaten track.

So wherever you go, stop casting every once in awhile and soak up the whole experience. After all, fly fishing is a lot more than just catching fish. It requires a little knowledge of biology, some physical endurance, dexterity of fingers, love of nature, and the heart of a gambler.

NORTHEASTERN UNITED STATES AND CANADA

Historically, more books have been written about fly fishing in the northeastern U.S. than about anywhere else, and with good reason. The main population centers of the country initially were

173

A lone paddler on an Adirondack pond, fishing while sunlight sparkles on the clean water—the perfect way to clear the mind.

and Atlantic salmon, but as time and circumstance reduced the numbers of these fish, they were replaced by brown trout from Europe and eventually a few rainbow trout from the West Coast. A dedicated fly fisher can still find brookies, but they are likely to be tiny—6 inches or less. (Big brookies, up to 7 or 8 pounds, are still available in some of the lakes in eastern Canada). Atlantic salmon also have almost disappeared from the Northeast, but the situation is improving. There are more spawning Atlantic salmon in the Connecticut River and Penobscot River in Maine than in the recent past.

On the coast, northeastern saltwater species have been added to the list of fish favored by fly fishers. Bluefish and striped bass chase baitfish up the coastline every spring and summer as water temperatures rise. Martha's Vineyard is one of the most productive spots in the Northeast to catch blues and stripers. Atlantic salmon still go up New Jersey's remote Miramichi River and spawn in its many tributaries. Considered by many to be the best fish

located near the Eastern seaboard, and most early fly fishers were looking for trout, so they traveled to the Northeast. Names of streams and mountain ranges have become ingrained in the minds of fly fishers everywhere: Beaverkill, Neversink, Willowemoc, Delaware, Connecticut, Battenkill, Penobscot, and Susquehanna; and the Catskills, Adirondacks, Broadheads, Alleghenies, and Poconos. It is still good trout country. Private fishing clubs own some of the best streamside lands, and most have a history of involvement in conservation activities to improve local fishing habitat.

Initially, interest centered on native brook trout

in the world to take on a fly rod, the Atlantic salmon continues to attract fly fishers from all over the world. Canada has also helped by allowing commercial fishing fleets to be bought out by the Atlantic Salmon Federation and others.

My introduction to the area came at forty years old, when I went to Vermont to visit the American Museum of Fly Fishing. My biggest surprise was the size of these famous streams—all of them were much smaller than I had imagined. What would be called a "creek" in the Rocky Mountains was a "river" in the Northeast. And the trees had been clear-cut four times. But the fly fishers I talked to and fished with (near Roscoe, New York, and Manchester, Vermont) were as avid as my friends out West—and, I had to admit, most of them were better fly fishers than I was. They had spent a lot of time on small streams. By contrast, I had been occupied with dumb trout in big rivers with relatively little pressure. That admission was (and is) embarrassing, but it is impossible to walk away from the facts. Fly fishers from the Northeast, visiting me in Idaho, have proven it time after time.

GREAT LAKES AREA AND NORTHERN CANADA

Each of the eight states that touch any portion of the five Great Lakes has good fishing. So does Canada's Ontario province to the north, which hovers like a protecting mantle over the Great Lakes. The western half of Ontario has hundreds of lakes, and they continue up through Manitoba and Saskatchewan provinces, and throughout the Northwest Territories. Fly fishers frequenting these northernmost areas can expect to see northern pike and some other big fish: brook trout (7 pounds), lake trout (30 pounds) and Arctic char (15 pounds).

As good as the fishing is up there, however, keep in mind that the further north the destination, the shorter the summer fishing season. In the States, the native fish are brook trout, northern pike, largemouth, and smallmouth bass, and of course lake trout in the Great Lakes. Today steelhead and salmon fisheries exist on most tributaries of the Great Lakes. Friends in Michigan have shown me photographs of a fly-hooked steelhead more than 2 feet long thrashing around in a spawning stream just 15 feet wide. It's enough to make a fly fisher nervous, but

fly fishers from the Great Lakes region have always been quite dedicated. They fish through the winter if they can, and some streams are open for trout (rainbows, browns, and a few brookies) and steelhead all year long.

Some of the most famous fisheries are in the Lower Peninsula of Michigan. Rivers like the Au Sable, Manistee, and Pere Marquette are near towns mentioned in fly-fishing books for decades: Grayling, Roscommon, Traverse City, Wellston, and Baldwin. Fly fishers around the Great Lakes like to fish for big brown trout on summer evenings. One fly fishers meeting I was attending broke up about 10 P.M. so that everyone could start fishing the big 2- and 3-inch yellow mayfly called the Hexagenia—at midnight.

In the U.P., as local residents refer to Michigan's Upper Peninsula on the northern side of Lake Michigan, anglers can fish the Two Hearted River, featured in some early Ernest Hemingway short stories, and the Escanaba River, among many others. Near the town of Escanaba, I once hooked and landed a big chinook (also called a king salmon), at the base of a

The modern fly fisher has all points on the compass as places to visit and pursue world class fly fishing opportunities.

dam where the fish were looking for a passage to Alaska. But the U.P.'s greatest fly-fishing treasure has to be Robert Traver, lover of secluded brook trout ponds and author of such fly fishing classics as *Trout Magic* and *Trout Madness*.

Wisconsin and Minnesota offer their own special waters, with muskie, pike, and bass, as well as many miles of spring creeks loaded with trout. Smallmouth bass, pike, and muskie are favorites on the St. Croix River, a national scenic waterway that is part of the border between Minnesota and Wisconsin. Chequamegon Bay of southern Lake Superior has some of the best trophy smallmouth fishing in the U.S., with local guides who understand fly fishers and support catch-and-release fishing. Also on the south shore of Lake Superior is the famous Brule River, where five U.S. presidents have fly fished and Calvin Coolidge set up the summer White House in 1928. The Wolf River in central Wisconsin is just like a western freestone trout fishery (a freestone fishery is one that is rock-lined, as opposed to lined with vegetation). For warmwater fly anglers, the lower Wisconsin River runs free for 120 miles, with sand bars, broad vistas and a variety of pike, bass, cisco, and even gar that can be readily taken on flies.

SOUTHERN STATES (EXCEPT FLORIDA)

Bass is the name of the game in many of the southern states. Largemouth and smallmouth are the most popular species, but dozens of other species are readily available to the dedicated fly fisher. Some bluegill reach up to 2 pounds (most notably in Texas and Alabama) and a trophy bluegill can put quite a bend in a fly rod. Landlocked striped bass have taken hold in many southern reservoirs. They have produced a whole new sport—and a reason to buy 8-, 9- or 10-weight rods for freshwater fish. Stripers weighing in at 20 pounds or more are being taken fairly regularly in Arkansas, Alabama, Kentucky, Tennessee, and Georgia during the winter months.

It always pays to investigate what the fishing is going to be like when you go someplace new so you can take the right fly patterns. I once was invited by a friend to fish the Tennessee River in Alabama. I asked him if the water would be clear. He assured me that it would. Suspicious, I asked him, "If I took a weighted nymph, dropped it over the edge of the boat, and let it sink 6 feet, would I be able to see it?" To which he replied, "Well, its not *that* clear."

We had great fun on that southern trip. My friend also introduced me to "stump knockers," "punkin" seeds, and bream (pronounced "brim," like on a baseball cap). All were new territory and new species for me, and I had a lesson in true selective feeding as I watched a little bluegill

High mountain ponds from Vermont to California provide spectacular opportunities.

pick the legs off a floating crane fly, one by one, delicious appetizers before the small-mouthed critter finally got to suck in the insect's body as the main course.

As part of the same visit, a friend from Houston introduced me to personal flotation devices on a sportfishing pond, located on a huge commercial catfish farm just outside of Galveston. I also found out that many southern states have truly wild strains of trout. People fish for trout in south central Texas, in the Blue Ridge Mountains National Park east of Knoxville, Tennessee, and in the mountains of the Carolinas. The White River in northern Arkansas has some tremendously large brown trout, some more than 20 pounds. The record brown trout—40 pounds, 4 ounces—was caught in the Little Red River in Arkansas.

A sight to make any salt water fly fisherman's mouth water: The tantalizing opportunities that appear from the casting platform of a flats boat.

Smallmouth bass, native to tributaries of the great Mississippi, are found in many places in the South. These fish, sometimes called bronzebacks because of their overall coloration, are very sporting in still water and in streams, just as difficult and as much fun to catch as trout. Lefty Kreh has repeatedly gone on record as saying that if he could fish for just one species of freshwater fish for the rest of his days, he would pick the glorious bronzeback. And he would not be lonely; quite a few other people feel the same way. Tim Holschlag, founder of the Smallmouth Bass Alliance, openly declares that trout simply do not have the fight or endurance of smallmouth bass.

FLORIDA

What can you say about Florida other than that it is fantastic? Managing the growth of human population is the state's biggest problem. Many fly fishers retiring from work in a northern state move to a southern state for year round fishing for a multitude of warmwater species. Fly fishing is part of their retirement plan. But a newly relocated fly-fishing retiree's main concern is: "What should I fish for today?" Popular species with fly fishers are bonefish, sailfish, tarpon, permit, redfish, snook, striped bass, certain sharks, and spotted sea trout. It's a tough choice, because there are usually two or more species to pursue every month of the year—and some months there are considerably more (see the Monthly Calendar section below). Several organizations deserve credit for bringing the nearly endangered redfish back as a sportfish: especially the Florida Sportsmen Association and the Gulf Coast Association. Conservationists have done a good job bringing back other species as well: bluefish and striped bass have been brought back from near extinction caused by commercial fisheries and other environmental hazards. But those are just three of the dozens of fish species available to the fly fisher. The battle over conservation of habitats will go on forever, but there are plenty of freshwater species for

THE EPICUREAN FISHER: AMERICAN TROPICS

From the southern U.S. through Central America, fly fishers in search of the good life can find extraordinary tropical options. Some fly anglers enjoy the "barefoot elegance" of a luxury resort like the Cheeca Lodge in the Florida Keys. Slouching into a lawn chair on the veranda to quaff a frosty rumrunner seems a justifiable reward. The vivid sunset brings on an equally intense hunger, but a first course of savory conch fritters will stave starvation—and then the platter of stone crab claws, with mustard sour cream sauce, arrives from the award-winning kitchen.

On Little Palm Island, also in the Keys and accessible only by water, alert anglers might witness small but undaunted Key deer swimming the channel from Big Pine Key to feast on the carefully tended hibiscus bushes nurtured by the Little Palm staff. Fly-fishing guests, however, will likely prefer the smoked-salmon parfait with Belgian endive and green apple or the lobster soup, finished off with the coconut cream-filled chocolate ravioli with praline sauce.

Such icons of hospitality tend to pamper bone-weary anglers, whether tired from the actual stalking of fish or merely frustrated by piscine refusals. Soft towels can refresh a sun-fried attitude. A Yucatan hideaway named Espiritu Santo Lodge offers one cabana with a bathroom large enough to rinse off fly rods in the shower while leaving them fully strung up. Add to this

Florida Keys

refinement the freshly made pastry called pastel nuez, a rich nut-flavored torte, and the disdain with which the bonefish treated your perfectly cast fly fades with the twilight.

Not every tropical destination offers opulent quarters, but epicurean fly fishers might still register surprise at the resourcefulness of kitchen staff in remote camps—for instance, the wonder of pizza-from-scratch—three cheesy, fennel-redolent varieties served for lunch on private Cannon Island in isolated Brus lagoon in Honduras. With blue morpho butterflies floating silently through a jungle of a hundred tints of green, even a frustrating morning where every tarpon came unbuttoned on its third jump elevates from disappointment to exciting fish story.

Permit have a reputation for instilling humility in anglers who try to fool them into biting a fly, and those off the Bay Islands of Honduras hold up their end. As one wades the flats of Guanaja all day, the chase tests resolve and saps magnums of energy. Such circumstances naturally call for a draft of Port Royal, the good local brew. Sip it out on the deck while a scarlet macaw squawks from surrounding jungle. Morning at Bayman Bay Club brings a made-to-order omelet, warm-from-the-oven rolls and smoky Honduran coffee strong enough to reset any angler's button.

—Sandy Rodgers

fly fishers in Florida, too, with bass and bluegill in the trophy classes.

The Everglades and Florida's West Coast provide different opportunities for the fly fisher. South America's peacock bass have been introduced into the canals around Miami and are doing quite well. Every fly fisher traveling to Florida on business should schedule a few off days and pack appropriate equipment and fly patterns—or enough money to buy them from local fly fishing or general fishing shops. They are all over the state, and most of them provide or refer customers to fishing guides, boat ramps, and bridges.

ALASKA

Doomsayers have been predicting the end of fly fishing in Alaska for decades. "Too many people," they say. "It's ruined. Too many lodges, too many planes, too many anglers. Almost had to stand in line last time I went."

Not true, folks. Today hundreds of lodges operate in Alaska, most of them accommodating fly fishers very well. Some of these lodges have been at it a long time, and many of their customers are repeat business. Customers and outfitter-guides often become like family, and fly fishers will come back time after time for the great fishing, usually in one of these three places: the towns of Bethel or Dilingham, or the general area of Bristol Bay, the most southern area mentioned. But fishing is also quite good in and around the capital city, Anchorage.

The Wood River Lakes near Dillingham feed a number of productive streams. Illiama Lake and the Copper River in the Bristol Bay area are favorites of many.

Bethel is the most northerly of the three popular areas mentioned. Consequently, it has a shorter summer, and so timing is everything. A lot of the land west of Bethel is dedicated to wildlife preserves so fly fishers often enjoy the company of wild animals.

For some visitors, the price of an Alaskan trip is so high that they have to save money for years; others go back exactly the same week of the same month, year after year. There are still some budget-minded options, however. A little investigative research, a few long-distance phone calls, or a few

Lake Kagoti in Alaska: Fly-in fishing can bring anglers to lodges with their own private fleet of boats to provide the fishing experience of a lifetime.

King Salmon Lodge, Alaska: Lodges in the bush don't necessary mean roughing it. Gourmet meals, luxurious rooms, and, of course, great fishing, are offered—for a price.

Fly fishing in Alaska serves up a wide range of culinary delights, and most lodges take well-warranted pride in their fresh baked goods and dishes created from local game.

Streamside, many guides prepare a shore lunch to bolster their anglers' strength. Upon catching a salmon right from the sea, the guide filets it, leaving the skin on. Out of his back-pack cook kit comes the grate, and it goes over the coals of the fire he has built. He then places the filets skin side down onto the grate and sprinkles lemon pepper on the other side, perhaps, or dabs of butter and lemon juice. He cooks the filets until the skin peels easily from the flesh, and then flips the seasoned side down. He seasons the newly peeled side and finishes cooking the filets just until they flake. If the waters of the day contain grayling, he might place a whole fish or two right into the coals to roast, a cooking method possible due to these fish's thick, tough scales. Meanwhile, the guide may have sliced home-fried potatoes and crisped them in a skillet, or heated a can of corn from his backpack. When fishing near a shady area where ferns grow, the guide can pluck fiddle-heads and sauté them for a rustic version of Brussels sprouts beside the water. Fresh fruit may appear from the guide's pack, or mounds of freshly picked blackberries or huckleber-ries might provide the dessert.

—Sandy Rodgers

hours on the World Wide Web, and you can custom-pick your trip to Alaska. Many lodges are listed on the Internet; start with the single word, 'Alaska,' to take you through a simple search.

It's worth it. Pike, char, rainbow trout, and grayling flourish, in addition to steelhead and various species of Pacific salmon. For obvious reasons, Alaska is not a winter alternative, but for every month they are open, each lodge knows which species will be present and on the fly.

ROCKY MOUNTAINS

Wide-open spaces and big, aggressive trout are the goal of most fly fishers who travel to the eight Rocky Mountain states and their neighbors, where most streams depend on winter snow for summer water.

Some waters are open all year, and any day in December, January, or February with a little sunshine and air temperatures in the forties will see fly fishers casting for dimpling trout with Snow Fly patterns, Griffith Gnats, various midges, and new inventions. People who live closest to the trout streams have a distinct advantage.

Each state boasts some well-known streams. Montana has the Bighorn, Big Hole, Yellowstone, Madison, Missouri, Clark, and Gallatin rivers. Idaho is home to Silver Creek, Henry's Fork, Boise River, the south fork of the Snake, the main Snake River, and the Salmon River. Wyoming's great waters include the Snake, Green Wind, and Bighorn rivers. In Wyoming's southeastern corner, the North Platte has the famous "Miracle Mile" between two reser-

The Alaskan experience offers fly-in trips to pursue several species of salmon, trout, and grayling. It is not unheard of for anglers to fish until their arms ache from catching large fish, not from just empty casting.

The mountains of the American West provide fly fishers with room to ramble from stream to river to lake in search of willing trout of paintbox hues. The acoustics of waterfalls and riffles may soothe jangled nerve endings, but it remains for the lodges and outfitters to keep an angler's physical motors stoked and contented.

Tucked into the Bitterroot-Selway mountain range, which runs between Montana and Idaho, Bear Creek Lodge rewards fly-fishing guests with its namesake stream at their doorstep. Fish right there, raft with a guide in the nearby Bitterroot River, or try out the Big Hole or Clark Fork a short drive away.

Blackbird's Lodge on the Bitterroot River offers guests rooms with poster beds looking over a lush English tea garden. An English slate pool table, a 1,000-foot redwood deck and barbecue area offer diversions for the fly angler fresh from the river.

"Let's go camping" may suggest franks and beans to some. The discriminating fly fisher, however, prefers more stylish dining at the end of the trail. When urban burnout strikes, a getaway horseback trip into Montana's Bob Marshall Wilderness can both mend the spirit and nourish the body. With pack mules to carry large wall tents, anglers ride from a headquarters lodge in Swan Valley over dusty trails in needle-padded forests to what outfitters call the "Shaw Creek Sheraton." The camp is complete with privy tent, shower, and heat in the sleep tents. Campers doze on cots with mattress pads and wake up to the sounds of horse bells and the smell of pine and spruce.

Savor crispy trout and cowboy coffee for breakfast, and then ride out past cold, clear pools and cascading waterfalls to fish alpine lakes and feeder streams of the South Fork of the Flathead River. Longer trips move onto the South Fork and, if time is available, to ride to the top of the Chinese Wall, an escarpment of the Continental Divide twelve miles long and 1,000 feet high. Fish below Scar Face Mountain, ride to the Ice Caves, or see the Flathead Alps.

Catch too many cutthroat trout or Dolly Varden on dry flies, or watch mountain goats on the crags as the trail horse moseys back to camp. From sheepherder stoves, simple contraptions built of two sheet-metal boxes with a stove pipe, come unmistakable aromas of roast beef.

The North Umpqua River in Oregon has long held a special place in the minds of fly anglers for its natural beauty, and on its banks, the Steamboat Inn furnishes pine-paneled streamside cabins. River suites boast fireplaces and soaking tubs overlooking the river. During the summer-run steelhead season, the inn closes at dusk to all but guests and those who have made dinner reservations. At this time, the staff devotes itself completely to guests at their Fisherman's Dinner, a special event where epicures can gather in the library to sip an aperitif and recap the fishing day while sampling hors d'oeuvres. Special events such as winemaker's dinners also take place regularly, featuring samplings from such Oregon vineyards as Domain Drouhin Oregon and Willakenzie Estate.

—Sandy Rodgers

voirs. Utah's best spots are the Green River, Provo River, and the huge Lake Powell reservoir behind Glen Canyon Dam in the southeastern part of the state. The reservoir is home to numerous species, including striped bass.

Colorado abounds with trout streams. The Roaring Fork and its well-known feeder stream, the Frying Pan, are near Aspen in the central part of the state. The Gunnison River, and the town by the same name, are a little southwest of that. The Delores River is an excellent trout stream in the southwestern part of the state; the South Platte runs right through Denver, flows north, and eventually exits in the state's northeastern corner. Headwaters of the North Platte are in the northwestern corner of Colorado. The Colorado River, which forms in north-central Colorado, has some two dozen feeder streams added to its flow before it exits the western part of the state near Grand Junction.

The most famous trout stream in New Mexico is the San Juan, in the northeast corner of the state. This is a so-called tailwater fishery, with the flow coming from a bottom discharge dam. The best trout-producing stream in Arizona is the Colorado River itself, just downstream from the massive Glen Canyon Dam and upstream from the Grand Canyon. Arizona also has lots of warmwater sport fisheries in all parts of the state and more trout fishing in its high mountains. Nevada boasts the Truckee and Humboldt rivers as well as Pyramid Lake on an Indian Reservation north of Reno. Pyramid Lake harbors the Lahontan cutthroat, which years ago used to

Yellowstone River: The upper Wyoming section of the river is a popular fly fishing destination, holding an abundance of gaudily-colored, easy-to-catch native cutthroat trout.

The Madison River of Montana is world-renowned for its rainbows and browns.

A fly fisher is surrounded by the brilliant red-backed sockeye salmon pooling prior to upstream spawning movement.

reach 20 to 30 pounds. Now many residents of San Francisco spend a lot of weekends in Reno—fishing, not gambling.

NORTHWESTERN U.S. AND CANADA

One big draw in Washington, Oregon, British Columbia (B.C.), and, to a degree, Idaho, is steelhead. These ocean-roaming rainbows have excited the human imagination for over 150 years. The Columbia River drainage in the States and the Fraser River drainage in southern B.C., have dozens of feeder streams to accommodate spawners. The Babine and the Dean, further up the coastline of B.C. have good runs of Pacific salmon and steelhead. Fly fishing for steelhead and five species of Pacific

salmon is big business in the Northwest. There are many fishing lodges, guides, and bush-plane pilot services. Some coastal streams have bigger runs of sea-run cutthroat than they did just a few years ago. That is because badly needed conservation efforts were put into place, which worked. It is not uncommon to catch a spawning cutthroat that will go 21 to 22 inches and weigh 3½ pounds. Any fly pattern that has red, orange, or rust colors in it will attract a salt-fresh cutt.

The Yakima River in Washington and the Deschutes River in central Oregon are good trout streams. For that matter, many streams on the east side of the Cascade Mountains in Oregon have pretty good trout fishing. The biggest current problem for fisheries in the Northwest is rapidly declining popula-

Green River, Oregon. A popular way to fish western rivers is the float boat.

tions of steelhead and most species of salmon. Coho and chinook are approaching endangered levels, a situation serious enough that the governement of British Columbia has banned all fishing for coho.

Saltwater fly fishing is on the increase in the Pacific Northwest. Black rock bass can be caught from the rocky shorelines of northern California, Oregon, and Washington. They are willing takers of the fly and strong fighters. Ling cod, barred sand perch, and starry flounder are also being added to the fly fishers' list of fish species being caught.

BAHAMAS

A trip to the Bahamas is the stuff of dreams. Islands in the sea, blue sky that lasts forever, sunning, swimming, snorkeling, wonderful exotic meals, tropical drinks garnished with little paper umbrellas—and some terrific fly fishing. Tarpon, bonefish, and big permit (more than 20 pounds) are the main draws for fly fishers. Billfish, tuna, and barracuda have their fans as well. Andros Island, the largest and one of the southernmost of the Bahamas, is considered by many fly fishers to be the best place in the world for bonefish. There are plenty of fish, plenty of flats, and plenty of local residents working as guides for well-established lodges. Trophy-sized permit patrol the tide flats around all the islands, as do many other species.

MEXICO

Mexico's famous resort cities—Acapulco, Cancún, and Cabo San Lucas—have long been known as great fishing hangouts. Deluxe resorts, good airline connections, the availability of dozens of saltwater gamefish species, exotic foods from sidewalk cafes, and low prices have made Mexico a saltwater fishing heaven for decades. Some things have changed over the last fifty years—Mexico is no longer as inexpensive as it used to be, especially at the showy resorts—but the country is still cheaper and nearer to the U.S. than any other exotic destination, and backroad communities are still economical options for housing and meals. If your goal is to live cheap and fish hard, a budget-style Mexican vacation may be just what you're looking for.

Back in the days when Zane Grey and John Steinbeck frequented Baja California and mainland Mexico, many captains of charter boats, and even some guides in the smaller 16, 18, or 20-foot "pan-gas," wouldn't allow a fly rod in their boat. Today even the most tradition-bound bluewater charter captains recognize that catch-and-release practices improve their odds of keeping the family business alive; in some cases, the legacy stretches back over a hundred years.

Panga guides were the first to capitalize on fly fishers. Any day a Mexican guide doesn't have a sport-fishing client in his boat, he must turn to commercial fishing, so panga guides keep their prices reasonable. Fly fishers respond predictably. Friendships are formed, and repeat business becomes common. If a fly fisher can get six or eight dorado a day, the guide will probably take home one or two fish, the fly fisher most likely will take one back to the hotel and have it grilled (with a lime juice and *cerveza* chaser), and all the other fish will go back to the sea.

Schools of small to midsize tarpon offer exciting and challenging game to the fly fisher. More mature tarpon approaching 100 pounds provide perhaps fly fishing's greatest quarry, with powerful runs and acrobatic display.

Access in Mexico is also better now. There are more saltwater destination cities, such as Mazatlan, Puerto Vallarta, Manzanillo, and several smaller cities on the west coast of the mainland. The improved road down through Baja California, along with a few new airports, has generated more commercial campgrounds, motels, and hotels in Baja's east coast cities such as Loreto, La Paz, and Buena Vista. Cabo San Lucas continues to draw big crowds to the southern tip of the peninsula. Cabo boasts a new fly shop with specially designed power boats to accommodate fly fishers, including a wraparound knee brace that helps landlubbers keep their balance while they cast.

In addition, there is good freshwater bass fishing in northern Mexico that wasn't there fifty years ago. Reservoirs built to serve growing human populations in need of electricity and drinking water now host a plentiful supply of big smallmouth and largemouth transplants. Anglers from California, Arizona, New Mexico, and Texas enjoy south-of-the-border trips often, while those from the frozen northland usually come during the winter for bass and the warm sun.

The current hot spot for bass in northern Mexico is near the town of Los Mochis, in the state of Sinola, a city with enough lodgings to accommodate the growing number of visitors. There also are U.S. own-

ers to provide good input on what "Norte Americanos" like and do not like in a fishing lodge. Just as an example, Texans report that the fried chicken and barbecued beef are excellent, so we know that the border states' expressed needs have been met.

Another area of Mexico very popular with fly fishers is around the city of Cancún on the northeast tip of the Yucatan Peninsula. Isla de Mujeres and Isla de Cozumel are nearby, with decades of service to fly fishers from all over the world. Offering a choice of travel plans ranging from the budget to the spectacular, the Yucatan is best in winter, though it's pretty good all year long.

CENTRAL AMERICA

From Cancún, the Mexican coastline runs south to the small, English-speaking country of Belize and its offshore Turneffe Islands. Bonefish are the initial attraction in this part of the globe, but there are tarpon and permit, too, making the traditional saltwater Grand Slam an attainable goal. Further south, Guatemala, Nicaragua, Honduras, El Salvador, Costa Rica, and Panama all have warmwater and saltwater fish. Costa Rica is the most publicized, with most of the attention going to marlin and sailfish off the Pacific coast. The extreme northeast corner of Costa Rica, where the Colorado River forms the boundary with Nicaragua, is one of the world's best locations for big snook and tarpon. Some lodges have been open for half a century, and fly fishers have been courted for a couple of decades now. If you like to catch big saltwater species with a fly rod, Central America is one place you should investigate.

Miami International Airport has connecting flights every day to each of these palm-studded countries. A little research on the Internet or in back issues of various fishing publications should

The wily permit, another flats reward.

Moody mangroves line miles of virgin flats on the Turneffe Islands off the coast of Belize. They are rich in the small fish and crustaceans that draw bonefish, permit, and tarpon.

reveal phone numbers to call for detailed information and lodge literature. Panama and Nicaragua are currently the budding fly fishing destinations in the region. Less developed and less known than some of the lodges, resorts, and public campgrounds in Costa Rica and Belize, they offer new frontiers for the experienced traveling fly fisher. Those rabid individuals looking for world records on a fly rod often fish all of Central America. It is an area of the world in which good advance planning will make a huge difference. Once you get there, an easygoing attitude will help you enjoy a culture where punctuality is not a priority.

SOUTH AMERICA

Of the dozen countries in South America, only a few have reputations for fishing, yet all have potential for the fly fisher who likes adventure. Most anglers have heard of the rainbow and brown trout fishing in southern Argentina and Chile, in the area of Patagonia. W. H. Hudson wrote about it a century ago, Joe Brooks a half-century ago, and dozens of other experts have offered their observations during the last several decades.

Winter in North America is summer in South America, and so thousands of anglers go south every winter to specific lodges or specific streams to fly fish for trout. Some say the experience is like fishing the western states of the U.S. forty or fifty years ago. That's nice, but it gets better than that. Two towns next to the international airport on Venezuela's northern shore are virtual Shangri-las for marlin and bonefish: Maiquetia is just a short taxi ride west from the airport, and a few miles east of the airport is La Guaira, another town stocked for sport fishing. The well-publicized Los Roques Islands are just a short boat ride north from either town. Several sportfishing operations are represented in Los Roques, now a national park, serving people from around the world, all year long. Inland, Venezuela boasts lots of fishing lodges for peacock bass and payara (a saber-toothed–looking critter). These stops range from

If you venture to New Zealand to fish the legendary waters of Lake Taupo or to pursue rainbows in the Tongariro River, consider a stop at Auckland's Empire Hotel on the way. Wild rainbow trout and brown trout average 4 pounds in the Taupo system, and hauling in such over-sized fish earns big appetites and deep sleep. Tongariro Lodge also provides fly fishers a chance to recover while comparing yarns over an evening meal of New Zealand game, before retiring to a private chalet. The high-tech angler can schedule a helicopter trip over scenic volcanic craters and lakes.

The Waikato River flows from Lake Taupo, which was formed in an age-old caldera of collapsed volcanoes. Tucked under majestic trees on the riverbank and surrounded by acres of lawns and gardens, Huka Lodge features gourmet dining that employs the freshest and best of New Zealand produce. Blazing log fires soothe, while the more energetic can partake of tennis, the heated spa, golf, shooting, riding, and rafting. Founded as a fishing resort in the 1920s, Huka Lodge is known for its solitude and idyllic setting within Wairakei Park nature reserve.

Gourmet fly fishers who venture back west to Chile or Argentina might well encounter the local tradition of streamside cooking called the "asado." The name refers to the grilling of meat—often lamb, goat, beef, sausages, and chicken. Around midday the fishing guide builds a fire, removes a grate from his kit, pokes stakes into the ground, and then puts the pieces of meat on the grill. On even an ordinary day of fishing, the guide unpacks salads, *empanadas*, and aji salsa, a spicy hot sauce made of aji chili peppers. He uncorks wine, whether *tinto*, the local red, or *vino blanco*, the white. While an asado always counts as an occasion, some events call for more celebration than do others. On special days with larger groups, a whole pig will be roasted, with music and gaiety and much passing around of the bota bag, and streaming of the *tinto* into the mouths of thirsty anglers, their casting arms outstretched.

—Sandy Rodgers

The majestic peaks of the Andes provides a dramatic backdrop for anglers in Argentina.

tent-sheltered bush camps to full-service lodges with amenities such as daily laundry service, gourmet chefs, and private commuter planes or private boats.

Colombia and Peru have had bad press for years, but adventurous fly fishers have been visiting trout, warmwater, and saltwater lodges there regularly for more than twenty-five years—and they usually want to go back. Both countries have seashores, high mountains, and a piece of the greater Amazon basin, so you can plan your dream trip by location or by fish species.

Ecuador, Bolivia, Paraguay, and Uruguay are seldom mentioned in South American fishing articles. All are relatively small countries with limited developed facilities catering to fly fishers, but there are a variety of fly-gobbling fish species in each country. Trout live in Ecuador's and Bolivia's high mountains and lakes; some lodges there cater to hunters as well

as anglers. Weeklong trips can be planned with time for dove or white-crowned pigeon hunting and trout or warmwater fly fishing.

Some say bringing in a dorado from one of Paraguay's large freshwater rivers is like taking a small tarpon with nasty teeth. This freshwater dorado is not the same fish as the saltwater version prevalent off Mexico's coastlines, which is also called a dolphin fish or mahi mahi. The freshwater dorado of South America is found in every stream that drains into the Rio Plate, and that includes parts of five different nations. Sometimes this fish is referred to as a golden dorado, because in Spanish the word "dorado" means golden. It's kind of like saying "pizza pie."

BRITISH ISLES AND EUROPE

England, Scotland, Ireland, Wales, Norway, Sweden, Denmark, and all other continental European coun-

The rugged Okyel River is among the justly famed Scottish waters known for Atlantic salmon fishing.

In England's Hampshire County runs the historic River Test. Famed for its scenic beauty as well as its famous fishing, it is regarded as holy water by many fly anglers, for these banks saw the footprints of Walton and Cotton. Its clear chalk-stream character presents a challenge to the stealthiest angler, with dry-fly-only sections to satisfy the purist at heart. Anglers can stay at a seventeenth-century manor house, recap the day's fishing at a coat-and-tie supper, and shoot clay pigeons when not busy casting for trout.

Pubs such as the Fox in the Test River Valley also offer clay-pigeon shooting on selected days of the week, or anglers can slip away to hear live music from the best Celtic rock groups at the Air Balloon, another local pub. When weariness strikes, sip bitters by a real log fire at the Happy Cheese Inn and taste traditional English food such as bubble and squeak. Anglers with an eye for architecture will notice the thatched, one-and-a-half story cottages, often referred to as "bun cottages." Here in Jane Austen country, with the River Itchen nearby, the cottages appear to have sprouted from the countryside, with their eyebrows of thatch over half-dormer windows and rounded outlines that curve down to half-hipped ends.

The River Wye, considered the best salmon river south of Scotland, has its source on Plynlimon, which means "five peaks," a 1,600-foot mountain in Central Wales that also gives rise to the Severn and the Rheidol. The upper reaches of the Wye, as well as its feeder streams, offer good trout fishing, while below, the river winds through farming country into Hereford and back, lending its many elbows to charming towns and villages, until the mouth of the Wye spills into Severn Estuary, which runs along the border of southeastern England and Wales. In the Welsh village of Trelleck, anglers can enjoy swapping fish tales at the Lion Inn, completed in 1580.

The border country of Scotland also contains a wealth of fly fishing history to further enhance any angling excursion. Fly fishers can lodge in an Edwardian country house at Walkerburn in the Tweed River Valley while fishing for sea trout, browns, and rainbow trout. A short way down the road stands Melrose Abbey, rumored to be the burial place of Robert the Bruce's heart. Nearby lies Tranquair, Scotland's oldest inhabited house, which dates back well over a thousand years.

Another of Scotland's infamous salmon rivers, the River Spey, has gained a reputation for requiring patience and energy among the anglers who try its waters. One of its beats, the four-rod Upper Easter Elchies Beat, approximately one mile long, flows conveniently through the backyard of the Scotch whiskey distillery that owns it. Fly rodders can lean back at the Craigellachie Hotel in the evening, look out over the blooming gorse and rhododendron of springtime, and lift a dram of smooth malt whiskey in tribute to *Salmo salar*, which is the Latin term for Atlantic salmon.

—Sandy Rodgers

The River Itchen in England.

tries have maintained private fly-fishing waters for centuries, and public waters are almost nonexistent. Nonetheless, England should be on every serious fly fisher's list as a destination fishing trip. Modern tools, techniques, and writing about fly fishing started there. Though trout fishing is a reserved privilege for members of private clubs or guests at fishing lodges, it is accessible—and completely dreamlike. There are plenty of lodges on "private" waters where you can fish these old and noble waters. Many who have fished there say the ghosts of Walton, the Dame, and Skues are all around them. Enlarging the circle to include all of Great Britain, there are Scotland, Wales, and Ireland for trout and Atlantic salmon.

The Aberdeenshire Dee River in Scotland has been a mecca for Atlantic salmon fishermen for many years. Steve Raymond, in his 1998 book *Rivers of the Heart*, talked about using a long two-handled spey rod on the "storied river."

Fly fishing in continental Europe is also popular. The rules regarding who can fish for what and when vary from country to country, but almost all fly fishing is done on private waters. Guests are assigned "beats," quarter-mile (or 300-yard) stretches of riverbank to which they have to restrict themselves for the day or half-day. Strange as it sounds, most who have tried it admit it is more enjoyable than they might have expected.

Atlantic salmon fishing in Norway and Sweden probably attracts the most U.S. anglers because the trout there are so huge. All countries in Europe have beautiful trout enclaves, but if you plan on going to Spain, Portugal, France, or Austria, do your research. Many of those countries have beautiful waters that, like England, are private. But also like England, they have private fishing lodges that can be discovered very easily by using the Internet.

NEW ZEALAND AND AUSTRALIA

Fishing New Zealand and Australia has been popular for many years. For fly fishers, the appeal has been big trout, usually rainbows or browns, in clear waters on remote streams with sharp-eyed guides. Trout are not native to either country, but officers in the Royal British Army saw to it that European browns filled that void, and an enterprising resident of the U.S. later brought in rainbows. I had a chance to fish in the northwestern part of New Zealand's South Island a few years ago and was intrigued by the remoteness and solitude of the location.

Trout fishing "down under" is largely a summer affair, which translates to a dead-of-winter getaway for fly fishers living well north of the equator. November through February are the safest bets, but adding a month on either end provides a few oppor-

Signposts in New Zealand point the way to a variety of back country fly-fishing experiences.

tunities that are not otherwise available. New Zealand's South Island, with a population of just one million (60 percent of whom live in the largest town), has the greatest concentration of trout and a

Ahuriri River, New Zealand. Known for its enormous rainbow trout and stunning scenery, New Zealand has become a popular destination for serious fly fishermen.

large number of fishing lodges to accommodate anglers. Some of the lodges are rustic; most are geared specifically to fly fishers. A few high end—and high-priced—lodges have private fisheries, and guests are well rewarded with service and scenery for the money they spend to stay there.

Saltwater species are gaining more attention from fly fishers in Australia and New Zealand. Big billfish have been a draw here for generations. The number of fish species off Australia's west and northwest coasts is phenomenal and include yellowtail tuna, swordfish, yahoo, and even 1,000-pound black marlin. While a few of these saltwater species are available in just certain months of the year, others are around all year long. Barramunda, for example, is a colorful, exotic lungfish that inhabits coastal streams in Australia.

Like bird-watchers, fly fishing species-hunters like to build lists of species they've encountered—or rather, caught. Australia and New Zealand are great places to catch species not found anywhere else in the world. Each country has its own commercial airline, both of which service major airports around the world. No matter where you live, you are not far from the chance to take one of the longest airline flights in all of fly fishing. Plan on sixteen hours in the air once you leave the West Coast of the U.S. Many flights stop in Hawaii and/or Tahiti on the way; some spouses (with children) prefer to deplane there for a week while their significant other is fishing in Australia or New Zealand.

BEYOND "WAY OUT THERE"

Russia is one of the current hot spots for fly fishing. Most trips are directed by Americans to streams in extreme eastern Russia, where anglers fish for species that are more or less (sometimes exactly) like the Pacific salmon and steelhead species that spawn in Alaskan streams. The Russian versions, however, routinely weigh more than 20 pounds and have been known to reach 50 pounds. The first Americans went some time ago, and those early visitors came back with fantastic tales that got everyone excited. A lot of quick Russian-U.S. business contacts were made, but some of the next series of trips bombed. Some trips got stranded at airports. Some were rained out completely, day after day, with no way out from the camp. Sometimes it was the fault of the organizer, sometimes it was the fault of the Russian contact, sometimes mere bureaucracy got in the way and anglers showed up at destinations that had neither fish nor guides nor lodging. (Most visitors went fishing anyway.) All of which illustrates one important point about booking a fishing trip to Russia: Use a reputable outfitter, travel firm, or fly shop owner. Call more than one firm, and ask for references from anglers who have gone to Russia. Fly fishing in Russia is a growth sport and industry, but beware of one last dreary detail: It ain't cheap. But the potential is boundless.

There's an old saying that "anywhere the British army went [during their colonization period] they found brown trout." The origin is that the officers were accustomed to fishing for brown trout at home, and they wanted to do the same in India, South Africa, New Zealand, etc. But trout weren't the only fish that officers were catching in exotic waters; everyone who has caught a tigerfish in Botswana, the country immediately north of South Africa, says it is one of the meanest fighters anywhere. Big ones weigh 20 to 30 pounds, but most fly fishers'

catches weigh 2 to 20 pounds. Regardless of the fish's actual weight, there's an innate savagery in these fish that is most impressive. Tigerfish are found only in Africa, from the Nile in the north to Botswana in the south.

Papua New Guinea, the eastern portion of the island of New Guinea not belonging to Indonesia, is developing as a fly fisher's dream destination for the freshwater niugni, or New Guinea bass. Considered to be arguably the strongest and most ferocious freshwater fish in the world, the niugni is in the same genus (*Lutjanus*) as the Cubera snapper, a popular saltwater game fish off Florida's coast. And this is one destination where the scenery is as distinct as the species being sought.

In his memorable book *Death of a Riverkeeper*, Dennis Schwiebert wrote "Iceland is quite beautiful, once you can accept its emptiness." Iceland might be eerily empty, but it also rates as one of the world's truly special places for the highly prized Atlantic salmon. Located approximately midway between Greenland and the Faroe Islands north of Scotland, Iceland boasts lodges of a European feel, with great dining, and plenty of solitude, but it is not an option

These prehistoric-looking behemoths can occasionally be seen inshore, due to their tendency to feed in the shallow waters of the Atlantic.

200 Best Fly-Fishing Web Sites. A unique new publication listing internet home pages and e-mail addresses for more than 200 institutions involved with fly fishing, including dozens of on-line publications. Web surfers can search for fly-fishing contacts in different areas of the world, list a species and see how many locations come up, or try a few of the many weather services to see what the weather is like in the next state or halfway around the world.

John Merry, 200 Best Fly-Fishing Web Sites, P.O. Box 218, Cameron Park, CA 95682; (530) 676-7271; jm@200bestflyfishing.com

The Angling Report. A monthly newsletter featuring current information on fishing locations throughout the U.S. and the rest of the world.

Don Causey, The Angling Report, 9300 S. Dadeland Blvd., Suite 605, Miami, FL 33156, (305) 670-1918, (800) 272-5656; www.anglingreport.com

Black's Fly Fishing Guide. An annual publication self-proclaimed as "the complete angler's guide to equipment, instruction, and destinations." Very good listing of lodges and guides, by state and nation.

Black's Fly Fishing Guide, P.O. Box 2029, 43 West Front St., Suite 11, Red Bank, NJ 07701; (732) 224-8700; blacksporting@msn.com

Fishabout. A travel firm that specializes in sportfishing adventures. Its catalog lists fishing destinations all over the world. The company has been in business a number of years;

The Colony Hotel of Kennebunkport, Maine, offers the chance to walk out the gate and cast in the surf or off the jetty into the frigid waters in pursuit of pollock, bluefish, mackerel, and the mighty striper.

write or call for the catalog.

Fishabout, P.O. Box 1679, Los Gatos, CA 95031; (800) 409-2000; trips@fishabout.com

Fishing Travel. A veteran of more than thirty years in the travel fishing business, this firm has been a part of the Bass Pro operation since mid-1995. It handles fly-fishing trips all over the world and has a breadth of opportunities spanning everything from fish camps where a bunch of buddies go to fish and fend for themselves, to resort lodges with professional guides. Fishing Travel has good contacts in all of Latin America and uses a houseboat for a lodge in Brazil. Any fish species, anywhere, and pretty much anytime is possible through this firm.

Valerie Baad, Fishing Travel, World Wide Sportsman, 81576 Overseas Hwy., Islamorada, FL 33036; (800) 327-2880; bblake@basspro.com; www.outdoor-world/wws/owrisl.htm

Frontiers. A giant in the industry, the firm has been in business 28 years. Its principals claim to be international fly-fishing travel experts, and many satisfied customers use them year after year. Frontiers is distinctive in fly-fishing travel services by offering some first-class gourmet trips (mostly in Europe) that have little or nothing to do with fly fishing; just have fun spending the grandkids' inheritance.

Frontiers, P.O. Box 959, Wexford, PA 15090-0959; (800) 245-1950; info@frontierstrvl.com

Bob Marriott's Travel Center. Send your inquiries to Kory Ferrin or Mike in the travel center. This is the Los Angeles fly-fishing connection to the rest of the world. Trips to Russia, Mexico, Alaska, and the western U.S. for trout are all part of its regular business. You do not have to live in southern California to compare prices and destinations with those of

other services. Again, customers come back year after year.

Bob Marriott's Travel Center, 2700 West Orangethorpe Ave., Fullerton, CA 92833; (714) 578-1880; bmfstrav@bobmarriotts.com

Orvis. What can be said about Orvis that has not already been said? In business since 1856, Orvis has an Approved Lodge program, and a large number of lodges all over the world wear the title proudly. All Orvis-approved guides and lodges know their local fishing conditions well and can offer support and assistance to beginning or experienced fly fishers.

Orvis Company, Rt. 7A, Manchester, VT 05254; (800) 333-1550; www.orvis.com

Pan Angling Travel Service. Another veteran travel service for fly fishers, in business since 1962, Pan Angling covers the world and has good connections with lodges of various price ranges for specific countries or species every month of the year. The company publishes a monthly newsletter highlighting upcoming hot spots and carrying photos of trophy fish caught on recently completed trips.

Pan Angling Travel Service, 180 N. Michigan Ave., Chicago, IL 60601; (800) 533-4353; www.spav.com/panangling

Rod & Reel Adventures. A travel firm on the West Coast representing many lodges in western Canada, Alaska, and all of Mexico, Central America, and South America. The rest of the world works with this fourteen-year-old firm, too, including some exotic lodges in Africa and New Guinea. Look in the back of its catalog, under Potpourri, right after New Zealand.

Rod & Reel Adventures, 556 Thompson Lane, Copperopolis, CA 95228; 800-356-6982; rod-reel@sonnet.com; www.worldwidefishing.com/rodandreeladv.htm

for those who have concerns about cost. Competent, experienced guides take anglers to assigned beats each day. The fish are big, bright, and available. Schwiebert and others vehemently maintain that every true fly fisher owes it to himself or herself to fish in Iceland at least once in a lifetime.

MONTHLY CALENDAR

If you could call several well-traveled fly fishers and ask them where they would go each month of the year to fly fish for any species, what would they say? The following list of choices came from Lefty Kreh, a well-known fly fisher who has experience and skill on his side no matter where he fishes. The author and editor have added their two cents here and there, but largely, it is Lefty talking.

January and February: The South Island of New Zealand is in prime condition for big rainbow and brown trout. Another excellent choice is the north central basin of the Amazon River in Brazil for peacock bass. Nearby, Venezuela's Ventuari River is good for peacocks and the saber-toothed payara. Arizona offers good fly fishing for trout just upstream from the Grand Canyon.

March: The Florida Keys offer the best fly fishing for giant (big, mature) tarpon. Mexico's Yucatan, Belize, South Florida, and the Bahamas have good fishing for permit.

April: Many midwestern and eastern states (Maryland, Michigan, New York, Pennsylvania, Wisconsin, and Virginia) have their opening day of trout fishing. By mid-month, fly fishing for trout is extraordinary. Success depends largely on air and water temperatures, but thousands of fly fishers

A fly fisher pauses midstream to search for flies to match the hatch on the world-famous Big Hole River in Montana.

across the northern states, from Minnesota to New York, prepare for April every year. Off the southwest coast of Florida, snook and tarpon are active. Hickory shad start spawning up mid-Atlantic streams.

May: One of the two best times of the year for fly fishing for bonefish, in both the Bahamas (especially around Andros Island) and the Yucatan. In England, the best mayfly hatches of the year come off, bringing trout to the surface more than at any other time. White shad and striped bass runs start in the rivers of the mid-Atlantic region. The Outer Banks of North Carolina are particularly popular.

June: Fly fishing for striped bass really takes off in New York and New England. Fishing is usually best from mid-June through July. The Kennebec River in Maine fishes extremely well. Most of the saltwater spawning baitfish species that the stripers follow inland are moving back to the ocean by mid-July. Alaska has its best dry fly fishing for rainbow trout this month, because the trout are hungry and there are no salmon in the streams to provide salmon egg snacks. Also, late in the month, the really big king or chinook salmon start coming up Alaskan streams. Fly fishing for bass and pike are generally excellent in the upper Midwest and into Ontario.

July: Idaho and Montana fish well during the middle of summer because the high altitudes and nearness to high mountain snow banks keep water temperatures at a level trout find invigorating. Rainbow, cutthroat, brown, brook, and even Dolly Varden are sometimes present, with most Rocky Mountain states having at least two or three trout species available and on the hatch all month long. Montana rivers such as the Big Hole, Bighorn, Missouri, Clark, Madison, and Yellowstone all fish well. In Idaho, fly fishers like Henry's Fork, Kelly Creek, Silver Creek, and the south fork of the Snake. Off the East Coast, from Virginia to Maine, small striped bass are busting the surface, feeding on baitfish enough to earn the nickname "breakers."

August: The upper part of Florida Bay, around Flamingo, is at its peak for redfish. Reds fish well this month around much of the Gulf of Mexico, includ-

ing the shores of several states. Alaska has its best fishing for silver salmon (coho), the most coveted of the Pacific salmon.

September: The flats around Key West, Florida are at their absolute best for trophy permit. Smallmouth bass fishing in streams in mid-Atlantic rivers like the Susquehanna, Potomac, Shenandoah, and Juanita is excellent this month.

October: Mid- to late-October provides the best weather and fishing opportunities for bonefish in Florida and the Caribbean. That includes lots of countries, islands, and possibilities. Brown trout start spawning in Rocky Mountain streams about midway through this month. They are much more aggressive when they are spawning and will strike at colorful, sparkling streamer patterns or the infamous, fast sinking, "black and uglies." In good years, western brown trout fishing will continue through mid-November.

November: The first two weeks of November provide the best fishing of the year for false albacore on the eastern seaboard. Called little tunny by some (and probably "bonito" by Southern California visitors), this small species of tuna provides great sport for fly fishers in all the mid-Atlantic states. The best location is at Cape Lookout, North Carolina, called "the mecca for albies" (anglers fishing for false albacore tuna). The best weather of the year for the Bahamas and resident bonefish occurs early in November. It is also the best time of the year for the light; there is less glare than other months for the fly fishers' comfort.

December: The Patagonia area of both Argentina and Chile fishes exceptionally well in December, since it is summer in the Southern Hemisphere, and both brown trout and rainbows react to fly hatches and hunger like they do everywhere else in the world. At the same time, sailfish are abundant off the southern Atlantic shore in the U.S., especially off Florida's eastern shore.

THE LITERATURE OF FLY FISHING

BY SANDY RODGERS

There are said to be over three thousand modern books on the topic of fly fishing. Perhaps that explains why Alfred W. Miller (who wrote under the pen name of Sparse Grey Hackle) went on record to claim that, "The best fly fishing occurs in print."

Fly fishing often seizes the imagination of anglers with a contemplative and studious nature. They welcome the prospect of a life well spent, absorbing the thousands of particulars that comprise the immense volume of fly-fishing knowledge. Perhaps this hunger that fishermen possess for amassing minutiae explains why more has been written about fishing, and especially fly fishing, than any other outdoor pursuit.

An attempt to definitively address over five centuries of fly-fishing literature could pack a bookshelf. Particularily since many reviewers hold that much of the best writing about fly fishing has occured in the last century, which has mustered a proliferation of worthy titles. Still, a representative selection can provide a decent survey. The following bookshelf sampling might even serve as a library starter kit. In this very short list (of the many possible titles), a fly angler will find books that primarily instruct and initiate. If entertainment and theory are of interest, a little research at a local library or fly-fishing shop will reveal hundreds of additional titles.

FLY TYING

A. K.'s Fly Box (1996), by A. K. Best. Offers just what it says—a peek into the flies used by a world famous fly tier. It provides full-color illustrations of natural mayflies, stoneflies and caddises, with a few grasshoppers and ants thrown in, along with instructions on crafting their imitations.

The Basic Manual of Fly Tying, Revised Edition (1978), by Paul N. Fling and Donald L. Puterbaugh. This book carries a reputation as one of the best basic instructional manuals. With more than 700 illustrations to lend clarity, it also provides insider tips and techniques from tying experts.

The Book of Fly Patterns (1987), by Eric Leiser. This is a definitive guide to the huge variety of fly patterns, with illustrations and color plates.

The Dry Fly: New Angles (1990), by the venerable Gary LaFontaine. Sometimes called the "new bible for serious anglers" because of its detailed work on imitation, its keen observations on attraction can add to an angler's understanding of the dynamics at work streamside.

Flies for Atlantic Salmon, Bass, Saltwater, Steelhead, and Trout (1992), by Dick Stewart and Farrow Allen. This mini-library series of instructional books presents fly tiers with directions for virtually all the most popular patterns in each of the specialty areas.

Ernest Briggs, *Sea-Trout Fishing River, Scotland*, 1880

A Fly-Fisher's Guide to Saltwater Naturals and Their Imitation (1994), by George V. Roberts, Jr. This book won the United Fly Tyers book of the year award in 1994, with its complete treatment of marine organisms and corresponding directory of patterns.

Fly-Tying: Materials, Tools, Techniques (1963), by Helen Shaw. This book remains the classic that has taught serious fly tiers the basics for years. Instruc-

tions with over 250 life-size tying sequences help to clarify every step.

A Modern Dry Fly Code (1950), by Vincent Marinaro. A modern classic described as among the most innovative of its time, it gives insight into dry-fly dressing, as well as the habits of feeding trout, and even insect behavior.

Rare and Unusual Fly Tying Materials: A Natural History, Volumes I and II (1994), by Paul Schmookler and Ingrid V. Sils. Gives sources and geography on both standard and rare materials, and its remarkable illustrations can stand alone as a form of entertainment.

Salmon Flies: Their Character, Style and Dressings (1978), by Poul Jorgensen. Covers basic low-water patterns, Spey flies, and fully-dressed salmon patterns that could work as frameworthy art.

Saltwater Fly Patterns, Fully Revised and Augmented Edition (1995), by Lefty Kreh. With over 350 fly patterns in an edition large enough for use at the tying bench, this book can keep the hands and imaginations of saltwater fly fishers busy while they plan their next outing on the brine.

The Soft-Hackled Fly: A Trout Fisherman's Guide (1940, reprinted 1993), by Sylvester Nemes. No bookshelf should be considered complete without this small but important volume.

Talleur's Basic Fly Tying (1996), by Dick Talleur. A standard by this well-known tier, contains more than 300 color photographs to illustrate his helpful techniques and shortcuts to proficiency.

Tying and Fishing the Fuzzy Nymph (1965), by E. H. (Polly) Rosborough. Lives on with its painstaking examples of a grand old fly tier's style.

Universal Fly Tying Guide (1994, 2nd ed.), by Dick Stewart. One of those essential references for the beginning fly tier, this book teaches basic skills and describes materials for all the standard patterns.

Western Trout Fly Tying Manual, Volumes I (1974) *and II* (1980), by Jack Dennis. Has been updated to cover newer tools and materials. The two volumes remain vital to fly fishers who want to tie generously hackled flies for brawny Western rivers.

ENTOMOLOGY

Approach to Fishing and Tying with Synthetic and Natural Materials (1994), by Harrison R. Steeves III and Ed Koch. This books serves as a reference for tiers who want to fish with ant, bee, and spider type flies, and contains dozens of patterns.

Aquatic Trout Foods (1992), by Dave Whitlock. This book has been described as the most down-to-earth, practical volume on fly fishing entomology. It is very amply illustrated by the author, whose eye to detail reveals his training as an engineer.

Art Flick's New Streamside Guide to Naturals and Their Imitations (1988), by Art Flick. A pocket-sized basic that informs an angler what trout eat and how to fashion an imitation.

Caddisflies (1981), by Gary LaFontaine. Reviews the basic issues of the caddisfly life cycle, discusses why existing patterns are not effective, and then describes the unique work he has undertaken to develop more effective flies to imitate the enigmatic caddisfly This work exemplifies the science and the art of fly fishing.

Emergers (1997), by Doug Swisher and Carl Richards. The behaviors of emerging trout stream aquatic insects are thoroughly examined, along with patterns and instructions for tying.

Hatches II (1995), by Al Caucci and Bob Nastasi. Provides emergence dates and common names for the hatches of aquatic insects on North American trout streams.

Matching the Hatch (1955), by Ernest Schwiebert. Enjoy Schwiebert's perfectionism for realistic flies in this meticulous consideration of trout-stream insects and the flies that best resemble them.

Mayflies (1997), by Malcom Knopp and Robert Cormier. This large book thoroughly explores the life cycles of these widely-varied, gauzy-winged bugs, and augments the text with precise illustrations.

Naturals: A Guide to Food Organisms of the Trout (1980), by Gary A. Borger. Learn to recognize and understand the preferred diet of trout and what materials and methods work best to duplicate them.

Nymphs (1973), by Ernest Schwiebert. This book is a bible for nymph fly fishers, with good illustrations and research that draws from the entire U.S.

Selective Trout (1989), by Doug Swisher and Carl Richards. This book provides insights into mayfly imitation and technique that are found nowhere else. The photographs and illustrations in this book set the stage for all future efforts.

Stoneflies for the Angler (1990), by Eric Leiser and Robert H. Boyle. Another favorite trout food, stoneflies are identified, mapped, and carefully emulated here. Color photographs will help anglers get a handle on these important insects, as will the fishing strategies for their use

Tricos (1997), by Bob Miller. Offers detailed tying instructions for trico nymphs and other patterns, with chapters on how to fish them effectively.

Trout Stream Insects (1991), by Dick Pobst. Gives anglers extensive coverage of hatches and imitative strategies.

CASTING AND TECHNIQUE

The Cast (1992), by Ed Jaworowski. Illustrates a fresh method intended to help anglers cast with greater facility.

Cathy Beck's Fly-Fishing Handbook (1996), by Cathy Beck. Geared toward beginning women fly fishers, this book covers casting and the basic principles of fly fishing.

Curtis Creek Manifesto (1989), by Sheridan Anderson. Takes a humorous approach to teaching beginning fly fishers. This straightforward guide contains hundreds of illustrations and practical tips.

The Essence of Fly Casting (1986), by Mel

Mayfly

Krieger. Comes supported by two of his videos, *Essence of Fly Casting I* and *Essence of Fly Casting II*. The exuberant Mel extols the benefits of practicing the motions of casting until they become so ingrained as to seem automatic.

Joan Wulff's Fly-Casting Accuracy (1997) and *Joan Wulff's Fly Casting Techniques* (1995), by Joan Wulff. Learn the basics of every cast needed by a fly fisher from this sixteen-time champion fly caster. Another book from this fly fishing veteran, *Joan Wulff's Fly Fishing: Expert Advice From a Woman's Perspective* (1991), teaches technique with the beginning woman angler in mind.

New Standard Fishing Encyclopedia (1965), by A. J. McClane, outfits modern readers with a comprehensive reference for all categories of fishing and provides a key to fish identification, from aawa (Hawaiian black-spot wrasse) to zipola (common name for speckled rockfish).

Presentation (1995), by Gary Borger, delves into strategy. Line handling and fly delivery tactics take their cue from his predator-prey approach to the angler-fish relationship.

Spey Casting: A New Technique (1994), by Hugh Falkus. Offers expert instruction on casting the two-handed rod as it is used in traditional English salmon fishing, as well as in steelhead fishing and competition.

A Trout and Salmon Fisherman for Seventy-five Years (1950), by Edward Ringwood Hewitt. This classic summarizes the findings of the man who created the Neversink spider skater fly, helped establish nymph fishing in America, and fostered the popularization of dry-fly fishing for salmon.

TROUT FISHING

Brook Trout (1997), by Nick Karas. Commemorates North America's native trout. Photographs and drawings illustrate the trout's history and explore its future.

Fly Fishing Stillwaters for Trophy Trout (1998), by Denny Rickards. Provides a system for finding and catching larger trout in Western lakes.

Anglers swarm from throughout the Northeast to fish the venerable water of Vermont's Battenkill River.

Joe Humphrey's Trout Tactics, Revised Edition (1993), by Joe Humphreys. An updated classic that contains discussions on the whole range of skills required for outwitting trout.

Lake Fishing with a Fly (1984), by Ron Cordes and Randall Kaufmann. This book is a classic on fishing trout in lakes, with excellent illustrations, detailed entomology, and numerous insights for the fly fisher.

Reading the Water (1988), by Dave Hughes. Teaches anglers how to find trout in a variety of waters. It provides an understanding of stream structure and discusses trout food.

Stillwater Trout (1980), edited by John Merwin. This book offers ideas and information for fishing lakes for trout from fifteen fly fishers, including Lefty Kreh, Steve Raymond, and Hal Janssen.

Strategies for Stillwater (1991), by Dave Hughes. Describes the basic methods for finding fish and specifies ways to fool them with any of the whole range of flies available.

Trout (1938), by Ray Bergman. The timeless classic that "makes you want to quit reading and go fishing instead."

Trout Biology (1981), by William Willers. This book, written by a professor of biology in an accessible tone, is a must for any fly fisher wishing to appreciate the key features of these exciting fish.

Trout Fishing (1972), by Joe Brooks. In this, Joe's final book, he went beyond his previous concise and informative works and wrote a tribute to "the universal charisma of trout."

Trout on a Fly (1990), by Lee Wulff. Urges anglers to think like a predator to increase their success.

The Way of a Trout with a Fly (1921), by G. E. M. Skues. Offers his contention that different conditions call for different flies, and that neither wet nor dry should rule as the ultimate in flies, an opinion considered heresy in his day.

The Wildlife Series: Trout (1991), by Judith Stolz and Judith Schnell. This 384-page reference work on trout contains information on trout anatomy, distribution, origins, and more, with color photographs.

Mailbox outside the Hungry Trout, a fishing gear shop in the Adirondack Mountains.

The Year of the Trout (1985), by Steve Raymond. Invokes a powerful and familiar yearning that resounds in the heart.

SALMON AND STEELHEAD TROUT

The Atlantic Salmon (1958), by Lee Wulff. Remains required reading if an angler wants to learn about this noble fish. Natural history, behavior, and proven techniques are covered.

Atlantic Salmon Flies and Fishing (1995, reprint), by Joseph D. Bates, Jr. The classic reference book, which details the fish's habitat and behavior; it also describes the type of tackle and best techniques to use. New color prints add visual cues.

The Steelhead Trout (1971), by Trey Combs. The author broke significant ground in this important text, one that steelheaders look to as the indispensable manual for steelhead fishing.

Steelhead Water (1993), by Bob Arnold. This book is an enjoyable way to become familiar with steelhead as a gamefish and the approaches taken by fly anglers to catch them.

SALTWATER SPECIES

Backcountry Fly Fishing in Salt Water (1995), by Doug Swisher and Carl Richards. Provides information on fishing mangrove-fringed estuaries, salty shoreline creeks, brackish rivers, and coastal canals.

Baja on the Fly (1997), by Nick Curcione. Gives anglers the benefit of Nick's forty years of fishing the bountiful waters of this peninsula.

Bluewater Fly Fishing (1996), by Trey Combs. Covers what many consider the new frontier of fly fishing, pursuing ocean gamefish all over the world.

Fish and Fishing of the United States (1849), by Frank Forester (the pen name of remittance man Henry W. Herbert). Attests to the eagerness of striped bass to strike a fly. Forester/Herbert also advocated a higher status for shad and the other species of fish that he discovered would rise to a fly.

Fishing the Flats (1983), by Mark Sosin and Lefty Kreh. This serves as a vital textbook for any angler lured by the dream of catching permit, bonefish, tarpon, or other shallow-swimming saltwater species.

Fly Fishing in Salt Water, Third Revised Edition (1997), by Lefty Kreh. This book is so essential that many anglers consider it the saltwater fly fisher's bible.

One of the most crucial pieces of safety equipment for the wading angler is the staff, like this portable model pictured above.

Fly Fishing the Tidewaters (1995), by Tom Earnhardt. Covers techniques to bring success in the sounds, bays, and inlets of the East Coast.

Inshore Fly Fishing: A Pioneering Guide to Fly Fishing along Coldwater Seacoasts (1992), by Lou Tabory. A real predator when it comes to fly fishing, Lou shares his considerable understanding of this fishery.

The Striped Bass (1993), by Nick Karas. Includes fish biology, tackle, and methods to catch these fish and even the best boats and vehicles to use to approach them.

The Striped Bass Chronicles (1997), by George Reiger. Offers personal accounts along with the his-

tory of this game fish that now provides fly rodding fun for thousands of anglers on the Eastern seaboard.

WARMWATER FLY FISHING

Bassin' with a Fly Rod (1995) and *The Sunfishes: A Fly Fishing Journey of Discovery* (1995), by Jack Ellis. Both offer insights gained when the author moved from Western trout stream country to Texas and its warmwater fishing. Both books are filled with fly patterns and techniques for success in warm water.

Bass on the Fly (1994), by A. D. Livingston. Takes a clear approach to the distinctions of bass fishing, with tips on how to fool the big ones.

Black Bass and the Fly Rod (1993), by Charles Waterman. Takes you through all the necessary steps in selecting tackle for both largemouth and smallmouth bass.

The Fly Fisher's Guide to Warmwater Lakes: A Natural System for Finding Bass, Pike, and Panfish (1995), by Cliff Hauptman. Cliff outlines how an angler can learn to study shorelines, light, yearly cycles of the waters, and the individual biology of the fish, and then use that knowledge to locate fish and enhance his catch ratio.

Fly Fishing for Smallmouth Bass (1996), by Harry Murray. Covers the use of poppers, streamers, nymphs, and bugs, as well as flies.

Fly Tying and Fishing for Panfish and Bass (1989), by Tom Keith. Discusses fishing strategies and basic fly tying, with a particular emphasis on panfish.

L. L. Bean Fly Fishing for Bass Handbook (1988), by Dave Whitlock. This well-illustrated introduction serves up useful tricks and lessons to give anglers a boost in their pursuit of warmwater gamefish.

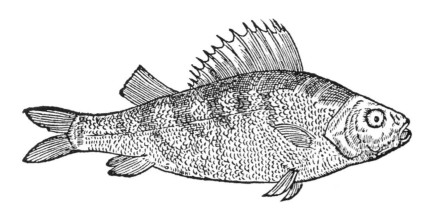

Smallmouth Strategies for the Fly Rod (1996), by Will Ryan. Gives tips on how to catch these fish in all types of habitat and at any time of year.

STORIES, ART, AND OTHER FLY-FISHING FASCINATIONS

American Fly Fishing (1987), by Paul Schullery. Details the rich and colorful history of fly fishing throughout this country, and includes historic photographs, prints, and drawings.

The Book of the Tarpon (1911), by A. W. Dimock. This classic, which details the author's struggles with these man-sized fish using greenheart or bamboo rods from canoes, makes current methods of catching tarpon from seaworthy kevlar-enhanced skiffs using space-age graphite tackle seem effortless.

Flip Pallot's Memories, Mangroves, and Magic (1997), edited by Neal and Linda Rogers. Combines Flip's reminiscences, from billfishing to bonefishing, with more than 100 brightly hued photographs.

92 in the Shade (1973), by Thomas McGuane. Brings to life the struggles of a wannabe fishing guide in an earlier Key West.

The Origins of Angling (1963), by John McDonald. Not only contains a facsimile edition of Dame Juliana Berners's *A Treatyse of Fysshynge wyth an Angle*, but also explores the many questions that surround the historic volume.

A River Never Sleeps (1991). Like other books and stories by Roderick Haig-Brown, this one has inspired many subsequent fly fishers to tramp through mossy woods in search not only of steelhead, but of Roderick's distinctive vision.

A River Runs Through It (1976), by Norman Maclean. This novella and its 1990s movie version, stirred many to take up the fly rod. It evokes images of lives that have the constant of fly fishing running through them like blood through the veins.

The River Why (1983), by David James Duncan. Charms with a fictional tale of the clashing of angling styles within a household.

Saltwater Fly Fishing Magic (1993), edited by Neal and Linda Rogers. This collection of hundreds of daydream-inducing photographs bestows a look at this rapidly growing aspect of the sport.

The Seasonable Angler (1988), by Nick Lyons. Can slow you down, make you notice things, maybe enough to boost your enjoyment of those very things missed in the rush to squeeze every moment from a day of fishing.

Silent Seasons (1978), edited by author/artist Russell Chatham. Contributors to this collection of short stories and essays include Jim Harrison, Tom McGuane, Harmon Henkin, Jack Curtis, and Chatham himself, with each narrative representing its author's unique view on fly fishing, from one's aesthetic yearnings to another's aching for that one more choice bit of tackle.

Trout: An Illustrated History (1996), by James Prosek. Feeds the needs of art lovers and trout lovers alike with its seventy original watercolors.

Trout Bum (1988), by John Gierach. Point to this book when one's fishing addiction raises eyebrows.

Trout Madness (1960) and *Trout Magic* (1987), both by Robert Traver. Both are very entertaining non-fiction accounts of fishing in Michigan, written by a Michigan Supreme Court Judge and author of the popular fly fishing mystery, *Anatomy of a Murder*.

BY SANDY RODGERS

A side from fishing itself, perhaps the most popular pastime for fly anglers is sharing information. Because the sport has so many facets—entomology, unusual casting methods, tying techniques, specialized lines and customized leaders, high-tech rods, endless kinds of fly-tying materials—fly anglers appear to be especially drawn to these more social aspects of the sport.

FLY-FISHING SHOWS AND EVENTS

The naturally social inclinations of fly fishers, coupled with the substantial growth of the sport over the last decade, has made fly-fishing shows very popular. It is possible, especially in the spring before the fishing season starts, to attend a different fly-fishing show every weekend. These shows provide anglers access to factory representatives who can answer technical questions about gear and usually offer seminars on various specialized aspects of fly fishing. Generally, a special venue is set up so anglers can also ask questions of fly tiers

and watch, up close, as flies are tied. Beginning fly anglers can learn more at a well-organized show in two or three days than they can in a year on their own. Those who are uncertain about whether they want to pursue fly fishing can explore their interests in detail—without purchasing expensive tackle and clothing—by first spending a couple of days at one of these events.

Many of these shows put the spotlight exclusively on fly fishing, while others feature fly and other fishing, along with the latest in boating and tackle technologies, as well as a raft of lodge or outfitting services. The fly-fishing-only shows tend to be more intimate and useful. For many of these shows, proceeds are used to sponsor conservation projects and fly fishing education programs. For ease of access, these events are listed by the month in which they traditionally have been held.

JANUARY

California: *Sacramento International Sportsmen's Show*. Contact John Kirk at (800) 545-6100. *San Mateo International Sportsmen's Show*. In late

January at the San Mateo (California) County Exposition Center; contact John Kirk at (800) 545-6100.

Illinois: *Midwest Fly Fishing Show*, Northern Chicago. This is the kickoff event of the year and, due to the excellent attendance, it draws representatives from many of the major fly tackle manufacturers. Fly tiers and seminars are a big draw.

Maryland: *The Fly Fishing Show*. Reckford Armory on the University of Maryland campus, in College Park, Maryland; (800) 420-7582.

New Jersey: *The Fly Fishing Show*. Founder Barry Serviente claims that this is one of the oldest, largest, and most successful of the shows that concentrate strictly on fly fishing. At the Garden State Exhibit Center in Somerset, New Jersey; (814) 926-2676. Generally takes place early in the month.

Oregon: *Portland International Sportsmen's Exposition*. This takes place at the Oregon Convention Center. Early January; contact John Kirk at (800) 545-6100.

Pennsylvania: *Greater Philadelphia Sport, Travel and Outdoor Show*. Held at the Fort Washington Expo Center in Fort Washington, Pennsylvania, during the last part of January; (215) 641-4500.

Washington: *Washington Sportsmen's Show*. Held in late January at Western Washington Fairgrounds in Puyallup; Call (800) 343-6973 for exact dates.

FEBRUARY

Colorado: *International Sportsmen's Exposition in Denver*. Not exclusively a fly fishing show, but has much for the fly angler to see and do; contact John Kirk at (800) 545-6100.

Iowa: *Hawkeye Fly Fishing Association Annual Meeting and Show*. When all waters are frozen, Midwestern fly fishers travel to Iowa for two days of fly tying and seminars; contact the FFF national office at (406) 585-7592 or visit the FFF website at www.fedflyfishers.org for dates in a given year.

Massachusetts: *Eastern Fishing and Outdoor Exposition*. At the Centrum, Worcester, Massachusetts.

Michigan: *Central Michigan Fly Fishing Show*. This is generally held in the greater Flint, Michigan area. Hosted by the Greater Flint Muddler Minnows and other FFF clubs; contact the FFF national office for dates in a given year at (406) 585-7592 or visit the FFF website at www.fedflyfishers.org.

New Jersey: *The Northeast Fly Fishing and Wingshooting Show*. Held in New Jersey; contact George Katilus at (732) 892-1400.

Oregon: *Pacific Northwest Sportsmen's Show*. Held at the Portland Expo Center in early February; Call (800) 343-6973 for details.

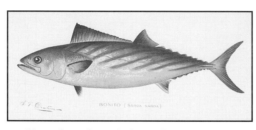

Many shows have dealers selling old fishing ephemera such as book and prints.

Virginia: *Capital Sport Fishing, Travel, and Outdoor Show*. Held at the Capital Exposition Center in Chantilly, Virginia; (703) 802-0066.

Washington: *Seattle International Sportsmen's Exposition*. Held at the Kingdome; contact John Kirk at (800) 545-6100. *Washington State Council of FFF Fly Fishing Jamboree and Auction*. This show, in its fourth year, is generally held in the Seattle area; contact the FFF national office at (406) 585-7592 or visit the FFF website at www.fedflyfishers.org for dates in a given year.

MARCH

California: *San Francisco Bay Area Fly Tying Festival*. The Northern California Council/Federation of Fly Fishers (NCC/FFF) sponsors this event, heralded the greatest concentration of fly tiers in the state of California; contact the FFF national office at (406) 585-7592 or visit the FFF website at www.fedflyfishers.org for dates in a given year.

Florida: *Great Outdoors Adventure Show*. Held at Cypress Gardens in Winter Haven, Florida. Late in the month; the show schedule is available from Scott Clack at (800) 282-2123.

Massachusetts: *World Fly Fishing Exposition*. Held at the Shriners Auditorium in Wilmington, Massachusetts. Mid-month; for specific dates call (603) 431-4315.

Michigan: *The Midwest Fly Fishing Exposition*. Always at the Southfield Civic Center, Southfield, Michigan, in March. This show, hosted by the Michigan Fly Fishing Club, has been going on for almost twenty years and is the oldest of its kind; further details can be obtained from Diane or Ron at (248) 486-4967.

New York: *World Fishing and Outdoor Exposition*. In Suffern, New York, at the Rockland Community College Field House, early in the month; call (603) 431-4315.

Oregon: *Northwest Fly Tyers Exposition*. Held in Eugene, Oregon, this show is over ten years old and is under the auspices of the Federation of Fly Fishers Oregon Council; contact the FFF national office at (406) 585-7592 or visit the FFF website at www.fedflyfishers.org for dates in a given year.

Pennsylvania: *Fly Fishers' Symposium*. Held at Seven Springs Mountain Resort, Champion, Pennsylvania; more details available at (814) 926-2676.

APRIL

Federation of Fly Fishers Great River Council Fly Fishing and Headwaters Conclave. Contact the FFF national office at (406) 585-7592 or visit the FFF website at www.fedflyfishers.org.

Idaho: *East Idaho Fly Exposition and Federation of Fly Fishers Western Rocky Mountain Council Conclave*. This is a great show for western fly fishers, and particularly for flytiers; contact the FFF national office at (406) 585-7592 or visit the FFF website at www.fedflyfishers.org.

Ontario: *Canadian Fly Fishing Forum*. Held in the Toronto area, hosted by the Izaak Walton Fly Fishing Club. This annual event grows in popularity every year, drawing from both southern Canada and the northern U.S.; call (905) 855-5420 or e-mail danm@globalserve.net.

Wisconsin: *Badger Fly Fishers Spring Opener*. Usually in Madison, Wisconsin. This local FFF club

has been hosting a meeting for fly fishers for over ten years; contact the FFF national office at (406) 585-7592 or visit the FFF website at www.fedflyfishers.org for dates in a given year.

MAY

Texas: *Texas Fly Fishing and Outdoor Show*. Held in Kerrville, Texas, this show is sponsored by the FFF and several local fly fishing clubs and is held annually; contact the FFF national office at (406) 585-7592 or visit the FFF website at www.fedflyfishers.org

JUNE

Southeastern Council of the Federation of Fly Fishers Annual Show and Conclave. This event focuses on warmwater and saltwater fly fishing, in addition to trout, and is held near good fishing from Florida to North Carolina in any given year; contact the FFF national office at (406) 585-7592 or visit the FFF website at www.fedflyfishers.org for dates in a given year.

Michigan: *Great Lakes Council of the Federation of Fly Fishers Annual Summer Show and Conclave*. At the MacMullen Center in Roscommon, Michigan, this small but very friendly show is held at an inexpensive and rustic meeting site very near the best waters of the Au Sable River; contact the FFF national office at (406) 585-7592 or visit the FFF website at www.fedflyfishers.org for dates in a given year.

AUGUST

The Federation of Fly Fishers Annual Conclave and Show. This show, now running for more than thirty

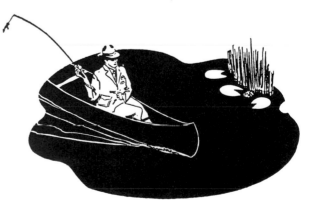

years, is usually in the western U.S., near great trout water. Every five to eight years it goes somewhere in the East. This show features the largest number of international fly tiers (over 125) and workshops (nearly 100) of any in the world; contact the FFF national office at (406) 585-7592 or visit the FFF website at www.fedflyfishers.org for dates in a given year.

OCTOBER

Great Lakes Council of FFF Steelhead Outing on the Pere Marquette River. This event features access to over ten miles of private water as well as fly tying and great food, all for a reasonable price; contact the FFF national office at (406) 585-7592 or visit the FFF website at www.fedflyfishers.org for dates in a given year.

Arkansas: *Federation of Fly Fishers Southern Council Conclave and Show*. In Mountain Home, Arkansas, this popular event has been held at the same site for at least ten years. It is a favorite of fly fishers from across the country; contact the FFF national office for dates in a given year at (406) 585-7592 or visit the FFF website at www.fedflyfishers.org.

Florida: *The Fort Lauderdale International Boat Show*. This show features an extensive array of fishing and boating products. Usually held at the Fort Lauderdale, Florida Convention Center. *The Shallow*

The latest gear is on display at the shows, such as these brightly colored wraps used in rod building. Innovations in design and materials continue in fly-fishing gear as the sport's popularity soars.

Water Fishing Expositions. This show is held at Fort Pierce, Florida, at the St. Lucie Auditorium, and in Houston, at the Astro Arena; inquiries can be made to Mark Castlow at the Castlow Group, (56) 562-5069.

New Hampshire: *Annual Fly Fishers Exposition*. Held in New Hampshire in at the Gunstock Recreation Area in Gilford; contact Bob Mitchell at 603-668-9748.

NOVEMBER

Federation of Fly Fishers Mid-Atlantic Council Fly Fishing Show and Conclave. This show is generally held in the Maryland-eastern Pennsylvania area; contact the FFF national office at (406) 585-7592 or visit the FFF website at www.fedflyfishers.org for dates in a given year.

California: *Educational Fly Fishing Fair at Bob Marriott's Flyfishing Store*. Held in Fullerton, California; call (800) 535-6633. Free admission gives access to fly-tying and casting demonstrations, manufacturers' booths and representatives, lodges, guides, outfitters, and fly-fishing celebrities.

FLY-FISHING SCHOOLS

Fly-fishing success depends on both technical knowledge and physical skill. With time and patience, all the necessary abilities can be acquired from books, videotapes, and friends. However, a popular fast-track alternative is to attend one or more fly-fishing schools. These vary from a half-day to a week or longer, with both basic and advanced skill development. Some schools are very focused—say, on casting, or on fishing a particular species—while others cover the entire gamut of fly fishing. If you are eager to reach proficiency as a fly angler, a fly-fishing school may be worthwhile. The following list offers many choices. You are advised to ask questions and get details to make sure your expectations will be met.

American Fishing Schools, 2850 Creekwood Lane, Lawrenceville, GA 30244; (770) 717-0837. American Fishing Schools offers a Trout Trickery seminar that is conducted nationwide, along with a fly-fishing school and youth fishing schools.

Balsams Grand Resort, Route 26, Box 1000, Dixville Notch, NH 03576; (603) 255-3400, offers an all-inclusive fly-fishing school during the spring months.

Birkholm School of Fly Casting, P.O. Box 1959, Poulsbo, WA 98370; (360) 697-3905, holds fly-casting classes and seminars.

The Bonefish School. This school is aimed at helping fly fishers who want to learn how to catch these hard-to-fool fish. Beginners spend a week soaking up sunshine and atmosphere in Georgetown, Exuma, in the Bahamas, where the classroom curriculum gets reinforced by four days of guided fishing. The school was founded by Jake Jordan, at Bob Hyde's Peace and Plenty Inn; the 20-student classes are taught by Jake, Bob, Steve Rajeff, Jamie Dickinson and Tony Weaver. Hopeful bonefishers can contact the Bonefish School at P.O. Box 500937, Marathon, Florida 33050-0937; (305) 743-0501, keysjake@aol.com.

Cabela's Fly Fishing Schools operate in both the eastern and western U.S. The two-day eastern school on Yellow Breeches Creek in Pennsylvania runs from April through mid-September, and the three-day western school, based out of Twin Bridges, Montana, operates from late April through early August. The courses include instruction, equipment, accommodations and meals; prospective students can obtain further information at (800) 237-4444.

California School of Flyfishing, P.O. Box 8212, Truckee, CA 96162; (916) 587-7005, operated by Ralph and Lisa Cutter, gives introductory through advanced fly-fishing instruction and seminars.

Castizo Fly Fishing School, at P.O. Box 12526, Albuquerque, NM 87195; (505) 831-4335, provides fly-fishing instruction and workshops for limited groups, with private classes for brown, cutthroat, and rainbow trout.

Dan Bailey's Fly Fishing School, based in Livingston, Montana, holds specialized clinics for fly casters who want to improve skills, or who only need to master special techniques like the double haul. Rather than pre-structuring classes, these sessions

Teaching the basics of casting: Schools and clinics in fly-fishing techniques are springing up across the country, with men and women of all ages involved.

are available in response to client interest, based upon requests received throughout the fishing season. Bailey has also set up a few weekend schools especially for women who want to learn fly fishing, and these are offered from spring through fall. Lyn Dawson, at (800) 356-4052, can supply details to interested anglers.

Eagle Associates, 5 Amara Court, of Woodlands, TX 77381; (281) 367-7646, offers fly-casting instruction from beginner to advanced, and fly-fishing seminars and classes for fresh or saltwater.

Educated Angler, P.O. Box 733, Centerville, UT 84014, provides beginning fly-fishing instruction.

The Florida Keys Fly Fishing School. This fly-fishing school, established in 1989, specializes in teaching fly anglers of all skill levels how to sight fish on the tropical flats: tarpon, bonefish, permit, snook, and redfish. It also covers bluewater (far from shore) fly fishing, including essential subjects such as fighting fish, wind problems, and flats etiquette. The staff of instructors includes director Sandy Moret, Steve Huff, Rick Ruoff, Chico Fernandez, Flip Pallot, Craig Brewer, and Tim Klein. Aspiring flats fishermen can obtain school dates and brochures at P.O. Box 603, Islamorada, FL 33036; (305) 664-5423.

Double Haul Ltd., 101 Cordova Reina Court, Ponte Vedra Beach, FL 32082; (904) 285-5411, presents **The Fly Fishing School at Ponte Vedra Beach**.

Fly Fishing with Bert & Karen, 1070 Creek Locks Road, Rosendale, NY 12472, is a fly-fishing school in the Catskill Mountains, with Bert Darrow (914) 658-9784 and Karen Graham (914) 339-8164 as instructors.

Great Glen Trails, P.O. Box 300, Pinkham Notch, Gorham, NH 03581; (603) 466-2333, has multilevel programs in fly fishing, starting with three-hour introductory programs.

Harry Murray's Fly Fishing Schools operate out of Murray's Fly Shop, P.O. Box 156, Edinburg, VA 22824; (540) 984-4212. Harry features on-the-stream schools in Shenandoah National Park.

International School of Fly Fishing. Mel Krieger began teaching fly casters the double haul on the lawns of Golden Gate Park during the 1960s. His former students now number in the tens of thousands. Mel is an active member of the Board of Governors of the Federation of Fly Fishers Fly Casting Instructor Certification Program. He also has chartered the International School of Fly Fishing in conjunction with The Fly Shop. As head instructor in classes with a three-to-one student-teacher ratio, he coaches both beginners and those who want to polish their skills. Distinguished by his ability to teach newcomers, Mel also gives private lessons and conventional fly-fishing clinics, as well as spey and two-handed rod clinics. Instructor workshops, combination golf and fly-fishing seminars, and a fly-fishing camp for children, ages 11 through 15 round out the school offerings. Peter Holman at The Fly Shop serves as the administrator for Mel's school at (800) 669-3474, or www.theflyshop.com.

Joe Humphrey's Fly-Fishing Schools are held at Allenberry Resort Inn and Playhouse, Box 7, Boiling Springs, PA 17007; (717) 258-3211, on weekends, with student fishing access to Yellow Breeches Creek in Central Pennsylvania. Joe, Ed Shenk, and Norm Shires serve as instructors.

Kaufmann's Streamborn. This Northwest fly-fishing school schedules its fly-fishing programs at its riverside house on the Deschutes River in Oregon, during the spring, summer, and early fall. It offers individual instruction according to each angler's skill level, and students have ample time to fish for rainbow trout or steelhead during the three-day schools. Fly-tying and spey-casting schools are also available. Randall or Jerry, at (800) 442-4359, can furnish dates and prices, or inquiring anglers can gather details about these Kaufmann's Fly Fishing Expeditions on the Internet at www.kman.com.

Kinzua Fly Fishing School, 44 Parkview Avenue, Bradford, PA 16701, svarka+@pitt.edu, takes place in the Allegheny Mountains.

L. L. Bean. Famous for its outdoor gear, L. L.

Bean set up a fly-fishing school around 1980 to provide educational support for users of their equipment. The school initially was directed by Dave Whitlock, with input from fly-fishing notables such as Lefty Kreh. L. L. Bean has since modified the format to include a range of Outdoor Discovery schools while retaining the same objectives. The school now operates entirely under the supervision and management of the L. L. Bean staff, most of whom are certified instructors. Instructors are selected for their high degree of interpersonal skills and enthusiasm. Instructors consider it their mission to coach students in the entire gamut of fly-fishing skills—casting, flies, tackle, knots, safety, etiquette—so that the novice can fish with a measure of confidence and understanding. Sim Savage works as program coordinator for these L. L. Bean Schools; his number is (800) 341-4341, extension 26666, or www.llbean.com.

North Country Angler, Route 16 North Main Street, North Conway, NH 03860; (603) 356-6000, holds fly-fishing schools in the White Mountains of New Hampshire.

Obscure Anglers, 715 S. 6th Avenue, Bozeman, MT 59715; (406) 587-4335, teaches novice through advanced fly fishing.

Orvis. The long-established Orvis company opened America's first fly-fishing school in 1966, in Manchester, Vermont. Orvis now holds schools in Colorado, Florida, Massachusetts, New York, and Vermont, where students learn how to tie the essential knots, read the water, select flies and equipment, wade safely, and carefully release fish. Essential fly-fishing etiquette and conservation topics help insure that protocol and responsibility maintain their presence in the fly-fishing world. Prospective students can find out dates and details by contacting Orvis fly schools at (800) 235-9763 or at www.orvis.com.

Sauk-Suiattle Fly Fishing Expeditions, at 5318 Chief Brown Lane, Darrington, WA 98241; (800) 462-1106, offers fly-fishing schools near Snoqualmie National Forest.

Sea Island Saltwater Fishing School, at the Lodge at Cabin Bluff, (800) 732-4752, includes five days of instruction, as well as lodging and meals.

Trout Magic, P.O. Box 321, Bend, OR 97709-0321; (541) 383-FISH, offers private, personalized fly-fishing lessons.

University of Fly Fishing & Wingshooting, 33855 La Plata Lane, Pine, CO 80470; (303) 838-2203, gives fly-fishing and wingshooting instruction to groups and individuals.

West Virginia Council of Trout Unlimited Fly Fishing School, 608 Seventh Street, Marietta, OH 45750; (740) 373-4924, hosts a weekend fly-fishing school.

Wild Trout University, 2251 Knapp Street, Suite 4D, Brooklyn, NY 11229; (718) 646-0583, willdaskal@aol.com, organized by Will Daskal, presents the Wild Trout University Fly Fishing School on the Beaverkill River.

Wulff School. From the late 1970s until 1991, Lee and Joan led every class of students at the Wulff School of Fly Fishing themselves. Joan carries on the personal touch with a student-instructor ratio of four-to-one at the school, which is located on a hundred acres in the upper Beaverkill Valley. Courses offered are Trout Fishing Theory and Environment, and Techniques of Fly Casting, with books by Lee and Joan Wulff to guide the instruction. More information can be obtained from Royal Wulff Products, 3 Main Street, Box 948, Livingston Manor, NY 12758; (800) 328-3638.

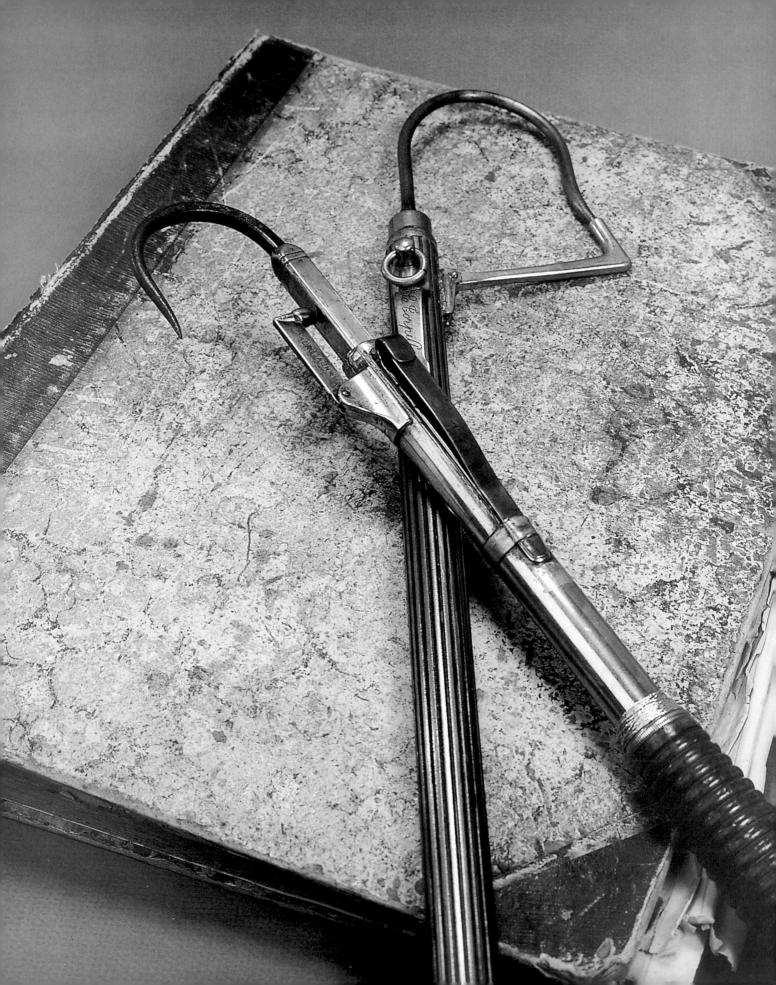

TERMINOLOGY

BY SANDY RODGERS

Fly fishing, like many specialized avocations, has a unique vocabulary with many words not found even in unabridged dictionaries. Terms like scud, beadhead, or tippet fall into this category. Worse perhaps is the fact that fly fishing contains many familiar words used in unfamiliar ways. For instance, to a seamstress the word mend refers to clothing repair. To a fly fisher it is a term that involves adjusting the fly line on the water to prevent its pulling unnaturally on the floating fly. While admittedly abridged, the following short glossary is a thumbnail sketch of essential fly-fishing jargon.

action: The bending resistance of a fly rod. "Fast-action" rods bend principally at the tip, are usually stiff overall, and will generate high line speeds to aid in distance casting, especially into the wind. By contrast, "slow-action" rods tend to flex their entire length, giving them a softer feel.

anadromous: Referring to fish that migrate upriver from the sea to spawn in fresh water, like salmon (*also see* catadromous).

angler: One who fishes for sport with a rod, reel, line, and hook or lure. The Sanskrit word *anka* means "to bend or angle, or to fish with such"; it forms the root word for *angler* and *angling*.

anti reverse: A type of fly reel in which the spool handle does not turn when line is pulled from the reel.

ant (Hymenoptera): In fly fishing, a fly tied in imitation of the insect and used as a lure.

aquatic: Referring to insects that begin life in the water and the flies that imitate them, such as caddisflies, mayflies, and stoneflies.

attractor: A type of fly that is generally unlike a natural food to the fish but nevertheless is effective in eliciting strikes.

arbor: The center shaft or spindle of a fly reel around which backing line is wound.

backing: The strong braided line tied to the fly reel, to which the fly line is attached.

badger: A hackle feather that is brownish-black

to black at the center of the quill, shading to ginger or white on the outer edges.

barbless: A hook on which the barb has been flattened, making it easier to release a fish unharmed.

barbules: The tiny spikes that connect the barbs of feathers together. When fly tiers set about to produce patterns which require certain looks from feathers, they must pay attention to seeing that all the barbules connect between the individual strands.

beadhead: A nymph or wet fly fashioned with a small, weighted metal bead at the head, which helps it sink more quickly.

belly: The larger midsection of a fly line.

Bimini twist: A knot frequently used for tarpon leaders; it forms a double line with a loop.

blank: A fly-rod shaft without guides, wrappings, or reel seat.

blood knot: A knot used to tie tippet material to the end of a leader, and to tie links of similar diameter material together, as in building a leader.

bobbin: A tool used in fly tying to hold the spool of tying thread.

bobbin threader: A fly-tying tool used to pull the tying thread through the tube of the bobbin.

bodkin: A tool used in fly tying to apply cement or lacquer to the head of a fly.

breakoff: The breaking of a tippet by a hooked fish.

bucktail: A fly tied with a long hair wing (usually from a deer's tail), to resemble a minnow or other bait fish.

butt extension: An added piece below the reel seat of a fly rod, which gives more leverage when fighting big fish.

butt section: 1. The thick end of a tapered leader that is tied onto the fly line. 2. The thicker or bottom section of fly rod of two or more pieces.

caddisfly (Trichoptera): An insect common to trout waters and a common food of trout. They are born in the water and have tent-shaped wings. Also, the flies tied to resemble them.

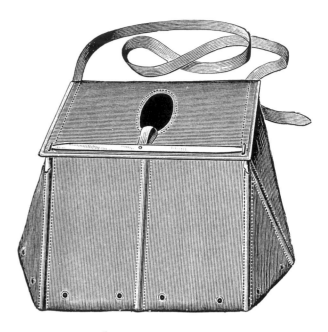

Canvas creel

capacity: The total length of backing and fly line a reel can best hold.

cast: 1. The act of delivering a fly to the fish by using a fly rod and fly line. 2. To throw the fly line and fly toward a target.

catadromous: Referring to fish that migrate from freshwater to the sea for spawning (*also see* anadromous).

catch and release: The practice of letting the fish one has caught swim away unharmed.

caudal fin: The tailfin or tail of a fish.

char: A subgroup of freshwater fish that includes brook trout, lake trout, arctic char, and Dolly Varden.

click drag: An inexpensive system on many fly reels that resists the pulling out of line, thus slowing and tiring a running fish. A clicking sound is made as a triangular piece of steel slips from one tooth to another over the reel spool gear.

collar: The part of a fly that is immediately behind the head.

cranefly (Tipulidae): Long-legged insect that serves as trout food and is therefore tied as an imitation.

creel: A basket, usually wicker, that holds fish.

damselfly (Odonata): A large aquatic fly that resembles a small dragonfly. The term also refers to its nymphal form; flies tied like either make good lures.

dapping: An early-nineteenth-century method of fishing in which the angler dangles the fly delicately on the surface of the water, using a very long rod and the shortest possible bit of line.

dead drift: The natural movement of a fly downstream with the current and without line drag.

disk drag: The method of creating resistance to line that is being pulled off a fly reel. Applying pressure between two disks causes a smooth friction that is adjustable.

dorsal fin: The prominent fin on the back of a fish.

double haul: The term for the cast in which the caster quickly pulls and releases the line on both the back cast and the forward cast. It is used to create greater line speed, enabling the caster to reach farther or cut through wind (*also see* haul).

double taper: A fly line that tapers at each end.

drag: 1. The resistance placed on a fly line by internal mechanical actions of a reel in order to slow the amount of line taken off the reel by a hooked fish. 2. The effect of the fly line and leader on a floating fly, which makes that fly move unnaturally (usually creating a "V" wake in the water).

dry fly: A fly tied to imitate insects that float upon the surface of the water, constructed of lightweight and waterproof materials.

dubbing: Small bits of material (including fur and synthetic fibers) twisted onto a waxed thread and wrapped around the hook as part of the body of an artificial fly.

Duncan's loop: A knot used principally to tie a fly to a monofilament tippet. Also called a Uni-Knot loop.

dun: 1. The stage of life of an aquatic insect that has just emerged from the water and has the ability to fly. Dry flies imitate this stage, also called the subimago stage. 2. A gray or dull color common to mayfly adults or duns.

emerger: A term to identify an aquatic insect in the stage during which it swims to the surface to hatch or change from a nymph or pupa to an adult.

false cast: Making forward and back casts without allowing the fly to drop onto the water. This lets the angler either add to the distance of the cast by feeding more line out or change direction of the cast. It is also used to dry off a fly.

ferrule: Derived from the Latin word meaning "little bracelet," this refers to the place where fly-rod sections are joined. The end of one section fits inside the end of another in an overlapping fashion.

flat: Area of shallow water with a sand, marl, mud, or grass bottom, often partially exposed at low tides.

floatant: A substance applied to fly lines, leaders, and flies to assist in buoyancy.

float tube: A one-person fishing craft originally built from a tractor or truck tire inner tube, in which the angler sits, allowing the fishing of waters that are too deep or soft-bottomed to wade in. Swim fins attached to the angler's feet supply the propulsion.

fly: An artificial lure, traditionally very light in weight and constructed of feathers and hair.

fly fishing: Fishing with a rod that uses the weight of the line to cast the leader with its fly.

fly line: The weighted line attached to the backing on the fly reel at one end and leader at the other.

fly reel: A fishing reel designed especially for holding fly line, which attaches to the butt section of the fly rod. Many fly reels include a mechanical means of adding resistance to outgoing line, thus assisting in fighting a hooked fish.

Big, fancy-sounding words alone don't catch fish. It may be fun, if a bit snobbish, to rattle off names like *Hexagenia limbata*, *Paraleptophlebia adoptiva*, and *Pteronarcys californica*, but many of the scientists who use those monikers every day don't fish at all. They're aquatic entomologists with an insatiable curiosity about the structure, function, habits, and habitat of these insects. To them, these names are merely terms.

A scientific name includes the genus and species of the organism. It's given in Latin because Latin is a dead language that is not subject to change by usage. Since Latin words are frozen in their meaning, when a scientist names an organism, that name remains permanent.

The scientific name allows anglers, just like scientists, to communicate accurately with one another. If I'm traveling to England to fish, and someone there tells me that mayflies will be hatching, I really don't have much information. But if they tell me that *Ephemera danica* will be hatching, I know exactly what flies to tie, what tippet sizes to carry, what rod, line, and reel I'll need—and exactly how excited I should be. In other words, knowing the exact insect that is hatching allows me to prepare for catching fish.

Knowing the scientific name also allows fly fishers to understand scientific literature. Armed with the genus and species name, I can learn what scientists—and other anglers—the world over know about a particular insect. It's much easier, and more complete, than the trial-and-error approach to knowledge. For example, knowing that a large mayfly is *Hexagenia limbata* and not *Hexagenia bilineata* is of precious little value to actually catching fish. They both hatch at the same time, are nearly the same size, are similar in color, behave the same during hatching, occupy the same types of bottom strata, etc. In this case, the insects can be grouped into the "Spring Hexes." However, knowing the insect is *Hexagenia atrocaudata* and not one of the other species of *Hexagenia* is very useful. This is the "Autumn Hex," which hatches in August and September, not in the spring, and hatches in the day, not at night. The spinners fall just at dark, not in the black of midnight, and so on.

Simply speaking, scientific names improve your understanding of what fish feed on. Learn the names and use them to dig out information that will increase your catch. Use them to communicate accurately to others. Then you'll be using them for their intended purpose, not merely as a way of impressing other anglers with fancy words.

—Gary Borger

Realistic stonefly nymph (Plecoptera), by Kevin MacEnerny.

fly rod: A fishing rod especially designed for casting a fly line. It is constructed of graphite, fiberglass, or bamboo, and in modern times carries a weight designation that permits one to match fly rods and fly lines for balance.

freestone stream: A river or stream that gets most of its flow from runoff or snowmelt. Typically, a freestone stream has a bottom of coarse gravel or rubble.

fry: A juvenile fish.

forceps: Pliers with a long, slender nose, typically associated with medical procedures, which is used to remove a hook from the mouth of a fish. Also called hemostats

furnace: Feathers that are brownish-black to black along the quill of the feather, with a gradation to light browns on the outer edges.

gaiters: A legging-like covering worn over the tops of wading boots to keep stream debris from entering.

gillie (also ghillie): An ancient Gaelic word meaning "boy." A fishing gillie is a term for a fishing guide, mainly used in the United Kingdom.

graphite: A material, used in the manufacture of fishing rods, that offers high elasticity with relatively low weight.

grilse: Small/adolescent Atlantic salmon.

grip: The handle of the fly rod, usually made of cork.

grizzly: A hackle with a barred V pattern in black and white or light and dark gray.

guide: 1. Graduated metal loops carefully spaced along the length of the fly rod, through which the fly line passes. 2. A local fishing expert who is paid to take anglers on fishing excursions.

hackle: Neck or back feathers wound around the hook on an artificial fly to create the appearance of insect parts, such as legs. Feather tips also are often used to imitate wings on dry flies and streamers.

hackle gauge: An inexpensive measuring device to determine the length of feather fibers (barbules) in relation to different hook sizes.

hackle pliers: A set of special spring-loaded grips used to wind hackle around a fish hook without breaking feathers.

hairbug: A surface fly typically for used bass, in which the body and head are formed from buoyant (hollow) deer, elk, antelope, or caribou body hair.

hair stacker: A tool used by fly tiers to get the tips of a bunch of hair lined up for placement on the fly.

hatch: The period when any species of aquatic insect swims to the surface of the water and works itself free from its shuck and transforms itself into a flying insect.

haul: An action associated with fly casting whereby

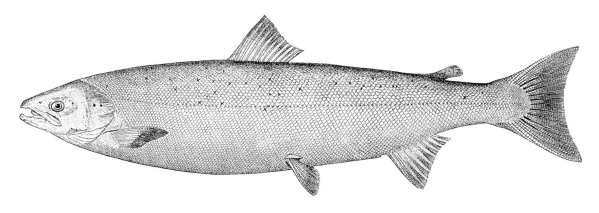

Atlantic salmon

the line speed is increased with an extra pull during line pickup, back casting or forward casting (*also see* double haul).

hook size: A standardization of hooks that is determined by the distance between the hook shaft and the hook point. Most hooks for fly fishing range from #2 (large) to #24 (very small).

improved clinch knot: A strong and easy-to-tie knot used to attach a fly to a tippet.

keeper: The small wire ring above the grip of a fly rod where a fly can be hooked when the angler moves around with his rod fully strung.

kick boat: A one-person fishing craft that is generally larger and more elaborate than a float tube. It can be powered by swim fins, oars, or a small electric motor. Also called a pontoon boat.

kype: A hook-shaped cartilaginous protrusion from the lower jaw of a male spawning salmonid.

landing net: A net with a fixed rim, used to catch a hooked fish and hold it while it is being unhooked for release.

leader: A clear segment of tapered monofilament line attached between fly line and fly. The section near the fly may additionally include a tippet.

lie: Locations along a river used repeatedly by fish, whether as feeding stations for resident fish or resting spots for migratory fish.

line dressing: A compound applied to fly line to clean it and/or make it float or cast more smoothly.

line weight: A system of measurement for fly line, referring to the weight of the first thirty feet of line but without regard to line strength. A "1" weight represents the lightest fly line.

loading: The term for the bending of the fly rod during the cast, caused by the weight of the line and the impetus given the rod by the caster's hand.

loop-to-loop: A term describing the joining of a fly

Choosing a fly

line to a leader or a leader to a tippet, whereby closed loops at the ends of each piece are used to make the connection.

marabou: Small and soft underfeathers from a turkey, chicken, or other domestic fowl.

mayfly (Ephemeroptera): Widely varied aquatic insects characterized by upright wings. Many trout flies are tied in imitation of these insects.

mend: To lift or roll a fly line in order to keep wind or water currents from pulling on it and creating an unnatural drift (line drag).

midge (Chironomidae): A very small (nonbiting) insect, or the dry fly tied to resemble it.

monofilament: A single strand of nylon used for leader or tippet material.

multiplier: A fly reel with gearing that increases the ratio of revolutions of the reel spool to the turns made on its handle.

nail knot: A knot commonly used to attach the fly line to the backing and the leader to the fly line.

nymph: An undeveloped aquatic insect in its underwater stage, and an important food source for fish. Also refers to the fly that imitates these insects.

palmered: A hackle wound around the entire length of the hook shank.

parr: A young salmon in its first two years of life, when it lives in fresh water. Also, the young of various other fishes.

pelagic: Referring to fish and other creatures that reside in the open sea.

Perfection loop: A knot commonly used to put a loop in the butt end of a leader as a means to attach the leader to the fly line in a loop-to-loop connection. Also used to connect a tippet to a leader in a similar loop-to-loop fashion.

polarized sunglasses: Eyewear designed to allow anglers to see beneath the surface glare of water.

pool: A section of stream where the water runs slower and deeper, forming a holding place for fish.

popper: A floating lure that produces a popping sound when retrieved, thus attracting the targeted fish.

presentation: Delivery of a fly to the feeding station of a fish.

pupa: The stage between the larva and adult form of caddis or midge aquatic insects. Also, the fly imitation of these insects.

reach cast: A cast used for adding extra slack in the line, or when fishing downstream, in order to provide a more natural float.

redd: The hollowed-out nest in a stream bed where a fish deposits its eggs, a behavior typical of most nesting salmonids.

reel seat: The part of the fly rod—made of aluminum, wood, or graphite and located just behind the grip—where the fly reel is attached.

retrieve: The method of stripping in the fly line that gives the fly action. Also, a term used to describe whether fly reels have a left-hand or right-hand cranking movement.

rise: The act of a fish coming to the surface to feed.

roll cast: A cast that consists of a long slow lift of the rod, followed by a downward punching motion. It literally rolls the flyline over the top of the water, thus propelling the fly to the target without the necessity of the backcast.

run: 1. The swim a hooked fish makes in trying to escape. 2. A place in a stream characterized by shallow water over a rocky stream bed that flows into a pool.

scud: A small freshwater crustacean that serves as a food source for trout. Also, a fly tied to imitate such organisms.

sea-run: A term describing trout that mimic the salmon life cycle of hatching in fresh water, migrating to the sea to mature, and returning to fresh water to spawn. Some brown trout, cutthroat trout, and rainbow trout (steelheads) do this.

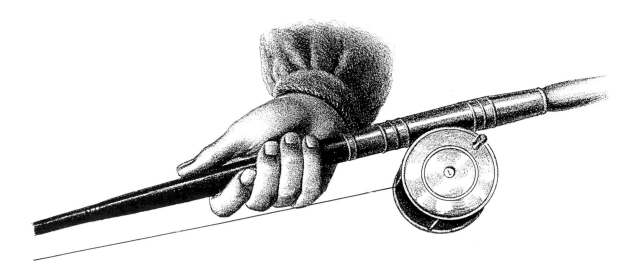

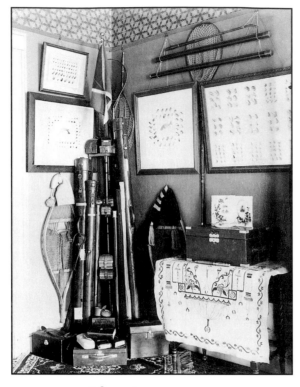

Fishing gear

seating (as in seating a knot): A term used to describe all the parts of a knot pulling together, as they must to form the knot.

setting the hook: An angler's response to a fish striking a fly that assures that the hook penetrates. Usually an upward motion of the fly rod.

seine: A small screen held under water to catch aquatic insects, to help the fly fisher determine what the local fish might be eating and so select the appropriate fly.

shooting head: A type of fly line with nearly all of its weight in the front 30 feet of line, and attached to a dacron, monofilament, or fine-diameter fly line, used as running line. It is used for making long casts in fishing in saltwater, in warmwater, and for steelhead.

shooting the line: Releasing extra fly line held by the line hand during the forward cast, which serves to extend the length of the cast.

single-action: A fly reel of simple design that retrieves line at the rate of one revolution of the spool per turn of the handle.

sink tip: A floating fly line with a sinking section about 10 feet long at the front end.

smolt: A young salmon in the stage at which it migrates to the sea.

snake guides: The S-shaped, rounded metal arches commonly used on the smaller sections of the fly rod to guide the line smoothly through to the loop-shaped guide at the tip of the rod.

spawn: The reproductive behavior of fish. Also, the eggs produced by the fish.

spey: A style of fly casting with two-handed rods, using a modified roll cast. Named after a river in Scotland where the technique was developed.

spinner: The end stage of a mayfly, when it falls onto the water after mating, making it an easy target for trout. Also called the imago stage.

spinner fall: An instance in which a great number of spinners fall to the water and die.

spring creek: A stream originating from a natural spring in the ground, rather than snow melt or runoff; generally provides a stable source of water with constant or near-constant temperature.

steelhead: A rainbow trout that spawns and lives the early part of its life in freshwater streams and then two to three years in oceans or large freshwater lakes.

stonefly (Plecoptera): A large aquatic insect that crawls out of the water onto a rock, splits its outer covering and becomes a flying insect with wings that lay on its back. Stonefly nymphs are a large, favorite trout fly.

streamer: A fly that imitates small baitfish or other organisms in a fish's diet, such as, leeches, crayfish, and salamanders; traditionally constructed from longer animal hair, such as, bucktail, or long, soft feathers.

strike: The taking of a fly by a fish. Also, the movement the angler makes in order to hook the fish.

strip: The retrieval of the fly line in increments to give action to the fly. Also, the pulling of the fly line loose from the reel in preparation for a cast.

stripping: Retrieving a fly in a provocative manner by a series of short or long pulls on the fly line.

stripping guide: The first guide forward from the grip of a fly rod, larger than the snake guides. Some rods have two stripping guides, graduated in size.

surgeon's knot: A knot often used to tie tippet material to the leader. Stronger than a blood knot and better for connecting unlike materials.

tail out: Lower end of a pool, where it becomes shallow.

tailing: A reference to the exposed caudal fins of feeding fish in shallow water.

tailwater: A river or stream that obtains its water from a large manmade dam.

terrestrial insect: Insects that are found on land and breathe air, including, most notably, ants, grasshoppers, crickets, and beetles. Also, a fly tied to look like a land insect.

tinsel: A metallic tape used in fly tying, often for ribbing.

tippet: Monofilament of small diameter tied on the end of a leader.

tip section: The small, top section of a fly rod.

tip-top: The fly line guide that is fitted over the end of the fly rod.

Uni-Knot: This knot, according to its inventor, Vic Dunaway, can be adapted for use in virtually any situation, whether tying the hook of the fly to the leader or joining lighter sections of line with those heavier test.

variant: A type of dry fly with oversized hackles but otherwise tied the same as the standard pattern.

wader belt: A belt worn at the waist over waders to help keep water out.

waders: Waterproof pants used to keep anglers warm and dry, either stockingfoot or with attached boots.

wading boots: Boots worn over stockingfoot waders; they usually have felt soles or stream cleats to enhance traction.

wading staff: A pole to help when wading in fast or deep water; some can be folded and stowed in vest.

weight forward: A fly line with most of its weight concentrated in the front thirty feet of line. The larger-diameter section of this line is referred to as the belly, which is usually around twenty feet long, with a long tapering of the line toward the front and a short tapering of it back to a thinner running line.

wet fly: A type of fly fished below the surface of the water, such as a nymph or a streamer.

whip finisher: A special fly-tying tool used to compactly and securely wrap the fly-tying thread on the head of a fly.

winding: The thread that holds the guides onto the fly rod.

X: A rating system to describe the diameter of leader and tippet material, with 0X representing a larger diameter (.011 inches) and 6X (.005 inches) representing a small, light diameter.

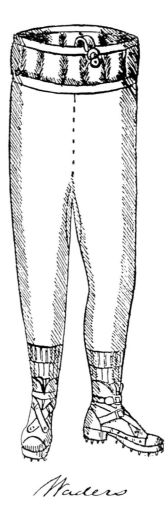

Waders

PHOTOGRAPHY & ILLUSTRATION CREDITS

PHOTOGRAPHS

Copyright © R. Valentine Atkinson: pp. 154, 179, 180, 182, 183, 186, 188, 189, 191, 192, 194, 195, 198

Copyright © Barry and Cathy Beck: pp. 134, 141, 185, 190

Copyright © Dennis Bitton: pg. 193

Copyright © Jason Borger: pp. 30, 31, 32, 34

Copyright © f-stop fitzgerald Inc.: pp. ii, iii, vi, x, 4, 18, 22, 26, 28, 36, 45, 49, 52, 57, 60, 65, 68, 70, 72, 73, 75, 76, 77, 78, 80, 81, 82, 83, 84, 87, 88, 89, 90, 91, 92, 93, 94, 95, 97, 98, 100, 103, 104, 105, 106, 107, 108, 109, 110, 111, 112, 113, 114, 115, 116, 117, 118, 120, 125, 128, 132, 136, 137, 138, 140, 142, 144, 146, 147, 148, 149, 151, 153, 155, 156, 158, 163, 166, 167, 168, 169, 170, 172, 174, 175, 176, 177, 178, 187, 196, 200, 204, 205, 206, 208, 212, 213, 216, 220

Copyright © Steve Moore: pg. 152

Copyright © Brian O'Keefe: pp. 181, 184

Copyright © Orvis: pp. 24, 25, 86, 96, 99

ILLUSTRATIONS

Painting copyright © Tim Borski: pg. 127

Knot illustrations by Susan Canavan: pp. 54, 55, 56, 58, 59, 60, 61, 62, 63, 64, 66, 67

Rod illustration by Kristen Couse: pg. 38

Lines and leaders illustrations by Aram Song: pp. 40, 41, 42

AMERICAN MUSEUM OF FLY FISHING COLLECTION

Courtesy of the American Museum of Fly Fishing: pp. viii, ix, 1, 5, 7, 10, 11, 12, 13, 14, 16, 17, 19, 29, 37, 46, 53, 69, 85, 101, 121, 122, 130, 133, 139, 145, 159, 160, 162, 164, 171, 173, 201, 203, 209, 214, 215, 217, 218, 222, 224

Douglas Adams, lithograph, *Salmon Fishing: A Likely Pool*, 1890: pg. 165

The Badminton Library of Sport and Pastimes (1885): pg. 225

Ernest Briggs, lithograph, *Sea-Trout Fishing River, Scotland*, 1880: pg. 202

S. F. Denton, lithographs, circa 1900: pp. 124, 129, 135, 143, 210

George Brown Goode, *The Fisheries and Fishery Industries of the U.S.* (1884): pp. 131, 150, 221

Frederic M. Halford, *Dry-Fly Fishing in Theory and Practice* (1889): pp. 71, 223

Frank Oppel, *Fishing in North America* (1876): pg. 21

Ogden Pleissner, oil on canvas, *The Battenkill*, circa 1960: pg. 15

Louis Rhead, *Fisherman's Lures and Gamefish Food* (1920): pp. 47, 126

Rondelet, *Histoire Entierre Des Poissons* (1855): pp. 123, 207

Genio Scott, *Fishing in American Waters* (1869): pg. 79; *Fishing in American Waters* (1875): pp. v, 6, 27, 74, 119

Scribner's Monthly, *Trout Fishing in the Rangeley Lakes* (February 1877, vol. XIII, no. 4): pg. 23

Sea Trout Fishing (1876): pg. 9

Striped Bass Fishing (1877): pg. 157

Izaak Walton, *The Compleat Angler* (1653): pg. 8

Wulff, Lee, *Lee Wulff's New Handbook of Freshwater Fishing* (1939): pp. 3, 43, 161, 211, 219

Acknowledgments

Many thanks to all the writers who have contributed herein, as well as the photographers; special thanks to Gary, Stick, Sean, Randall, Kate, Bebe Bullock, Dick Finley, Margot Page and Brooke, and all the staff at the American Museum of Fly Fishing in Manchester, Vermont, for their kind assistance in allowing my research and photography in their limited space. Thank you to Paul Ferson, Tom Rosenbauer, and Ryan Shadrin, and everyone at the Orvis Company for allowing use of their equipment and for sharing their knowledge as I prepared the photography. Thank you to Lee and Joan Wulff for allowing use of their text and time, and for being so creative in the sport, and to Tom Akstens and the Hungry Trout in the Adirondacks for showing me the joys of their Dream Mile. Thank you to my editor Constance Herndon, associate publisher Annik LaFarge, and publisher David Rosenthal at Simon & Schuster for their support on this project. Assistance beyond the call of duty from Sandy and Bob Rodgers in the Keys was greatly appreciated. For logistical support, thank you to the Vermont Travel and Tourism Board, Paul Kaza Associates, the Manchester, Vermont, Chamber of Commerce, the South Carolina Department of Travel and Tourism, the Hilton Head Island Chamber of Commerce, the Maine Office of Tourism, Nancy Marshall Communications, Visit Florida Tourism Department, the Greater Miami Chamber of Commerce, and the Florida Keys Tourism division; for generous accommodations, the beautiful Equinox hotel in Manchester, Vermont, was especially helpful, as was the cozy Battenkill Inn, the grand Colony Hotel in Kennebunkport, Maine, and the Goodspeed House in Camden, Maine. Thanks to Carol Ann Traynor and the staff of Nikon Professional Services for photographic technical services and equipment loans. At Balliett & Fitzgerald Inc., many thanks to designer Sue Canavan for creating a beautiful book under duress. Thanks to Peter Burford and Nick Lyons for great fly-fishing publishing; thanks to Sparse Grey Hackle, a writer with a greater name than mine. Thanks to guides Bob Young at The Equinox, Bob Rodgers in the Keys, Seth Taylor of Maine Sport, Adam Redman in Miami, Jim Dion of the Northeast Angler, Ian Cameron of Penobscot Driftboats, Captain Marvin at Shelter Cove on Hilton Head, and artist Tim Borski.

Finally to my wife, Judith and my children Genni and Weston, for time spent on the water with all of them, over years past and those yet to come, many thanks now and forever.

—*f*-stop fitzgerald

Aberdeenshire Dee River 193
action 24-26
Adams fly 73, 79
Aelianus 6, 19-20
Alaska 179-181
Albright, Frankee 11
American Museum of Fly Fishing 3
America's Favorite Fishing (F. Philip
    Rice) 133
Angling in All Its Branches (Samuel
    Taylor) 71
Antony, Mark 19
arbor knot 67
arbors 33-34
The Art of Angling (Richard Bowlker) 8
Assyria 19
Atherton, Jack 76
Ausable Wulff fly 80
Australia 193-194

backing 30
back-to-back uni-knot 63-64
Bahamas 186
bamboo 21-23
Banks, Joseph 9
Barker's Delight (Thomas Barker) 8
barramunda 194
barrel knot. *See* blood knot
basic cast 105-106
bass 123-124
    bass bugs 14, 138, 139, 140
    black rock 186
    exotics 131, 142, 189, 195
    fishing 134, 176, 188, 199
    fly patterns 14, 139
    largemouth 94, 123, 135
    smallmouth 123-124, 177, 199
    striped 129-130, 151, 176, 183, 199
Basurto, Fernando 8
Bates, Joseph 16
Bavaria 7-8
Becket bend 64
belly boats 135-137
belts, wading 98
Bergman, Ray 133
Berners, Dame Juliana 10, 207
Billard, Christian 78
billfish 11, 130, 194
    See also marlin; sailfish
Bimini twist 53
Black Crowe Beetle fly 80
blood knot 49, 62-63
bluefish 129, 150-151
bluegill 176-177
bobbins 83

bodkins 83
bonefish 127, 149, 188, 189, 199
bonito, ocean 150
Book of the Black Bass (Dr. James Hen-
    shall) 14
Bowlker, Richard 8
braided-loop connector 65
Brodney, Kay 11
Brule River 176

Cahill fly 80
calendars
    event 209-212
    fishing 198-199
Canada 174-175, 175
carp 130
Cass, Beulah 11
casting 101-119, 203-204
    delivery 50, 73, 119
catch and release 98, 162, 163-165,
    167, 169
Catskill Curler fly 81-83
Central America 188-189
char, Arctic 175
China 19
chinook 125
    See also salmon, Pacific
clinch knot 55-56
clothing 95-96
Clouser Minnow fly 129, 156
clubs, early 12
Coffin Fly 5, 6
coho 125, 199
    See also salmon, Pacific
The Compleat Angler (Izaak Walton) 8,
    20-21, 70
connections 53-54
    backing to line 65-67
    leader to tippet 48, 50, 51, 59
    line to leader 50, 64-65
    loop-to-loop 49, 59-60, 65
    tippet to fly 45
conservation 142-143, 157, 161-163,
    166-170
Cotton, Charles 8, 20-21, 70
crappies 131
creels 119, 218
Crosby, Cornelia "Fly Rod" 10
crosswinds 115

Dahlberg Diver fly 80, 139-140
dapping 101
Darbee, Harry 73-76
Dave's Hopper fly 80
de Bergara, Juan 70

Dette, Edward 73-76
*Dialogue between a Hunter and a
    Fisher* (Fernando Basturo) 8
disk drags 32, 33
dolphin. *See* dorado
dorado 121, 126, 152
double haul 117
double taper (DT) lines 39
Douglas, Dorothy 72
drag, surface 112-114
drag systems 32-33
drum, red. *See* redfish
Dry-Fly Fishing in Theory and Practice
    (Frederic Halford) 13
dubbing bags 70
Dunaway, Vic 56-58
Duncan loop 58

Egypt 19
Elk Hair Caddis fly 80
England 13, 20, 193
entomology 70, 202
etiquette 170-171
exotics 160, 169-170
The Experienced Angler (Robert
    Venables) 8
eye protection 91-94, 104

false albacore 152, 199
fiberglass 23
fish
    anadromous 14
    big game 52, 57, 137-138
    saltwater 205-206
    See also by name, e.g., trout, tarpon
flats fishing 147, 149
Flick, Art 73, 203
flies 13, 14-16, 80, 220
    Atlantic salmon 71, 72
    attractor 69-71, 76
    collector's 78-79
    dry 13, 73, 79-80, 88
    heavy 25, 50-51
    matching 69-70, 71-74, 76, 78, 79
    saltwater 77-78, 156-157
    warmwater 138-141
floatants 88-89
Floating Flies and How to Dress Them
    (Frederic Halford) 13
float tubes 135-137
Florida 146-149, 177-179
flounder, starry 186
The Fly and the Fish (Jack Atherton) 76
fly boxes 87-88
A Fly-Fisher's Guide to Saltwater Naturals

and Their Imitation (George V. Roberts, Jr.) 78, 202
fly-fishing-only regulations 163-165
fly retriever 90
fly tying
    books 10, 11, 201-202
    kits 70-71
    materials 77, 78-79, 81-83
    saltwater 77
Franck, Richard 70
freestone fishery 176

gaffs 216
gear 103
    cold-weather 95
    rain 95
Glass Minnow fly 77
Gold-Ribbed Hare's Ear fly 75, 80
Gore-Tex 96, 97
Grand Slam 126
graphite 23-24
Gray Ghost fly 11, 80, 82
grayling 180
Great Lakes area 175-176
Green Drake fly 5, 80
Gregory, Myron 16
grip, in casting 103-104, 223
grips, rod 26

hackles 70
Halford, Frederic 13, 74
Hall, Henry 13
Hanson, Carl 77
hatcheries 122, 163, 168, 169
Hauck, Ross 35
hauling line 115-117
Hazzard, Albert 164
Hendrickson fly 79
Henry's Fork Hopper fly 80
Henshall, Dr. James 14, 134
Hewitt, Edward 73
high-speed runs 32
Hintlian, Mike 149-151
history 6-9, 14, 134
A History of Angling (Charles Waterman) 16
Hoffman, Richard 7
Homer Rhode loop 58-59
hooks 8, 13, 80-81, 93, 165
Hornberg fly 80

Iceland 195-196
Inchworm fly 80
instruction 101-119, 212-215
Itchen, River 192

Just Fishing (Ray Bergman) 133
King Eider fly line 38
knots 53-67
    leader 49, 60-64, 64-65
    saltwater 57, 58-59
    terminal 54-59
    tippet 51
    See also individual knots
knots, wind 115
korkers 97
leaders 37, 43-47
    building 48-51
    care of 51
    design 44, 46-47
    designations 45
    material 44, 48-49
    performance 47-48
    ready-made 45-47
    saltwater 154
    silkworm gut 8
    tarpon 57
Ledlie, David 9
Lefty's Deceiver fly 156
Leisenring, James 73
Leisenring lift 109-110
Letort Cricket fly 80
Letort Hopper fly 6
light, artificial 94
line guides 27
line rating systems 38-39
lines 36, 37-43, 40, 41
    care of 44
    designations 39
    development of 12-13, 16, 38, 42-43
    floating 38
    saltwater 153-154
    sinking 41-42
    two-handed 43
line weights 30, 39
Llama fly 80
Logan, Bill 79
luggage 98-99
lures 16, 164

Macedonia 6, 19-20
magnification 93-94
El Manuscito de Astorga (Juan de Bergara) 70
Marbury, Mary Orvis 10
marlin 188, 189
    See also billfish
Marryat, George Selwyn 13
Martuch, Leon 38
Maxima 46, 48-49
mayflies 71, 175, 203

imitation 5, 6, 76, 77, 80
McBride, Sara Jane 10
McCusker, Joe 78
McMurray Ant fly 80
mending line 111-113
Mexico 186-188
Mickey Finn fly 80
microjigs 139, 140-141
Minor Tactics of the Chalk Stream (George Edward Mackenzie Skues) 13
Miracle Mile 181-183
Modern Development of the Dry Fly (Frederic Halford) 74
Montana Stonefly 80
Moore, Winston 155
Muddler Minnow fly 16, 80, 82
muskellunge 131, 137

nail knot 49, 64-65, 66
needle knot 49, 64
neoprene 96-97
nets, landing 98, 158
New Zealand 193-194
night feeding 94
no hackle duns 77
non-slip loop knot 58-59
Northeastern United States 149-151, 173-175
Northern Memoirs (Richard Franck) 70
nymphs 80

offshore fishing 151-152
Okyel River 191
Orvis Company 168
overhand knot 54

panfish 134, 140-141
Papua New Guinea 195
pawl drags 32
payara 189
peacock feathers 52
De Peculari Quadam Piscato Macedonia (Aelianus) 19-20
perch, yellow-barred 143
perfection loop 59-60, 61
permit 127-128, 188, 199
Pheasant Tail fly 80
pike, northern 71, 131, 137, 138, 199
pliers, hackle 83
pollock 125
The Practical Angler (W. C. Stewart) 73
Prince Nymph fly 80
Pulman, G. P. R. 71-74

Quill Gordon fly 80

rating systems 38-39
reach cast 113
redfish 129, 130, 147, 149
  conservation 177
  fishing 145, 199
Red Fox Squirrel Nymph fly 80
reel boxes 4
reels 28, 29-30, 34, 100
  capacity 33-34
  care of 34-35
  construction of 31-32
  saltwater 154-156
  selection of 33
  types of 31-32
reel seats 26-27
Rice, F. Philip 133
Rio Grande King fly 80
Roberts, George V., Jr. 78
Robinson, Helen 11
rods 19-27
  bamboo 12, 19, 21-23, 24
  beginners' 25-26
  care of 27
  and casting 101-102
  development of 7, 17, 19-21
  fiberglass 23, 101
  graphite 22, 23-24, 102
  materials 20-24
  parts 18, 25, 26-27, 38
  saltwater 153
  selection of 20-21, 24, 27
  telescoping 20
roll cast 108-109
roll cast pickup 109-110
Ross Reels 35
Royal Coachman fly 79, 81
Russia 194-195

sailfish 188, 199
  See also billfish
salmon 124-126, 175, 180, 205
  Atlantic 124, 174, 193, 195, 221
  flies 71
  Pacific 124-125, 185-186, 199
saltwater gear 35, 77-78, 152-157
sand perch, barred 186
S-cast 113-115
Schwiebert, Ernest 76-77, 203
Scientific Anglers 38
scientific nomenclature 220
shad 126, 199
Shakespeare Company 23
sharks 130
Shaw, Helen 11, 202
shoes, wading 95, 97-98

shooting line 116-118, 117
short hauls 115
single haul 116-117
sinkers 88-89
Skues, George Edward Mackenzie 13,
  71, 73, 205
slack, in line 113-114
Smith, Bonnie "Bonefish" 11
snook 188
sockeye 185
  See also Pacific salmon
Southern United States 176-177
South America 189-191
Spain 8
Spey, River 192
spiders 73
spit shot 89
spools 30, 156
spring-and-pawls 32-33
staffs, wading 98, 206
steelhead 124-126, 175, 185-186, 205
  See also trout, rainbow
steeple cast 110-111
Stevens, Carrie 11
Stewart, W. C. 74
streamers 14-15, 80
  Gray Ghost fly 11, 80, 82
  saltwater 153-154, 155, 156
Streamers and Bucktails (Joseph Bates) 16
strike indicators 140-141
striped bass. See bass, striped
stripping line 107-108
sun protection 94-95
surgeon's knot 49-50, 62
surgeon's loop 59, 60

tailing 148, 149
tailing loops 106, 115
taper 37, 39-41, 42, 44-45
tarpon 129, 131, 170, 187, 188
tarpon fishing 198
Taylor, Samuel 71
technology 12-13, 14-17, 42-43, 44
The Tegernsee Fishing Advice 7-8
terrestrials 80
tides 147-148
tigerfish 195
tippet class records 47
tippets 37, 47-48, 50, 51, 57
  diameters 45
Tonkin cane 22-23
tools 89-91
  catch and release 167
  fly-tying 83
  knot-tying 49, 60, 65

travel agencies 196-197
Traver, Robert 176, 207
A Treatyse of Fysshynge wyth an Angle
  6-7, 8, 10, 20, 70, 207
"Trilene" knot 56
trout 94, 122-123, 204-205
  brook 122, 123, 160, 174, 175
  brown 45, 122, 123, 167, 177
  cutthroat 122
  fishing 119, 198, 199
  golden 122
  introduced 161, 189, 195
  lake 122, 175
  leaders 46, 48
  native 160-161
  rainbow 122, 123, 161, 198, 199
  See also steelhead
Trude fly 80
Tube Bodiz 78
turbine drags 33
Turle knot 55
Two Hearted River 175
Tying and Fishing the Wet Fly (James
  Leisenring) 74

uni-knot 56-58, 63-64
Upper Easter Elchies Beat 192

Venables, Robert 8
vests 86-87
Vincent, Jim 42-43
vises 83, 92

waders 96-98, 223
Walton, Izaak 8
warmwater 14, 135-137, 142, 206-207
watercraft, personal 135-137
Waterman, Charles 16
The Way of a Trout with a Fly (George
  Edward Mackenzie Skues) 13, 205
web sites 196
weed guards 48, 140
weight-forward (WF) lines 39-40
Western United States 181-186
whip finishers 83
Whitlock, Dave 47, 77, 80, 203, 206
Woolly Bugger fly 80
Wulff, Joan 11, 204
Wulff, Lee 11, 86, 128, 205
Wulff triangle taper (TT) lines 40-41
Wye, River 192

Zugbug fly 80